TAKEN BY SURPRISE

"Let me go, you bloody English dog!" With all her might, Cecelia kicked at Noah's shins. She knew a moment of pure, triumphant pleasure as her foot connected and he grunted in pain.

"You little guttersnipe!" Noah growled threateningly.

Cecelia's moment of victory was lost as Kincade snatched her to him by her shirtfront, almost lifting her from her feet to shake her in anger, the action knocking her hat from her head. Released from its bondage beneath the tricorn, Cecelia's glorious mane of thick curls fell in riotous, satiny waves to her slim shoulders, revealing to Noah for the first time her true gender and, after a stunned moment, her real identity.

"Let me go!" Cecelia demanded, her breasts heaving in agitation.

"Oh no, *Miss Demorest*." Noah smiled wolfishly as he studied her feminine features closely. "I've suffered enough of your insults. It's time I demanded and received some satisfaction from you." He dipped his head to allow his lips to claim hers in a dominating kiss, a kiss designed to humiliate and conquer . . . and a kiss that swept them both so forcefully and powerfully with passion that it caught the two adversaries quite unawares. . . .

CAPTIVE PRIDE

BOBBI SMITH

ZEBRA BOOKS
KENSINGTON PUBLISHING CORP.

*This is for Sylvie Sommerfield,
author and friend extraordinaire*

Prologue—England, 1773

Wraithlike tendrils of fog clung tenaciously to the trees surrounding the clearing, lending an almost spectral aura to the moment, and not even the pale clarity of the rising sun could dispel the mood as the cold, deadly sounds of the clashing steel blades rent the early-morning silence.

Bodies tense with expectation, weapons held in readiness, the two men engaged in the duel faced each other, each trying to anticipate the other's next move. In a graceful dance of death, they moved about the clearing . . . testing . . . probing . . . each searching in his own way for his opponent's weakness, but each failing to find that fatal flaw.

They were the best of the best, these two. Equals in the fine art of swordsmanship, they were peers of the realm and dashing figures of men. One, tall and dark, his body tightly muscled, his movements lithe and sure, was hawklike in visage. His gray eyes were sharp and glinting as they reflected his intense concentration, his chiseled mouth firm in his determination to win. The other was blond and as tall as his rival, but his body tended to fat rather than muscle. His aristocratic features reflected a love for excess in the puffiness there. His full lips were curved in a taunting, confident smile. His pale blue eyes, still bloodshot from his intemperance the night before, shone with an almost maniacal light as he strove to prove his superiority over his foe.

Grim-faced, the dark-haired combatant reacted to his enemy's mocking expression violently, pressing his attack in a powerful series of maneuvers. He would not, could not yield to defeat at this man's hands. He would defend his honor to the death. The remembrance of his opponent's cutting, publicly issued insult left him a man possessed. He challenged his foe again and again, the strength of his rage fueling his already considerable strength.

His rival suddenly seemed to sense the driving desperation in his renewed attack and grew nervous as he realized that the challenge he'd taken up so casually the night before could only end in one way . . . with one of their deaths. No longer regarding the duel as mere sport, he responded in earnest, knowing that his very life depended upon his own talent. But his years of undisciplined living had taken their toll, and he was no longer a real match for his fit opponent.

The dark-haired man parried his lightning thrust and feinted to his left, countering with a vicious lunge. His swiftly flashing sword pierced his adversary's momentarily unprotected shoulder and drew blood.

As hot crimson stained the swordsman's white shirtfront, a collective gasp escaped those who had gathered at this early-morning hour to watch. Their expressions mirrored their stunned disbelief as the realization dawned on them that this would indeed be a fight to the death; that the shedding of blood alone would not satisfy the graveness of the insult.

Knowing that he now had the advantage, the man pressed his attack with ruthless intent, penetrating again and again his enemy's ever-weakening defenses. He was methodical in his gory siege, his silver eyes reflecting the cold deadliness of his vengeful desire. Driven by demons even he didn't fully understand, he inflicted wound after debilitating wound

8

upon his foe, wanting to humiliate him as thoroughly as he himself had been humiliated the night before. His fury firing his prowess, he tortured his opponent heartlessly until the overpowering need to put an end to what had become a farce of a duel drove him to sink his blade deep into the other man's chest.

Silence hung in a deathlike pall over the dueling ground as the physician who'd accompanied them raced forward to examine the downed man.

"It's done. He's dead," the doctor said tonelessly as he glanced up. He had never before witnessed such a savage end to an affair of honor, and he wondered suddenly if perhaps everything that was being said about this man was, indeed, true.

In the aftermath of his surging rage, he stood tensely above them, his bloodied weapon still in hand, his eyes still glazed with the primitive blood lust that had possessed him during the fight. It was only after the physician's words penetrated the haze of his blind fury that he realized it was over. He had won.

As sanity gripped him once again, he saw for the first time with rational eyes the brutal carnage he'd wreaked. A look of disgust crossed his handsome features. Throwing his weapon violently aside, he turned away.

At the edge of the dueling field, seventeen-year-old Matthew Kincade stood pale and shaken as he clutched his older brother Noah's coat tightly in both hands. He had never seen this side of Noah before—this pitiless, cold-blooded side—and the discovery that his brother could kill with such callous expertise left him stunned. He knew Noah to be warm and loving; yet the man who had just so viciously put an end to James Radcliffe's life seemed a stranger to him. Matthew swallowed nervously at the memory of the final, deadly sword thrust and he forced his gaze away from Radcliffe's still, prone form to search quickly for his sibling. He caught sight of Noah heading for their waiting carriage and, forced from his stunned immobility, hurried after him.

Noah Kincade strode quickly toward his conveyance, the hatred and strength of purpose that had possessed him earlier purged from him now by the success of his violent encounter with Radcliffe. He wanted to get away from the ugliness this moment would always represent to him, and it was only the sound of Matt's voice that stopped him from entering their carriage.

"Noah?" Matthew's call was hesitant, filled with uncertainty and perhaps even a little fear.

Noah swung around to face him, his features stony, his eyes dark now with fathomless emotion.

"Your coat . . ." he offered quietly in a way of explanation as he held the garment out to him.

As Noah took the coat, his gaze met and locked with Matt's, and for a brief instant they regarded each other in studied silence. Noah had always understood his brother, and he could easily read the turbulence of his feelings in his strained expression, but there was nothing he could say or do to change the outcome of all that had happened. They would have to go on from there. There could be no going back. . . .

He made short order of donning his frock coat, and then, without so much as a glance toward the field of death, he climbed into the coach, leaving Matthew to follow.

Chapter One

Staring out across the fading green of the autumnal countryside with unseeing eyes, Noah stood rigidly at the window behind his desk in his study at Kincade Hall. Though the early-afternoon sun shone warmly through the glistening glass, he felt none of its warmth. Chilled to his very soul, his handsome features frozen in an inexpressive mask, he turned back to the room to face Ronald Perkins, his father's attorney. The lawyer was seated in the leather wing chair on the opposite side of the massive, scarred oak desk, his papers spread out before him in studied disarray.

"Then it's gone. . . . There's no chance of saving it. . . ." His tone was bitter as his gaze seemed to come alive, flashing silvered fire at the lawyer.

The rotund barrister was nervous and sweating, his hands unsteady as he removed his wire-rimmed glasses and dabbed at his broad brow with a wrinkled white handkerchief. "Uh . . . yes, m'lord. I'm afraid so. The house and grounds have already been sold to meet a portion of your father's debts."

Noah's jaw tensed in anger as he stalked forward to plant his hands firmly on the desktop, leaning forward menacingly. "Were you aware that these conditions existed *before* my father's demise?"

Lord Noah Kincade was an intimidating man in the best of times, but here, confronted with the loss of his beloved home and the majority of his family fortune, the power of his outraged personality was near to overwhelming. Ronald, a cowardly soul, knew a moment of true physical fear as he stared helplessly up at the demanding nobleman.

"I did," he answered honestly, knowing that it would not do to lie to Noah.

"You knew . . ." Noah's eyes went blank for a moment as he considered this news. This man had known that his father was squandering the family's resources at the gaming tables and yet made no move to stop him. "And yet you did nothing?"

"Sir." Perkins cleared his throat and straightened uncomfortably in the chair. Not willing to tolerate any attacks on his professional character, he summoned all his inner fortitude to answer. "I was employed by your father. It was not my job to criticize him."

"Could you not have advised me so I could have prevented this from happening?" Noah asked heatedly.

"Lord Kincade," he began in righteous indignation, "your father paid me well for the job I did. Any time I ventured to offer advice to His Lordship concerning the state of his finances, I was firmly reminded of my expendability. Your father hired me because I was discreet. It was a quality he valued most highly in those he kept in his employ."

The anger suddenly seemed to drain out of Noah as his broad shoulders slumped. When he looked up at the lawyer again, his face was haggard and pale, and he appeared far older than his twenty-six years. Dragging a hand through his thick, dark hair in a gesture of weary defeat, Noah nodded slowly as he dropped into his chair.

"Then it's settled. It's gone. . . ."

"The house and grounds, yes. That transaction was completed two days ago. I am in the process now of finalizing the sale of the town house in London," Perkins reported with as much professional dignity as he could muster. "You and Matthew are not totally devoid of funds, as you know, for you both still retain your independent trusts from your mother's estate."

Noah quickly calculated in his mind just how far their trusts would go in maintaining their current lifestyle, and he grew even more overwhelmed. His mother's family had been comfortable, but their holdings had not come anywhere near the fortunes of the Kincades.

"I have one other bit of information here that may prove uplifting," he offered tenuously.

"Oh?" One dark brow lifted slightly in angry disbelief as Noah regarded the lawyer cynically.

The knowledge that he'd lost his home was devastating to him and he found it most difficult to imagine anything that could possibly be interpreted as *uplifting* in this whole sordid affair. He was financially ruined, and all of his future prospects were in a shambles. Not so long ago, Noah was heir to the vast Kincade shipping fortune and one of the most sought after of bachelors about the *ton*. But when the rumors of the Kincade family's cataclysmic losses had begun, Noah's "friends" had become acquaintances, shunning him and retracting invitations issued months before. Even Lady Andrea Broadmoor, his light-o'-love for some months, had cut him loose upon hearing the gossip, and her desertion, in particular, was one lesson he would never forget. He clenched his fists in utter frustration at his own helplessness. As things stood now, Perkins's *uplifting information* was the only hope he had, and he knew he couldn't allow himself the luxury to trust in that for any real help.

"Yes . . . the ships . . ."

"Kincade Shipping . . ." For just an instant, his spirits rose at the thought that their prosperous shipping firm might still be intact, untouched by their father's excesses. If so, he knew he still held a modicum of control over his life.

Perkins hastened on, "The company itself is lost."

Noah's last hope was dashed and bitter emotions welled up inside of him. He held himself in rigid control, refusing to betray any weakness or despair before the attorney's watchful gaze.

"Go on," he urged icily.

"There are two ships, however, that you and Matthew do retain joint title to." He shuffled through his papers until he found the one he was looking for. "The *Lorelei* was your father's pride and joy. He made special provisions in all of his dealings that it would not be included in any settlement against him."

Noah nodded at the knowledge that they owned at least one fleet ship.

"And the *Sea Pride*," Perkins concluded. "She's an older merchant ship, but still serviceable."

"I see," was his only reply. In his discomfiture, he suddenly was eager for the barrister to be gone, and he asked sharply, "Is there anything else you have to tell me?"

Again the lawyer nervously cleared his throat. "Yes . . ." he hesitated, "and this is the most difficult for me to relay. . . ."

"I don't see how anything you could have to say to me now could possibly be any worse than what you've already told me," Noah remarked sarcastically, striving to stay master of his riotous emotions.

Perkins gave a curt nod and blurted out hastily, "It seems the new owners of Kincade Hall want to take possession right away. Their request is that you vacate the premises by the end of the week."

For a second Noah almost lost what little control he had on himself, but his stubborn, unrelenting Kincade pride wouldn't let him. He would reveal to no one the misery that rocked him over the loss of his family estates, not now and not in the future.

Noah accepted, agonizingly, the reality of his situation.

With that acknowledgment came a plan of action. The power of wealth had just been painfully demonstrated to him. Before, he had always taken his vaulted position for granted, but no longer. Vowing silently to himself, he swore that he would recoup all of their father's losses. He would redeem the Kincade name among his peers and reestablish the family so firmly that future generations would be immune to such tragedy.

He knew it was not something that would happen overnight, but Kincade Hall would not remain in the hands of strangers for long. It had been in the family for generations. He would buy it back just as soon as he could raise the funds, and he *was* going to raise the funds. Nothing would deter him. Nothing.

"Perkins, I thank you for your help in these matters." His voice was steady, his manner icily calm as he rose. It was a signal to the barrister that his audience with Noah was at an end.

"Oh . . . fine, my lord . . ." He gathered his papers together and hurriedly stuffed them into his portfolio. "If I have any more news, I'll be in touch."

"I'd appreciate that."

"Do you know where you'll be staying after the end of the week?" Perkins hated to ask, but it was essential that he know His Lordship's whereabouts should anything of an urgent business nature come up.

Nerves stretched taut, Noah answered through gritted teeth, "Should you need us for anything, you will be able to reach us through Captain Russell of the *Lorelei.*"

"Fine, fine." Perkins could sense the tension in the air and he was eager to be on his way back to London. With a quick bow, he started out of the room. "Until later."

"Yes . . . until later . . ." Noah's tone was grim and final.

When the family retainer had gone and he was alone, Noah turned slowly back to the window. His heart felt like a stone in his breast, and he refused to admit that the prickling, burning sensation in his eyes was anything besides weariness.

The last two weeks had been disastrous and he wondered if things could possibly get any worse. First there had been his father's death in a hunting accident and the systematic dismantlement of the Kincade empire as his father's creditors had come forth, like vultures, to feast on the remains.

Exhausted, Noah massaged the back of his neck, trying to work out the tightness in the muscles there as he gazed out across the low, rolling hills painted now with the faded colors of the dying season. He thought, philosophically, how his life was like the land that was spread out before him . . . his glory days of summer over and only the bleakness of winter ahead. The goal he had set before himself to regain his lost fortunes and prestige seemed insurmountable at that moment, but he knew that the longest of journeys is accomplished by only one step at a time. Still . . .

No longer able to deny the depths of despair that had been tormenting him since the beginning of his ordeal, Noah repeatedly smashed his fist against the wall, venting his fury upon the polished dark wood panels.

How could his father have gambled away their very livelihood? Had Radcliffe been partially right in his slimy insult? The thought sent a shaft of denial through him. No matter what else, his father would never have done what Radcliffe had claimed.

Remembrance of the duel heightened his agony, and he did not feel the damage he was wreaking on his unprotected hand. Finally, as he became aware of the futility of his actions, he stopped, all emotion temporarily drained from him. He sensed no physical discomfort, but looking down at his bloodied knuckles, Noah knew it would come later . . . later when the shock had worn off and the ugliness that was reality settled over him like a stifling mantle.

*   *   *

Lord Thomas Kincade had spared no expense when he'd purchased the *Lorelei,* for he'd meant her to be the showpiece of his fleet. The captain's cabin, where Noah now sat in conference with Lyle Russell, the *Lorelei*'s master, reflected his father's expensive tastes. The bunk was wide and comfortable-looking, the walls paneled, and the furniture dark and heavy. It was a restful room, a haven from the harshness of life at sea, and both Noah and Lyle were enjoying the small bit of peace they'd found there.

"All the arrangements have been made," Noah was saying as he handed the contracts over to Lyle.

"How soon do we load?" the captain asked, one hand stroking his bushy, gray-streaked beard thoughtfully as he quickly perused the documents. At fifty years of age, Lyle Russell had spent most of his adult years working for Kincade Shipping. He had been shocked by his good friend Lord Thomas's death and by the subsequent revelations concerning the nobleman's overwhelming debts. The sale of the shipping firm had seemed almost a physical blow to him, and he was determined to help Lord Noah as much as he could.

"The *Lorelei* will berth and start loading the day after tomorrow," Noah informed him. "The *Sea Pride* is another matter entirely."

"Oh? Is there a problem?" Lyle extracted the contract for the merchant ship from the sheaf of papers he held and read it over carefully, surprise registering on his face as he noted what type of merchandise the *Pride* would be carrying. "I didn't know you were planning on shipping war materials. . . ."

"It's a risky move on my part, but the payoff could be substantial."

"There's a market for the goods?"

"According to those I talked with who were in authority, there is a kettle of unrest brewing in the colonies, and violence could break out there at any time. Should that happen, agents here agreed that a shipment of arms could be *very* profitable."

"It is a daring plan, but if you stand to reap a suitable reward for your efforts, I see no reason to hesitate." The ship's captain nodded in approval of the younger man's farsightedness as his gaze rested warmly upon him. As aggressive and determined as Lord Noah was, perhaps the recovery of the lost Kincade fortunes was not as impossible as it seemed.

"Either way there's a pound to be made, and who knows? Maybe His Majesty's troops will be in desperate need of cannon and shot by the time we arrive. That could jack the asking price up considerably. I certainly see no reason why we shouldn't make every effort to take advantage of the situation." Noah's eyes glinted at the thought of the full purse he could conceivably earn. "According to the agent I dealt with, however, the *Pride* won't be able to load for some weeks, and that puts us dangerously close to the winter season on the North Atlantic."

"There's no reason why the *Lorelei* has to remain in wait. Why don't we sail on ahead? You can make the necessary contacts in the colonies, and by the time the *Pride* arrives, all will be in readiness."

"How soon can you be ready to sail?"

"If the loading is completed on schedule, we can probably set sail within four days."

"That will be fine." Noah stood and started toward the door of the cabin. "I've yet to tell Matt the news, so I had better return to the inn and let him know."

"You'll be there, should I need you?"

"Yes. We'll remain in our rented quarters there until you dock to load, then we'll come aboard." Absorbed in his thoughts, Noah forgot his bandaged hand and reached out for the doorknob. He grimaced at the painful contact.

"Your hand . . . Are you all right?" Lyle asked with quick concern.

Noah glanced up to meet his captain's worried regard and

he slanted him a cunning smile. "I think, for the first time in quite a while, Lyle, that I'm going to be just fine." And for the first time since he had learned the complete, devastating truth, he believed it.

It was growing late and the taproom in the inn was becoming increasingly crowded and noisy. Noah took little notice, though, as he sat at a secluded table in a back corner of the room, his expression pensive as he drank deeply from his tankard of ale. Matthew had retired to their rooms earlier and Noah was taking advantage of the time alone to sort out his thoughts about their upcoming voyage to the Americas.

Though he'd heard much about the colonies, Noah had never had any desire to visit them. Now, fate had intervened. Within six weeks he would find himself aboard the *Lorelei* docking in Boston City of the Massachusetts Colony. The thought did not lighten his spirits. The trip was a necessary evil, and he would tolerate the inconvenience only because of the money to be made. His goal was to return to England in the spring with his pockets well lined. He knew that one successful trip would not restore all his lost inheritance, but once he made the necessary business contacts in Boston, he was confident that their future would be bright.

Noah was so deeply lost in thought that he did not notice the stranger approach his table. It was only when the man spoke that he glanced up.

"Lord Noah Kincade?" the man asked.

"Yes. I'm Lord Kincade," Noah responded, wondering at the interruption and frowning a bit as he cautiously assessed his visitor. The stranger was tall, but not overly so. His coloring was swarthy, and the clothes he wore were clean and well cared for, yet essentially nondescript. He was the type of man who could blend in with a crowd and never really be noticed. The man appeared slightly nervous, as if he was constantly on guard, and his dark eyes shifted uneasily about the room.

"May I join you, my lord? It's important." The stranger leaned slightly forward as he added the last in an undertone.

"Oh? I don't know you, sir, and I fail to see how we could have any important business to conduct."

"The fact that you don't know me is irrelevant," he said cryptically. "The business we have to conduct concerns your ship the *Sea Pride*, my lord."

"The *Pride*? What have you to do with the *Pride*?" Noah demanded, his eyes narrowing in anticipation of new trouble. What did this man want? Was there to be another claim laid against the already ravaged remains of the estate?

"Nothing, my lord. At least not yet, and that's what I need to talk with you about." There seemed an underlying urgency to his words.

Noah was relieved that his first suspicion had proved wrong, and since the man's manner was nonthreatening, he waved him into the opposite chair.

"What is it? What do you want?"

"I don't want anything. I'm here to make you an offer." At the sound of the taproom's door opening, the stranger glanced sharply in that direction, relaxing again only when he'd noted who'd entered the establishment.

"The *Sea Pride* is not for sale," Noah said firmly.

"It's not the ship we're interested in." He met Noah's gaze across the table. "I've heard through certain reliable sources that you'll be shipping arms to the colonies aboard the *Sea Pride*. If that is true, then I'm prepared to make you an offer for that shipment."

Noah stiffened, irritated that his private business should be so widely known, and he asked imperiously, "Who are you, sir?"

"I'm an Englishman who's angered with the unfair treatment the colonies are receiving from the Crown," the stranger answered.

"You're approaching me with an offer to purchase my

shipment of war materials for possible use against England? Are you mad? Do you think I'm a traitor to my country?"

"I think you're a smart businessman, or at least I had hoped you were," the other shrugged. "It's not a matter of loyalties. It's a matter of money. Our offer would be considerably higher than any others you're likely to receive." The man gazed levelly across the table at Noah, trying to read his response, but Noah was careful to disguise his true feelings as he wrestled with the unexpected proposal. "There's no need for you to decide now. Think about it." Reaching into the pocket of his coat, he withdrew a folded piece of paper. "You'll be docking in Boston. This note contains the name of the person to contact if you decide to take up my offer."

He shoved the paper slowly across the surface of the table and then stood up. "Good night, Lord Kincade."

Noah sat immobile, staring at the note. That single folded piece of paper represented to him the final proof of the magnitude of his losses, yet he could not stop himself from reaching out for it. The memory of his friends' rejection and the forfeiture of Kincade Hall was too real . . . too consuming. He would do whatever he had to do to survive. As his hand closed around the note, he looked up, but to his surprise, the stranger had gone.

Cecelia Demorest sat sedately with the group of women, listening idly to their chatter about the upcoming ball at the Spencer household on Saturday night.

"Spencer's party Saturday night should be marvelous," Marianna Lord twittered as she sipped delicately from her cup of tea. A plump, happily married lady in her early thirties, Marianna always enjoyed these afternoons when the ladies of her social set met for tea and gossip. "I understand that several of the local dignitaries will be there, *and* Lord Radcliffe and Lord Townley."

It was all CC, as Cecelia's friends called her, could do to contain her feelings and not grimace at Marianna's breathless mention of the aristocrats. Though CC's father was an important agent for the British government in Boston and dealt with these men on occasion, she personally found them hard to tolerate. Those she'd had the misfortune to meet had been very puffed-up with their own consequence, and most high-handed. Her father, an Englishman through and through, thought nothing of their pompous, demanding ways, but CC, born and raised in the Americas, thought the noblemen not an endearing bunch. As far as she was concerned, everyone in the colonies would be better off if the aristocrats stayed in England, where they belonged.

"I know I'm looking forward to it," Margaret Kingsley agreed, and then added slyly, "And who knows? Perhaps by Saturday Eve Woodham will be ready to announce her engagement to Lord Radcliffe."

"Really?" Marianna immediately perked up. "I knew that they were seeing each other, but I had no idea . . ."

"Well, they've been quite close, you know, and there's no denying Eve is looking for another husband. She couldn't do much better than an English lord, now could she?"

"That's a matter of opinion," CC stated derisively, unable to resist the temptation to add her own thoughts on the matter.

"Really, CC . . ." Marianna was surprised by her statement. Wasn't it every girl's dream to marry a rich, handsome titled gentleman? "Can it be jealousy we're hearing?"

"Hardly, Marianna," CC replied, not in the least stung by her friend's assumption of envy. "You forget that my father deals with these noblemen all the time. I've been singularly unimpressed with them."

"CC!" The other women were stunned. "Surely you're jesting!"

CC laughed in delight at their shock. "Really, ladies, think about it. Most of the noblemen we've met have been fat and ugly or very effeminate, haven't they?" She watched in satisfaction as the ladies exchanged looks, unable to argue. "I have to admit that Lord Radcliffe is relatively attractive, but looks don't make the man. We all know he's an arrogant ass."

"He's certainly the perfect partner for Eve, then," Caroline Chadwick put in cattily, and the others laughed at her frankness.

Eve Woodham was a classically beautiful blonde who had been widowed several years before. Well aware of her attractiveness, Eve used her position in society to her best advantage. The other women knew that no man, not even their own husbands and boyfriends, would be safe from her charms, should she decide to make one of them her quarry.

"Indeed he is," CC agreed, her emerald eyes alight with mischief.

"Well, if you aren't out to catch a nobleman, then what do you want in your perfect partner?" Marianna teased.

A long-time friend, Marianna had known her for over ten years. She had watched in delight as CC, a rather gangly, awkward child, had blossomed into a lovely young woman. With her auburn hair and green eyes set off by the perfection of her peaches-and-cream complexion and softly curved figure, CC was strikingly attractive. It was a mystery to Marianna why she had never picked one of her ardent suitors and settled down. Lord knows, at twenty-two, she'd been courted by many, but she'd never seriously encouraged any of them.

"Oh, I don't know, Marianna." CC frowned slightly. "I really haven't thought about it much."

And that, in fact, was the truth, for, unknown to her friends, CC was not even the least bit interested in marriage and babies. There was something far more important in her life that drew all her interest, but it was something she could not reveal to anyone.

"You must have some idea, CC," Margaret chided. "Come

23

on, tell us. What's your dream man like?"

With a light laugh, CC allowed herself to fantasize for a moment; her expression grew slightly distant and rapturous as she tried to envision her perfect mate. "All right, I'll tell you. He'd have to be tall, dark, handsome, and as fair and honest as my father."

"You're certainly not asking for much!" Caroline teased. "But what about riches? You didn't mention that. Doesn't your future husband have to be wealthy?"

CC actually considered that for a long moment before answering, and then, when she finally did respond, she surprised her friends again. "I would never judge a man by how well his pockets were lined. It's his personal integrity that counts."

"You mean you'd be willing to marry a poor man?" Marianna was curious.

"If he was the man I loved, then yes. It wouldn't matter," she replied with conviction. "A lack of money will never be a deciding factor in my falling in love with a man."

"How noble of you. Shall I send word to all the tall, dark, handsome men of Boston to come courting no matter what their finances?" Marianna bantered.

"Don't you dare, Marianna!" CC laughed, her eyes twinkling merrily.

"What about John?" Margaret asked, knowing that CC had been seeing John Robinson steadily for some time.

"I like John, but I'm not in love with him." She said it almost regretfully. John was a good man and they got on well together, but CC could never even consider a lifelong commitment to someone she didn't love. Besides, the secret that she and John shared was far more important than love. "I'm more than happy to continue as I am until the right man does come along," she added, giving her friends hope that she did indeed want to marry.

"And he will," Marianna said sagely. "Mark my words. When you least expect him, you're going to look up and there he'll be."

"How heavenly!" Caroline sighed.

"It happens that way often," Margaret agreed.

CC smiled noncommittally at their musings, silently thinking that they were all hopeless romantics. She'd been courted by far too many attractive men to think that some handsome stranger was going to sweep her off her feet, but she decided to humor her friends.

"Well, when it finally does happen and I do fall in love," CC promised, "you'll be among the first to know."

Chapter Two
Boston, Six Weeks Later

The taproom at the Red Lion Inn was crowded as Noah and Matthew made their way to the only vacant table in the establishment. Noah, deep in his own thoughts, paid little real attention to their surroundings, but Matt was alert, trying to absorb every facet of life in the colonies.

Since they'd arrived in port that morning, the younger man had become intrigued with Boston. Noah had left him to his own devices while he and Captain Russell had dealt with the port authorities, and Matt had taken the opportunity to tour the city on foot. He'd left the crowded wharf behind with its clog of merchandise and, steering clear of the tenement section of town as Russell had advised, had followed the narrow, winding streets through the multitude of small shops and businesses to the elegant area overlooking the Boston Common. Stately mansions stood in regal testimony to the type of life that could be had in the colonies, and Matt found himself becoming more and more impressed with America. There was a vitality in the air, a freshness of spirit that he'd never seen in London, and he marveled at it.

"You know, Noah, I could come to like this town," Matt remarked as he slipped into the chair opposite his brother's.

"It's certainly different," Noah answered unenthusiastically. He'd had little time to see the sights and, in fact, was unexcited about doing so. His business interests were foremost in his mind right now; that and returning to England.

Polly, the comely, well-endowed barmaid, sidled up to the table to take their order. "Good evening, gents. What can I get for you tonight?" She eyed both men with interest, for they were not only gentlemen of the highest caliber, but they were good-looking, too. Noah ordered succinctly, requesting that their ale be brought right away, and Polly hurried off to do his bidding, returning quickly with two brimming mugs of brew.

"Your meal will be ready soon," she related as she placed their tankards on the table before them. They were handsome, these two, and she thought the resemblance between them startling. Though both men were tall and their dark coloring similar, she thought the older man more attractive. He seemed to have an innate animal magnetism in the firm slant of his lips and the steely depths of his gray eyes, and she found him irresistible.

"Thank you," Noah replied as he tossed her a coin for her efforts, and she rewarded him with a wide smile that held more than a hint of an invitation.

"If you need anything else, just say the word. My name's Polly." She let her gaze meet Noah's knowingly before hurrying away to her other duties, her heart beating wildly at the thought of what it would be like to share his bed and passion.

Had Noah been of a mind, he might have taken her up on her obvious offer, for she was a pretty enough girl, and clean-looking, too, but at the moment he was not so inclined. Instead he was thinking about his appointment the following afternoon with Edward Demorest, the British agent he was to deal with, and on the mission he'd assigned to Russell. He was growing concerned over the length of time the captain was taking and he wondered why he had heard nothing from him.

It was then, as he attempted to sit back and relax, that a man's sharply worded protest rang out clearly above the din of conversation. The man's tone was so outraged that both Noah and Matthew glanced concernedly in his direction.

"Damn it, Arthur! The world's gone mad!" the man, fat and red-faced in his upset, bellowed at his companion, thumping the table in front of him as he spoke for even further emphasis. "What can they be thinking of?!"

"I don't know, Leland," the man named Arthur commiserated. "It's a bad situation."

"The mobs seem to be controlling the town!" Leland complained worriedly. "Ever since word came about Parliament passing the Tea Act, things seem to have gone from bad to worse!" He paused and took a deep drink from his mug of rum before continuing. "The protesters are threatening me and all the other merchants who agreed to sell the tea! It doesn't make sense! Our price here is lower than what Englishmen are paying at home! Drink the tea and enjoy it! Who cares if there's a tax on it as long as the asking price is still cheap!?"

"It's this damned newspaper." In disgust, Arthur tapped the copy of the *Boston Gazette* that lay on the table in front of him. "Agitators! The whole God-awful bunch!"

The shopkeeper nodded in agreement. "Everyone I talk to says they're loyal to the king, but you can't help but wonder when you hear of all the trouble. If everybody is loyal, then who are the rioters in the streets?" He shook his head in profound distress.

"Well, the men who write these articles in the *Gazette* certainly aren't trying to help matters any."

"That's true," Leland agreed solemnly. "There may be only a few of those hotheads, but they seem to know their business. They're always trying to stir something up."

"Their latest rallying cry is completely foolhardy. Have

you heard? Independence for the colonies . . ." Arthur snorted in derision. "Independence, indeed."

"It's ridiculous. Why would they want independence? We're a part of the mightiest empire in the world," Leland bragged to no one in particular.

"His Majesty's troops are the most efficient fighting corps in the world. We just defeated the French, for God's sake! If we turned our troops loose on the idiots who are stirring up all the trouble, they'd rid Boston of them in no time." Arthur drained his mug with gusto. "It'd be quiet again then, the way it should be."

"It'll never happen, but I wish it would. Business would be normal again. . . ." Leland partook of his own rum and suddenly became rather philosophical. "I'm just hoping that it'll all blow over, like it did all those years ago when everybody was in an uproar over the damned stamp tax."

"Me, too," Arthur remarked, having no taste for confrontation or violence.

Noah and Matthew had been listening with interest to the colonists' conversation, and Noah shot Matt a smug look. It looked like the risk he'd taken with the war materials shipment was about to pay off, and pay off big. He lifted his tankard in a silent salute.

"It seems, dear brother, that our shipment may be quite timely in its arrival." Noah smiled in satisfaction. The news that there was trouble brewing pleased him tremendously, and if Russell could just manage to make the necessary contacts . . .

"All too," Matthew agreed. "It looks like contracting the arms shipment for the *Pride* was a wise move. From the sound of their conversation, it seems our troops may be needing them soon."

"It certainly does, doesn't it?" Noah felt his old confidence return now that he knew his instincts had been proven correct, and mentally he rubbed his hands together in anticipation of the profit. He had not revealed to Matt his mysterious conversation with the stranger, and he had no intention to do so. This was business, and he was in charge.

"Still . . ." Matt began, a slight frown marring his handsome features, "it seems a shame that this trouble between the colonies and the Crown can't be worked out in some other way."

Noah shrugged his disinterest. "Pray that it doesn't, my boy."

Matt stiffened at Noah's attitude. He had kept relatively quiet until now, trusting his brother to take charge of their lives without question, but he was finding that the changes in Noah's personality were more far-reaching than he'd originally suspected after the duel and the loss of Kincade Hall. Noah seemed terribly patronizing, causing Matt to wonder if he had really become so obsessed with money that all else paled in importance. As his brother continued speaking, Matt was shocked to discover this was true.

"There's a fortune to be made by being at the right place at the right-time with the right product," Noah continued, his thoughts on the money to be made, not the lives that would be lost.

"You seem almost eager for a war. . . ." Matt frowned, verbalizing his thoughts.

With a slight lift of his shoulders, he answered, "I'm a businessman, Matthew, not a bleeding heart. It doesn't matter to me who fights whom, or where. What matters is that I can provide the materials they need, when they need them. It's a simple matter of profit and loss. Nothing more."

Before Matt could reply, Polly returned with plates of steaming, appetizing food, and the moment to debate the issue with him was lost.

Polly was quite conspicuous in her desire to attract Noah's attention and she flashed him her most charming smile as she bent over to place his platter before him, her action giving him an unrestricted view of her ample cleavage.

Noah's smoky gaze darkened with sensual promise as he

30

saw the tempting flesh. Though he was still concerned about Russell's progress, his spirits had lifted considerably since hearing the rumbles of discontent from the two colonists, and the thought of bedding the winsome wench after his long weeks of celibacy was now most appealing. She read the invitation in his heated regard and was thrilled to know that he wanted her. Polly could hardly wait for the evening to pass so she could go to him.

"If you will be needing anything else, just let me know," she told him flirtatiously as the barkeep's impatient call drew her away.

Matthew couldn't prevent a wry smile as she moved off to do her job. "You do have a way with women."

"It's a burden I've tried my best to live with," Noah quipped dryly as he began to eat.

"I should be so burdened," Matt grumbled good-humoredly, and Noah chuckled.

"Your day will come," he assured him.

There was a moment of warmth between them then that had been rare during the past weeks, and Matt completely relaxed. "I've been quite impressed with what I've seen here."

"Really," Noah replied without enthusiasm.

"You don't like Boston?" Matt asked, hoping that, after all the bitterness they'd suffered in leaving England, his brother might be open to an opportunity to change their lives.

"I don't intend to be here long enough to find out whether I like it or not, Matthew," Noah answered. There was only one thing he wanted to do, and that was to make as much as he could on this arms shipment and then return to England to reclaim what was rightfully theirs.

"But, Noah . . . think about it. . . . This would be the perfect place to make a fresh start. . . ."

Noah's eyes narrowed as he turned a cold, silver regard upon his younger brother. "I had one reason and one reason only for coming here, and that is to make the most money

31

possible in the least amount of time. You've heard the talk. There's going to be trouble soon, and though I have every intention of making a profit off that trouble, I have no desire to get caught up in it. As soon as I've concluded our business dealings here, little brother, we're going to be on our way back to England with our pockets well lined."

Matthew's usually mellow temper flared at his dictatorial manner. Noah had their entire future all planned out and yet had never bothered to discuss it with him. "I resent your making decisions that will affect both of us without consulting me. I will, after all, be eighteen before the month is out."

Noah was surprised by his sudden show of defiance.

"I do believe I'm aware of your age, Matthew. I was, after all, a full eight years old when you were born," Noah drawled derisively. "As for my decision making, I have done, and will continue to do, those things that I feel will be of benefit to the both of us. Right now our primary concern—as you well know—is money and, to be more specific, a lack of it."

"I realize that but—"

Noah cut him off. "There are no 'buts' about our situation. We have lost nearly everything. Don't you remember the humiliation we suffered when we departed Kincade Hall for the last time?"

"I haven't forgotten," he answered defensively, flushing at the painful memory.

"Then where is your pride? I intend to reclaim the heritage that was stripped from us, Matthew. That is my only purpose right now, and it should be yours, too. . . ."

The sense of camaraderie that had existed between them ruined, Matt fell silent before Noah's determined onslaught, for he could voice no convincing argument against his plans. Obviously, to Noah, his suggestion to start anew here in Boston had seemed cowardly, as if he were cutting and running, but Matt knew that wasn't true. Feeling slightly bereft and not understanding why, Matt directed his attention to the meal before him, his appetite suddenly diminished.

The plaintive call of the night watch announcing the midnight hour echoed through the deserted streets of Boston as Noah stood, glass of wine in hand, at the window of his room. Though rum was the primary drink of the area, he had disdained the recommendation of the house and ordered a bottle of their best wine sent up to his room when he and Matthew had retired. He'd found the wine drinkable and had proceeded to imbibe most of the bottle to ease the tension that gripped him.

Matthew's rare display of contentiousness had troubled Noah, and he wondered how his brother could dismiss their life in England so easily. Hadn't Matt attended the best schools? And hadn't every door opened for him at the mention of the Kincade name? Didn't he miss their old lifestyle, and didn't he long to return to Kincade Hall? With an imperceptible shake of his head, Noah drained his glass and then refilled it.

Matt's attitude made no sense to him. The idea of them taking up permanent residency in the colonies was ludicrous. He counted on his brother coming to his senses and putting the ridiculous thought from him. Certainly it must have been just the throes of early manhood encouraging him to test his own independence against the powers that be.

A soft knock at the door disturbed his thoughts and he moved quickly to answer it, hoping that it was Russell finally returning with important news about the contacts he'd made. Noah was only mildly surprised to find Polly waiting outside in the semidarkness of the hall.

"Polly . . ."

"I was just wondering if there was anything more I could do for you before I left for the night. . . ." she said boldly as her gaze roamed hungrily over his tall, broad-shouldered form. The knowing, sensual smile he gave her excited her.

"Come in." Noah's deep voice caressed her senses, and she felt hypnotized by his very presence.

"I was hoping you'd still be awake. . . ." Polly smiled widely as he stepped back to allow her entry into his room. Striding forward, she made certain to brush suggestively against him, and the contact sent chills of expectation through her.

"Would you care for a bit of port, my dear?" He indicated the near-empty bottle.

"Wine was not what I had in mind," she told him archly.

"Nor I."

Noah knew that a night of unbridled sensual passion, free and clear of any involvement save the cost of her favors, was just what he needed. Following the sordid death of his relationship with Andrea, he had been far too involved with his other problems to give female companionship a thought. Now, his mood enlightened by the discovery that his instincts had once again proven accurate, he felt the need for a celebration of sorts, and Polly seemed just the thing. Closing the door, he turned to the serving wench and dragged her into his arms.

Polly needed no encouragement as she looped her arms about his neck and pulled him down for a long, passionate kiss. The feel of her lush, soft curves pressed so tightly to him stirred his long-denied desires, and Noah wasted no time in sweeping her up in his arms and carrying her to the bed. She was a willing female and he wanted her, and that was all that mattered. He released her long enough to shed his own clothing and he watched with hidden amusement as she eagerly began to strip off her own garments.

Polly finished undressing first and was ready and waiting for Noah in the center of his bed when he came to her. Her eyes rounded as she stared greedily at the magnificence of his broad chest and long, strongly muscled limbs. She thought him the most perfect man she'd ever encountered and she

34

went into his arms without pause when he stretched out on the bed beside her.

Their animal passions flared hotly as they came together in a blaze of lusty need. Noah caressed her silken flesh with learned expertise until she was mindless in her craving for him, needing the satisfaction only he could give. Overwhelmed by his sensuality, Polly cried out for him to take her and he moved over her, parting her thighs and seeking out the hot depths of her aroused body.

They crested the peak of physical gratification quickly, and Polly held tightly to him as the pulsing waves of her pleasure surged through her. She was no innocent miss, having worked at the inn for several years now, yet she knew that this man was special. Never before had a lover excited her so much. He had seemed to anticipate her body's every craving and had not hesitated to please her. She was still quivering as she lay passively in his arms, the ultimate joy he'd just given her having rocked her to the very center of her being.

Noah lay silently savoring the deliciousness of his release.

"You're wonderful," Polly sighed, gazing into his eyes when at last she was able to speak.

"So were you," he countered with a smile that twisted her heart, and when he ran his hands down her back to cup her rounded buttocks and draw her closer, she gasped.

"Ooooh!" she exclaimed as she felt the heat of his hunger building again. She had never known a man to be so virile, and she wriggled against him already eager for more.

Noah needed no encouragement as he thrust avidly into her, seeking again the momentary thrill of physical forgetfulness. His rhythm was hard and steady as he strove for the pinnacle, and it was only the sound of the knock at the door that brought him crashing back to reality. Noah stopped, frowning at the interruption.

"Who is it?" he demanded curtly, his body still aching with unsated desire.

"It's Lyle, Noah."

"Just a minute," he called out as he quickly extricated himself from Polly's possessive arms.

Polly watched and pouted as he moved from the bed and began to pull on his clothing, for the evidence of his desire was still proud and full. "What about me?"

"This is business, wench," he told her abruptly. "Get your clothes and be gone."

"But I don't mind waiting. . . ." she cooed sweetly, not at all anxious to leave his bed.

"I mind." He fixed a frosty silver glare upon her.

Experiencing Lord Noah Kincade's displeasure for the first time, she scurried without further arguments to get her clothing.

"Shall I come back later?" she asked huskily as she adjusted her full, heavy breasts more comfortably in the confines of her gown. Her body was still alive with the need for completion, and she hoped he would want her to return.

"Not tonight." Noah's answer was brusque as he tossed her several coins. "Here."

Polly stared down at the generous amount he'd given her with disbelieving eyes. "Thank you." She gave him a wide smile as she started from the room.

Noah finished buttoning his shirt and strode forward to open the door for her, ushering her out.

Captain Lyle Russell, master of the *Lorelei*, was standing respectfully in the hall as Noah opened the portal, and he eyed the disheveled Polly with a seagoing man's avid interest as she hurried off.

"Lyle." Noah was both happy and relieved to see him, and his tone reflected his emotions. "Come in."

"Pretty wench." He nodded in Polly's direction.

"Perfect to ease a man's needs," he answered with a quick grin as he ushered the captain into his room.

"Indeed." Lyle smiled wryly as he saw the rumpled bed and he gave a hearty chuckle. "Sorry to interrupt."

"You have news?" Noah asked, quickly changing the subject. He closed the door to ensure their privacy, and then crossed the room to light a candle, the flickering yellow light adding a shadowy intensity to their meeting.

"Yes, and I think you'll be pleased. I made the inquiries, as you instructed. It wasn't easy, but I finally was able to make contact with Joshua Smith," Lyle supplied.

"Go on." He was anxious to hear it all.

"Smith was reluctant to speak openly at first, but once I showed him that note and explained to him your reason for wanting to make contact, he agreed to try to gain you admittance to the next meeting of the dissenters."

"When is it?"

"He didn't say, and I don't believe he really knew himself," he answered truthfully. "Evidently, these men are very serious about their cause, for everything is carried out with the utmost secrecy."

"I see. Do you have any idea how soon we'll be hearing from him?"

"I told him where you were staying, and Smith said he'd get in contact with you directly when he had an answer, one way or the other."

"How will I recognize him?"

"He's about fifty, I guess, tall and thin. His hair was gray, he didn't bother with a wig, and the most prominent feature about him was his arm. . . ."

"What about it?"

"He's lost use of his left arm," Lyle explained.

Noah nodded and reached for the warm bottle of wine. "You've done well, Lyle, and I only wish I had something more suitable to celebrate your success." He offered the bottle to Russell, and the captain took a deep swig, emptying the contents.

"Thanks." He handed the empty bottle back.

"Matt and I dined here at the inn. Judging from the general tone of the conversation we managed to overhear, there is definitely unrest stirring in Boston."

"If that's the case," Lyle said thoughtfully, "I think your timing in this matter may prove impeccable, just as you'd originally hoped."

"We shall see," he said quietly. "As you know, my meeting with Demorest is set for late tomorrow afternoon, so I'll be getting in touch with you regarding the *Lorelei*'s shipment as soon as I've completed dealings with him."

"Good." The captain would be glad to get at least that much settled. "I think I'll be heading back to the ship now. If you need anything before tomorrow, just send word."

"I will." Noah saw the captain out.

He felt most pleased with himself as he locked the door behind Lyle. Things were progressing nicely. After his meeting with Demorest the following day, during which he planned to close the sale of the *Lorelei*'s goods, he hoped to have a tidy sum that would keep both Matthew and him in the style to which they were accustomed well into the new year. That would take care of all the more pressing matters. Then he could devote himself entirely to his concerns with the radicals, so that by the time the slower-paced *Pride* arrived, he would have everything under control.

Noah was about to prepare for bed when another knock sounded at his door. Giving a rueful shake of his head, he answered it quickly, for he was certain it was Polly returning to pick up where they'd left off. He was amazed to find Matthew standing there, fully dressed.

"Noah? What's going on?" Matt's expression was worried as he moved into his brother's room.

"What do you mean?" Noah tried to play the innocent, not wanting to involve Matt in the seamier side of his wheelings and dealings.

"I mean"—Matt flashed him a strained look—"what was Russell doing here in the middle of the night? It's well after midnight."

"Just a business matter, that's all," he replied nonchalantly.

"Business at after one in the morning? Surely it was something out of the ordinary or he would have waited until morning. Besides . . . I heard . . ." As he started to confess to overhearing a bit of their conversation, Noah turned on him.

"Just exactly what did you hear, little brother?" His tone was deadly serious. "And why were you eavesdropping?"

His reaction honestly startled Matt, and he stared at Noah as if seeing him for the first time.

"I wasn't eavesdropping!" he denied heatedly. "I woke up when I heard Lyle's knock. I thought he might have important news of some kind, so I got dressed and started over to see what the problem was."

"Go on."

"I was about to knock when I heard him mention something about a Joshua Smith and secret meetings. It was then I realized that you had no intention of coming for me, so I went back to my room," he finished angrily. "I want to know what's going on, and don't try to hedge."

"It's a business matter. Nothing to concern yourself with." Noah tried to pass over his inquiries, but Matthew was not about to let the matter slide.

"On the contrary, I think there is every reason to concern myself. I told you how I felt about your excluding me. Obviously you're planning something, and I want to know what it is." He was greatly irritated by the fact that, again, his brother had not consulted with him.

"The only thing I'm planning is the fastest way for us to make money," Noah bit out, finding his younger sibling's growing habit of challenging him most annoying. "In detail, if you must know, when we made port I instructed Lyle to try to make contact with Joshua Smith in hopes that the group he represents might be interested in purchasing the *Sea Pride*'s arms shipment."

"I see. And what group is it this Smith represents that you have to conduct your business with him in secrecy meetings?"

Noah answered coolly, "I was given Smith's name by a contact in London."

"What contact?"

"I don't know. It was all done very furtively. He did not give me his name, nor did I ask for it. It seems Smith is a middleman for a very active rebel group here in the colonies, and that his group is definitely interested in purchasing the *Pride*'s arms shipment."

Matthew's expression was aghast. "You're not serious?"

"I am most serious. I have the goods that, hopefully, these people want, and I intend to get the best possible price for them. As I said, it's a simple business matter," Noah dismissed easily.

"There's nothing simple about betraying your own country!" Matt was suddenly outraged.

"Matthew"—Noah's voice was icy—"weren't you the one who earlier today was ready to forsake our dear old homeland and settle here?"

"There's nothing treacherous about my wanting to remain here and begin life anew. These colonies are a part of the Empire. But, Noah . . ." His confusion over the changes in his brother's personality was very real. "I don't understand what's happened to you. You've become so cold-blooded . . . so mercenary. It started with the damned duel, and now . . ."

At the mention of the duel, Noah's piercing silver gaze glittered dangerously, but he didn't speak as Matt continued.

"How can you even consider selling the weapons to the highest bidder regardless of affiliation? Where is your conscience? If you sell those arms to the men who are advocating independence for the colonies, they might be used against soldiers of the Crown. You already heard that merchant in the taproom saying how dangerous things have become."

Noah shrugged coolly. "It's not my concern who uses the weapons or for what cause they're used. All that matters is that we get the best price for our merchandise. Whoever pays the top price will get the goods." The steely edge to his tone left no doubt in Matt's mind that he was very serious.

"It seems to me that you're selling your soul," Matthew disparaged.

"I have been forced by circumstances to become a businessman. Nothing more, nothing less."

"There's more to this than business."

Noah's stance was rigid. "I'm sure I don't know what you mean."

"Making money has become your obsession! Damn the cost! You won't be satisfied until you've made enough to return to England and resume our previous social status!" Matthew had never before spoken so openly or so critically to his older brother, and he surprised even himself by his outburst.

"And as much as you have the audacity to argue the point, you will be a direct beneficiary of what you call my 'obsession,'" Noah returned sarcastically. "If we are to return home and reestablish ourselves—"

"You're the one who's so intent on returning to England! I never said that I wanted to go back, let alone 'reestablish' myself!" he declared furiously.

"We will be going back. Never doubt that for a moment." The fierce determination of Noah's words chilled Matthew. "Now, if you don't mind, it's late and I would like to get ready for bed." The rebuff in his tone clear, Matt knew it was useless to continue the confrontation.

"Of course." Stiffly, he excused himself and then stalked across the room, closing the door firmly behind him as he made his exit.

As he entered his room, Matt was still angry and frustrated as he bitterly pondered the fate that had changed his once easygoing brother into a man so totally obsessed with wealth. Allowing his thoughts to wander, he tried to come to grips with the man his brother had become.

Striding to the window, he parted the curtains and stared out across the night-shrouded city. How had it all come about? Just a few months ago they had been happy. Their father had been alive and the lucrative Kincade Shipping firm had been flourishing. Now he and Noah were at the brink of financial ruin, the strain of which was tearing them apart.

Matt shook his head sorrowfully as he remembered the trauma of the duel with Radcliffe. It seemed to him now, as he pondered it, that the changes in Noah had already occurred by then, but he had been just too naive to realize it. Though Noah had never related exactly what had been said by Radcliffe the night before their fateful encounter, the insult that was issued had stirred a cold, deadly resolve within Noah and sealed, possibly forever, the transformation of his very being.

Sighing in resignation, Matt turned from the window. He knew he would get little rest this night. As he stretched out, still dressed, on the comfort of the wide bed, he couldn't help but wonder if Noah would ever be the same again.

Chapter Three

"Marry me, CC. You've kept me waiting long enough." John Robinson's proposal was ardent as he held the woman he loved within the possessive circle of his arms. "I've spoken with your father and he has no objection. It's up to you now. You know how I feel."

CC regarded her longtime beau, John Robinson, from beneath slightly lowered lashes. She cared for John and didn't want to hurt him, but she knew that she did not share the same feelings that he did. He was her friend and her confidant in many things, but love . . . no, she didn't love John.

"I'm sorry, John," she demurred softly. "I care about you. I truly do, but I'm not ready to marry yet."

John's temper flared. As a gainfully employed, very attractive, very eligible bachelor, he was sought after by many women, all of whom were eager for his attentions, but he had spurned them for CC. She was the only woman he wanted, and yet, after paying serious court to her for months, she was still aloof. It was maddening!

Of course, John knew that he'd been warned. Many men before him had tried to win her elusive heart, and none had succeeded. Now, to his despair, it looked like he, too, was to suffer their same fate . . . unrequited love.

Still, no matter how he tried to downplay it, her answer hurt, and he couldn't stop himself from pressing her for some kind of more definitive answer besides "I'm not ready to marry yet."

"When will you be ready to marry, CC?" he challenged. "You're twenty-two. Most women of your age have settled down and—" John got no further as the copper-haired vixen reacted sharply to his statement.

"I am not most women, John Robinson," she told him haughtily, her green eyes flashing in the heat of her sudden anger. How dare he relate her age to her marital status! No man was ever criticized for waiting to marry; indeed, they were often congratulated by their comrades for having avoided the "trap" for so long. Annoyed, she moved quickly out of his embrace.

John quickly realized the mistake he'd made and he hastened to make amends. "I know you're not like other women, CC. You're different . . . special. That's why I love you and want to make you mine." Going to her, he tried to take her back into his arms in hopes of smoothing things over, but she would have none of it.

"No, John." CC coolly avoided his embrace. "And if your feelings are as serious as you say, then maybe we shouldn't continue to see one another."

John's declaration that he wanted to *make her his* grated on her nerves. She would belong to no man. The man she would marry, if indeed she ever did marry, would have to accept her as an equal, no less. She would not be chattel. His superior attitude erased the slight guilt she'd been feeling and convinced her more firmly than ever that John was not the right man for her.

"But, CC . . ." he came toward her.

She held up a hand to stop his progress. "I don't want you to think that there's more to our relationship than what exists openly between us."

John stood silently for a moment staring at her. She was

lovely, his heart's desire, and yet his wounded pride almost prodded him to agree to end their relationship. His heart, however, refused to even consider an existence without her.

His dark eyes fixed upon her, John spoke slowly. "I love you. I have for a long time."

Though she longed to erase the past few minutes and resume their friendship as it had been, CC knew it was impossible and that from now on things between them would never be the same.

"I'm sorry, John, but I'm just not ready to think about marriage yet. You, of all people, should know that."

John grimaced inwardly at the truth in her claim. He knew very well in what direction her interest lay, and it certainly wasn't in hearth and home. "But don't you realize that the danger is growing? It isn't safe for you to be so involved any longer."

Again, his domineering attitude screeched through her. Who was he to tell her what she could and could not do?

"John. I will not allow you or anyone to dictate my life. If you insist on continuing to try to do so, I'll put an end to our relationship right now," CC told him emotionally. "And as far as the movement is concerned, I've been involved in it for a long time, and I intend to stay involved."

John sighed. He loved her. He wanted to marry her and keep her at home having his children, away from the violence that was sure to erupt soon, but she would have none of it. Resignedly, he realized that he would have to bide his time and hope that she would someday come to accept that he was right. Until then, he would continue as he had, loving her, but never having the right to claim her as his own.

"All right," he agreed in temporary defeat. "You've made your point and I see no reason to discuss this any further."

"You understand?" she asked hopefully, for he had been a good friend and she did not want to lose his companionship.

"I'm trying, CC. Believe me, I'm trying." He sounded disgruntled.

45

"Thank you, John." She smiled sweetly at him, and as usual, John felt himself melt before her considerable charms.

"I almost forgot. . . ." John spoke in low tones, forcing his thoughts back to reality. "Tomorrow night, eleven o'clock, the room in back of the stables of the Green Dragon Inn."

Her expression grew suddenly serious. "I'll meet you as usual."

"Fine," he agreed as he realized that there was nothing more to discuss. "Well, I'll be going."

"John?"

He gave her a quizzical glance.

"You'll still be my guest at our ball, won't you?"

Heartened that she still wanted him to escort her, he smiled. "I wouldn't miss it."

"Just remember," she confided. "Father made out the guest list, and everyone he invited is a loyalist."

"I'll be my usual Tory self," John assured her, for he'd become a near master at hiding his true feelings toward the king and Parliament.

As she crossed the room to accompany him to the door, John was unable to resist one last kiss, and he took the opportunity to boldly sweep her into his arms.

"John . . ." she gasped, surprised by his ploy.

"Just because I accepted your refusal gracefully doesn't mean I don't want you, CC," he murmured as his lips claimed hers in a passionate kiss.

CC was not a stranger to his embrace, and she remained passive, finding his kiss neither exciting nor repulsive. When he finally released her, she moved away, his kiss leaving her womanly depths untouched by desire's fiery blade.

John, however, was not so unaffected by the exchange, and his breathing was rasping as he convinced himself that someday she would finally admit to loving him. He left the house then, murmuring in quiet promise, "Tomorrow . . ."

As the door closed behind him, CC hurried down the wide center hall to her father's study, where she knew she would find him awaiting her. As she reached the door, she met Gilbert, their butler, on his way out.

"Be sure to bring him in to me as soon as he arrives," Edward Demorest was saying.

"Yes, sir," came the polite reply as the servant held the portal wide for CC.

"Father?" she spoke softly and hesitated only briefly until she saw his welcoming smile.

At fifty-three, Edward Demorest was the picture of good health, and as always, CC marveled at the vitality he exuded. He had been a dashingly handsome young man, as evidenced by the oil portrait of him that hung over the fireplace in the parlor, and his dark good looks had not faded with the passage of time. Trim and fit, his black hair streaked with silver, his hazel eyes glinting with good humor, he was still a very attractive man. He'd been a widower for some ten years now, and more than a few of the ladies had set their caps for him. Edward, however, was not interested in remarriage, though he cut a wide swath through their numbers. CC's mother, Sarah, had been his soul mate. No one else would ever be able to take her place in his affections.

"Come in, come in." Edward waved his daughter into the private haven that was his study.

CC smiled engagingly as she entered the room. "Do you have a business appointment soon?"

"Yes, Lord Kincade arrived in Boston yesterday and we've a meeting set up for this afternoon," he explained.

CC couldn't help but wrinkle her nose slightly in distaste at the thought of the English nobleman. Though she'd never met this Lord Kincade, her encounters with other egotistical, supercilious members of the *ton* had left her completely unimpressed. CC hoped that she would be able to avoid this newcomer when he finally arrived, for no doubt he would be just as foppish as all the others she'd known.

"I see." Her reply did not hide her already established dislike of the as yet unseen Englishman. Her father cast her a

47

sharp glance.

"He will be here on business." His tone was sharp, as he had intended it to be. Edward knew of his daughter's low opinion of the members of the peerage, and he had no desire for a possible run-in between the newly arrived Kincade and outspoken CC.

"Then I will endeavor to stay our of your way," she teased with a lightness of spirit.

"Vixen," Edward growled, his eyes dancing with amusement. "Now, to matters at hand . . . ?" He led the conversation, anticipating good news regarding a change in her present marital status.

"What matters, Father?" CC kept her features schooled into a mask of wide-eyed innocence as she strolled casually to the floor-to-ceiling casement window that looked out over their spacious garden.

"Blast it, girl! Don't play coy with me!" Edward had known her far too long to be taken in by her mischievous ways. "Tell me what you told the young buck! Am I to have a chance at grandchildren soon or not?"

"I'm afraid it's not quite your time yet, Papa," she told him kittenishly, and she was rewarded with a frustrated groan. CC couldn't stop the chuckle that threatened, and she laughed as he scowled at her blackly. "Oh, Father," she sighed as she came to stand behind him, looping her arms affectionately around his neck and giving him a sweet hug, "I'm sorry, but I'm just not ready to marry yet."

"Sorry, bah!" he snorted in derision. "You're twenty-two years old, my lass. Well past the time for marriage! Why, when your mother was your age, she had already been married four years and had borne you."

"I know that, Papa, but I am not Mother," CC answered gently.

"It wouldn't hurt for you to try to be more like her. She was a wonderful woman, and I shall always mourn the day she was taken from me," he related in a solemn tone as he thought of his dear departed wife, Sarah.

CC tightened her arms about his neck for just a brief instant in sympathetic understanding before moving to sit in the chair opposite his desk.

"Well, you might as well tell me everything," Edward grumbled, studying the beautiful woman who was his daughter. How like her mother she looked, he mused as he gazed at her with loving eyes. Her hair was long and russet. As was her custom during the day, she'd pinned the sides up and away from her face, framing her perfect features with a tumbling array of thick, glossy curls. Her eyes were the mirror of her soul, as her mother's had been. Vividly green and reflecting a quick, keen intelligence, they could be sparkling with joy one moment or flashing fire the next. Her complexion was perfect, her nose slender, her mouth wide and given to easy laughter.

Edward knew CC was a woman to be reckoned with, for she was an educated woman of opinion. He also knew that he was the one responsible for having raised her to think as freely as she did, and he was now ruing the day. Though he loved her as no other, they seemed at odds on just about every subject. True, CC always gave the appearance of being in deference to his masculine mandates, but Edward somehow sensed that it was all an illusion, that underneath she held very firm convictions from which she would not be swayed—a less than desirable trait she'd inherited from him. His daughter was not a malleable female, and that thought bothered him. The ability to surrender to a man's will and submit to him as head of the household was the main quality that most men wanted in a wife. He wondered if his child would ever find her mate.

"What did the poor lad do that made you reject him?"

"Nothing, and there's not a lot to tell, Papa," CC began. "You know that John and I have been seeing one another for some time now."

"Yes, yes . . . so go on. . . ." he encouraged impatiently.

"So, unknown to me, John's feelings had developed into something deeper than friendship," she explained.

"And yours didn't?"

"No. I don't love John," she replied honestly. "He's a good man, and kind, too, but I feel nothing more for him than friendship."

Edward thumped the top of his desk loudly. "Don't you see, woman, sometimes love comes after marriage! John's a good man. You said so yourself. His affiliations are the same as mine, and he brings in a good living. He'd be the perfect husband for you! He's not bad-looking either, if I'm any judge of men, and you'd certainly make handsome babies together."

CC flushed at his last statement. "I will not marry a man I do not love, Father. After all, you were in love with Mother when you married her, weren't you?"

"I give up!" he muttered in exasperation, and she immediately brightened at the thought.

"Do you really?" she queried hopefully.

"Never," he came back quickly, smiling despite his heartfelt disappointment. "The right man for you is out there somewhere." He steepled his fingers in a thoughtful gesture as he regarded her.

"I don't doubt that for a moment, Papa," CC agreed easily.

"Just don't wait too much longer to find him! I do want to live to see my grandchildren."

She laughed lightly. "If that's your only worry, I'd say I have a good long time to work with."

Edward growled good-naturedly as a reluctant smile curved his lips.

"Now, about the ball Friday night . . ." CC ventured, glad to be off the subject of John and marriage.

"Yes, what about it? Is there a problem?"

"No. Everything's running smoothly. It's just that there's another couple I'd like to invite."

"It's a bit late for that, isn't it?" He frowned, trying to imagine who he could have forgotten. "Was there someone I forgot?"

"Ryan Graves and his wife, Rachel."

"What?! Graves?! He's a Whig! I'll not have him in my house!" he thundered as he thought of the outspoken supporter of John Hancock and Sam Adams.

"Papa, they're very nice," CC said determinedly.

"And just how would you know?" Edward had long been aware of CC's interest in the political affairs of Boston, but he had not known that she was involved to the extent that she would have made the acquaintance of someone of Graves's caliber.

"I met them at Faneuil Hall some weeks ago. They seemed very—" she got no further.

"Faneuil Hall?!" He looked at her aghast, for he knew that Faneuil Hall was the main meeting place for the rabble that wanted to stir up trouble in Boston. "What were you doing at Faneuil Hall?"

"There was a meeting and I—"

"You were at a meeting there?! I'll tell you about those meetings, miss! They're nothing but a gathering of malcontents. Why, if those fools have their way, this town would be in a shambles in a week! Stay away from those gatherings. God only knows what might happen one of these nights."

"There is a lot of truth in what's being said there, Papa," she insisted.

"Truth? Bah!" he snorted derisively. "It's only the truth as those rabble-rousers see it! Don't you realize that our allegiance is totally to the king? We owe everything we have to the Crown. This house, your education . . . why, our very safety is ensured because the troops are here."

"And they certainly provided safety for us several years ago, didn't they?" The thought of the troops quartered in Boston always angered her, for she had been there the night that several soldiers on sentry duty had opened fire on a

51

crowd of unarmed colonists. She had seen it all . . . the death, the misery . . . and she would never forget it. It was burned into her memory—a bloody, fiery image of dying men. It was that remembrance that fueled her driving compulsion to be involved in the rebel movement.

Edward's expression turned grave as he remembered the night when she had come in totally distraught over what she'd seen. "I know it was a terrible thing for you to witness, but the courts ruled it was self-defense. They were exonerated, and that settled it in my mind."

"Well, it didn't settle it in mine!"

He shook his head slowly. "I don't understand how you can even think about going against England. By God, I'm a loyal Englishman! Just because we live here in the colonies doesn't make it any less so."

"Then why doesn't Parliament treat us like Englishmen?" CC demanded sharply. She understood well all the politics of the times and wanted more than anything to show her father the validity of the idea of independence for America.

"They're treating us better than Englishmen!" her father argued, believing in his heart that they were privileged to live under British authority. "Why, we can buy tea here cheaper than they can in London, and yet these insurgents are still running around complaining about the minuscule tax on it."

"It's more than just the tax, and you know it. They're trying to establish a monopoly in the tea market, and if we allow them that much, where will it end?" She did not back down.

Edward's dark-eyed gaze hardened. He loved her, but enough was enough. "You are a woman, Cecelia Marie, and as such, you shouldn't be concerning yourself with these matters.

CC was so infuriated by his attitude that she felt as if she were about to explode. He had encouraged her education, encouraged her readings, encouraged her to develop her own opinions. Now that she'd formed them, he fell back on the old, trite adage, *You're a woman and you shouldn't be concerning yourself*. Her frustration was so great that she wanted to scream!

"You are under my authority," Edward was continuing, "and until you take a husband, you would do well to remember that."

For a brief instant the idea of marrying held vast appeal; at least then she would be away from his repressive attitude. As quickly as she thought it, though, CC knew she loved him too much to marry just to free herself of his domination. Besides, the law dictated that a woman was completely under the control of her husband, too. So unless she chose her future mate wisely, she would probably end up more stifled than she was now.

Knowing that she had pushed her father as far as she could hope to for the moment, she employed her outwardly submissive strategy to calm him. "I'm aware of my place in life, Father."

As CC had hoped he'd be, Edward was caught off guard by her quick change of mood, and he cleared his throat nervously at her suddenly sweet demeanor.

"But, Papa . . ." she continued.

"What?" he asked abruptly, not completely trusting her transformation.

"*You* were the one who taught me to think for myself." An angelic smile accompanied her words.

Blustering good-naturedly, Edward admitted gruffly, "That I did and it's a good thing, too. You must always remember, though, that thinking something and saying it are two different things. You may think whatever you wish, but as a woman, you must never expound upon it."

As much as CC loved him, his censoring words sent another sharp pang of bitterness through her. How unfair it seemed that social convention dictated that, because she was a woman, her opinion was deemed of no consequence. The injustice of it was staggering.

53

"Yes, Papa," she said a bit sadly as she went to him once more and pressed a soft kiss on his cheek. "I know." CC realized that her father was not responsible for the dictates of society, even though he lived by them.

"Good." He patted her hand. "Now, run along like a good girl. I have much to do and little time."

"I'll go . . . but the Graveses . . . ?"

"The guest list stands as is. I want no agitators in my home. Is that clear?"

"Yes," she replied with suitable humbleness, all the while wondering what he would think should he learn of John's and her affiliation with "agitators."

"I expect that you'll mind your tongue with our guests. I don't think Governor Hutchinson or Major Winthrop would appreciate your expounding on ideas of taxation without representation or independence from the king," he dictated as she moved toward the door. "I know I wouldn't. This will be a purely social affair."

"I promise I'll not embarrass you, Papa." CC considered with some humor how outraged his loyalist guests would be if they ever discovered her true thoughts.

"Good . . . good. Now, be off with you. I've work to do before my meeting with Lord Kincade." He hesitated just an instant before adding, "Wait . . . there just might be another guest."

CC had already opened the door to leave and she paused, halfway out of the room, to glance back at him questioningly. "Oh? Who?"

"Lord Kincade, of course. I'm surprised I didn't think of this sooner. I shall invite him this afternoon, and if he accepts and honors us with his presence Friday night, I expect that you will graciously make him feel welcome."

CC had not heard the butler admit Noah to the house and she did not know that he was guiding him directly to the study, as Edward had requested earlier.

"But, Father," she insisted, ignorant of Noah's presence

54

just behind her in the hall, "you know how I feel. I mean, it's going to be miserable enough tolerating that ass Lord Radcliffe, and now you're including another nobleman. . . ."

Noah and the servant could not help but hear their conversation as they stood a few steps from CC. The butler was about to make their presence known, but Noah stilled him with a restraining hand.

The woman, who was obviously Edward Demorest's daughter, did not mince words as she continued her argument, and Noah listened with interest as he gazed upon her from behind. Though the vitriolic diatribe she was spouting was nothing short of a character assassination of him, he found himself intrigued by her slender, womanly form and the rich, glossy thickness of her hair as it tumbled about her shoulders in soft, natural curls. He wondered idly what she looked like. No doubt, he thought, with a tongue like that, she had the face of a shrew.

"Cecelia . . ." Edward was threatening stonily.

"I know he's going to be just like all the other aristocratic noblemen I've met," CC derided, not looking forward to meeting this newcomer. "He's either going to be old, fat, and ugly or so much of a mincing fop that he's more of a miss than I am!"

"Cecelia!" He was shocked at her outspokenness.

"Papa, why be so surprised? You know it's true. Why, that awful Lord Ralston who was here last year was nothing but a—"

"Silence!" he all but bellowed, knowing exactly what Ralston's unusual preferences had been. He found her knowledge of his oddity distressing. Where had he gone wrong?

"Yes, Papa," CC replied with a slight smile, relieving him considerably. "And at your insistence, I'll do my best to make Lord Kincade feel welcome."

"You most certainly will, young lady. I must say that I'm appalled by your attitude, and quite disappointed, too," he

55

lectured, shaking his head ruefully. "Not all noblemen are like Lord Ralston, you know."

"I'm only speaking the truth, and you know it," she returned saucily. "And now, I'll go and let you get back to work, for I see there is absolutely no point in discussing this anymore."

"Indeed," he remarked dryly, turning his attention back to the papers spread before him.

"I'll see you at dinner." CC took a step backward into the hall and gasped suddenly as she encountered the hard, solid wall of a man's chest. A pair of strong hands gripped her shoulders to help steady her as she almost lost her balance in her surprise. She spun quickly around, breaking that contact, to see who had dared eavesdrop on her private conversation with her father.

The man who towered above her was well over six feet tall, and CC stared up at him blankly for a moment, trying to place him in her memory, but she knew beyond a doubt that, had she met him before, she would have remembered. His features were lean and handsome and he was deeply tanned, as if he spent much time outdoors. His hair, worn unpowdered, was dark and his eyes . . . Lord, his eyes were fascinating, she mused distractedly. . . . They were gray, she was certain, but at the moment they seemed almost silver, revealing nothing of his inner emotions. As if reading her thoughts, he smiled down at her mockingly, and a shiver of expectant excitement chased down her spine.

Having listened attentively to her critical assessment of his finer points with cynical amusement, Noah had fully expected her to be ugly, reasoning that her prejudiced opinion of aristocrats was directly related to a well-earned set-down some peer had issued. He was caught totally by surprise when she whirled about, and he found himself staring down into a pair of the most beautiful green eyes he'd ever seen. The sight of her face sent a shock of awareness through him unlike anything he'd ever experienced before, and he stood perfectly still for a moment as their gazes clashed. She was lovely, and he was astounded. No horse-faced miss, this chit; far from it. Her features were so arresting that even the determined tilt of her chin as she glared challengingly up at him could not detract from her beauty.

With the strict self-discipline that he always practiced, Noah brought his turbulent thoughts under control. Women were the last thing he needed to concern himself with these days. Polly would suit. He had no need or desire for any involvement with any other female, especially not a shrewish, viper-tongued one, no matter how gorgeous she was. Noah gave her his most sardonic smile as he spoke.

"May I introduce myself?" His deep, accented voice was a velvet caress on her senses, and she could only nod as she awaited his pronouncement. "Lord Noah Kincade, at your service." He bowed elegantly as she stood speechlessly before him, and he was smugly pleased by her obvious confusion.

A flush of embarrassment stung CC's cheeks as she stared at him wide-eyed in her acute mortification. He was Lord Kincade, and she had no doubt that he had heard every word she'd just so scathingly spoken. She swallowed nervously as she tried to think of an appropriate response.

Edward, wondering at the commotion in the hall, stepped out of the room just as Noah introduced himself to CC.

"Lord Kincade? By Jove, you're here! Delighted, absolutely delighted." He was nervous as he wondered just how much of CC's derogatory declarations the nobleman had heard. "I'm Edward Demorest, and this is my daughter, Cecelia."

"Mr. Demorest." Noah greeted him cordially before turning back to the young woman. "And Miss Demorest . . ." Noah spoke her name slowly. "Charming," he intoned drolly. His gaze swept over her in cool assessment before swinging back to her father, the effect being one of complete and indifferent dismissal.

At his abrupt, arrogant manner a spark of embarrassed anger seared through CC's momentarily stunned senses, and she glared at him venomously.

"Indeed, Lord Kincade," she shot back, wondering why she found his snubbing so irritating. He was a titled gentleman. Hadn't she come to expect such behavior from them? They were all so pompous . . . so obnoxiously vain. The fact that she found him attractive had nothing to do with it, she declared to herself vehemently. CC gritted her teeth as she gave her father a sweet smile. "Father, if you'll excuse me, I'll leave you gentlemen to your business. . . ."

"Of course, dear." Judging from Kincade's calm manner, Edward felt certain that Kincade had not overheard his daughter's disparaging comments, and he was exceedingly grateful. "Come in and have a seat," he invited, leading the way back into the study. Directing Noah to the chair before his desk, he shut the door behind them.

CC stared at the closed portal for a moment before turning away to find the butler still standing there.

"I'm sorry, Miss CC," Gilbert apologized humbly, knowing how embarrassed she'd been by the Englishman's presence, "but the gentleman hushed me when I started to announce him."

"He did, did he?" That news infuriated her all the more. The damned scoundrel! He had deliberately eavesdropped! How dare he!

"Miss CC?" He read the range of emotions on her expressive face and knew a moment of disconcertion.

CC was angry, but not at the butler. "Don't worry about it, Gilbert. It's not your fault that he's a conscienceless cad who would deliberately listen in on someone else's private conversation."

He was relieved that her irritation wasn't directed at him. "Can I do anything else for you?"

"No, Gilbert, I'm fine, thank you."

"Do you think Lord Kincade will be staying for dinner?" the servant inquired.

"I hope not," she muttered under her breath in annoyance as she walked off.

"Miss CC?" he ventured again, not having heard her answer. "I'm sorry. I didn't hear you."

CC paused to answer. "You'll have to check with my father. I'm not sure if their business meeting will last that long or not."

"Yes, ma'am. I'll do that."

Hoping she'd seen the last of the obnoxious Lord Noah Kincade, CC again started off to her room.

Chapter Four

Edward smiled in satisfaction as he regarded Noah across his desk. They had been poring over contracts and manifests for more than an hour and had finally come to a mutually beneficial agreement regarding the *Lorelei*'s current load of merchandise.

"A toast to an agreement well met?" he offered as he rose and strode to the liquor cabinet across the room.

"Thank you, Edward," Noah agreed. He had found him a tough but fair man to deal with and he was pleased with the terms they'd finally settled upon. The profit from the *Lorelei*'s goods would keep Matthew and him comfortably until the *Pride*'s arrival.

"Bourbon? Or sherry, perhaps?"

"Bourbon will be fine."

Edward poured two generous tumblers of the golden liquid and handed one to Noah. "To our future business dealings. May they be as successful as this one."

"I see no reason why they shouldn't be." Noah nodded in accord as he sipped of the potent brew, but even as he said it, his thoughts were on the possibility of his upcoming meeting with Smith.

"You say you have another ship due in port soon?"

"The *Sea Pride*," he provided. "The best I can figure,

depending on the weather, she should make port sometime around the first of the year."

"You'll be staying until spring then?"

"Yes. Atlantic crossings are hardly the thing during the winter months, so Matthew and I will remain until the weather breaks."

"Wise choice. I made the voyage once, several years ago, and I vowed never to do it again if I could possibly avoid it," Edward said with a rueful shake of his head. "We encountered storm after storm and I spent most of my time belowdecks, fighting off seasickness. The entire trip took four months and it seemed more like four years." He laughed at his own remembered discomfort as he placed his now empty glass on his desktop. "But enough of that. Let's speak of more enjoyable pursuits. I'd be honored if you'd agree to stay and dine with me."

"Thank you." Noah was pleased at the invitation, for he knew it would be to his benefit. In cultivating Edward, a most loyal British agent, he would be laying the groundwork for preventing any future suspicion regarding his activities.

"Wonderful," Edward said as he rang for a servant.

"Will your wife and daughter be joining us?" Noah asked casually.

"I'm a widower, my lord," he answered.

"My deepest sympathies, sir."

"I appreciate the thought, but my beloved Sarah has been dead for many years now." Sadness reflected in his eyes as he spoke. "It's just CC and me."

"CC?"

"Cecelia, my daughter," he offered quickly, grinning. "CC's a pet name. She's always been a spirited lass, and somehow it just suits her."

Noah nodded, but he hardly agreed with Demorest's description of his daughter. Spirited was not quite the word he would have used to describe Cecelia Demorest. The chit possessed a sharp tongue for such an attractive woman, and it was a fault that Edward, as her father, would do well to see curbed.

When the butler appeared at the door, Edward ordered, "Gilbert, Lord Kincade will be staying for dinner. Please inform Cook, and then tell CC that a guest will be joining us."

The servant left hastily to do his master's bidding, wondering all the while what Miss CC was going to think of the news he was about to relay.

"Are you serious?" CC flared in annoyance as Gilbert imparted the news moments later.

"Yes, ma'am," Gilbert replied respectfully. "They concluded their business and your father invited him to stay. Cook says the meal will be served in about an hour."

"All right," she groaned in dismay, accepting the inevitable. "You may tell Father that I'll be down to join them as soon as I freshen up."

"I'll do that, ma'am." He backed discreetly from her room, leaving his mistress to her thoughts.

When he'd gone, CC stalked to her wardrobe and threw wide the door. Standing, hands on hips, she stared at her vast selection of gowns. She didn't know why she was concerned about it, but some bit of pride within her refused to allow the arrogant Kincade to see her at less than her very best. He had dismissed her earlier as if she were little more than a guttersnipe, and she was determined to show that pompous fool that she was no easily forgotten rustic miss. Impatiently, she began to sort through her clothing, hoping to find the perfect dress to wear. Spying her favorite yellow silk, CC whisked it from the closet. It was perfect . . . not too dressy, yet not too ordinary, and the pale yellow-gold was a very good color on her.

She rang for her maid, Anna. When the young girl appeared, she requested a bath be sent up. By the time her bath was ready, CC was waiting, clad only in a silken wrapper.

"Shall I help you bathe, Miss CC?" Anna asked.

"No, but I would like you to lay out the rest of my things before you go," she instructed. "I'll be wearing the yellow silk."

"Yes, ma'am." The maid quickly set about her task, asking as she did, "Did you see His Lordship, Miss CC?"

"Yes, I saw him." Her less than enthusiastic answer drew a questioning glance from her servant.

"Did you not think him the most gorgeous man you've ever seen?" Anna sighed, her excitement at the handsome lord's presence obvious.

"Frankly, Anna, I thought the man an overbearing idiot, just like the rest of his breed!" CC snapped shortly.

"Lord Kincade?" The maid was astounded. "But, ma'am, he's tall and ever so good-looking! Why, I've never seen such a fine figure of a man before.... And to think he's a nobleman besides!" Anna remarked dreamily.

"And there's the rub," CC retorted as she slipped out of her robe and stepped into the bathtub.

"If you say so," the servant quickly demurred, not wanting to incur her wrath. "But, frankly, Miss CC, I wouldn't mind a handsome lord like him sweeping me off my feet and taking me back to live on his estate in England!"

"Well, believe me, Anna, you'll get no competition from me." She lowered herself carefully into the steaming bath and sighed in contentment as the hot, scented water caressed her. "He's all yours."

"If he looks my way, I'll remember that." The maid laughed in delight at her own fantasy of the fabulous Lord Kincade carrying her off into the sunset. "Now, will you be needing anything else?"

"No . . . that's all, but you might come back in a few minutes to help me with my gown."

Anna nodded and disappeared from the room to allow her

mistress her privacy.

Though CC knew she should hurry in order to help her father entertain his guest, she found the bath's welcoming warmth infinitely preferable to the thought of seeing Lord Kincade again. With leisurely delight, she soaked. It was long minutes later when she finally finished washing and rose in sleek, dripping splendor from the soapy depths of the tub. CC started to reach for the towel Anna had left out for her when she noticed her own reflection in the full-length mirror across the room. She stared at herself with interest, studying her body for the first time with a critical eye. Her breasts were full, but not to the point of being heavy. The trimness of her waist emphasized the firm roundness of her hips, and her legs were slender and shapely. As she wrapped the towel about her, CC felt good about herself. She knew she was an attractive woman, and after she completed her toilette and took the extra time to artfully style her hair up and away from her face tonight, she knew she would feel confident enough to handle the *very smug* Lord Kincade.

"I can't imagine what's keeping CC," Edward complained as he moved to the doorway of the parlor and glanced up the staircase for what seemed like the hundredth time. "Been well over half an hour now. . . ."

"It seems the way with women." Noah commiserated easily from where he sat on the sofa.

"Not CC," he stated flatly, used to his daughter's punctuality and puzzled by her tardiness.

"Really? Then she must be the exception to the rule." Noah quirked a brow as he watched his host move about the room. He wondered idly why she was taking so long. Had she been so embarrassed by their earlier run-in that she didn't want to face him? Noah felt certain that that had to be the reason.

"CC is the exception to many rules, I'm afraid," he began.

64

"Wait . . . here she is now." Edward went swiftly to her as she descended the stairs, and Noah rose from the sofa to acknowledge her as she swept into the room on her father's arm.

"Good evening, Lord Kincade," CC said, facing him.

For the briefest of instants, Noah was struck almost speechless. Only the long years of jaded living in London that had perfected his self-control enabled him to maintain his air of cool aloofness as he stared at Cecelia Demorest, for she was, without a doubt, the most beautiful woman he'd ever seen. He had thought her most pretty before, but nothing had prepared him for this. Her complexion was creamy and flawless, her burnished hair perfectly coiffed, and her gown fit her exquisitely, molding the sweet curve of her bosom in a caress of golden silk. Noah could only envy the sensuous cloth.

With an effort of will, he kept all expression from his face as he greeted her politely. "Miss Demorest."

CC's emerald eyes sparkled with deceptive innocence as she gazed up at him. There was no denying it, she thought with dismay. Anna was right. Lord Kincade definitely was one gorgeous man. Still, CC refused to let herself be affected by his striking good looks. He might have the advantage over the other aristocrats she'd met because of his physical attractiveness, but he was still the arrogant titled Englishman who'd eavesdropped on her conversation, and she wanted nothing to do with him. She would treat him nicely only to please her father, and that was that.

"How wonderful that you could stay and sup with us." She kept her voice soft to disguise the underlying sarcasm she was feeling.

"It was kind of your father to invite me," Noah returned, putting her beauty into perspective. Lovely or not, this was the same woman who had voiced such a scathing opinion of him, and quite without provocation. "May I say how lovely you look this evening?" he offered perfunctorily.

"Thank you, my lord," CC answered with equal coolness, feeling somehow a bit disappointed that he was less than overwhelmed by her. She had wanted to put him in his place, to show him just how sophisticated she really was. Yet he'd given no indication at all, other than his offhand compliment, that he found her in the least attractive. "I do believe the meal is ready to be served. Shall we go into the dining room?"

Leading the way, CC started into the splendidly appointed room and she was surprised when Kincade moved to hold her chair for her. She glanced up at him trying to read his expression, but his features were a mask of polite civility.

"My lord." She nodded slightly in acknowledgment of his gentlemanly act.

The touch was a simple thing, the mere resting of his hand at the small of her back as he guided her to her seat. Still, the sensation the contact aroused in CC was shocking, and she stiffened in response to it. He had only lightly touched her in a courteous, impersonal gesture, for heaven's sake, and yet a thrill of excitement tingled through her unlike anything she'd ever experienced before. Her breath caught in her throat, her heart skipped a beat, and beneath the satiny fabric of her gown, her breasts swelled and tautened, their sensitive peaks pressing pointedly against the restraining confines of the material. Desperately she fought to subdue her rampant reaction.

Worrying that Kincade had noticed her disquiet, she cast a sideways glance at him as he moved to take his own seat. CC was relieved to find that he seemed totally unaware of the fact that his nearness had sent her senses reeling, and she breathed a little easier. *What in the world was wrong with her?* she berated herself as she tried to resist the feelings that were flooding through her.

Though he gave no outward indication, Noah was irritated as he took his seat opposite CC at the table. He had felt her sudden tenseness as he'd guided her to her chair and

66

he wondered if the dislike she had for him truly ran so deep that a simple touch could affect her so. The thought irked him more than he was willing to admit. Not that he cared. However, it was just that women had always found him attractive, and the idea that CC, a simple colonial, thought him less than desirable was annoying.

Edward had stood back and allowed Noah and CC to lead the way into the dining room. His eyes were shining with pride as he watched them walk ahead of him, and he couldn't help but admire the handsome couple they made. The idea of a match between then suddenly occurred to him, and the thought was not without merit, he decided. Kincade was pleasant enough, and the possibility of his daughter marrying a wealthy aristocrat pleased him immensely. He knew that if he could arrange a marriage between them, he would have done his best for CC. Still, Edward wondered in dismay how he could possibly encourage it when CC had already ardently proclaimed her dislike of all English noblemen. It was a tricky situation, and he realized that he would have to use the utmost discretion in whatever he tried to do. Hurrying forth, he joined them at the table and set about to enjoy the repast.

"So tell us of your home in England," Edward invited as the servants set the main course before them some time later. "You have family there, of course?"

"Actually, no. My younger brother Matthew is my only family, and he traveled with me this trip."

"He's here in Boston? We could have sent the carriage for him. . . ."

"He knew that I was coming here on business and that there was a possibility I would be delayed," Noah explained. "So I told him before I left the inn to avail himself of the services there."

"Perhaps another time then?"

"Of course."

CC was paying little attention to their small talk as she sat at the table opposite Noah. The titillation of his touch had left her disturbed and distracted, and she was still wondering, in some confusion, why she had reacted the way she had. What was there about this man that he had the power to unsettle her with such a simple touch? Surely, CC tried to rationalize, it was only because Kincade was handsome, and nothing else. But even as she made the effort to convince herself of that, she knew that she had been with good-looking men before and had never experienced any reaction like this. Finally, unable to find a logical answer, she determinedly put all thoughts of it from her and busied herself with the meal.

"We're having a formal ball on Friday evening, and we'd be honored to have both you and your brother attend," Edward invited.

"It's most kind of you to include us, Edward," Noah replied graciously, hoping that the rebels he needed to meet with did not hold their next meeting that night.

"Then you'll come?"

"Matthew and I would be delighted."

"That's wonderful." Edward smiled widely as he glanced at CC. She had been quiet during the dinner, too quiet, and he wanted to bring her into the conversation. "Don't you agree, CC?"

"Oh, definitely, Father." CC forced a smile as she looked up. She fought to keep her expression pleasant, but when her gaze unwittingly locked with Noah's, she couldn't hide the irritation she felt at knowing that he would be in attendance Friday night. Thank heaven she had John! At least with him as her escort, she would be able to avoid Kincade as much as possible.

Noah saw the flicker of annoyance in CC's face, and his eyes narrowed as he regarded her coldly. CC found herself staring into his impenetrable silvered gaze. Though she was unnerved by the complete lack of warmth in his mirrored regard, she held his eyes levelly, breaking away only when the sound of her father's voice broke the mood.

"Good, good," Edward was saying cheerfully. He had been so absorbed in his food that he had missed the sudden tension between them.

Desperate for something to say to prove to him that she had not been affected by his frigid glare, CC asked, "How old is your brother, Lord Kincade?"

"Matthew is seventeen, although he'll be the first to tell you that he'll be eighteen within the month," Noah smiled.

It was the first time that CC had seen him smile, and the transformation in him was nothing short of amazing. His features before had been so cruelly arrogant, so set and hard. Yet when he smiled, he seemed a different man. His whole countenance had been softened by the power of that one gesture, and she wondered distractedly what it would be like if he ever smiled at her that way.

Her musings were interrupted then as the dessert was served, and when they'd eaten their fill of the chef's creamy concoction, they retired to the parlor to savor an after-dinner drink.

CC wanted nothing more than to retire to her room, to get away from Kincade's disturbing presence, but she knew she had no good reason to go to her chambers early. She had to remain and help entertain her father's guest.

"The dinner was delicious, Edward," Noah complimented as he accepted a snifter of brandy from his host. "Extend my best to your chef. He's a talented fellow."

"Indeed he is. I'm most fortunate to have him in my employ," Edward agreed as he presented CC with her liqueur before seating himself beside her on the sofa. "You'll have to come to dinner often. We'd be delighted to have you."

Noah sipped casually of his brandy. "Your hospitality is most welcome. I appreciate it."

CC almost choked on her liqueur at her father's open-ended invitation. That would be all she'd need . . . Lord

69

Kincade to dinner regularly. It took all her willpower not to show her displeasure at the prospect.

They chatted idly for a while, Noah filling Edward in on things back in England, and he, in turn, describing the pleasures of life in Boston.

"Tell me of the political scene," Noah ventured, wanting his opinion on what he'd heard the day before. "Yesterday at the inn, Matthew and I overheard a conversation between two merchants regarding unrest here. Is there any truth to the talk?"

"I'm afraid there is some truth to it."

"Oh? What's the problem?"

"The troublemakers are nothing but blithering idiots! That's the problem," he told him heatedly.

"Who are they?" His question was mildly put, a mere request from someone who wanted to know what was going on.

"The refuse of the earth," Edward snorted in disgust.

"Is it true that they want independence from the king?" Noah tried to sound incredulous.

"They're always trying to stir up trouble, but this time they're going too far. It won't work. We're loyal here. Have no doubt about that."

"Oh, I don't doubt your loyalty to the Crown, Edward. I was just trying to understand why anyone would want to break away."

"I don't understand it." He took a drink of his brandy. "It seems outrageously drastic to me to scream for independence over a simple tax on tea. There have been arguments in Parliament before over taxes. I'm sure there always will be."

CC tensed as her father tried to dismiss as unworthy the grievances of the dissenters.

"Indeed?"

"The agitators have been stirring mobs to action. They're trying to encourage an open rebellion against the king, but it won't work. This stupid tax on tea they're complaining about is negligible, and this argument that England now holds a monopoly on the tea trade is a most ridiculous complaint. . . ."

"Father . . ." CC's tone was hard as she sat stiffly next to him, and Edward glanced at her with warm affection.

"My daughter is of a differing view, I'm afraid."

"Oh?" Noah looked to CC, noticing the high color in her cheeks and the way her eyes flashed with an inner fire.

"She thinks it's wrong that—"

"I can speak for myself, Father," CC cut in righteously, completely forgetting her father's admonition to keep her opposing opinions to herself. "It's a fact that Parliament has given the British East India Company a monopoly on the tea trade in our country. The point is, we cannot stand by and allow this to happen!"

"You say 'our country,'" Noah pointed out. "England and her colonies are one and the same."

CC gave a cutting laugh. "Hardly. We are not treated fairly, Lord Kincade. You Englishmen tax us without giving us a voice in our own affairs! We are—"

"Enough, daughter!" Edward interrupted, embarrassed by her cutting frankness. "Lord Kincade, I'm sure, is not interested in any of this."

Silence hung tautly in the room as CC stood, breathless and magnificent in her barely restrained anger. It had been a long day—first, John's domineering attitude, then her father's. CC knew that if she didn't leave the room, she might say something she would later regret.

"As you can see, my father and I do differ on several major points of political interest. So if you'll excuse me? I believe I shall retire for the evening." Without waiting for an answer, CC swept from the room.

"My apologies," Edward began humbly, hoping his daughter's outburst hadn't discouraged Kincade's interest in doing business with him. "As I said before, CC is a most spirited young woman and—"

71

"That she is," Noah replied dryly, "but there's no need to apologize."

Noah had never known a woman to speak out so forcefully, and he found himself intrigued. She had the beauty of an angel, yet her temperament was fiery, her tongue sharp, and her convictions deep. Noah wondered why Edward had even allowed her to voice an opinion. Such was generally unheard of in England. Still, the news she'd imparted helped. It seemed there had to be truth to the talk of revolution if even the women were getting involved. He smiled slightly. All indications were that the *Pride*'s shipment was going to be just the thing.

"You weren't offended?" Edward was surprised by his attitude.

Noah answered wryly, "Hardly, but I have to admit I was taken aback to find two such differing opinions in one household."

Sighing, Edward rose and went to the liquor cabinet to refill his snifter. "I made the mistake of encouraging CC to grow intellectually, to think for herself, and to form her own opinions. I never dreamed hers would be so at odds with mine."

"The curse of many a parent, I would think," Noah replied nonchalantly as he swirled his brandy in the snifter before drinking of the heady brew.

"I'm sure," Edward agreed. "You seem most interested in the unrest. Have you any thoughts on the matter?"

"I'm afraid I don't know quite enough about it yet to have full understanding of the incidents. I was asking more for business reasons."

"Business reasons?"

"As you know, my other ship, the *Sea Pride*, is due in port soon."

"Yes, so?"

"The *Pride*'s carrying a full shipment of military supplies," he informed him.

Edward nodded pensively before saying slowly, "As much as I hate to admit it, I'm afraid they may be needed by our troops."

"I had been advised before I set sail that arms might be the most profitable of cargoes, but as an Englishman, I had hoped not," Noah lied as he looked slightly remorseful.

"And I, too, but you see how easily tempers flare. . . ." He shrugged, the action reflecting what seemed to be a weariness of soul over the matter. "There are powerful men involved in it now—rich merchant John Hancock, for one—and they're determined that there will be changes. He has quite a following, he and Sam Adams."

"Sam Adams?" Noah frowned. "I don't believe I've heard his name mentioned before. What's his connection with this?"

Edward went on to explain the fiery orator's involvement with the Whig party and his dealings with the shadowy group called the Sons of Liberty, unaware that CC was on the staircase listening intently to their conversation. It wasn't that she had been trying to hear their discussion, but their words had carried out into the hall. CC had been unable to ignore Kincade's statement that his ship was transporting war materials to the colonies. *Damn him!* she thought in outraged fury. He was one of those directly responsible for bringing in the military arms that would be used by the hated redcoats to maim and kill innocent civilians.

Her small fists clenched in futile fury, despising Lord Noah Kincade even more than she had before, she ran up the steps, anxious to seek out the solitude of her bedroom. He was dealing in war supplies. He would profit from their use. No wonder he'd wanted to know about the political situation!

CC was glad when she reached her room to discover that Anna was not there waiting for her. The last thing she needed was her maid asking her endless questions about "handsome Lord Kincade." *Ugh!* she thought forcefully. She undressed on her own, pulled on her nightdress, and plopped down on her bed in frustrated irritation. Kincade was a pompous ass . . . an unprincipled cad . . . a . . . a . . . Yet even as she condemned him, CC couldn't help but remember the way her body had responded to his touch, and she wondered what it was about him that he could destroy her cool equilibrium with just a caress.

The disquieting remembrance stayed despite CC's best effort to banish Kincade totally from her mind, and when she heard the carriage pull to a stop in front of the house, she quickly climbed out of bed and rushed to the window. There, safely hidden behind the heavy velvet drapes, she watched in silence as Kincade strode purposefully to the conveyance and climbed in. It was only after the carriage had disappeared down the street that she returned to the warm comfort of her bed and sought elusive sleep.

Chapter Five

CC couldn't believe her luck as she dutifully walked her father to the front door late the following evening.

"I hope everything goes well for you, Papa," she told him, kissing his cheek as she bid him goodbye.

"I don't understand why this meeting is so important that it couldn't wait until tomorrow morning, but I shall endeavor to make the best of it," he groused. "As it's late already, I'll no doubt be delayed past midnight. Don't wait up for me. I'll just see you in the morning."

"Yes, Papa," CC answered respectfully as he started down the steps to his waiting carriage. "Good night."

"Good night, CC."

She watched until his conveyance was out of sight before moving back inside and closing the door against the slight chill in the night air. It was with a great sigh of relief that she gathered up her skirts and darted for the staircase. Now that he was out of the way, it was time to move, and move quickly. Hurrying to her bedroom, she locked the door securely behind her and began a breathless search through the darkest corners of her armoire to find her hidden cache. When at last she had the secret bundle in hand, CC tossed it on the bed and began to undress. She was busy struggling to unbutton the buttons of her dress when the knock came at her door.

"Miss CC?" Anna's call was muffled through the locked door.

"Yes, Anna. What is it?" CC took care to keep her tone relaxed.

"I was just wondering if you were going to be needing me anymore tonight."

"No, I don't think so. Why?"

"Well, I'm not feeling real good. I thought I'd go to bed early, if it's all right with you, of course."

"You go on to bed. I'll be just fine. In fact, I was thinking about retiring early myself.

"Thank you, Miss CC."

"Good night, Anna. Get some rest."

"Yes, ma'am. I'm sure I'll be fit as a fiddle in the morning. Good night."

CC smiled to herself as she considered how perfectly everything was going. She had worried that she would have difficulty sneaking out of the house undetected at this late hour, but her father's unexpected imperative business meeting and now Anna's illness had rendered her escape a most easy matter.

Conquering her stubborn buttons, CC slipped out of her gown and quickly shed her petticoats and chemise before moving to the bed to untie the parcel she'd retrieved from her armoire. With eager hands, she pulled on the wrinkled, dark-colored boy's clothing, buttoning the loose-fitting shirt over her full breasts and tucking it into the waistband of the knee breeches. White stockings and heavier, low-heeled boy's shoes were donned, along with a baggy, nondescript vest to camouflage the swell of her bosom. Anxious to be gone, CC moved quickly to the mirror to pin her heavy mane up. That done, she snatched up the tricorn that completed her disguise and carefully anchored it on her head.

A quick glance in the mirror confirmed that any resemblance between her current self and young Miss Cecelia Demorest was remote. The breeches were skintight, as the young boys wore them, hugging her hips and thighs revealingly, but the baggy shirt and overlong vest helped to conceal her more feminine curves. She felt a sense of freedom whenever she wore her boyish garb, and she took secret delight in these times when she got to carry out her masquerade.

Though she knew she was being outrageously daring every time she ventured into town so disguised, she also knew that there was nothing more important in her life than being involved in the movement to rid the colonies of the hated British domination. It was necessary for her to pretend to be a lad in order to move about the city unobserved. A woman traveling alone at this time of night would draw undue attention to herself, but the sight of a boy walking the streets after dark was not uncommon.

Satisfied that even her father would have trouble identifying her should they meet on the dark Boston streets, she straightened her room and arranged her pillows under the covers on her bed to resemble a sleeping body, just in case someone decided to come checking on her. After unlocking the bedroom window that opened nearest the massive oak tree, CC took one last surveying glance around the chamber to be certain that all was set to rights, and then climbed nimbly out into the tree's thick, supportive branches.

Though he had spent the entire day on board the *Lorelei* going over the ledgers and manifests with Lyle, Noah was not particularly tired as he retired to his room that night. If anything, he felt strangely tense, as if a huge spring were coiled deep within him. Accustomed to being in complete control of himself, he found the stress annoying. Still, he knew the cause. It had been two days and he had not yet heard from Joshua Smith. He was certain that the rebel would contact him eventually, but that knowledge didn't make the waiting any easier.

Restlessly he moved to the washstand, poured a bowl of water, and then began to strip off his shirt. Bared to the waist, he idly rubbed the taut muscles in his neck, wishing that the inn boasted bourbon of the same caliber as he'd had at Demorest's home the night before. Certainly a glass of the smooth, strong liquor would help to settle the unusual uneasiness that gripped him.

The memory of the evening at Demorest's brought a fleeting thought of Edward's daughter, CC, and Noah grimaced. Lovely though she was, her profession of disliking him even before they'd met had done nothing to endear her to him. Not that it mattered, of course, for he had no intention of becoming involved with any woman. Still, it had been a most amusing scene when she'd turned to find him standing behind her in the hall. A slight smile curved the grim line of his mouth as he remembered her startled expression and the becoming blush that had stained her cheeks upon his most gallant introduction. Certainly, since she'd promised her father to do her best to "make him feel welcome," the ball Friday night did promise some amusement.

The knock at Noah's door interrupted his thoughts, and thinking that it was probably Polly, he did not bother to pull on his shirt as he strode forth to open it. The sight of a tall stranger standing impatiently in the deep shadows of the hall, his left arm hanging uselessly at his side, took him by surprise.

"Kincade?"

"I'm Lord Kincade," he replied, regarding him levelly.

"I'm Joshua Smith." Smith eyed the half-dressed Englishman skeptically. He had no use for these fancy aristocrats, and he took an immediate dislike to this one.

"Mr. Smith . . . please come in." Noah held the door wide and then closed it securely behind him. "Have you come with an answer for me?" he asked quickly as he snatched up his shirt and began to dress.

"There are a few matters we have to discuss before we get to that," Smith answered obliquely, waiting until he had Noah's complete attention before bluntly speaking his mind.

"Didn't Captain Russell tell you everything?" Noah was immediately on the defensive.

"He told me some."

"And?"

"And we don't trust your kind, Kincade. Might as well get that out in the open right now."

"I see." Noah's tone was icy. "What is it that you feel you need to clear up about me?"

"I've cleared up a lot on my own, but what I haven't been able to find out is exactly why you're interested in selling to us and not the government. It seems rather odd to me that a nobleman like yourself would be willing to turn your back on your own kind."

Noah's gaze turned steely as the man's question touched a nerve, and he replied with cold precision, "Why I'm doing this is none of your business. Either you are interested in what I have to sell or you're not. And if you're not, I'm certain there are others who would be more than willing to pay my price. It's that simple."

They stood glaring at each other for a long moment, measuring one another's worth.

After weighing all he knew, Smith gave an abrupt nod. "The meeting's tonight. We have to leave now."

Noah nodded tersely, not revealing any weakness to the rebel. The last thing he'd wanted was a discussion of his motives or a disclosure of his more recent past. It was private. Something he would never discuss again. "Fine, I'll—"

A sharp rap on his door cut him off.

"Noah?" Matt called out.

"Who is it?" Smith's tone was angry.

"My brother."

"Russell didn't say anything about you having a brother. Get rid of him."

Noah partially opened the door to speak to Matt. "What is it?"

"I thought I heard voices, and I thought something might be wrong. . . ."

"There's nothing wrong, Matt," he dismissed curtly. "Just business."

"I see." He knew that he had heard voices, and he now understood exactly what was transpiring. The rebel contact . . .

"I'm going out," Noah informed him in a tone that brooked no response. "I'm not sure when I'll return."

"I'll be up," he answered. Though he did not approve of his brother's plan of action, he wanted to know exactly what was going on.

When Noah turned back to Smith, the colonist was watching him with narrowed eyes. "How much does he know?"

"Only the business end of the deal. Nothing else. There's no need for him to be involved."

He studied the nobleman for a long moment. "Get ready. We have to go. And wear something dark. We don't want anybody taking notice of you when we're in the back streets."

Noah pulled on his dark coat and quickly followed Smith from the room.

John Robinson was waiting for CC several blocks from her house, and they started on the trek to the Green Dragon Inn together, shoulders hunched, eyes downcast lest they run into someone they knew.

"Did you have any trouble getting away?" he worried.

"No. Luckily father had a business meeting he had to go to. As I figure it, I should make it home before he does," she told him, matching him stride for manly stride as they trudged on toward the inn.

"CC, you don't know how I worry about you. . . ." John began hesitantly. "Are you sure you want to continue this charade? You know the risk you're taking."

He glanced at her quickly, and the look he gave her reflected his disgust with her outfit. He thought it much too dangerous when she disguised herself to attend the meetings. She was a lady and should act like one.

"John . . ." The unspoken threat was in her tone as she halted and faced him squarely, hands on hips.

"I know," he replied, annoyed by his inability to control her. As much as he loved her, he found himself growing more and more disenchanted with her whenever he came up against her independent, headstrong ways.

"Then let's go." She stalked off. CC had hoped that their conversation the previous day had blunted his feelings, but he seemed just as possessive and dictatorial as ever.

They reached the Green Dragon Inn without speaking again and, after giving the appropriate password, were admitted to the secluded room above the stable where the meeting was to be held. Greetings were exchanged among those present along with news received from the other colonies by the Committees of Correspondence.

"I've heard that an outsider is coming tonight," Jack Dearborn, a small, nervous man who moved in the inner circles of the group, confided to CC and John as they settled in around the large table.

"Who?"

"Don't know his name, but I know there was a lot of arguing among the leaders as to whether to deal with him or not."

"Why did they decide to do it?" CC wondered. "Is he someone important?"

"More importantly, is he someone we can trust?" John asked.

81

Jack shrugged. "Don't know. All I know is that Joshua is bringing him. They'll probably show up a little later."

John and CC exchanged puzzled glances as they tried to imagine why a stranger would be admitted to their midst. Times were treacherous enough without risking the sanctity of the meetings.

A respectful hush fell over those gathered as John Hancock entered, followed closely by Sam Adams. They were a study in contrasts, the rich merchant and the fiery orator. Hancock, impeccably groomed, was a perfect example of the successful Bostonian. Adams, his gray wig askew, his brown suit badly in need of pressing, his shoes scuffed, tended to look as if outward appearances meant nothing to him.

All listened attentively as Adams, furious and indignant over the news he'd just received, addressed the group first. In his usual impassioned manner, he bombarded those present with the outrageous revelation that, along with the terrible monopoly given the British East India Company over colonial trade, Governor Hutchinson had cleverly arranged to have his own sons appointed as agents for the tea, thus ensuring their own future riches at the expense of everyone else. Graft and corruption! Monopoly!

Local merchants would be driven out of business by the English dominance! The people would starve! And if Parliament could ordain a monopoly on tea, what was to stop them from setting up other singular controls?!

Those at the meeting responded with indignant fury at the news Adams imparted, and a rumble of protest swept through the room.

"There is only one solution to these abuses!" he declared. "We must be freed from tyranny! We must be independent! It's the only answer!"

Cheers of agreement answered his call, and Adams then relinquished the floor to Ryan Graves.

"I think we all are in accord with Sam's assessment of our situation. We are sending notice to the other colonies

82

through our Committee of Correspondence to try to block the sale of English tea, and while this may help, it will not end the problem."

"Here, here!" someone shouted in a patriotic frenzy.

"There is only one way to end Britain's stranglehold on us . . ." Graves's tone lowered as he prepared to deliver the most important bit of news. "There is only one solution, and it's inevitable. We must be ready! It is precisely for that reason that I have agreed to meet with a man Joshua Smith tells me could help our cause."

A sudden quiet settled over the meeting until one voice called out in question, "How?"

"Joshua has informed me that he's made contact with a man who is interested in selling us arms."

The silence that gripped the room was deafening. It had finally been spoken aloud . . . the dreaded possibility that had been considered by all, but quickly denied. They did not want to fight, but they also realized, if it came to conflict, they had to be physically prepared or face almost certain annihilation at the hands of the British regulars.

"How do we know we can trust this man? How do we know he's not some kind of spy working for Governor Hutchinson?" another asked.

"It's a chance, at this point in time, that we have to take. Let there be no mistake," Graves warned ominously. "The day will soon be upon us when we will be needing the military supplies."

CC was frowning, troubled, when she whispered and looked at John. "He's right, you know. They've pushed us too far this time. Full independence is the only answer." The prospect sent a shiver of trepidation through her even as she supported the effort completely.

Graves began to speak again, but he paused as the guard at the door moved to admit a late arrival. When Joshua Smith stepped into the room, all eyes turned in his direction. Hope and distrust mingled in their expressions as they waited, and a hush fell over them as they watched a mysterious, tall, dark-haired man follow Joshua inside.

Mysterious, that is, to everyone but CC. Aghast, CC stared in horror as Lord Noah Kincade strode to the head of the table and shook hands with the leaders gathered there. Anger and outrage filled her as she shifted her chair, unnoticed, farther back into the shadows. What was Kincade doing there?! He was the enemy! A nobleman! A liar! Last night he'd been casually sharing a drink with her father, telling him of his arms shipment and how distressed he was over the thought of possible fighting in the colonies. Now . . . now he was here at a meeting of the rebels!

What game was this slick, arrogant fool trying to play? Just who was Noah Kincade, and what did he stand for? Was he truly a rich English lord who was possibly spying for the governor, or was he an amoral opportunist who would sell anything to anyone for the right price? Both possibilities hardened her heart even more toward him. As she watched him speak privately with Graves, Adams, and Hancock, she wondered if she should reveal all that she knew.

John noticed then that CC had become silent and shifted position when the stranger arrived. He asked her in a low voice, "What's wrong?"

"Nothing really. I just didn't want to take a chance with my disguise. I don't like outsiders being invited to our meetings." CC didn't know why she refrained from telling John the truth, but she held her tongue and she was grateful when Graves started to speak and drew John's attention from her discomfort.

"This is Lord Noah Kincade," Graves introduced him.

Noah's title did nothing to endear him to those present, and their expressions reflected their hatred and mistrust.

"He owns several ships, one of which is currently en route to Boston laden with military supplies. He is willing to sell those arms to us."

"Why?" a gruff voice challenged from the back of the

room. "You're an Englishman, right?"

A derisive smile twisted Noah's lips as he addressed the question coolly. "I am an Englishman, but I am more so a businessman."

Several snorts of mocking disbelief were heard.

"How long till the king's soldiers come pounding on the door, Graves?!" someone else shouted. "The man could be a spy!"

"I've checked him out," Joshua Smith related firmly.

Noah spoke up, "I am no spy and you need not fear that I will reveal any of what passes here tonight to the authorities, even if we do not come to an agreement. You see, I have as much to lose as you do, if my dealings with you are disclosed."

The gathering quieted as he went on to tell them more.

"Before I sailed from London, I was advised by a nameless contact to get in touch with Mr. Smith here when I arrived in Boston. The contact said you might be interested in what I have to sell. Knowing that there is a great possibility that hostilities might erupt soon, and being the businessman that I am, when I made port I directed my man to attempt to locate your leaders. He met with Smith to tell him of our shipment, and after clearing things with Mr. Graves, Smith came to me. Smith saw to it that I was blindfolded for the major part of the trek to your meeting place. The location of your rendezvous point will remain your secret."

There was a murmuring of approval at the tactics so far employed.

"I am here strictly to offer you a product for a price," Noah relayed dispassionately. "If you're not interested, there are others who are."

"What are you selling and how much?" a cautious voice called out.

"Three thousand pounds," Noah intoned emotionlessly, "for a shipment of the finest-quality flintlock muskets, gunpowder, rounds, and cartouche boxes. The *Pride*'s also carrying field guns, cannon shot, and grapeshot. I doubt, gentlemen, that you'll get another opportunity like this one."

Dead silence gripped the room as leaders and followers alike tried to grasp the enormous amount being demanded for the goods.

"Would you be willing to sell us only a portion of the shipment?"

"It's all or nothing, sir. As I'm sure you're aware, I do have other alternatives. I'm sure agents of the Crown would be more than willing to pay my price." Noah was unbending in his response.

CC gritted her teeth as she heard his last remark. Agents of the Crown! Her own father! Kincade was a mercenary of the first order!

"Sir, it will be necessary for us to discuss this further," Graves said, deferring an immediate decision. Indeed, if it had come to that, he would have been forced to decline. Money was the problem.

"Of course. If you like, I can wait outside."

"Smith . . ." Graves called for the man to escort him from the inner chamber to allow them privacy.

The discussion that followed was lively, as those present argued both for and against the purchase of the weapons. John joined in, ardently opposing the purchase. He was one of many who feared that by buying the weapons, they would be admitting that there was no further hope for peaceful negotiations with Parliament to rectify the very real problems that existed between them.

CC, however, was too caught up in her own emotions regarding Kincade's treacherous appearance, and she intended to get to the bottom of his ploy, whatever it was. Drawing as little notice to herself as possible, she left her seat at John's side while he was embroiled in the discussion with the others and exited the meeting room, heading in the same direction as Smith had taken Kincade. She came upon them, standing in silence in the darkness just beyond the rear door of the stables below.

"Smith," she called out to Joshua, "I'm sure they'll want your input. I'll stay with our *guest.*"

The unusual inflection CC gave the last word caused Smith to pause, but he shrugged off her obvious distaste for Kincade, believing her to be one of those who opposed the purchase of the war supplies. With a nod, he left her in charge of the Englishman as he returned to the meeting to add his opinion to the discussion.

Noah thought the youth's voice sounded familiar, but his thoughts were too filled with anticipating the rebels' decision to give it much consideration. Perhaps, he thought distractedly, the boy worked at the inn and he'd met him there at some other time.

"You! You lowlife swine!" CC's volatile temper flared to full fury as she glared at him through the night's enveloping gloom. She didn't bother to wonder why his duplicity annoyed her so much. She had disliked him from the first, and this discovery of his true character only built on that initial aversion.

"I beg your pardon?" Noah glanced at the short youngster with mild amusement.

"You're despicable! You think that if you play both sides against the middle, you'll come out a winner either way, don't you?" she seethed self-righteously.

The challenge in her words was unmistakable, and Noah pivoted to face her, keeping his expression carefully blank.

"I'm sure I don't know what you mean, son. And besides, aren't you a little young to be involved in such goings on?" he questioned derisively, hoping to shut the boy up and put him in his place.

"You're a double-dealing coward!" CC couldn't believe his audacity. He was amoral and two-faced. He claimed to be a loyal Englishman, and yet he showed no hesitation in turning around and selling the arms to the very people who would use those weapons against the British.

Her words hit her mark. The last man who had referred to a Kincade as a coward was dead. Noah instinctively reacted to the insult, his hands snaking out to viciously grab her by her upper arms and drag her forcefully closer. CC had meant to berate him, but she had never expected him to respond with physical violence. She struggled against his overpowering strength, twisting and tugging in her need to be free of his bruising hold.

"Let me go, you bloody English dog!" With all her might, she kicked out at his shins, and she knew a moment of pure, triumphant pleasure as her foot connected and he grunted in pain.

"You little guttersnipe!" Noah growled threateningly.

CC's moment of victory was lost as Kincade snatched her to him by her shirtfront, popping several buttons off. He paid little attention to the damage to her garments as he almost lifted her from her feet to shake her in anger, the action knocking her hat from her head. Released from its bondage beneath the tricorn, CC's glorious mane of thick auburn curls fell in riotous satiny waves to her slim shoulders, revealing to Noah for the first time her true gender and, after a stunned moment, her real identity.

Noah went still as he stared down at her in disbelief. Cecelia Demorest? How could it be? What was she doing dressed as a lad? And, more important, what was she doing involved in this group?

"Let me go!" CC demanded, her breasts heaving in agitation. She ached all over from the mauling she'd just received at his hands, and she was very aware of the firm grip he had on her now ruined shirt, for his clenched knuckles were pressing firmly against the softness of her disguised bosom. The contact created an unfamiliar stirring deep within her loins, and she twisted, trying to pull herself free and get away from the pressure.

"Oh no, *Miss Demorest.*" Noah smiled wolfishly as he studied her closely. "I've suffered enough of your insults. It's time I demanded and *received* some satisfaction from you."

"I don't know what you mean." Her words were a breathless whisper as she stilled and stared up at him, emerald eyes wide with fright. CC had felt no fear in attacking him before, but now something new pulsed through her, and the strength of the unknown emotion frightened her. Her expressive features mirrored her terror, and Noah read her perfectly. It pleased him, oddly enough, to think that he had her at a disadvantage.

"Then I will show you what I mean. . . ." he growled, his head dipping to allow his lips to claim hers.

It was a dominating kiss—a kiss designed to humiliate and conquer. CC again began to struggle, wanting—no, needing—to be away from him, but Noah would have none of it. His free hand reached up to tangle in her hair firmly and hold her immobile. With masterful intent, Noah possessed her mouth, his tongue penetrating and pillaging the inner honeyed sweetness.

Had CC remained passive, Noah would have soon tired of the game, but she refused to submit gracefully to his attempt to overpower her. With all her might she fought against his hold, until in a moment of desperate desire, she tried to yank free. The cloth of her shirt gave way, revealing in the night's deep shadows the full, round perfection of her breasts.

The sound of the tearing cloth penetrated Noah's thoughts, and he drew back sharply to look down at the ragged piece of material he clutched in his hand, and then at her. Cecelia Demorest, Noah decided rather distractedly, had a beautiful body. Her hair . . . her eyes . . . and, bare for him to see for the first time, her breasts. Pale-hued and pink-crested, they rose and fell with the uneven tenor of her rapid breathing, and Noah could not stop himself from dropping the shred of cloth and reaching out to touch their creamy, hard-tipped perfection.

CC stood still, watching dazedly as he reached out to touch, ever so lightly, the swelling, taut fullness of her breast before moving to tease the pert, aching peak. The thrill of those practiced fingers caressing her most sensitive flesh was so unbearably erotic that CC felt her knees weaken, and she began to shiver. It was only with the sound of a low moan, one she realized later had come from her own throat, that reality intruded. Jerking quickly away from his questing, arousing touch, she desperately attempted to cover herself with the frayed material.

"No! Get away from me, Kincade!"

Noah, not used to being denied, was not about to let her put him off. She had been playing with fire, and it was time she learned that he was the one in control.

"Oh no, my little hellcat. . . ." He leered at her appreciatively as he took hold of her shoulders, and the shirt once again gaped open. With slow, torturing precision, he drew her inexorably to him. "You started this, and by God, you're going to finish it!"

"I hate you!!"

"I know." His mouth curved in an almost demonic slant as he bent to her. "You've hated me from the first. . . ."

Why not? Noah thought as the need for release pulsed hungrily within him. Obviously the chit had the morals of a streetwalker if she was dressing up like a boy and involving herself in such volatile, masculine matters as the policital underground. Noah felt certain he wouldn't be the first to taste of her lovely charms, and he knew he surely wouldn't be the last.

Crushing her to his chest, he kissed her hungrily. He wanted a woman, she was there, and despite her protests, Noah could tell by the response of her body that she was not as averse to his touch as she wanted him to believe.

CC was scared, more scared than she'd ever been in her life. Kincade's hands were everywhere, touching, probing, exploring, and yet all the while preventing her from escaping his dastardly clutches. Her breasts, bare and sensitive, were throbbing as his fingers worked their magic on their pink crests. When his mouth left hers, moving lower to suckle one hardened peak, her legs buckled. Only Noah's strong arm about her waist supported her, and she was unable to fight . . . unable to flee. She was mindless in her need. Never before had a man touched her so, and never in her wildest dreams had she ever considered that a man's caress could bring such physical ecstasy.

As his lips and tongue continued their mesmerizing play, Noah slipped one hand lower to cover the sweetness of her heat. Suddenly he wanted more from CC than just to ease his manly need in the depths of her body. She was a flame of excitement to him . . . the feel of her . . . the scent of her. His senses were enraptured by her nearness. The desire for a passionate union with this woman surged through him, and Noah knew he would settle for no less.

CC didn't understand exactly what was happening to her, but the languid weakness that had spread through her at the touch of his lips on her breast became now a driving force, urging her to move against the hand he pressed so tightly, so intimately to her most secret places. Noah accommodated CC's movements, matching the thrusting of her hips to massage her expertly to heights she'd never known existed. He wanted to please her and to show her the ecstasy only his touch could give.

Hands that had fought him earlier gripped his shoulders now in rapturous desperation . . . wanting . . . needing . . . craving. CC's breathing was strained, panting as her body responded wantonly to Noah. When he moved to kiss her again, bringing her hips full against the hardness of him, a rainbow of rapture shot through her at the alien contact that suddenly seemed so right. He held her hips pinioned to his, letting her move against him in feverish rhythm until she crested the peak her body had instinctively known would come. Shudders of spendor wracked her slim form as she collapsed in his arms, her head thrown back in sated ecstasy, her eyes closed, savoring the delights her body had just revealed to her.

It pleased Noah to find that she was so responsive to him and that he could pleasure her so easily, and he laughed softly as he held her cradled victoriously against the hardness of his chest.

It was that arrogant, deep-throated chuckle as his lips sought once again the soft flesh of her exposed throat that jarred her back to reality. CC blinked in shocked realization of what she'd done. She had allowed him liberties she'd never allowed another, and now he was laughing!

"Now, love, you shall know true satisfaction," Noah was saying as he started to strip her pants from her in preparation of introducing her to the joy of love's completeness. He was caught totally by surprise when CC let out a high-pitched shriek of indignity and pushed away from him full-force. Stunned to find herself out of his restrictive embrace, she backed nervously away from him.

"How dare you!? You are more vile than I ever dreamed!" she cried, clutching her arms about herself protectively as she stared up at him with wide, terror-filled eyes.

How could this have happened to her? Somehow she had to get away! She had to!

Noah loomed threatening above her, his face dark with anger, his eyes narrowed and glittering. "So it's a tease you are, is it?" he thundered, not willing to let it end so easily between them. His body was on fire with desire for her, and he had no intention of letting her flee from him. He reached out to her, wanting to finish what they'd started.

CC backed desperately away from him, but she found herself pinned against the wall of the stable. He moved forward, his expression so ominous that she knew there would be no escaping his wrath. She thought about running, but he was blocking her only path of escape.

"No . . ." She held up one hand to ward him off, turning her head against the sight of him, so tall and dark and foreboding.

"Oh yes, my little hellcat. Even a tease has to pay the price sometime, and your time is now." Noah's tone was unyielding, as were his hands as he reached out and grasped her by her upper arms. The sweetness of the moment was gone. Before she could protest again, his mouth swooped down to cover hers as his hands slipped within the waistband of her trousers to touch the womanly core of her that he so longed to penetrate.

Only the sound of the door to the meeting room opening and low, muffled voices coming their way saved CC from Noah's full possession. Hearing the others coming, Noah gave a growl of complete frustration and released her abruptly, stepping away. He eyed her disdainfully as he straightened his clothing with a casual nonchalance.

"I would suggest you cover yourself or leave," he advised dispassionately. "Unless, that is, your friends are used to your doing this. In fact," he added in a low tone, "if you wish, you may come to my room at the Red Lion Inn later. Then we can see this to a proper end."

"How dare you?!" She gasped at his words and struck out at him with all her might, the sound of her hand connecting with his cheek rending the night.

"This is not the end, CC. Not by any means." His expression carefully blank, Noah stared down at her for a brief moment before turning away and walking off into the stable to meet the men who were coming for him.

Numbly unaware of the compromising danger of her situation, CC stood stock-still staring after him as he disappeared into the building. When he'd gone from sight, the harsh truth of the moment assailed her. She knew she had to get home, and get home fast, by the darkest, most out-of-the way route possible.

Clutching her shirt across her bosom, CC ran from the scene. She was scared, but that was not the overriding emotion that was driving her as she skirted the more populated areas of town and stayed hidden deep in the shadowy cover of the night. No, hatred for Lord Noah Kincade was the fuel that was guiding her flight homeward. It was a hatred that burned so fiercely it left her wondering if she would ever be able to look at him again without wanting to wreak very real vengeance upon his person.

Gasping for breath, she finally reached the haven of her tree, and with her last ounce of energy, she climbed it's protective branches to the safety of her own bedroom. Secure within the protective surroundings of her own locked chamber, she moved unsteadily to her four-poster bed and collapsed weakly across it.

Her heart pounding, CC lay panting upon the softness of the counterpane. As she stared up at the ceiling, her thoughts were of Kincade, and Kincade only. She despised him. He was everything she'd thought he was and worse! And to think that he had the gall to suggest she come to his room later! The thought embarrassed her, and she rolled quickly over to hide her burning face against the coolness of the covers. Still, the despicable visions of his unwanted kiss and touch would not be so easily dismissed, and a shudder wracked her as she remembered in humiliation the way her body had responded to him.

The memory of the ecstasy she'd experienced at his hands troubled CC, and she drew a long, ragged breath as she thought of all that had happened. How could she have done it? How could she have sought his touch so eagerly when he'd brought her full against him? CC blushed as she remembered how she was all but climbing all over his lean, hard frame. A dull, hungry ache started anew within the heart of her as she recalled the heat of his mouth upon her breast and the taste of his passion-inducing kisses, and, frowning, she timidly touched herself. CC gasped at the sensation that shot through her and gritted her teeth as she climbed off the bed. What had that fiend done to her? She had never felt this way before, and it was all his fault!

Her distress evident in her actions, she viciously stripped

off the boy's clothing and poured herself a bowl of cold water at her washstand. Vigorously she scrubbed every inch of her body, wanting to erase his scent from her skin, but even as she washed, thoughts of the way her breasts responded to him haunted her, and she threw the damp washcloth across the room with violent force.

"Damn him!" she uttered in frustration. Why couldn't she put the memory of him from her mind? He had used her . . . abused her. . . .

CC stormed to her armoire and rummaged through, looking for her nightdress. Finally locating the soft, filmy garment, she tugged it on impatiently, trying to ignore how sensitive her nipples were now to the material's silken caress. Bundling up her boy's things, she hid them carefully again in the back of her wardrobe.

After climbing back into bed, CC curled on her side and tried to rest, but sleep would not come. Instead, her exhausted mind replayed again and again her degrading, outrageous encounter with Kincade. She had been helpless against his formidable charms, and she was devastated by the realization. He had manipulated her body just as he manipulated people. Though CC forced herself to acknowledge that she had responded to his touch, she vowed never to allow him near her again. She would see him Friday night only because circumstances forced her to, and after that he could fall off the ends of the Earth, for all she cared. She hated him. She despised him.

CC wondered for only a brief instant if there was any possible way she could use her knowledge of his activities against him, but she knew the answer even as she thought about it. There was no way she could confess to her father the truth of his double-dealings without revealing to him her own involvement. Caught in a web of intrigue, she knew she had to remain silent.

Clutching her pillow to her breast, CC hugged it tightly and sighed. If she could just make it through the ball Friday

95

night, she would probably never have to see Lord Noah Kincade again. Yawning, she closed her eyes and, after lying quietly for a long time, finally drifted off into a deep, dreamless sleep.

It was late, well after midnight, and Noah was frustrated in more ways than one as he sat alone in the taproom of the Red Lion Inn. Signaling Polly to bring him another tankard of ale, he accepted the mug of brew and was grateful when, after tossing her a coin in payment, she moved off to tend to her other duties, leaving him alone with his thoughts.

Nothing had gone as he'd expected this evening. He had thought that his offer of arms would be snatched up eagerly by the insurgents, but they had hedged on making a firm commitment to him. He was now being forced to cool his heels while they bickered among themselves. He'd returned to the inn then, temporarily thwarted, but confident of ultimate success.

He held out small hope that Cecelia Demorest would be eagerly awaiting him in his bed, and he stifled a sardonic chuckle as he thought of her reaction to his advances. Her display of "maidenly" nervousness had not amused him and certainly hadn't convinced him of her innocence. No, CC was definitely not the sweet little virgin her outraged actions would lead a lesser mortal to believe. She had definitely known what she was doing with that lovely body of hers, and he wondered just how she would react when they came face-to-face Friday night at the ball. His own body tensed in remembered excitement as he saw in his mind's eyes her naked beauty, and Noah knew that there was still much unfinished between them. Friday night was definitely going to prove an interesting evening.

For a brief instant, Noah worried that CC might betray his business maneuverings to her father, but he knew she would keep silent. In betraying him, she would have to explain how she came about her knowledge of his activities, and there would be no way she could do it without revealing her own unsavory connections. Satisfied that he was safe from interference by agents of the Crown, he finished off his brew and headed for the stairs, intending to retire.

The light shining from under his bedroom door brought him up sharply in the hall, and Noah frowned. Had CC come to him? His breath quickened at the thought, but as he opened the door his excitement rapidly died. He had forgotten. Matthew was waiting for him.

"Well?" Matt stood as Noah entered the room, and he watched him expectantly. "What happened?"

"Nothing." Noah was tired and in need of sleep and had no desire to discuss the meeting.

"Nothing?" He glanced at him in disbelief. "You've been gone all this time and you're trying to tell me nothing happened?"

"That's right. I made my offer, and the man I'm dealing with said that they needed to think it over . . . that they'd be in touch."

"It's not too late to change your mind, you know," he prompted. "There's no reason why you have to be involved in the dirty side of things."

Noah's face was blank as he stared at his brother. "I'm not involved in anything. I'm merely trying to arrange a business transaction, and frankly, Matt, I'm not in the mood to debate the issue with you."

"Then I'll say good night," Matt told him tersely as he made his exit. "I hope you sleep well."

Though Matt meant his comment as a subtle curse in reference to the arms deal, Noah knew he wouldn't be sleeping well; and it wouldn't be because of the damned war supplies. He would find no rest this night, because the fire the damned Demorest vixen had stirred in his loins refused to abate. Every time he thought he had his desire under control, the memory of her luscious nakedness and wanton response to his lovemaking sent a shaft of pure excitement through him. Yes, he thought with some agony as he stretched out on the bed, he and Miss Demorest definitely had some unfinished business.

"Sir?" The woman's soft call penetrated Noah's thoughts and he rose quickly to open the door.

"Polly?" Noah was surprised by her presence.

Polly had sensed his need to be left alone when he was downstairs in the taproom, but her desire for another taste of his passionate possession had driven her to approach him.

"I was hoping you might be wanting me. . . ." She was not quite as brazen as she had been the other night, for he had made no move to encourage her when she'd waited on him downstairs.

Noah stared down at her, taking in her warm expression and the supple curves of her rounded figure.

"Oh yes, Polly. I'm wanting you. . . ." he growled as he drew her into the room.

Polly was thrilled to know that he did, and she wasted no time in coyness, quickly divesting herself of her restrictive garments.

"I'm glad I came to you." She smiled at him invitingly when at last she stood before him in all her glory.

"So am I," Noah admitted as he led her to the bed and followed her down upon its softness. "So am I."

Chapter Six

Matthew wanted to sleep. He did not want to lie there alone in the darkness of his room, tense and miserable, dwelling on the chasm that had developed between him and Noah. Yet no matter how he turned and tossed, the peace and forgetfulness of rest would not come.

It was very late, nearly three in the morning, when he finally gave up the struggle. He found his rented quarters stifling and knew a need to get away from the confining closeness. Rising, he pulled on his clothing, took up his tricorn, and strode impatiently from the room.

The taproom below was empty, and only the soft glow of a single lamp lit Matt's passage as he left behind the safety of the inn. Outside, the city seemed quiet, and the narrow, deeply shadowed streets were deserted. In the distance, a lone church bell hollowly rang out confirmation of the lateness of the hour.

Matt paused and drew a deep, invigorating breath of the fresh night air before starting off. He had no idea where he was bound. He only knew that he needed to walk to rid himself of the agitation that was disturbing him. Hands thrust deep in his pockets, dark head down, he strode briskly through the maze of winding thoroughfares, paying little attention to direction or purpose.

The scream, when it came, was blood-chilling. Matt stopped dead in his tracks, looking around himself with awareness for the first time since he'd left the inn. The deep, rumbling sound of drunken male voices came to him, and he glanced about trying to ascertain from which direction they'd come. Finally, pinning down the source of the ruckus, Matt sprinted quickly in that direction.

"Keep your hand over her mouth, Cecil, and hold her hands!" the red-coated soldier urged his companion as he lifted the woman's skirts and tore at her underclothing. "The stupid wench probably woke the entire city!"

"Nobody'd care," Cecil remarked with a sloppy grin as he pinned the struggling girl's arms above her head with one hamlike hand and clamped the other more tightly over her mouth. "She's only a damned colonial. Worst we'd get is a slap on the wrist, if anybody even found out. Now, hurry, Reggie! I been a long time without a woman, and this one looks real willing." He glanced at the girl's panic-stricken, pale features and laughed lasciviously.

The soft material of her undergarments ripped easily under Reggie's avid pawing and he sought her femininity in a rough exploration. The girl started in complete surprise at the soldier's brutal touch, and she tried to scream again, only to find the cry muffled behind the man's suffocating hand. She squeezed her eyes shut against the sight of the lust on the two men's faces and tried to kick out at the one who was savagely exploring her.

"Stupid wench!" Reggie snarled as he viciously slapped the soft flesh of her inner thigh. The shock of his blow stunned the young woman, and she went limp beneath him. "That's better. Now, just lie still, and we'll be done real fast now. . . ."

"Come on, Reggie," Cecil urged.

Reggie's eyes glazed with desire as he ripped open the bodice of her gown. Excited to the edge by the sight of her naked bosom, he reached down to loosen his pants. He was—

alive with the need to take his ease in this woman's body, and he was positioning himself between her thighs when the sound of a questioning call and heavy footsteps coming their way drew a raging curse from both men.

"Damn! I knew somebody heard her scream! Let's get out of here!" Cecil was frightened.

"But what about her?" Reggie worried.

"What about her? She's a no-good woman. If she wasn't, she wouldn't have been out on the streets at this time of night. She won't tell. . . . And besides, nothing happened! Let's go!"

Still trying to fasten his breeches, Reggie got awkwardly to his feet and followed Cecil's frantic flight from the scene, disappearing with his friend quickly into the darkness.

Matt could hear the drunks' comments, and he had called out, hoping to frighten them as he'd hurried in the direction of the scream. Turning into an alley, Matt caught sight of two British soldiers racing into the night. He would have gone after them had he not seen the young woman lying lifelessly in the filth of the back street. He knew he should follow the soldiers, but the sight of the girl, her clothing torn, lying so still made his stomach lurch. She looked dead.

Matt knelt beside her and carefully lifted one delicate wrist, seeking a pulse. He was vastly relieved to discover that the woman was not dead, and he looked down at her for a moment, wondering if she'd just fainted or if the men had beaten her into unconsciousness. In the softness of the moonlight, Matt could see a dark bruise forming on her forehead, and he felt a surge of fury at the men who had so badly abused her. She was such a tiny thing, he realized as he held her small hand in his, and she looked so fragile. . . . Matt hadn't intended to stare at her, but his gaze drifted down her body, noting the smallness of her perfect breasts revealed beneath the torn bodice, and the sleekness of her bared legs.

Realizing what he was doing, Matt muttered a violent

101

curse at his own depraved behavior and quickly stripped off his coat. As gently as he could, he wrapped his garment about her and then lifted her protectively into his arms. The girl groaned faintly as he stood and started back toward the inn, but other than that, she did not stir. He reached the Red Lion in short order and pounded on the door, rousing Waddington, the innkeeper, from a deep sleep.

"What is it?" the rotund old man complained as he stumbled through the semidarkness of the taproom in his nightgown, rubbing sleepily at his bleary eyes.

"Waddington! Open the door! I've an injured woman here!" Matt ordered in his most imperious tone, and he was rewarded to see the man snap to action.

"Lord Kincade!" Waddington stepped back, his mouth open in stunned surprise as the younger of the two English noblemen strode into the room carrying an unconscious woman.

"Yes, damn it! Now summon a doctor, and be fast about it!" he snapped, not hesitating on his way up the stairs. "Call the authorities, too! This woman's been assaulted, and I want the men who did it arrested!"

"Yes, sir, my lord!" Waddington hopped to do his bidding as Matt hurried down the hall to his room.

With some difficulty, Matt finally managed to get the door to his room open, and then crossed the room to lay his lovely burden upon the softness of his bed. Matt carefully removed his coat from about her slim body and then covered her with a blanket to save her any embarrassment should she awaken. He lit his lamp and drew a chair up to the bedside to await the doctor's arrival. It seemed an eternity before a knock came at his door.

"I've sent one of the kitchen boys for the doctor," the innkeeper informed Matt when he answered.

"And the authorities?" Matt demanded sharply, blocking the innkeeper's entrance into his room. For some reason, he felt the need to protect the woman from prying eyes.

"He'll be getting them, too, on the way back," the innkeeper assured him, trying to catch a glimpse of the female the nobleman had tucked into his bed. All he had seen when Matt had carried her through the dimly lighted taproom had been a tumble of raven hair. "What happened?"

"I had gone out for a walk . . . couldn't sleep . . . and I heard her scream. There were two regulars. . . ."

"Did you see them up close?" he asked with great interest.

"No, I only caught a glimpse of the backs of their uniforms as they ran off." Matt glanced back toward the girl. "We'll know more once she comes around. Send the doctor up as soon as he arrives."

"Will you be needing anything else?"

"Bring some hot water and whatever else you think the physician will require," he directed.

"I'll be back." Waddington tried to get one last look at the woman before scurrying away.

Matt returned to his seat beside the bed, taking the time now to study the woman he'd rescued. Her hair was a rich, lustrous ebony and it curled softly about her face and her exquisite features. Her nose was small, her mouth soft and inviting. He wondered what color her eyes were as he noted the long, dark lashes that fanned out across her pale cheeks. Only the ugly contusion on her forehead marred the perfection of her loveliness.

What circumstances had led her to be in such dire straits? What had she been doing out on the streets of Boston during the middle of the night? Was she a barmaid on her way home from work or a strumpet out looking for business? Matt found himself frowning as he considered both possibilities, and he took up her hand in his, finding with some satisfaction that it was soft and uncallused. Whatever she was, this woman was not a barmaid, for the hands of women employed in that line of work were invariably chapped and

103

work-reddened. The possibility that she was a strumpet occurred to him again, and he dismissed it as ridiculous. Had she been plying her trade, she certainly wouldn't have screamed at the soldier's advances; more than likely she would have encouraged them. No, he decided. Her reasons for being out in the night alone were a mystery, and they would remain a mystery until she could explain herself.

Matt leaned forward, almost willing her to awaken, as he whispered in a husky voice, "Who are you?"

But there was no answer to his question as the beauty's eyes remained closed and her hand remained unmoving in his. Without conscious thought, Matt lifted it to his lips and pressed a soft kiss in her palm.

"Whoever you are," he swore quietly to himself, "you're mine from now on, and I swear no one will ever hurt you again."

He remained vigilant, not leaving her side until he heard the doctor and Waddington approaching. Then he rushed from the bedside to open the door. "She's in here, Doctor."

The physician, a short, balding man, bustled into the room. "I'm Dr. Spalding," he introduced himself.

Matt again blocked the innkeeper's entrance. "I'll call you if we need you."

Spalding was frowning as he looked from the young Englishman to the prone form of a girl. "What happened, young man?"

"She was attacked on the street by two British regulars. My arrival frightened the two men off. I don't know how badly she's injured. I brought her directly back here and then had Waddington send for you."

"Has she regained consciousness at all?"

"No. She's been like this since I found her."

The doctor nodded as he approached the bed.

"Do you recognize her, Dr. Spalding?"

"No, can't say as I do." The doctor took her pulse and then examined her forehead. "I'll need to do a more extensive examination, and I'd like you to step from the room, please."

Matt hesitated, not wanting to leave her alone, but common sense won out. "I'll be right out in the hall."

"Fine."

As Matt went outside, he found two serving girls coming down the hall with heated water and supplies for the physician, and he admitted them to the room.

Noah, roused by all the commotion, emerged from his room just as the servants headed back downstairs. "Matthew?" The graveness of the younger man's expression troubled him.

Matt glanced up as Noah came to join him. "Noah . . ."

"What is it? What happened?" He looked worriedly toward the closed door to his room.

"After I left you earlier, I couldn't sleep, so I went out for a walk. . . ."

"Yes . . . so?" he prodded impatiently.

"There were two soldiers abusing a girl in one of the back alleys. I managed to frighten them off, but the girl was injured. I brought her back here and had Waddington summon the doctor. He's with her now. . . ." Matt glanced solemnly at the portal.

"How badly was she injured?" Noah wondered at Matt's foolhardiness in charging into an unknown, dangerous situation unarmed, but he knew, as a gentleman of honor, he could have done no less. He was proud of him

"I don't know. She's unconscious. She has a bad bruise on her brow, and they'd . . ." Revulsion raged through him at the thought of the vile men tearing her clothing from her and assaulting her while she lay helpless beneath them. He said a silent prayer, hoping that he had arrived in time to save her virtue. Noah's hand on his shoulder comforted him as he imagined her terror, and Matt knew a sudden, driving need to be back by her side.

"Lord Kincade?" Waddington called from the foot of the stairs.

Matt and Noah exchanged glances as they hurried to see what the innkeeper wanted. "Yes?"

"The constable has arrived. . . ."

Matt nodded and went down to meet him. "I'm Lord Matthew Kincade."

"Jeremy Roberts." The constable, a tall, thin, harried-looking man, introduced himself. "Waddington here tells me that you had some trouble tonight?"

"I was out for a late walk and came across a young woman being assaulted by two British regulars. The soldiers fled, but not before they'd injured the girl. I brought her back here. She's in my room, and the doctor is with her now."

"I see. Would you be able to identify the soldiers were you to see them again?" he questioned.

"No," he replied, his tone deadly. "The cowards ran when they heard me coming, and I only got a look at their backs."

"I'm afraid there's not much for me to do then, other than to notify the young woman's family. Do you know her name?"

"She hasn't regained consciousness yet. I'm sure when she does, she'll be able to give you a full accounting of the incident."

"I see," Roberts nodded. "Then I shall check back with you first thing in the morning. Perhaps by then we'll have more information to go on."

"Indeed."

After the constable had gone, Matt and Noah sat together in the empty taproom. Though Noah tried to initiate a conversation, Matt was too concerned about his mysterious lady's condition to carry on a decent discussion. He responded in distracted, monosyllabic answers to all of his brother's questions. Noah finally gave up the attempt, and they remained in silent vigil, awaiting the physician's reappearance and his prognosis for the injured girl's recovery.

It was a long while before the doctor appeared at the top of the staircase. "Lord Kincade?"

Both Matt and Noah came to their feet at the sound of his voice.

"Yes, Doctor? How is she?" Matt went hastily to meet him at the foot of the steps.

The physician's mood was somber. "She still hasn't recovered consciousness yet, I'm afraid, but her general health seems good enough."

Matt breathed a deep sigh of relief. Her condition was not life-threatening.

"As you know, she's had a bad bump on the head, and has a few other bruises from their obvious mistreatment of her, but she should be fine."

Matt's throat tightened as he forced himself to ask, "Did they . . ."

"No," Spalding answered firmly.

"Thank God . . . I got there in time. . . ." He spoke softly, his distress greatly eased by the doctor's pronouncement.

"Indeed you did, and I'm sure the young lady will be very grateful to you for your rescue." He clapped Matt on the back. "Her clothing was filthy and in shreds, so I took the liberty of doing away with it."

"Yes, I know," Matt ground out. "The damned savages . . ."

"She's going to be just fine," Dr. Spalding quietly assured him again, "and I'm sure Waddington can help find something suitable for her to wear. Perhaps one of his servants . . . ?"

Matt nodded.

"Someone should stay with her through the night, just in case she should awaken and be frightened by her unfamiliar surroundings."

"I'll stay with her," Matt declared quickly.

"I'm sure Waddington employs a female servant who could—"

"I said, I'll sit with her," he stated with regal authority. "I have no designs on her person. I only want to see that she makes a full recovery."

"Well . . ." he hedged.

"It's done. Say no more. How much do I owe you for your services?"

The doctor quoted a price.

"Does that include a return visit tomorrow to make sure she's well?"

"Of course, my lord. I'll check back with you shortly before noon, if that suits you."

"It does." Matt was firm. "You'll be compensated for your help tomorrow when I'm certain she's recovering. Until then, Doctor, good night."

Noah listened to the conversation with nothing short of amazement. This was his little brother issuing orders as if he were born to it? The thought amused him. Matt had indeed grown up.

"You handled that very well, Matt, but are you certain you want to sit up the night with the girl? Surely there's a serving wench qualified—"

"No. This is something I've got to do myself," Matt told him seriously as he headed upstairs.

"Shall I sit with you?" Noah asked as they came to Matt's room.

"There's really no need for the both of us to lose a night's sleep. You can go to bed, and if there's been no change by midmorning, you can relieve me then," he responded. Matt led the way into the room and they found the lovely girl lying unmoving on the vast white expanse of his bed, the blankets discreetly covering her.

"She's beautiful, Matt. . . ." Noah was surprised. He had not expected a woman rescued from the streets to be so comely.

"I know." Matt glanced up at Noah quickly, his troubled gaze showing how deeply he'd been affected by the unknown woman's plight. There was a long pause before he added,

"You may as well go on back to bed. I'll be right here for the rest of the night."

"All right. If you need anything . . ."

"I'll be fine," he insisted. "I just hope she is."

Matt turned his attention back to the young woman as Noah let himself from the room.

The late-night hours passed. The black velvet canopy of night lightened to deep purple and then to red-streaked gold as the sun struggled to reclaim the land. Matt grew increasingly restless and worried as he sat beside the bed wondering why she hadn't come around yet. Had the doctor been wrong? Was there some injury he'd missed? Finally, unable to sit in silent restraint any longer, he stood up and moved to stare out the window.

Within the confines of the room at the inn, Faith Hammond stirred and opened her eyes. Everything was blurred for a moment, and she blinked in tired confusion as her surroundings slowly came into focus. It came as quite a jolt to find that she was in a strange room, and with that revelation came the terrible remembrance of the two soldiers and their assault. Terror seized her and she looked quickly about, spotting for the first time the tall, dark-haired man standing at the window, his back to her.

Horror-filled, Faith wondered what to do. If she remained quiet, she knew she might be able to effect an escape later if he left her alone in the room, but the memory of the attack drove her to try to flee now. She started to slip from the bed in the hope of making a dash for the door when she discovered her state of dishabille. What had they done to her? And where were her clothes? Desperate and more frightened than ever, Faith clutched the blanket to her and tried to get to her feet. Waves of dizziness washed through her and she couldn't stifle a moan of pure agony as she swayed unsteadily, one hand going to her throbbing brow.

Matt heard her groan and turned. The sight of her out of bed and standing truly surprised him. "Please . . ." Seeing her very real physical distress, Matt spoke quickly and took a step toward her. "You must lie down."

His gaze met hers across the width of the room, and he stopped. There, in the turquoise depths of her eyes, was all the fear and loathing she was experiencing, and it was directed at him. The thought that she believed him to be one of her attackers hurt, and he tried to explain, moving toward her again with his arms spread wide in protestation of his innocence. But the girl only backed toward the door as he came in her direction, her eyes rounding in terror.

"Wait . . . please. . . . My name is Matthew Kincade. You're safe. . . ." He crossed the distance between them slowly, hoping to keep her from panicking, but it didn't work.

Her head spinning, her nerves taut, Faith spun on her heel and raced as quickly as her unsteady legs would carry her to the door. She was fleeing for her very life, and she knew she had to get away. The blanket seemed her enemy as she made her attempt, tangling between her legs and causing her to stumble. The missed step gave Matt the time he needed to reach her.

"No!" Matt hadn't meant to speak so forcefully, but he knew he had to stop her from dashing out into the hall with only the blanket for protection. The fact that she tripped aided him in his efforts, and he quickly ensnared her in his grip. The moment he held her, he knew he'd made a big mistake.

The horror of the dark, dank alley and the grossness of the attempted rape assailed Faith then, and she began to cry, desperately beating at Matt with her fists and trying to strike him wherever she could land a blow.

Matt knew a moment of total disconcertion. He knew she was hysterical and that he should calm her, but he had no idea how to go about it.

"Miss . . . please . . ." he tried to explain in a soothing tone, but his efforts were fruitless in the face of her very real fears.

"You're safe from the soldiers. . . . Please . . ." When at last he managed to trap both of her fists in his, he pinioned her to his chest, holding her with quiet, steady force, until she ceased fighting him.

"Don't hurt me anymore. . . . Please, don't hurt me." Sobs wracked Faith as she stood weakly in his restrictive embrace. She knew it was useless. Her struggles seemed so feeble against this man's overpowering strength. Perhaps, she reasoned wildly, if she submitted quietly and stopped trying to escape, he would at least let her go when he had finished with her. . . .

Her plea pierced Matt's very soul, and he loosened his grip, lifting one hand to cup her cheek and tilt her face to his. "I have no intention of hurting you, little one."

A spark of sanity penetrated Faith's embattled senses. The man was talking to her, not attacking her. He was holding her loosely, not beating her or hitting her, and he had the clearest blue eyes. She stared up at him for a long, motionless moment. . . . And his face . . . had he been one of her attackers? Certainly his accent was English, but she didn't remember him as one of those who had loomed above her in the frightening darkness of the alley.

"Who are you?" she asked tremulously, her limbs quaking from the exertion of her struggle.

"My name is Matthew Kincade." Matt couldn't tear his gaze away from hers, the turbulent depths of her aquamarine eyes mesmerizing him. "Are you all right?"

"I . . . I . . ." Weakness washed through her and her legs suddenly folded beneath her.

As she sagged against him, Matt scooped her up in the warm strength of his arms. He placed her gently back on the bed, tucking the blankets around her.

"Should I send for the doctor again?" he asked worriedly as he studied her pale, pinched features.

"No . . . yes . . . I need to get help . . . I need . . ."

"Shh . . ." he hushed her, sitting down beside her.

111

"No! I can't be quiet. I need the doctor . . . my mother . . ."

Though the desperation in her voice was very real, Matt sensed this time that her upset had nothing to do with him. Holding her hand, he questioned, "Take it easy now and tell me everything. Who are you?"

Faith felt a bit of strength return as she lay quietly. "My name is Faith Hammond," she told him tonelessly, wondering how she'd come to be in this man's room. "How did I get here . . . in this room with you? The last thing I remember . . ." She trembled at the devastating memory of the two drunken soldiers, and the way they'd chased her and dragged her into the dark alley.

"Don't think about it," Matt commanded, his hold on her hand tightening unconsciously as he imagined all she'd been through.

As Faith looked up at him, an unidentified depth of emotion flickered in his eyes before he quickly shuttered his expression.

"It's over and you're safe, Faith," he was saying. It was the first time Matt had spoken her name aloud, and he liked the soft and feminine sound of it.

Faith gave a curt nod, wondering suddenly just how safe she was, lying unclothed in a bed with him sitting so casually beside her. He was so strong and handsome. Her heart gave an odd jump as she looked at him calmly for the first time.

"The soldiers got away," Matt said, knowing the questions she wanted answered, "but I interrupted them before they could harm you seriously, and that's all that really matters."

A flush stained her cheeks as she wondered if they'd had their way with her. Certainly she was sore all over. . . .

Matt read her thoughts, and his gaze was warm, steady as he met her eyes. "No, Faith, they didn't have time. I got there before they could. . . ."

The tears came then, and she made no effort to hide them from him. "Thank you," she murmured shakily.

His protective instincts aroused, Matt wanted to take her into his arms and comfort her, but he held himself in restraint, believing that any such move by himself would only traumatize her further. He forced the desire to hold her from him with some difficulty.

"You're welcome," he answered more stiffly than he'd intended. "We're in my room at the Red Lion Inn. The doctor has already been here to check on you, but he'll be back again later. I spoke with the constable, too, and he'll be returning to speak with you sometime this morning also. Is there someone I should notify? Parents?" He started to ask if she had a husband, but stopped. He didn't want to consider the chance that she could be married.

"Just my mother." Her eyes appeared enormous in her pale face as she explained. "She was the reason why I was out so late last night. . . . She's ill . . . running a terribly high fever, and I was going for a doctor when the soldiers cornered me. . . ."

Matt released her hand as he got quickly to his feet. "Where do you live? I'll arrange for the doctor to attend her right away."

Faith gave him the directions, and Matt strode to the door. "Stay in bed and rest," he instructed. "I'll be back as quickly as I can."

Faith lay quietly, staring at the door he'd closed behind him. Who was this man? She knew only his name and nothing more. Matthew Kincade . . . She said it softly to herself, thinking that the name suited him quite well. It was so masculine . . . so vital. . . .

Faith closed her eyes for a moment and sighed. She didn't know why, but here with Matthew Kincade she felt safe and protected. There was something about the tall, attractive stranger that had won her trust. Matthew had rescued her; he had treated her with the utmost respect and consideration. He had been wonderful, and she wished . . .

Her eyes flew open as she blocked the last thought that

113

had entered her mind, and she silently berated herself for her childish musings. It would not do to daydream about some strong, handsome man rescuing her from danger, falling in love with her, and taking her away from all her troubles. Faith had learned long ago that life was not like that.

Still, she couldn't deny that Matthew was handsome. His dark good looks and piercing blue eyes were almost breathtaking in their potency. Nor could she deny that he had saved her from a terrible fate, but, she told herself rigidly, he was not for her. He was simply a stranger who had not turned his back on her plight. He was being kind. That was all.

Faith knew she had been exceedingly foolish to allow herself to even imagine that there could be anything more. She was poor, while Matthew, obviously, was rich. How else could he afford to stay at this fine inn? No, she decided. She would leave here just as soon as she could, and when she did, her association with Matthew Kincade would be at an end. The thought distressed her, but she accepted it resignedly. A great weariness stole over her again, and she took a deep breath as she settled back against the pillows and closed her eyes.

When Matt returned to the room long minutes later, he found Faith seemingly asleep, and he entered quietly lest he disturb her rest. If anything, he knew she needed sleep most of all, for it would ease the sharpness of her dreaded memories and soften the impact of all that had happened.

Though his tread was soundless as he moved into the room, Faith seemed to instinctively sense that he'd returned. Her gaze followed him, her smile soft as she greeted him.

"You're back. . . ."

Matt was a bit startled to find that she was awake, and he smiled brightly in response. "Yes. The doctor is being summoned and will be on his way to your home with all due dispatch."

Faith hadn't believed before that moment that it was

possible, but when Matt smiled, he appeared even more handsome. His infectious grin added warmth to his already classic features.

"Thank you." Her heart was pounding as she watched him. "I don't know how I'll ever be able to repay you. . . ."

"There's no need to even consider repayment," he insisted. "I don't want you to give it another thought. My reward is seeing you well again."

"I'm feeling much better now," Faith told him.

"Good. Waddington managed to come up with these garments. I hope you'll find them suitable." He spread out an assortment of feminine attire on the bed next to her. Though clean, the quality of the servant's clothing had been less than he'd hoped to find for Faith, but at this hour of the morning he'd had to settle for what was available. He'd paid the price quoted without dickering.

"But where are my things?" She was embarrassed to think that he had seen her unclothed, but there was no telltale flicker of acknowledgment in his expression.

"The soldiers had torn them beyond repair and the doctor decided it would be best just to discard them."

"Oh." Faith mourned the loss of one of her two better day gowns, for her wardrobe was meager.

Matt wondered at the sadness that had been reflected in her face for just the briefest of instants, but before he could inquire, someone knocked at the door.

"G'morning, Lord Kincade." Mary, a plump, buxom serving wench, bustled into the room carrying a tray heavily laden with steaming food as soon as he opened the door. Beatrice, a skinny girl with a beaklike nose and squinty eyes, trailed behind her toting a small table.

Faith blinked at the maid's greeting. *"Lord" Kincade? Had the girl greeted Matthew as "Lord"?*

"Thank you," Matthew was saying politely as the two servants set the table for them.

"You're welcome, m'lord," they both cooed. They thought

115

Matthew Kincade irresistible and wished that the handsome nobleman would take notice of them. They had heard talk in the kitchen of the girl's misfortune and subsequent rescue by him and thought her a most lucky woman. Oh! To be saved by Lord Kincade! How romantic!

Matt, however, was unaware of their interest as he directed, "Miss Hammond needs your help to dress before we breakfast. I'll wait outside while you assist her."

Before Faith could say anything, Matt had gone from the room, leaving the two maids to attend her. *Maids?* she thought quizzically. She had dressed herself for her entire life, and yet Matt had assumed that she would need help.

"Is something wrong, ma'am?" Mary asked as she sorted through the garments.

"Did you call him 'Lord Kincade'?"

"Yes, ma'am. He and his brother are newly arrived from England this week," Mary told her, surprised that she didn't know he was an aristocrat. "Didn't he tell you?"

"No. I had no idea that he was a nobleman." Faith was astounded.

"Yes, ma'am," Beatrice said, "and he's such a fine good-looker, too."

"That he is," Mary agreed quickly, glancing toward the door. "Come now. Let us help you with these clothes. We don't want to keep him waiting long."

For the first time in her life, Faith allowed herself the luxury of attendants, but only because it would hasten her exit. She had to leave . . . had to get away. Lord Matthew Kincade was too dangerous for her peace of mind. Besides, she knew how little the aristocrats thought of colonials. Hadn't she heard the soldiers' mocking, degrading statements? She stood quietly as they helped her into the garments and then brushed out her long, dark hair. Though the dress and underthings were made for another, they fit reasonably well. Faith was feeling much more herself when she finally stood before them fully clothed.

"Now you look fine for His Lordship," Mary remarked, taking care to hide her envy. "We'll be going now."

The words screamed inside her as they hurried from the room. *You look fine for His Lordship*. Lord Matthew Kincade was the stuff of which fantasies were made, and she could not allow herself that dream. There was no point in remaining. She was fully recovered, except for a few bruises and aches, and her mother needed her. Self-preservation dictated that she go, now. She would not share the meal with him. She would not stay with him a moment longer.

The maids admitted Matthew on their way out and he thanked them warmly for their help before facing Faith.

"You look lovely," Matt complimented as he stood before her, his eyes glowing as his gaze skimmed over her. She was beautiful, despite the secondhand clothes. Her hair was glorious, tumbling unconfined down her back in shining splendor. Though the bruise on her forehead was more pronounced, the healthy rosy color in her cheeks seemed to assert that she was feeling better, and he felt a quickening deep within the heart of him. She was going to be fine. Without thought, guided only by his feelings, Matt bent toward her then, his lips brushing ever so lightly against hers.

It was a soft kiss, a gentle exchange, nothing like the disgusting advances of the soldiers. It sent a thrill of physical awareness through Faith unlike anything she'd ever felt before and made her all the more determined to flee. Breaking the contact, she darted toward the door, throwing it wide in her need to escape.

"Faith . . ." Matt was caught off guard by her action. Only when his startled eyes met hers and witnessed the wariness there did he think he understood his mistake. He shouldn't have touched her . . . shouldn't have taken advantage of her trust. She had been so abused, and he had frightened her away. "I'm sorry, I didn't mean . . . please stay. . . ."

"No . . . I can't. . . ." Faith had to get away from his overwhelming presence. The kiss had only emphasized the need. She was vulnerable, her defenses were down, and he was perfect, everything she'd ever wanted in a man, but he was beyond her reach. "I have to go. . . ."

With that she disappeared into the hall, dashing for the stairs. Matt stood perfectly still, stunned by all that had happened. She was gone. He hesitated only an instant before running after her, but as he started from the room, he ran headlong into Noah. The jolt of the impact jarred them both.

"Matt? What the hell . . . ?" Noah grasped him by the shoulders to steady them both.

"It's Faith. . . ."

"Faith?" he frowned.

"The girl. She just ran out, and I was trying to catch up to her." Matt shifted free of Noah's grip and hurried to the top of the staircase, only to find to his dismay that she'd already gone from sight.

"What happened?" Noah asked as he came up behind him.

Matt did not want to answer, for he believed that the blunder he'd made in kissing her had frightened her away, and he felt more than a little ashamed.

"Nothing," he answered curtly.

"Nothing? Then why were you chasing her down the hall?"

"I wasn't chasing her down the hall," he denied. "I just didn't think she should be up and about yet, that's all."

"Oh." Noah knew that there was more to the moment than his brother was ready to confess, but he let it drop. "Join me for breakfast, then?"

Matt wanted to race after her. He knew her address. He knew he could hire a conveyance and reach her home before she did, but he did not. He was certain that he was the last person in the world she would want to see.

"I've got a better idea," Matt remarked. "Why don't you join me?" And he led the way back to his room.

Chapter Seven

Standing before the mirror above the washstand in his room, Noah finished arranging his neck cloth into a precise style. He then donned his ivory satin waistcoat and quickly buttoned the polished gold buttons. Noah had always disdained the ornately embroidered fashions of his contemporaries, thinking them particularly dandyish, and instead had favored a more understated style, one that enhanced the man and not the clothes.

His peers in London had often chided him for not following the current trends, but the ladies had thought him daring. His elegantly tailored wardrobe had emphasized the lean power of his manly form, and the women had found him near to irresistible.

Noah was not remembering London society, though, as he drew on the unadorned black velvet cutaway coat he'd selected to wear to the Demorest's ball. Instead, he was thinking of CC. There was unfinished business between them, and he wondered how she was going to handle welcoming him to her home tonight. Would she welcome him openly and make him feel at home as she'd promised her father before their first meeting? A brief, leering smile played about his lips at the thought. Or would she try to stay out of his way and ignore him as much as possible? There was only

119

one thing he knew for sure. It was going to be interesting seeing how she handled herself in front of her father's loyalist friends. Turning back to the mirror, he surveyed himself critically. Satisfied that he looked his best, he paused to idly adjust his ruffled cuffs when a knock sounded on his door.

"Noah, it's me. . . ." Matt called out.

"Come on in," he responded.

"Are you about ready? It's well after eight," Matt told him as he let himself into the room. Since his fateful encounter with Faith Hammond early the day before, Matthew had thought of little else, and he was looking forward to the diversion the ball would present. The young colonial woman had haunted his thoughts ever since she'd rushed from the inn and out of his life. Though he had been tempted on several occasions to go to her home, he had held himself back. She had suffered enough. By leaving as she did, she had let him know how she felt in no uncertain terms, and he knew there was no point in pursuing it.

"Just about," Noah answered. Studying his brother's reflection in the mirror before him, he was impressed by the fine figure of a man Matt presented. Though his evening dress was not as starkly plain as his own, Matt had chosen well. Playing down the fancy embellishments so popular with others, he had opted for a simple gold-thread design on his dark blue vest, down the front of his matching coat, and about the deep cuffs. The results were striking on the younger man. Matthew was no fop, and Noah was pleased.

"Well done, Matt. You look quite the man-about-town."

Matt was pleased by his brother's compliment. He had always admired Noah's taste in clothes and had tried to emulate his style to a certain degree. "Thanks."

"No need to thank me. It's quite the truth," Noah assured him. "Has the carriage arrived yet?"

"Yes, it pulled up just a minute ago."

"Let's be on our way then," he encouraged, and they started below.

"Tell me about the Demorests," Matt urged a short time later as the conveyance they'd hired made its way through the winding streets of Boston toward the Demorest home. "You've said very little about them, save that Edward Demorest is the agent you're dealing with here in the colonies."

"There's little else to tell." Noah, immersed in thoughts of his upcoming confrontation with CC, wanted to avoid his brother's probing questions.

"I'm rather looking forward to making some acquaintances tonight," he went on. "My interest in the colonies has grown, and I want to learn more about their way of life."

"Don't get too enamored with the way things are here," Noah warned.

"I know, I know," Matt sighed. "We're returning to England in the spring, but still, there's no reason why I shouldn't find out all I can while I have the opportunity. Who knows? Maybe someday in the future I'll return on my own."

Noah could see no reason for his continued interest, but he let it go. If Matt's interest in the colonies kept him occupied and out of his way while he took care of business, he was all for it.

"Does Demorest have a family?"

"One daughter," came Noah's curt reply as a vision of CC dressed in her boy's garb danced before him.

"Oh? What's she like?"

The question was a simple one, but Noah found himself groping for an appropriate answer. How could he describe a chit who one moment had been spouting off about her dislike of English aristocracy and the next had been the picture of decorum? Or how could he explain her involvement in political intrigue and dressing as a boy? CC Demorest was a hotheaded, stubborn, and opinionated female; all the things a woman should not be, in his judgment. Yet the memory of her kiss and the smooth ivory

121

silk of her skin sent a rush of excitement through him. Yes, Noah vowed silently as he fought to subdue his desire, there definitely was unfinished business between them.

"She's pretty," he finally answered abstractly, gaining Matt's immediate attention.

"Really? Then why haven't you mentioned her before?"

"Why should I have?" Noah snapped, much to Matt's confusion.

"No reason. It's just unusual for you to ignore a good-looking woman," he quipped, his remark earning him a strained glance from his brother.

"As you should know, women are the last thing I'm concerned about right now," he replied harshly.

Matthew fell silent as he pondered Noah's complete change of personality. Just a few short months before, he had been a rake and a roué of considerable repute on the London social scene. With the beauteous Andrea Broadmoor at his side, he had been the envy of many, but now everything was different. Again Matt wondered, as he turned to gaze out the carriage window at the passing city, if his brother's more lighthearted side was lost to him forever.

Eve Woodham arched a finely plucked pale brow in approval of her own appearance as she studied herself in the mirror above her dressing table.

"You've outdone yourself this time, Peggy," the lovely widow told her maid. "This style is perfect, and the bird . . . Well, it's just a stroke of genius." Eve turned and twisted before the glass, admiring the new-fashion hairstyle Peggy had created.

"Thank you, ma'am." The servant, unused to compliments from her exacting mistress, smiled brightly, thankful that she'd pleased her. She had had her doubts about attempting the new arrangement, but knowing that the ball this evening at the Demorests was an important one to Eve, she'd taken the risk. Piling Eve's blond hair high over an oval wire frame, she'd powdered it and then artfully added the nesting bird to create what she hoped would be a trend-setting style for her fashion-conscious mistress. The results, she had to admit even to herself, were stunning. There was no doubt in her mind that Eve would be the most lovely woman at the ball.

"Hurry now and get my gown. I want to make an entrance tonight, but I don't want to be too late." Eve stood and moved to the center of the room. She slipped out of her dressing gown and let it fall unheeded to the floor, knowing that the maid would pick it up later.

With Peggy's help, Eve donned her hoops and then slipped into her new gown, an open-robe style of pale blue, ivory-shot silk. The low-cut bodice was most revealing, and Eve's slight smile was scheming as her maid approached her with the dainty fichu that was used to modestly cover that exposed delicate flesh.

"No," Eve stated flatly when Peggy would have adjusted the material over her cleavage.

"No, ma'am?" The maid's eyes were wide in wonder.

"I think not tonight, Peggy."

"But, Miss Eve . . ."

Eve's blue eyes flashed in crystal coldness as she spoke of her plan. "Tonight Lord Noah Kincade will be in attendance, and I fully intend to attract his attention."

"Lord Kincade?"

"He's just arrived from England. I haven't met him yet, but I've heard that a handsomer man has never walked the face of the earth," she confided, an edge of unswaying determination in her voice.

"Ooh! How exciting! No wonder you've been in such a tizzy getting ready for tonight."

Eve's smile was hard. "Mark my words, Peggy, I'm going to do whatever it takes to win him."

After coming out of mourning for her elderly first

husband two years before, Eve had been sought after by most of the bachelors of Boston. Gorgeous, intelligent, and extremely sensual, she made a practice of keeping men dangling. She had experienced one bad marriage, her dead husband having been very tight with his money and very jealous of her, and she was determined to select her second husband with more care.

Since being widowed and left with a comfortable fortune, Eve had discovered that she liked being in control of her own destiny. As she waited for the right man to come along, she had made the best of her widowhood, using it as both a device to attract suitors and a defense against too ardent ones. When she'd heard the talk about Lord Kincade, she'd become convinced that he was the right man. The colonies bored her, and having always longed to live in England, Eve was setting her cap for Lord Noah Kincade. Rumor had it he was tall, handsome, and very rich. She did not intend to fail.

"But what of Lord Radcliffe, ma'am?"

"Geoffrey?" Eve scoffed with an indifferent laugh. "He's a plaything to me, Peggy. He has no money of his own. He's the earl's youngest son and has been banished here by his father for his excesses."

"But he's certainly a good-looker."

"It's nice that a man is handsome, but it's not essential to my future happiness."

"I don't understand." The maid was truly puzzled. Eve and Lord Geoffrey had been lovers for some time now, and Peggy had always expected them to marry.

"Geoffrey's pockets are lined only out of his father's need to keep him away from home. He's totally dependent on his relatives for his income, and I might add they are not overly fond of him."

"And Lord Kincade?"

"I don't know much, just that the family owns Kincade Shipping and that they are very wealthy. Obviously, since Noah Kincade's here doing some of the negotiating himself, he must be intricately involved in the business. According to one source, he has every intention of returning to England in the spring." Eve whirled about to give Peggy a triumphant smile. "So, with any luck at all, before the year's out, I will be Lady Kincade and on my way to England to be lady of the manor."

"Oh, Miss Eve . . ." Peggy sighed. "He's everything you've ever wanted . . . an Englishman who's rich and titled and good-looking."

"I know," Eve agreed. "I've waited for a long time for Noah Kincade to come along, and I don't intend to let him get away. So"—she turned and posed for Peggy—"what do you think? Am I beautiful enough?"

"You're more than beautiful, ma'am. You're breath-taking. No man will be able to resist you tonight," she affirmed.

"Good." She went to her jewel box and selected her finest diamond eardrops and matching necklace. "Help me with these. We must convince Lord Kincade that I am every bit his equal money-wise, or he's liable to dismiss me as a mere colonial."

"Yes, ma'am." Peggy was truly surprised at the amount of effort her mistress was putting into catching His Lordship, and she wondered if all her careful planning was going to work.

"Peggy . . . run and tell James that I'm on my way down, and have him order the carriage brought around."

"Yes, ma'am." The maid hurried to comply.

CC descended the staircase gracefully and Edward stood in the hallway below, watching her with glowing eyes. She was beautiful, this child of his. Wearing a modestly cut emerald brocade gown of the open-robe style, its sleeves falling in graceful ruffles at her elbows, CC was dazzling, and he was not averse to letting her know how proud he was of her.

"You're lovely, my darling." Edward met her at the bottom step and pressed a fatherly peck on her cheek.

"Thank you, Papa." She smiled up at him, her eyes warm with affection. "I hope you're satisfied with the preparations I've made for the ball."

"I've gone over everything with Gilbert, and you've arranged things marvelously," he complimented. "The first of our guests should be arriving in the next few minutes, and the music is scheduled to begin in about half an hour."

"I'm glad you're pleased. I know how much this means to you, having the governor and Major Winthrop in attendance."

"They are very important men, and I hope the evening proves a pleasant one."

"It will." CC had spared no expense in planning for their guests. Taking her father's arm, she allowed him to lead her into the parlor.

"A sherry, CC?"

"Please." She accepted the crystal glass and sipped delicately of its amber contents as she moved to the window.

"Lord Kincade will be here, you know, as well as his brother," Edward offered.

A smile curved her lips, but did not reach her eyes, as she replied in a teasing tone that hid her very real aversion to the man, "I know, and I promise not to embroil him in any more political discussions."

Secretly, CC dreaded the upcoming confrontation, for she wasn't overly confident of her acting abilities. She despised Kincade from the very depths of her soul, and she hoped that she wouldn't have to speak to him at all beyond a welcoming greeting. After that initial encounter, she was going to make every effort to avoid him. Considering all that had happened, CC was certain that that arrangement would suit him, too.

For an instant the fear stabbed at her that Kincade might

reveal all to her father, but she quickly forced the possibility from her mind. He'd be a fool to risk exposing his own involvement with the rebels, and she knew, in spite of everything else, that Lord Noah Kincade was no fool.

The sound of a knock at the door and the servant answering signaled the beginning of the party, and Edward and CC went forth to welcome their guests.

Tall, blond, and stylishly attired in an intricately embroidered scarlet coat and matching vest, Lord Geoffrey Radcliffe, second son of the Earl of Radcliffe, stood at the edge of the ballroom dance floor savoring his tumbler of Edward Demorest's expensive bourbon and contemplating his lot in life. All in all, things weren't going too badly for him. Not that he relished living in the colonies, but when one had no alternative, one had to make the best of it. Money had never been a problem, as his father was more than happy to pay whatever amount it took to keep his "disgraceful" youngest son out of the way. He lived as comfortable an existence as possible in Boston and did not suffer too much the inconvenience.

Geoffrey's thin, cruel lips twisted into a cynical smile at the thought of his family's opinion of him, and he took a deep drink of his bourbon. He found their collective condemning of him amusing. Still, it did have the power to irritate. Who were they to criticize, when they were as immoral in their own vices as he had been in his? Only, he had had the misfortune of being discovered and, therefore, had lost favor with the king. It irked him that he was banished from his home, but he knew he was better off where he was. Certainly, had he been allowed to remain, he would have had difficulty tolerating his older brother James's constant criticism. Geoffrey had always hated James, the next in line for the title of Earl of Radcliffe, for his superior attitude, and he realized that the distance between them was a good thing.

127

The sound of more guests arriving drew his dark, brooding gaze to the main hall, and a glimmer of appreciation lit his expression as he caught sight of the fair widow Eve Woodham making her grand entrance. Geoffrey's pulse quickened as he remembered their last encounter, and he thrust all thoughts of his family from him. Eve was the main reason that his life here in the colonies was tolerable, and he could hardly wait until he could maneuver her into a secluded corner tonight so they could be alone. He was enamored with her lithe body and the wild spontaneity of her lovemaking. She was more enticing than any of the women he'd dallied with in England, and Geoffrey was totally caught up in the web of her sensuality.

Even though he wanted to hurry forth and claim her for his own, Geoffrey held back. He was a nobleman and his position dictated that it would not do to appear too eager for her company. He would wait patiently until she'd swept into the ballroom and charmed all those present before approaching her. Turning to a group of men nearby, he joined in their conversation.

"Eve . . . so glad you could come." CC greeted Eve with apparent warmth, for, though she had known her for years, she had never developed a fondness for her. Eve represented all that CC disliked in a woman because she used the "helplessness" of her femininity to entice men. CC knew better. There was nothing helpless about her; the woman was a vulture where men were concerned. She had observed her manipulations of her admirers for a long time and understood her motives perfectly—Eve Woodham was out to catch the richest husband she could. CC wondered why the men didn't realize it.

"It was so kind of you to have me," Eve returned sweetly as she eyed CC's emerald gown. She recognized the styling and craftsmanship as the work of one of the finest seamstresses in the city but decided that, attractive though the gown might be, it was not nearly as exciting as her own. She smiled to herself as the butler came to slip her wrap from her shoulders, revealing to all the daring cut of her décolletage.

"Eve, my dear, you look beautiful," Edward told her gallantly as he bent over her hand.

"Thank you, Edward," she preened under his flattery.

"Your gown is lovely," CC added, admiring the style but wondering why Eve had felt it necessary to bare so much of her bosom. Was there someone here she was trying to ensnare with her "charms"? "And your hairstyle is striking." Though not an admirer of powdered hair, CC had to admit that Eve's stylist had created something very eye-catching. *If the hair doesn't attract the man she's after tonight,* she thought a bit cattily, *the gown will certainly do the trick.*

"I had the gown made especially for tonight, and Peggy designed my hair. It's absolutely marvelous, isn't it?" Eve glowed as she leaned toward Edward. "Has he arrived yet?" she asked, lowering her voice to an almost conspiratory pitch.

"Yes, Geoffrey is—" Edward started, but she interrupted, touching his arm as she gave a light laugh.

"Not Geoffrey. Lord Noah Kincade. I've heard so much about him lately that I just can't wait to meet him."

"Lord Kincade . . . of course . . ." he blustered. "No, he hasn't made an appearance yet, but I'm sure he'll be arriving soon."

"You've met him already, haven't you, Cecelia?" Eve asked, keeping her tone casual lest she reveal too much of her excitement at finally having the opportunity to meet the nobleman.

CC didn't understand why, but the other woman's mention of Kincade annoyed her.

"Oh yes, I've met him," CC answered through gritted teeth. She remembered the last time she'd seen him, and his words— *You may come to my room at the Red Lion later*— rang through her mind.

"And?" Eve pressed, eager for any information she could

gleen about the rich lord.

"He's a very handsome, charming man." CC almost gagged on the lie. Handsome? Once she had thought him so, but no longer. And charming? Hatred flamed anew within her as she thought of that night. Noah Kincade had all the charm of a snake . . . the morals, too.

"Then I bet you're excited about seeing him again tonight," Eve ventured.

"He's only a business acquaintance of my father's, Eve." CC managed to disguise her uneasiness at the thought of facing him. "John is here, you know."

She glanced back toward the ballroom doorway and was pleased to see John making his way toward her, the pale blue velvet of his embroidered coat enhancing his blond attractiveness. He looked most handsome this night, and CC knew she should be thrilled to be the object of his affections, but somehow she wasn't.

"Of course; how could I have forgotten?" Eve flashed John the smile she reserved for men only, then brashly asked within John's earshot, "And just how long are you going to toy with John's affections, CC?"

CC stiffened at her inquiry and was tempted to tell her bluntly that it was none of her damned business, but she refrained. "If and when I decide to marry, Eve, you'll be among the first to know, I'm sure."

Eve wasn't certain whether or not there was a barb to her words, but she couldn't resist a parting shot. "Don't keep him dangling *too* much longer, darling. I doubt John will wait for you forever," she sniped before sweeping away toward the ballroom.

John greeted Eve as they passed, and then approached CC, his brown eyes alight with interest. "Do I note a possible change in your attitude toward our marriage, my love?"

"John . . . we've discussed marriage between us and—" she was answering when she heard her father behind her speak.

130

"Lord Kincade! How good of you to come." A chill of apprehension shook her as she heard his deep, mellow response.

"Good evening, Edward. May I present my brother, Matthew. Matthew, this is Edward Demorest."

"A pleasure to meet you, my lord," Edward greeted him.

"Thank you, sir, but please call me Matthew."

"Matthew, then." He was most pleased at being allowed the familiarity. "CC, darling . . ." Edward spoke to his daughter, who was standing with her back to them and appeared to be in deep conversation with John. "Lord Kincade and his brother Matthew have arrived."

Tensing, she forced the semblance of a sweet expression on her face as she turned from John to welcome him, but even as she spoke, her gaze remained hard and suspicious. "Lord Kincade."

"Miss Demorest . . . a pleasure to see *you* again." He read the distrust in her green-eyed gaze. Knowing the reason for it, he delighted in taking her hand and, with slow, gentlemanly ease, bringing it to his lips for an innocent-looking, yet very sensual, kiss. Noah deliberately let his gaze rest upon her bosom before rising up to look her in the face.

The hot brand of his mouth upon her hand, and the penetrating heat of his silvered regard as it seared her decorously clad breasts sent a thrill of remembered desire through her, but it was a sensation she was determined to resist. CC struggled not to give in to her indignity. She knew why Kincade was doing it. He was taunting her, daring her. He had told her that night that it was not through between them, and now she knew he meant it. It took nerves of steel for her not to snatch her hand from Kincade's grasp, and she was greatly relieved when he finally released her, his smile mocking and knowing.

Dragging her eyes away from his, she turned as quickly as politeness allowed to the younger man at his side. "This is your brother?"

"Matthew, may I introduce Miss Cecelia Demorest."

131

Matthew's smile was real in appreciation of her beauty, and he, too, took her hand and raised it to his lips. "Miss Demorest."

How odd, CC mused distractedly as she considered the effects of Matthew's touch compared to his brother's. The emotions she'd experienced when Noah Kincade had touched her were foreign and very frightening; yet when the younger Kincade touched her in the very same manner, she felt no threat at all. Glancing up at him, CC found warmth and cheerfulness in his blue eyes, eyes so unlike his brother's glacial gray ones. She responded to that glow of kindness as a flower responds to the sun.

"Lord Kincade." She smiled brightly. There was a great physical resemblance between the two brothers, but Matthew had a friendly openness about him that encouraged the same response in others.

"I would beg you to honor me by calling me Matthew." Matt found Cecelia Demorest enchantingly lovely.

"Matthew." She spoke his name softly and then realized that John was still standing there awaiting an introduction. "Lord Noah Kincade and Matthew, this is John Robinson."

Noah had heard John's remark to her about "our marriage, my love," and he stiffened as he eyed him askance. He recognized John almost immediately as one of those who'd been in attendance at the secret meeting, and he wondered how any man could allow the woman he professed to love to take part in such dangerous activities. Her father, he was certain, knew nothing of her involvement with the rebels, but this man, who was obviously her fiancé, was supporting her participation. The thought rankled, and Noah found himself wondering why. What did it matter to him that Cecelia Demorest was risking her life by working with the revolutionaries? Probably, he thought with age-old male cynicism, this John encouraged her in her pursuits and maybe even directed her to use her lovely body to help

132

further their "cause." His expression hardened as he acknowledged Robinson with distant disdain.

"CC, you and John stay and welcome any latecomers while I introduce Lord Kincade and Matthew to our other guests," directed her father. He then escorted them down the hall, leaving CC behind with John.

"Why didn't you tell me that Lord Kincade was an acquaintance of your father's?" John hissed for CC's ears only when Edward had guided the two Englishmen into the ballroom. "Is he the reason why you disappeared from the meeting the other night?"

"Yes, I was worried about being found out," she answered, glad to have that as an excuse.

"But why didn't you tell me about him before you left?"

"He had only been to the house once on business." Her tone was hushed, but sharp. "You know that Joshua checked him out. He's not a spy, though it would probably be easier to stomach his company if he was."

"Why?" Her remark mystified John.

"Because knowing he's not a spy reduces him to nothing more than a money-hungry double-dealer!"

"Aren't you reacting a little strongly?" he wondered.

"Hardly. The man's amoral. He has no true interest in our cause, save how much he's going to make off of us. If we don't meet his price, I have no doubt that he's going to turn around and offer the shipment, lock, stock, and barrel, to my father for the British troops. I know for a fact that they've already spoken of it."

"Then we'd better not allow Graves to waste any time in giving him our answer. Somehow we're going to have to raise that money before his ship comes in!" John knew a moment of anxiety, for he was certain that they would never get another opportunity to purchase military goods like this one.

"John, I don't want to think about this anymore tonight."

133

CC sounded weary. Her nerves were stretched taut at the thought of being in the same room with Kincade all night long.

"All right," he agreed reluctantly, though his thoughts were still on Kincade and how to raise the necessary funds to meet his demanding price. "Shall we join the others?"

"Please," she agreed after looking to see if any more carriages were arriving.

Chapter Eight

Edward made the rounds of the ballroom, introducing Noah and Matthew to all present. The music and dancing had already begun by the time he led them to where Major Winthrop and Lord Radcliffe stood in earnest conversation near the refreshment table.

Winthrop noticed their approach first, and he smiled broadly in welcome. "Edward . . . wonderful party . . ."

"Good evening, Edward," Geoffrey greeted his host.

"Good evening, Lord Radcliffe, and thank you, Harley. My Lords Kincade, may I present Lord Radcliffe and Major Winthrop." Edward made the introductions easily. "Lord Geoffrey Radcliffe and Major Harley Winthrop, this is Lord Noah Kincade and his brother, Lord Matthew Kincade." He was pleased to have such notables in attendance and hoped his distinguished guests would find that they had much in common.

"I'm honored, my lords." Winthrop, a tall, stout man in full military regalia, bowed in form.

"Major." Noah and Matt both returned his greeting.

Though he was careful to disguise it, Geoffrey eyed the Kincades with some displeasure. He remembered that Noah Kincade had had a reputation as being quite a ladies' man in England, and he did not like the thought of him being in

135

competition for Eve's favors. Certainly Eve was the most beautiful woman at the ball, and he had no intention of sharing her . . . not with Kincade . . . not with anyone.

Noah had been vaguely aware the James Radcliffe had had a younger brother who'd been banished to the colonies, but he'd never expected to meet him socially. He waited, nerves suddenly on edge, for Radcliffe's reaction to his identity. If word of the duel and his brother's death had reached him already, then Noah knew that a confrontation would be unavoidable. It was a confrontation he didn't want. He was here to conduct business as quickly and quietly as possible without the taint of what had happened in England interfering, and he hoped that Geoffrey had not yet received the news.

Though the moment was a tense one for both Noah and Matt, they were relieved when the other nobleman showed no sign of recognition beyond the usual social amenities.

"My Lords Kincade." Geoffrey nodded coolly in their direction. "What brings you two gentlemen to Boston?"

"Business, I'm afraid," Noah responded noncommittally as he took a glass of champagne from the tray of a passing servant. "And you?"

"I suppose you could say I'm here on business, too," he replied, thinking that his only business here in the colonies was the business of seeing to his own pleasure.

Eve had been keeping subtle track of Edward's progress about the room as she'd danced with one of her admirers, and as soon as she could break free from the man's persistent presence, she moved to join her host.

Her gaze was hot upon Noah Kincade as she drew near. She had recognized the nobleman at once when he'd entered the room shortly after she herself had arrived. He was tall and elegantly dressed in black velvet, and she found herself mesmerized by his overpowering presence. Noah Kincade, she'd decided, was every bit as attractive as the gossips had claimed, and Eve knew that somehow she was going to have him in her bed. She stilled a thrill of passion as she imagined his lips upon hers and his hands upon her body. How she would love parting her thighs to him! How marvelous it would be to be dominated by such a magnificent specimen of manhood! She could hardly wait to possess him completely!

Eve was cautious, though, and she schooled her features into a mask of polite interest as she approached. Geoffrey knew her too well, and it would never do for him to guess where her interests really lay . . . at least, not yet.

Edward noticed her coming to join them and introduced her. "Ah, Eve Woodham . . . I'd like you to meet Lord Noah Kincade and his brother Lord Matthew Kincade."

"I'm honored." Eve flashed Noah her most flirtatious look as he bent courteously over her hand.

"The pleasure is all mine, I'm sure," he replied with ease.

As he greeted Eve, Matthew quickly discerned her carefully concealed interests, for her gaze followed Noah instead of looking at him. Though she was being careful to hide her emotions, Matt had seen so many women pursue his brother that he could recognize almost instinctively those who were about the chase. Knowing the outcome before the game even started, he took his leave of them as quickly and politely as possible and moved off to sample the refreshments spread out in sumptuous array on the tables nearby.

If there was one thing Noah was accustomed to, it was beautiful women flaunting themselves before him in hopes of gaining his affections. It was not a matter of ego with Noah, merely a fact that he had learned to deal with through the years. Women found him attractive, and many were very open in revealing their desire for a liaison with him. As he considered Eve with seeming indifference, he could tell that she wanted him. It was in her eyes as she met his gaze with frank boldness and in the unspoken invitation of her innately sensual movements as she stood before him.

Geoffrey, too, noticed her posturing, and he felt jealousy

slowly begin to burn within him. She was his! How dare she flaunt herself before Kincade?! Downing his drink, he fought down the urge to grab her and drag her from the room. There would be time later to let her know of his displeasure.

"If you'll excuse me for a few moments, I see some late-arriving guests in the hall. . . ." Edward took his leave of them.

"Of course, Edward."

"How are you finding life in the colonies, Lord Kincade?" Eve asked with seemingly avid interest.

"Most interesting, Miss Woodham," Noah replied drolly.

"Oh, it's not Miss," she told him. "It's Mrs., but please call me Eve."

"And your husband?" He quirked one dark brow at her invitation.

"Alas," she sighed, "my husband has been dead for over two years now."

"My deepest sympathies, Eve," Noah responded.

"Thank you." Her smile was tinged with what she hoped was the right amount of respectful sadness. "But it's really not necessary. I've been out of mourning for some time now."

Noah thought her pretty in a full-blown way, but as he considered her charms, CC stole into his thoughts. . . . CC embarrassed by his overhearing her caustic comments on aristocrats, CC dressed in her outlandish boyish garb, and CC surrendering wantonly to his caresses in the darkness of the stables. A surge of desire filled him as he remembered that night, and as casually as he could, Noah lifted his head and glanced about the ballroom. As if by instinct, he found her, the emerald glory of her gown and the unpowdered, shining copper tresses drawing his gaze like a magnet.

Deep in conversation with Caroline Chadwick, CC suddenly felt uncomfortable, as if someone was staring at her intently. Looking up, her gaze collided with Noah's and

138

she felt heat flush through her body. Nervously she turned her back to him and tried to continue her discussion with Caroline.

"I'm sorry, Caroline; what were you saying?"

"I was saying, darling, that our dear, sweet Eve looks to have set her cap for a new man this evening," Caroline related. Her eyes narrowed as she observed the merry widow hanging breathlessly on Noah Kincade's every word.

"Oh? I hadn't noticed. . . ."

"How could you miss?" she commented dryly. "The woman's practically falling out of her dress. It's completely outrageous. Another inch and . . . Well, anyway, didn't you see her? Why, as soon as the allemande she was dancing with Fulton ended, she made a 'casual' mad dash to where your father was introducing the Kincades to Major Winthrop and Lord Radcliffe. It's disgraceful. Really, I don't know how the woman gets away with it. She's over there with him now just making a damned fool of herself!"

CC found herself growing irritated by all that Caroline was relating. She had made an honest effort to completely ignore Noah Kincade since he'd arrived, and had done quite well, until now. Now, since discovering his eyes upon her and listening to Caroline's barbed comments about Eve's behavior, she found herself shifting her stance so she could watch him covertly even as she continued conversation with her friend.

"Lord Kincade certainly is as handsome as everyone said," Caroline went on. "And his brother, too. Don't you think, CC?"

"I suppose," CC answered distractedly. She didn't want to care what Kincade did; in fact, she didn't want to know. Yet she found herself unable to look away from the sight of Eve fawning all over him. For some reason, she found herself wanting to slap the widow.

"You only *suppose*?" Caroline gave her a very disbelieving look. "My dear, do you need glasses? They're both marvelous-looking and, I understand, very rich. . . ."

"Yes, that's what I heard," she agreed. She was glad when the musicians began to play again, interrupting Caroline's endless chatter. CC was pleased when John appeared at her side and claimed her for the dance. Although she was tempted, she forced herself not to look over in Kincade's direction again, devoting all her attention to John.

As the music began, Geoffrey quickly took the opportunity to ask Eve for the dance. Eve had been hoping that Kincade would ask her first, but she accepted Geoffrey's invitation with outward grace. Inwardly, however, she was seething as he squired her through the intricate steps of the gavotte. Attractive and titled though he was, Geoffrey couldn't hold a candle to Noah Kincade, and she was determined to find a way to lay claim to Noah's affections.

Geoffrey's gaze was riveted upon Eve as they danced. She was everything he'd ever desired in a woman, and he felt most possessive of her this night. The thought that she might be interested in Kincade annoyed him greatly. He wanted to take her away from the glitter of the ballroom and make love to her until she cried out her need for him, and him alone. His dark eyes lingered on her low-cut bodice, and he burned with the need to caress that silken flesh. The memory of the Randolphs' ball several weeks before and of their wildly arousing tryst that night on the balcony beyond the ballroom sent molten excitement through his veins. He was hard put to keep his desires under control.

As the music ended, Geoffrey gave her no chance to leave him, taking her arm and escorting her out into the hall in hopes of having a moment alone with her.

"Geoffrey? Where are you taking me?" Eve demanded. She wanted to rejoin Kincade, not suffer any more of Geoffrey's advances.

"I want to be with you, darling . . . alone," Geoffrey whispered as he tried to guide her into the privacy of the deserted study.

"Geoffrey!" She refused to be drawn inside. "I want to socialize. The party has only just begun, you know, and we do have all night." Eve added the last as an enticement to give him hope that at some point later in the evening she would go with him.

Hearing her promise of "later," Geoffrey relented. "You know how much I want you, Eve. . . ."

"I know," she replied, giving him a sultry smile.

Thinking he was not going to protest, she started to return to the ballroom and Lord Kincade. However, Geoffrey was not ready to let her go yet, and he reached out to stop her.

"Did the few private moments we shared at the Randolphs' ball mean so little to you?" His expression was alive with excitement as he challenged her.

"Of course not. Don't be ridiculous," she purred, giving him further hope that she wanted him as much as he wanted her, while, in truth, she disdained the idea of ever making love to him again. She had her sights set on a man more worthy of her love. In Eve's mind, Geoffrey was now very definitely a part of her past. "It was a wonderful night. . . ."

Geoffrey smiled in arrogant male confidence. "I didn't think you'd forgotten. . . ."

The night of the Randolphs' ball, when they had made mad, passionate love on the balcony, had been forever emblazoned on his memory as the most sensual night of his life, and he felt assured that many more like it would follow.

"As you said, my love." He ran a caressing hand up her arm. "Later."

Eve managed a strained smile as she was forced to return to the ballroom in his company.

Noah nodded to some inane remark the major had made. He lifted his glass of champagne to his lips and took a deep drink of the heady brew. Though he gave the appearance of listening to Winthrop, his attention was really riveted on CC

141

and John as they moved about the dance floor. The memory of her passionate response to him taunted him, and the narrowing of his eyes as he watched her was the only outward sign of the state of his emotions.

With iron-willed control, Noah forced himself to look away, and he was pleased to see Eve returning to the ballroom. Though she aroused no great ardor within him, she would provide a diversion from his thoughts of CC. Noah had no desire to become involved with anyone, but he would have no objection to a casual dalliance, should the lovely widow be willing to oblige. Her charms were obvious, and perhaps it was time for him to relax and enjoy life a little more. Certainly he had no pressing financial problems at the moment, and it was just a matter of time before the arms shipment arrived, after which they would be well on their way to rebuilding their lives and their lost fortunes. Greeting Eve with a smile, he invited her to dance.

CC and John had rejoined a group of their friends after the music had ended, and she was enjoying a glass of champagne when she saw Kincade sweep Eve out onto the dance floor. Irritation surged. She didn't understand it. She just knew that it aggravated her immensely to see the other woman in his arms. Still, she had to admit that they were perfect for each other. Kincade was an amoral predator, just like Eve.

Feeling her determination to ignore Noah slipping, CC made a desperate effort to turn her full attention to John. When he suggested they dance again, she agreed almost too eagerly. John was thrilled to think that he was finally making some progress in winning her love, and he gloried in the thought that she was warming to him. Perhaps Eve Woodham's earlier prodding had made CC realize just how important his feelings for her really were.

CC's endeavor to concentrate on John was sharply interrupted when she discovered to her dismay that Noah and Eve had lined up next to them for the dance. Was there no way she could avoid this man? Her gaze seemed drawn magnetically to Noah, and she found him watching her, but his expression was fathomless. Biting her lip, she looked quickly back to John and was glad to find that he hadn't noticed her discomfiture.

The music began then. CC found herself dreading the moment when, because he was the gentleman to John's right, she would have to take Noah's hand and allow him to escort her through the intricate steps. A cold knot formed in her stomach as she anticipated his touch. Why did his very closeness affect her so? Did the touch of his hand really have the power to stir such dramatic feelings within her?

A terrible tenseness gripped CC as Noah stepped forward and extended his hand to her. Fighting down the shiver of apprehension that quivered through her, she moved mechanically to slip her hand in his. His hand was warm, enveloping her cold one in a firm, steady grip, and a myriad of electrifying sensations flooded through her at that simple touch. Her heartbeat quickened at his nearness, and as she caught the clean, manly scent of him, CC felt a surge of remembered excitement. Her mind screamed that it couldn't be so, but her body ignored all her logical protests, responding vitally to just the feel of his hand on hers.

Noah glanced down at her and a slight smile curved his mouth, almost as if he sensed her distress and found it amusing. His silver gaze raked over her then in a bold assessment. CC's heart jolted painfully in her breast as his words of the night in the stable echoed menacingly through her thoughts. . . . *Even a tease has to pay the price sometime. . . . This is not the end, CC . . . not by any means.*

It was with great relief that she found herself suddenly freed of his overwhelming presence. She continued through the motions of the dance completely unaware of anything save her desire to get away, to escape outside for a moment of peace.

John, totally ignorant of CC's distress, was so happy with

the way things were going between them that he did not object when she pleaded the need to be alone after the dance had ended. Before she could make her escape, however, Matthew Kincade approached them.

"Miss Demorest . . . may I have the honor of the next dance?" Matt invited.

CC had felt an immediate affinity with Matthew when they'd first been introduced, and she didn't hesitate to accept. "Of course, Matthew, but only if you agree to call me CC, as all my friends do."

"I shall be delighted, CC." Matt smiled at her.

"If you'll excuse me, John?"

"Of course," John answered. Earlier, having seen the flash of appreciation in Matthew's eyes when he'd first met CC, John would have worried at his intent, but now he felt confident enough to give her over to him without hesitation.

"Have I told you yet how lovely you look this evening?" Matt asked with courtly earnestness as he led her out onto the dance floor.

"No," she replied, smiling sweetly, "but I'm more than willing to listen."

Matt laughed out loud at her retort, drawing quite a few stares from the other dancers. The women of his social set in England could not hold a candle to CC, he thought with firm conviction. She was fresh and exciting, just like the land in which she lived.

"Your eyes are like the stars of night, your complexion, silken perfection, you—" he began in lighthearted good humor.

"Enough!" she protested. "I believe you!"

"Good, although there's more if you'd care to hear it," Matt added in mock confidence.

"Perhaps later." CC shot him a teasing look as she followed his lead through the intricate steps and glides of the allemande.

"Ah, then there will be a 'later.' . . ." He gave her the

humorously exaggerated look of a hopeful suitor.

"Are you always this outrageous?" she asked as the dance brought them back together again, and she was surprised when he frowned at her question.

"I don't know." Matt paused for effect before adding with mock seriousness, "Am I being outrageous?"

"Very." She smiled widely, enjoying his easy banter.

"Do you suppose your fiancé will be jealous?"

"My fiancé?" She was suddenly confused.

"John . . ."

"John's not my fiancé."

"Oh? I was under the impression . . ." Matt began, and then asked pointedly, "Then you're not in love with John?"

"Well, no. Why did you think that?" Admitting her feelings out loud made her understand once and for all that she really didn't love John.

"When Noah and I first arrived, you were talking to him about getting married," Matthew related as the music came to an end, and he offered her his arm.

CC took it without hesitation and then answered honestly as they walked slowly across the room, "John wishes it were so, but there will be no marriage between us. I won't marry a man I don't love."

"So you're a heartless heartbreaker. Are you?" He winked at her audaciously.

"At twenty-two, I think I'm past the heartbreaker stage," CC remarked facetiously.

"You can break my heart anytime." He said it so gallantly that she laughed.

It surprised CC to realize that the entire time she'd been dancing with Matthew, she'd hardly given his brother a thought, and she felt more confident than she had all night.

"I feel in need of a breath of fresh air. . . ." she remarked, not quite ready to return to John.

"Shall I escort you?" Matt offered willingly. He'd found CC a delightful companion and was in no hurry to leave her, especially since finding out that John Robinson was not her intended.

"I'd like that," she told him honestly. "Let's go out on the patio."

They stepped through the French doors and moved out onto the terrace, unaware that Noah was watching them from across the room, his expression fierce and cold.

Noah was livid. Watching CC laughing and flirting so boldly with Matthew had infuriated him. How dare she lead his brother on so openly! What was she plotting? Matthew was barely out of short pants and hardly her equal when it came to intrigue. Noah knew what kind of woman CC really was, and he wasn't about to let her take advantage of Matt's naiveté. Hadn't he just heard her discussing her upcoming marriage with John? What kind of woman shared heated embraces with him, planned marriage with another, and toyed with a third as the others looked on?

Noticing that John did not appear upset by her actions, Noah concluded cynically that they definitely had to be in this together. Why else would the man allow his fiancée to flirt with other men and lead them on? John, no doubt, had urged CC to seduce Matthew in order to gain influence over him. Then, once she had Matt within her power, they were going to use him to try to convince Noah to sell the shipment to the rebels at a lower price. The whole scenario certainly made sense to Noah, and his jaw flexed in anger. To think that CC had had the gall to accuse him of being double-dealing! She was nothing more than a conniving witch playing very treacherous games.

Noah turned and excused himself from Eve, who had been practically clinging to him since they'd danced. Then he started across the room to follow Matt and CC outside. All thoughts of Eve's seductive ways and the promise in her eyes were banished from his mind as he stalked his prey. Cecelia Demorest was going to learn a very valuable lesson this night. She was going to learn that Kincade men could not be used.

Light from the interior of the house shone brightly through the French doors and illuminated the terrace and gardens beyond in a dim, golden glow. CC and Matt were standing in the deep shadows near the edge of the terrace, and CC was laughing easily at something witty Matt had said when Noah strode purposefully from the house. He paused for an instant to allow his eyes to adjust to the darkness, and in that moment the lilting sound of her laughter came to him. As he glanced in the direction of her voice, his anger became a scalding fury when he saw CC lay a hand on Matt's arm in what looked to be a very intimate gesture.

"Matthew!" He forced himself to keep the anger he was feeling from his tone.

"Noah?" Matt turned calmly to greet his brother, completely ignorant of his mood. "Come join us. CC and I—"

"You're wanted inside, Matthew," Noah told him conversationally. "I believe Edward had something he wanted to speak with you about."

"Oh." Matt glanced from Noah to CC, but in the semidarkness could read neither's expression. "Well, CC, if you'll excuse me?"

"Of course," she replied, although she tensed at the thought of being alone with Noah. It was her worst imagining come true, and all her instincts were screaming for her to run from him, as far and as fast as possible. She trembled as she watched Matt disappear back inside the house. "It's getting slightly chilly. I think I'll go back in, too."

CC started to move past Noah, but he was too fast for her as he grabbed her by her wrist and stopped her flight.

"Oh no, CC . . . you aren't going back inside . . . not yet."

"You lied to Matt. . . ." Her gaze flashed with sudden icy contempt as she recognized his ploy, and her anger overcame her fear.

"Of course." His feral smile was fleeting.

CC stared up at him accusingly, but his features seemed carved in stone as he regarded her expressionlessly. She knew a feeling of very real dread then, for there was something terribly sinister about his manner. She swallowed nervously.

"What do you want?" CC forced herself to sound more furious than fearful.

"I think there's something you need to understand." He spoke tersely.

"Oh?" she challenged him with foolhardy disdain.

"I know what you and your fiancé are up to, and it's not going to work." His grip on her wrist tightened threateningly as he thought of her deceitful ways.

"Let go of me!" CC snapped, tugging against his bruising hold.

"In my own good time, my dear," he snarled, looking around the terrace. When he spied the steps that led away from the house, he started toward them, drawing her along with him down the short flight of stairs and into the deep, dark privacy of the gardens.

Panic seized her.

"Just what do you think you're doing?" CC cried as she found herself practically being dragged from the house. "I have no desire to be out here with you!"

"Would you prefer Matthew? Or perhaps your loving fiancé, John?" he derided hatefully.

"John is not my fiancé," she snapped.

Noah ignored her reply completely as he drew her on down one of the formal walks, and toward the secluded summerhouse near the rear of the garden. Usually CC loved the garden, but on this night the definite chill in the air and the leafless trees and shrubs of late autumn lent it an unnerving eeriness. She began to shiver as he led her onward, the lights of the main house fading in the distance until she was surrounded only by darkness and his overpowering male presence.

"I said to let me go!" CC dug her heels in and managed to stop his progress for a moment. "I don't know what it is you want, but you can tell me right here, right now." Painfully she twisted her arm, trying to free her wrist, but his hand was like a steel band.

"So your game is to play dumb? It won't wash," Noah sneered, turning on her. "I know what you're up to . . . the both of you."

"I don't know what you're talking about!" CC seethed, finding his cryptic statement baffling.

"You know damn good and well what I'm talking about!" There was an ominous edge to his voice that CC had never heard before, and she knew a true moment of fear.

"Let me go! You're a madman!" She began to struggle again, trying valiantly to break his grip. "You attacked me the night of the meeting, and now . . ."

Noah chuckled then, and it was a very unpleasant sound. "On the contrary, my dear little rebel, as I recall . . . and believe me, I remember everything about that night . . . *you* were the one who attacked me." The moonlight cast harsh shadows across his taut, angry features. "You're in too deep, little girl. It's time you learned that you have to pay the price, if you're going to involve yourself in men's affairs."

"What do you mean?"

Noah gazed down at her dispassionately. He found her innocent, terrified look most amusing, and he applauded her thespian skills.

"You really should take to the London stage," he told her sarcastically. "Your performance is quite believable, and if I was not aware of your true colors, I just might be convinced by your wide-eyed claim of innocence."

"It's no claim, and I have no idea what you're babbling about!"

"You're boring me with your denials, wench," Noah drawled.

"Why, you!" CC tugged forcefully and managed finally to free her arm from his punishing grasp. "You're everything I ever thought you were and worse!"

"Ah, yes. Let's see, I was either fat and ugly or a 'mincing fop'. . . . Wasn't that it?" His eyes glittered dangerously. "And we both know I'm no fop, don't we?"

In a lightning move he crushed her to him, his mouth swooping down with unerring accuracy to possess hers. The kiss was meant to punish. He wanted to show her exactly who was in control.

Though her arms were trapped between them, CC fought him, pushing with all her strength against the solid wall of his chest. She had been right to be afraid of him, and she should have run from him while she had the chance. What did he think he was doing? And what did he mean by all the mysterious accusations he'd just thrown at her? Her struggles to be free only heightened Noah's desire to dominate her, and he broke off the chastening kiss to look down at her with hard, cold eyes.

"Shall we see just how dedicated you are to this cause of yours? Do you do whatever John tells you to do, if it will help achieve your goal?"

CC stared up at him in horror, trying to grasp what he was saying. "John? I don't understand. . . ."

"Then let me make myself a little clearer. There's no need for you to waste your considerable charms on someone as inexperienced as Matthew when I am more than willing to sample the fare you have to offer." He bent to capture her lips again, his tongue delving within to duel and master hers in a ravishing exchange.

With all the strength she could muster, CC broke off the kiss. She raised her hand to strike him, but this time Noah anticipated her move and snared her arm in a vicelike hold.

"I wouldn't do that ever again if I were you. I might be inclined to hit back."

His grip was so fiercely unyielding this time that CC paled

and swayed, fearful that the bone might snap.

"You're despicable! Let me go! I want to go back inside!" she gasped, tears of pain filling her eyes.

Just an instant, seeing her very real distress, Noah felt a twinge of conscience and gave a fleeting thought to the possibility that he might be wrong about her. He stopped himself harshly. This was the woman who, despite her vows of hatred for him, had been in his arms eagerly the other night and had just tried to seduce Matt the same way. No matter how she tried, she could not deny it. She was nothing but baggage. She was deceitful and not above using her body as a tool to pursue her own ends. Why shouldn't he take her if he wanted her?

"Oh? How would your lover feel about that? Aren't you supposed to use this lovely body of yours to further the cause?" he growled as he pulled her to him. "I'm not averse to being tempted. Forget Matthew. I'm the one you should be concerning yourself with. . . . I'm the one who's in control. . . ." Noah was snarling as he brushed aside her fichu and slipped one hand within the confines of her bodice to fondle the fullness of her sweet, rounded breast.

"Please . . . no!" She tried to resist, but it was useless against his strength. She tried to make some semblance of sense of his words, but she was totally, mindlessly confused. Was he crazy? What did he mean, *use her body for the cause?*

But there was no time left to think or to question as he kissed her again, his mouth moving over hers in a demanding, potent exchange. CC's limbs were quaking as he held her pinned against him. She could not move, she could not protest. All she could do was submit to his bold, questing touch, and it infuriated her even as it frightened her. What did he mean to do with her? Her mind was on fire with the need to escape him, even as she felt the stirrings of desire deep within her. She refused to acknowledge her weakness, though, and held herself rigidly in his arms, determined not to give him the satisfaction of knowing her desperation.

151

But Noah understood women far too well, and realizing that force was not working, he changed his tack. With all the moves of a master, he set out to seduce her senses, softening his kiss to a bare whisper of contact and easing up on his controlling embrace. He would dominate her, but he would do it with her consent.

CC was surprised by the sudden change in Kincade, yet she still held herself stiffly against him. She hated him! She would not capitulate. She would not let him know that his every touch was wreaking havoc on her senses. Any moment now, CC felt certain he was going to become frustrated in his efforts and stop, and then she would be free.

Noah, however, had sampled her wanton passion once and meant to taste it again. With slow precision he stole kiss after burning kiss, until she was unknowingly meeting him halfway. Pleased that he was making progress, but still not satisfied with her response, he pushed her gown from her shoulders and lifted her breasts free of the soft confines of her chemise. With ardent, heated caresses, he toyed with that sensuous flesh until he felt the tenseness easing from her.

CC was becoming lost in a haze of forbidden desire. She despised Noah Kincade, but her body was defying her mind and betraying her ideals to the ecstasy of his thrilling caress. CC knew she should continue to fight him, to deny him the triumph she knew he would feel in conquering her resistance, but she suddenly had no will of her own. And when his mouth moved to explore the sensitive tips of her breasts, she gave up the struggle. Exquisite pulses of pleasure radiated to all parts of her body, and she found herself gasping in sweet agony. Even as she detested him and all he stood for, she wanted him and she could no longer deny it.

"Kincade . . ." She breathed his name in a half curse, half cry.

Noah pulled back, straightening above her to stare down at her moonswept beauty. "My name is Noah."

The stilling of his caresses left CC feeling oddly chilled

and she stared up at him, the fires of her need burning hotly within the womanly heart of her.

"Noah . . . please . . ."

"Please what, CC?" he growled, sliding both hands down the curve of her back until they rested, knowingly, on her hips. With inexorable pressure then, he pulled her forward until she was flush against him. "Please make love to you?" he taunted.

The coldness of the gold buttons on his vest cut into the softness of her bared breasts as he crushed her to him, and still he pressed her closer until she could feel the strength of his male arousal. The alien contact, even through all the layers of their clothes, brought a sudden gasp from CC, and she glanced up at him, nervously wetting her lips.

"Yes . . . oh yes . . ." she pleaded, hungry for that spiraling peak of excitement he'd given her when she'd been in his arms the other night.

"Soon, love, you'll know all of me. It won't be like the last time," Noah vowed as he brazenly took possession of her mouth again. His hands began an expert foray, tracing fiery patterns across the creamy flesh he remembered so vividly.

At some point in time—Noah could never recall exactly when—his intent changed. He no longer wanted simply to dominate her. Suddenly he wanted to make love to her. His senses were alive with the need to take her . . . they had been since the night of the meeting, although he'd tried to deny it . . . and he wanted her to share in the heat and passion of the moment. He wanted her to be a full and willing participant in their coming together.

Noah ignored the edge of uncertainty that threatened to dampen his driving desires. He was firmly convinced that CC Demorest was no blushing virgin. She was involved in underground activities. She was engaged to one man while openly leading on others. . . .

"Remember, I'm only taking what you're offering," Noah muttered in a strangely hoarse voice, as if to exonerate

153

himself of any possible guilt.

Somewhere in the back of her mind, CC knew she should tell him that he was wrong about her. Yet suddenly, at the sensual touch of his hand upon her breast and the insistent pressure of his manly pride against her maidenly softness, she had found herself inundated with wildly uncontrollable sensations, and she couldn't reply. She was enveloped in a flame of need, heat surged through her, coiling tightly in that secret feminine place between her thighs. CC felt herself losing all touch with reality. She knew she should fight, especially now that he'd completely released her and was sweeping her up in his arms to carry her the rest of the way to the summerhouse, but she couldn't. His erotic caress, his intoxicating kiss, and the very mesmerizing hardness of him had sent her senses skyrocketing. She was lost, to all but the desire for completion with this man.

Though Noah was caught up in the passion of the moment, too, he cynically applauded her acting abilities. What an accomplished little actress she was, he thought distractedly as he strode to the small house and entered its secluded interior. CC had gone from a fighting vixen to a surrendering whore in the space of a few exciting caresses. She had played both roles to the hilt, and he sneered inwardly at the change. *Had she thought he would enjoy a challenge more than a willing woman? Was that why she had fought so hard in the beginning?*

Noah knew he should taunt her with the knowledge that he had conquered her resistance and force her to admit her role in the plot with John, but there would be time for that later. Right now, his body was demanding satisfaction. He wanted her, she was willing, and he was going to have her.

Noah let her slide down the length of his body, and then kissed her deeply as his hands worked impatiently at the fastenings on the gown. CC knew only a moment of apprehension as he slipped the dress from her before surrendering without question to his demanding hands, and

154

he stripped her of her remaining garments. She stood before him then in all her glory and Noah paused to stare at her loveliness in silent appreciation. CC was perfect. Her breasts were full and proud, her waist small enough to invite his touch, her hips gently rounded above long, shapely legs. His breathing grew ragged as he stepped closer to pull her back into his arms, and she went willingly.

Gently he guided her down onto the cushioned sofa, fitting his still-clad body intimately against her defenseless one.

"You're beautiful, CC," he told her as he explored every inch of her satiny flesh, seeking out her pleasure points, first with his hands and then with his lips.

His sensual touch was evoking feelings of desire CC had never experienced before, and she was almost frightened by the power of her own arousal. Restlessly she moved beneath his welcome weight, seeking something more, needing that unknown quantity that only he could give which would make her feel whole . . . complete . . . satisfied.

Noah rose above her, bracing himself by his arms as he gazed down into her face. Her eyes had been closed, but they flew open as he drew slightly away. Desire flared openly in the dark emerald depths of her gaze as she met his smoky one. CC though vaguely that she'd never seen Noah's eyes reflect quite that color before, and she lifted both hands to frame his face, pulling him back to her for a tumultuous kiss.

It was the final invitation he needed, and he broke away from her almost painfully to shed his own clothes. He could wait no longer. His need to be buried within the hot, pulsing sheath of her was more than he could bear.

CC watched him, feverishly, as he shrugged out of his dark coat and quickly unbuttoned his vest. Her gaze was ravenous as she devoured him with her eyes, visually caressing the powerful width of his shoulders and the broad expanse of his furred chest. Wantonly, she knew a sudden desire to tangle her fingers in the dark hair that grew there and follow its tapering line of growth lower. Sensual heat surged through her at the thought, and in the night's covering darkness, she blushed. It didn't matter, though. Nothing mattered except having him back in her arms, touching her and creating those magic, mindless sensations within her again.

Noah stripped off the last of his clothes and turned to her then, giving CC her first unrestricted view of a man's body. Her breath caught in her throat as she stared at him in fascination. He was magnificent as he stood there bathed in the moon's fading glow. From his dark head to his slim hips and long, straight, strongly muscled legs, he was perfect. Timidly, CC avoided looking at his manhood, but Noah's deep voice commanded.

"Look at me, CC."

She glanced up, meeting his compelling gaze, and then trailed her line of vision lower until she saw him, full and powerful and ready for her.

"Noah . . . I . . ." She was nervous and uncertain, but he allowed her no time to waver as he came to her.

"I mean to have you, CC, and there will be no interruptions this time." His tone was serious as he moved over her.

His body was a scalding brand upon her cool alabaster flesh, and CC clasped him to her hungrily as she tried to absorb some of his warmth. Noah nudged her thighs apart with one knee and then positioned himself to take her, sliding his hands down to her buttocks to lift her to him. CC gasped at the exciting sensations his touch aroused, but she was totally unprepared for the foreign thrust of his hips as he probed her softness, seeking entry. She stiffened at the strangeness of it and tried to push away.

"Noah . . . stop . . . wait . . ."

"It's too late, CC, much too late," Noah groaned as he found the portal he sought and thrust eagerly forward.

Noah felt her tense as her feminine resistance tore before his passionate onslaught. He felt her virginal tightness as he

156

pierced her untouched depths and he froze, holding himself rigidly above her. His thoughts were chaotic. CC had been untouched until him. . . . She had been a virgin. . . . The enormity of the moment shocked him, yet he could not stop. The feel of her body, hot and velvet, holding him buried within her was driving him beyond all rational thought, and there could be only one outcome.

"CC . . ." He whispered her name hoarsely as he began to move, his body rocking slowly, gently against hers.

CC lay completely still. The passion she'd been feeling had vanished now that the pain of his penetration had ripped through her. She had never known there would be pain; she had thought his touch would only bring pleasure. She bit her lip to keep from crying out as he began to move in a foreign, yet somehow oddly familiar, rhythm.

Noah sensed the change in CC, and he brought his own surging desires under control with an effort. He was determined to make their joining good for her and he bent to kiss her, murmuring softly to soothe her fears.

"Easy, love. It'll pass. Relax. . . ."

CC gave a small, shaken sob as he claimed her lips, and Noah felt an even greater agony to know that he'd really hurt her. His kiss was soft and sweet, drawing her from herself and gradually easing the tension that pervaded her slim form.

CC had been stunned by all that had happened, but the gentle persuasion of his mouth on hers helped to calm her, and she sighed quietly.

"I want you, CC. . . . I have from the beginning," Noah told her as he trailed burning kisses down her throat and across her bare shoulder.

His action sent a shiver of awareness through her. CC was amazed to find that the knifelike agony of his possession had passed and only a pressing fullness remained. When his hands left her hips to cup and caress her breasts, she felt the faint stirrings of pleasure again and instinctively she pressed her hips to his, feeling a need for something more deep within.

A shudder of pleasure shot through Noah at her innocent invitation, but still he held himself in check. He had blundered once; he would not do it again. With patient care, he worked at arousing her once more, his hands skimming over her in an erotic play that teased her to the heights of desire and banished all thoughts of pain from her mind.

CC could not remain still beneath his burning weight. His masterful touch had transported her to rapture's precipice, and she needed him to show her the way to total fulfillment.

"Noah . . ." She whispered his name as she lifted her hands to frame his face and draw his eyes to hers. "Please, Noah . . ."

Her plea broke what little control he still had over his own passions. He began to move within her again, this time taking care to pleasure her as he went. He never stopped touching and kissing her as his hips drove in age-old rhythm into her welcoming softness, and when she reached her pinnacle of delight and cried out her ecstasy, he held her tightly. His own peak soon followed, the knowledge that he'd taken CC from pain to pleasure heightening the joy of his excitement. They crested and soared, completely immersed in the splendor of their joining, and then rested, wrapped sensuously, intimately in each other's arms.

Chapter Nine

A near-violent fury shook Matt as he stood in the study with a group of men listening to the conversation between Harley Winthrop and Colonel Thornhill praising the soldiers stationed in Boston.

"Gentlemen," Matt interrupted abruptly, his sudden anger overwhelming him, "it's been my experience that the troops stationed here are less than the professional soldiers you make them out to be. I should think that discipline would be one of your most pressing concerns."

Winthrop cast him a quick look of surprise as he wondered why His Lordship would be interested in military affairs. Colonel Thornhill, a tall British officer of ramrod-straight posture and a long, flowing mustache, frowned at his inference.

"How's that, Lord Kincade?" Thornhill inquired. He knew that the Kincades had only just arrived in Boston, and he wondered what possible contact this young man might have had with the troops.

"I had the occasion to rescue a young girl from two of your fine troopers several days ago," Matt informed them coldly.

"Rescue a girl *from* our troopers?" They exchanged puzzled glances. "I dare say—"

Matt cut them off. "She had been beaten, and had I not

arrived on the scene when I did, she surely would have been more sorely abused, if you understand my meaning."

"I hadn't heard of this infraction," Thornhill blustered. "Two soldiers attacking a young woman?"

Winthrop frowned in consideration and then shrugged, chuckling maliciously. "Must have been a colonial wench. She was probably a working girl. . . ."

"Sir!" Matt took offense at his remark. "Indeed she was a colonial, but she was no prostitute. She went out on the streets that night to fetch a doctor for her seriously ill parent. Your fine soldiers, instead of protecting her, were the cause of her terrible anguish! She might have died at their hands."

"Were you able to identify the soldiers?"

"No, all I saw was their backs as they ran away," he told them scathingly.

"And the woman?"

"I don't know if she followed up on the report I made to the constable or not," Matt answered uneasily.

Matt had wanted to check on Faith after that morning, to make sure that she was all right, but he had hesitated, believing that she wanted nothing more to do with him. When the doctor had returned to the inn the following morning, he had instructed him to attend Faith at her home and then report back to him after seeing her. Upon his return, Dr. Spalding had assured him that the young woman and her mother were doing fine. It had heartened him to know that Faith was better, but since she had sent no message with the doctor, he'd been forced to accept that there would be no further contact between them. He had directed the constable to her home, too, but the officer had never reported back to him with any findings or information, giving him reason to believe that Faith had been unable to identify her attackers.

"Evidently she didn't, Lord Kincade," Thornhill dismissed. "I'm sure it's all blown over by now. Usually these girls lead the soldiers on, you see. . . ."

"Our men do have their raucous moments, but all in all, they're good fighting men."

"No, I don't see, Thornhill. And Winthrop, I'm surprised by your attitude! You call attacking a defenseless woman a 'raucous moment'?" Matt was furious.

"Lord Kincade," Thornhill began with a rather mollifying tone, "you've only just arrived here in the colonies. You can't possibly know the way of things yet. . . ."

Matt's blue eyes turned icy as he faced the two officers. "Sir, I'm learning, and what I'm learning does not endear the military's presence to me!" He gave them both a curt bow. "If you will excuse me?"

And without another word, Matt strode with dignified aristocratic grace from the room. He was still angry when he reached the ballroom, and he stood stiffly in the open double doorway watching the dancers as they performed the minuet. A servant passed with a tray of champagne and he helped himself to a glass of the sparkling wine, downing it quickly in his disquiet.

His gaze searched the crowded room for some sign of Noah or CC, and noting their continued absence, he wondered at Noah's reason for wanting to be alone with her. After returning to the house as Noah requested, he had discovered that Edward had not been looking for him. The awkwardness of the moment had passed quickly as he'd joined the men in the study, but he still had been left to ponder his brother's interest in lovely Cecelia Demorest. She was definitely an attractive young woman, but the Widow Woodham seemed more Noah's type—sophisticated, worldly, sensual. . . .

Still, Matt knew he should be pleased that Noah hadn't changed so completely that he couldn't appreciate a beautiful woman. Matt just hoped that he wouldn't hurt CC in any way, for he sensed that she was an innocent in the ways of the world, and he didn't want his rakehell of a brother taking advantage of her naiveté.

Thoughts of innocence brought Faith to mind again, and Matt traded his empty glass for another full one. Faith . . . he could still see her in all her beauty as she'd rested on his bed, and the memory of the way they'd parted filled him with a strange emptiness. He thought of her terror upon awakening and how he'd calmed her fears, and he remembered the kiss. Matt had alternately cursed and treasured that one tender moment. Had he denied his sudden, obsessive need to kiss her, she probably would not have fled his company, but he had given in to his desire, and he had regretted it bitterly ever since.

He drew a deep breath as his gaze darkened in serious thought. If the opinions voiced by Winthrop and Thornhill were reflective of the Crown's general attitude toward the colonies, no wonder there was so much unrest . . . and maybe he'd been precipitate in arguing against selling the arms to the rebels. How arrogant the British officers had seemed! He recalled then the conversation between the merchants that he and Noah had overheard in the taproom their first day at the inn and he wondered now at the veracity of their complaints. If mobs of colonists were running about the city, then maybe there was a justifiable reason for it. That conclusion gave Matt pause as he glanced about the room filled with rich, successful loyalists. He found himself wanting to know more about the troubles that were developing, but he knew that this would not be the place to learn anything objective. Deciding to hold his peace for the time being, he set aside his troubled thoughts and rejoined the crowd in the ballroom. Tomorrow would be soon enough to delve further.

The faint stirrings of a chilling zephyr carried the soft strains of music across the stillness of the night-shrouded grounds. Within the darkness of the summerhouse, the sound of the melody intruded, borne on a bitter breeze.

162

Awareness crashed through Noah's drugged senses as reality and reason returned, and the icy fingers of the wind branded him with a cold, confusing thought. *CC had been a virgin.* . . . The realization both alarmed and aroused him as he lay still embedded within her warmth, and he fought down an unexpected surge of desire at the remembrance of her untutored passion. Keeping tight control over his body's urgings, Noah drew a deep, steadying breath as he considered the ramifications of all that had happened. He did not doubt for a moment that she had intended to bed him. She had taunted him at the stables, and had they not been interrupted, she would have given herself to him then. Tonight had been inevitable. CC had known it and so had he. And, Noah arrogantly assured himself, no matter how much she might try to deny it, she had enjoyed it.

Cynicism returned as he thought of Matthew, John, and the arms shipment. Irrationally, he found it angered him to know that CC was willing to use her body . . . to sacrifice her very virginity . . . just to further the rebel cause. Even as it infuriated him, though, the arousal he was fighting to control would not abate. If she wanted to persuade him, why not? Perhaps if she tried just a little harder, Noah mused harshly, he just might be convinced to lower his price. . . .

Heat throbbed anew through his loins as he gave free rein to his needs. It startled Noah to find that his desires could be so potent and forceful so soon. Never before, even with the most sensual of mistresses, had this happened to him, but he wasted no time thinking about it as he began to move within CC, driven by the need to possess her again.

Languidly secure beneath the protective warmth of Noah's big body, CC had been drowsily content, blocking out, in her sensual satisfaction, all thoughts of reality. Only when Noah hardened within her and began to move again was she forced to admit to herself what had happened. Stunned by her situation, she went rigid beneath him. How could this have happened? How could she have given herself to Kincade?

Noah felt the change in her, and believing she would willingly succumb to him once more, he murmured, "Relax, love. Let me—"

"Get off of me, Kincade!" she hissed.

Aware that his movements were stoking the embers of her forbidden desire again, she twisted her body and pushed against his chest at the same time in a burst of desperate energy, successfully dislodging him and almost dumping him on the floor.

"What the . . ." Noah managed to brace himself, and he drew back viciously to stare down at her.

But CC was not intimidated by his hate-filled glare and she took advantage of his momentary shock to scramble from beneath him. As she did, her gaze accidentally grazed his lower body, and she witnessed there the throbbing strength of his need for her. She bit back a groan and rushed to snatch up her chemise.

"You're the most loathsome man I've ever had the misfortune to meet, Kincade!" She refused to look at him.

"Indeed?" His mouth thinned as his eyes narrowed to silver slits. "You didn't think so just a short while ago, my dear."

"You . . ." she fumed, struggling with the buttons on her undergarment.

"If anything, sweetheart"—he sarcastically drawled the term of endearment—"you were begging me. . . ."

Emerald fury glittered dangerously in the depths of her eyes as she turned to face him, and her breasts heaved in agitated indignation beneath the soft, sheer covering of her chemise.

"The only thing I begged you to do was to stop!" she fumed, miserably aware, even as she said it, that he had spoken the awful truth. "Stay away from me from now on! You're a scheming manipulator, and I don't want anything to do with you."

"It will be my pleasure to stay away from you, but let me warn you, Miss Demorest." Noah spoke slowly and distinctly, lending a deadly seriousness to his words. "You leave my brother alone. Matthew is an innocent in all of this and knows nothing of your intrigue or deceitfulness. I won't allow him to be used as a pawn."

Noah's stance was menacing as he loomed over her, and even his unclothed state did nothing to detract from the power of his regal command. CC didn't understand what he could possibly mean by saying that she was using Matt as a pawn, but she refused to be cowed by him and stood up to his anger with more bravery than most men.

"You, sir, are the user. Not me! I have forfeited something more precious than gold at your hands this night!"

"What you forfeited was forfeited willingly, CC. You will not convince me otherwise."

Recognizing the undeniable truth of his statement, she flushed painfully and she was grateful for the concealing darkness.

"Get out . . ." Her tone was flat and unemotional. "Now."

Noah dressed quickly and strode from the summerhouse without another word. He paused on the terrace to check his appearance and then reentered the house with the nonchalant air of a man who'd just taken a casual, lengthy stroll through the gardens.

CC managed to pull herself together into some semblance of respectability, but she knew there was no way she could return to the ball without first returning to her chambers and securing Anna's help. Quietly she skirted the grounds and entered the house through the servants' entrance. Racing up the back staircase, she did not relax until she'd made it safely and undetected to her bedroom.

Eve was angry and restless. Noah Kincade had mysteriously disappeared after leaving her side and going out on the terrace. Though she'd searched as discreetly as possible throughout the house, she hadn't been able to locate him anywhere. Determined not to let anyone know of her unwavering interest in him, she had continued to lightly flirt with her numerous suitors and had even encouraged Geoffrey a bit, though she was wont to do it. His presence at her side had been a face-saver, though, for she had not wanted anyone to suspect that Kincade had left her without a thought. When she saw Noah return to the ballroom through the French doors, she was elated and she turned quickly to Geoffrey.

"Geoffrey, darling, would you mind getting me another glass of champange?" She gave him her most seductive smile.

"Of course, Eve. I shall be right back." Geoffrey hurried to do her bidding. He had been pleased when Kincade had disappeared from the scene and had taken full advantage of the opportunity to dominate Eve. She had been his usual attentive companion and he was eagerly anticipating the end of the ball. As he procured the glass of liquor, his blood raced excitedly as he imagined them in bed together, and he turned back in her direction, anxious to be with her again. Perhaps, he thought avidly, I can convince her to depart a little early. . . . But as Geoffrey started back, he saw her moving across the room toward Kincade, who had just come back inside from the gardens. He realized then that Eve had only used the pretense of wanting another drink in order to send him from her. The jealousy that had been born several hours before flared to life again as he watched her throw herself at the other nobleman.

Instead of returning to Eve's side, he drank her champagne himself, taking no time to savor it properly. The mixture of bourbon and champagne hit him hard, and he swore viciously under his breath as he saw Kincade escort Eve out onto the dance floor. A wildfire of emotion swept through him, but somehow he managed to hold himself back from making a scene. With all the dignity expected of one in his vaulted position, Geoffrey sought out another of the eligible young ladies and graced her with his presence.

Noah's smile was strained as he danced with Eve, but she did not notice. And though he gave the impression of listening to her senseless chatter, in truth his thoughts were far away, wrapped in the searing, exciting memory of CC's passion. At first, when he'd reentered the ballroom and Eve had joined him, he'd been grateful for the diversion she presented, but now he was finding her company stifling. He found himself constantly searching the crowd for some sign of the vibrant emerald gown and the woman who wore it. Cursing himself for being a fool to even think of CC, he forced all remembrances of the other woman from his mind and concentrated solely on Eve's less than stimulating conversation.

CC descended the front staircase to find John in the wide hall talking with Matthew. Her smile was shaky as she greeted them, but neither man seemed aware of it.

"CC, darling, I didn't know that you'd gone upstairs. . . ." John took her hand and kissed it as he met her.

"I needed to rest for a moment and freshen up a bit." Her words were not a lie. She enlisted Anna's help, and they had made short order of styling her hair again and smoothing the wrinkles from her gown. Anna had been smart enough not to question her mistress's unusual condition, and CC had been greatly relieved at not having to explain.

"I hope you weren't feeling ill." Matt was quick to worry, for he remembered her need to get a breath of fresh air.

"Oh no. Nothing like that," she reassured him.

"Good." His smile was warm with honest affection as he regarded her, and noticing her becomingly heightened color, he wondered what had transpired between her and Noah in the garden.

"CC? Would you care to dance again?" John invited.

"Of course," she accepted, glad that it had been John to ask and not Matthew. Not that she didn't like the younger

Kincade; she did, very much. It was just that she wanted to avoid any further contact with Noah, and dancing with Matt would have been like waving a red flag before an angry bull. "Matt, if you'll excuse us?"

"Until later." He bowed slightly as John led her back inside to join the dancers.

Eve's grip on Noah's arm was possessive as they stood together at the side of the dance floor.

"I'm so glad that you came tonight," she purred, pressing her full bosom against the hard-muscled strength of his forearm as she turned to look up at him.

"So am I," he replied evasively.

Realizing that it was getting late and that the ball would soon be over, Eve knew that she had to make her play for him now or risk losing him until the social scene brought them together again.

"There is no reason for our evening to end just because the Demorests' ball does." Her gaze upon him was openly brazen so there would be no mistaking the invitation she was offering.

Noah was about to decline as graciously as he could when he caught sight of CC returning to the ballroom on John's arm. She looked totally happy and completely at ease. Though he didn't quite understand why, he was suddenly furious, and he diverted his attention quickly to the lovely widow clinging to his arm.

"Is there a reason why we have to wait for the ball to end before making our departure?" he asked in low, seductive tones.

Eve's breath caught in her throat as she looked up at him with luminous eyes, unable to believe her luck. "No. No, of course not. . . ."

"Do you have your own carriage?"

"Yes," she breathed excitedly.

"Then shall we have it brought around?"

"Please . . ."

Noah took charge in his usual manner, and after speaking privately with Matt for a few moments in the music room, he searched out Edward to bid him thanks and good night. CC, it seemed, was nowhere to be found as he and Eve were making their departure.

"Edward, please relay my deepest appreciation to your lovely daughter for her hospitality this evening," Noah told his host.

"I shall do that," he agreed, puzzled by her absence. It was in the poorest form not to be available to bid her guests goodby. "Also, I had a private matter to discuss with you, and I was wondering if you could luncheon with me tomorrow."

"I'd like that."

"Shall I meet you at the Demorest home? Say about noon?"

"I'll be waiting."

CC had heard Noah as he'd ordered the Woodham carriage brought around, and though she'd tried to deny it, a shaft of pure agony had penetrated her heart. Kincade was the vile, amoral beast she'd thought him to be. He had gone from her to Eve without a pause, and just the thought of it left her feeling sick. CC disappeared from the ballroom when she noticed Noah and Eve moving toward the front hall. Seeking refuge in the seemingly deserted music room, she was determined to remain out of sight until they were gone.

"Is something wrong?"

The sound of Matthew's voice behind her surprised CC, for she had thought she was alone. Sweeping about to face him, she forced a cool expression.

"No, why do you ask?" CC was not about to reveal the truth of her feelings to anyone.

"No reason. I just hadn't expected to find you alone when you have a house full of guests," he shrugged.

"You're absolutely right," she said hastily, "and I suppose I'd better rejoin them."

Girding herself, CC started reluctantly toward the door, knowing that she would come face-to-face with Noah in the front foyer as she made her way back to the ballroom. Only Matt's next words stopped her.

"Please, CC," he spoke earnestly, "I wasn't criticizing you for taking a moment to relax. You don't have to rush back to the ballroom to be with your guests. After all, I'm a guest, too." The engaging smile he gave her lightened her heart. "Stay. We can talk for a while."

"I'd like that," she managed, relief stealing through her at being saved from a confrontation with Noah and Eve. "I'd like that a lot."

Chapter Ten

Anna greeted CC at the door to her bedroom when at long last CC finally made her way upstairs to retire for the night. Noting the strained exhaustion in her mistress's unusually pale features, Anna wondered what had really taken place during the long hours of the ball.

"Miss CC? Aren't you feeling well? Shall I help you undress and have a bath sent up?" Anna offered as CC sank down wearily on the bed.

"A bath would be heavenly, Anna. Thank you. . . ."

"I'll tell the others right away." Anna hurried off to order the bath, leaving CC alone for the first time in hours.

Exhausted, CC sighed as she slipped off her shoes, and then, eager to get to bed, she stood up and began to undress by herself. It was when she stripped off her chemise that she first noticed the smear of dried blood on the inside of her thigh. A potent rage filled her at the sight of the damning evidence that testified to her own weakness. How could she have been so stupid as to surrender to Kincade? She knew what kind of man he was! His behavior tonight only convinced her all the more firmly that he was an unprincipled opportunist.

Quickly, lest Anna return and discover her foolishness, CC rushed to the washstand to scrub the telltale stain. Even as she washed the reminder of Noah's possession from her flesh, she could not erase the memory of him from her mind . . . the sensual heat of his touch, the thrill of his kiss, the rapturous glory of his total possession. . . .

CC muttered a vile curse under her breath. Lord Noah Kincade was a filthy, arrogant . . . Her hatred of him at that moment was so fierce that she couldn't think of any expletives horrible enough to wreak on his character.

CC frowned as she reflected on all that had happened during the course of the night. Noah had assumed, just as Matt had, that she was engaged to John. He had accused her of attempting to use Matthew, though she wasn't sure how she was supposed to be using him or to what end. And even though she had fought him almost from the start, he had insisted that he was only taking what she was offering. . . .

Suddenly, in a rush of revolting realization, it all became clear to CC, and she shook her head in stunned, outraged bewilderment. As naive as she'd been, she hadn't understood Kincade's accusations before, but now a disgusting awareness dawned. Lord Noah Kincade had thought that she was prostituting herself in hopes of winning them over to the rebel cause. . . .

The knowledge that he had suspected her of such degrading behavior only served to intensify her already hostile feelings for him. He thought her no better than a common tramp! He had used her as such, and even the discovery of her untouched state had not altered his opinion.

Her anger was so powerful that she felt physically ill, and she was pale and trembling when Anna's soft knock came at the door. Snatching up her dressing gown, she pulled it quickly on, fearful that without it Anna might somehow know of her indiscretion. Bidding her servant to enter, she forced herself to present a calm front as the maid directed the belowstairs servants where to put the tub and then supervised as they filled it with hot water.

"Is there anything else I can do for you, Miss CC?" Anna

offered solicitously.

"No. I think I'll just soak awhile and then go on to bed."

"Shall I bring you a sherry? You're still looking rather peaked," she noted with concern.

The offer of a sherry did sound soothing, and CC agreed, "A small brandy might just be the thing, Anna. Thanks."

Quickly and efficiently, Anna directed the other servants from the room and then followed them downstairs to get the liquor for her mistress. As she poured the brandy into a crystal snifter, she pondered the situation. Something was amiss, but she wasn't sure just what it was. Usually after a party Miss CC was lighthearted and full of gossip and interesting tidbits of all that had happened. This unusual silence by her was troubling. Anna suspected that it all had to do with her earlier unkempt state, and she wondered if something terrible had happened. Something that maybe she should talk about.

Carrying the liquor, she returned to the room and knocked only once before admitting herself. It did not surprise Anna to find CC already soaking in the steaming tub, and she drew a small table near and placed the brandy upon it within easy reach.

"Thank you, Anna."

"You're welcome. So how was the ball, Miss CC?" Anna tried to encourage her to talk, hoping to discover the reason for her strange mood.

"Fine" came her answer.

"Did your father seem to enjoy himself?" she asked as she moved quietly about the room picking up CC's discarded clothing.

"I think so. He was quite pleased that everyone came."

"Indeed, there was a crowd, and Lord Kincade was here, wasn't he?"

At the mention of his name, CC couldn't prevent herself from tensing, and Anna noticed but did not comment on it.

"Yes, he came, and so did his younger brother, Matthew."

"Was the brother wearing dark blue?"

"I believe so; why?" CC cast a glance at her maid.

"I'd caught sight of him one time and thought him quite good-looking, too. Still, there is just something about the older one that's—"

"I know." CC cut her off sharply, not wanting to hear her sing Kincade's praises. Anna knew nothing about the man; she only saw the gift wrap, so to speak. "I'm really tired tonight, Anna. . . ."

Anna took the hint and started for the door. "Will you be needing me for anything else?"

"No. You go on. I'll be fine."

"Good night, then, Miss CC."

CC was glad when Anna had gone. Sipping from the relaxing liquor, she soaked in the hot, perfumed bath for a long time after her departure, wanting to ease all the unfamiliar aches from her slender body. Only when she felt drowsily content and free of Kincade's scent upon her did she emerge from the tub and dry herself. Clad in her most comfortable nightdress, she finally slipped beneath the covers of her bed.

Sleep should have come easily. She was warm, content, and safe in her own bedroom, but images of Kincade kept disturbing her rest. Whenever she closed her eyes, a vision of Noah as he had been in the summerhouse would loom before her, his silver eyes burning with passion, his hands reaching out for her with sensual intent. CC tossed and turned, growing more and more distraught over the heat that surged through her whenever he entered her thoughts. She hated him and all he stood for, yet he was haunting her. The memory of his touch alone had the power to send her pulses racing.

Getting up, she padded restlessly to the window. Parting the heavy drapes, she stared out across the quiet city as she tried to come to grips with the riotous feelings Noah Kincade stirred within her. From the very beginning, he had not fit

174

any preconceived mold she had of English noblemen. . . . He was not fat and ugly; he was not effeminate. What Kincade was, CC acknowledged grudgingly, was devastatingly handsome. She recognized now that he was the consummate rake and a masterful lover. Though she knew she hated him and his mercenary ways, her body had responded to him as to no other.

CC shivered and retreated to the warmth of her bed, protectively pulling her blankets up to her chin. She had given in to Kincade's sensual demands in a moment of weakness, and she vowed that it would never happen again. She was going to make every effort to ensure that their paths never crossed again. Feeling slightly reassured and a little more in control, CC curled on her side and closed her eyes.

The remembrance of Noah leaving the ball with Eve Woodham pierced CC's drowsy thoughts then, sending a pang of heart-pain echoing dully through her, and a silent tear was tracing a lonely path across the softness of her cheek as sleep finally claimed her.

Matt left the ball and returned to the inn a short time after Noah had departed with Eve Woodham. Since his discussion with the military men in the study earlier that evening, he'd found himself growing more and more aware of the loyalists' attitudes and more and more annoyed with their puffed-up ways until he finally felt the need to escape their stifling presence.

He was troubled as he settled himself at a quiet table in a corner of the taproom. The liquor he'd consumed that night had rendered him slightly philosophical and he found himself, for the first time, confronting and challenging his own aristocratic views of life. Savoring the cool tankard of ale Polly quickly served him, he almost wished that Noah would return from the merry widow's so he could discuss things with him.

A wry smile lifted the corners of Matt's mouth as he thought of Noah leaving Eve Woodham's company early. If ever there was a colonial woman guaranteed to attract Noah's attention, it was Eve. She was gorgeous, sophisticated, and most obvious in showing just how interested she was in him. It pleased Matt to know that at least some part of Noah's old self remained, and he knew that there was little chance of his brother returning any time soon.

Thinking of Noah, Matt wondered why his brother had wanted to be alone with CC in the garden. He knew that it had to have been important since Noah had gone to all the trouble of inventing an excuse to send him inside, but beyond that he had no clue as to the reason. At first, after discovering Noah's manipulation of the situation, Matt had suspected that he might have been interested in CC, but then, when he'd departed the party in Eve's company, he'd dismissed the thought. Whatever had passed between Noah and CC, it had not had to do with courtship. It would have made absolutely no sense for Noah to attempt to woo their lovely hostess and then leave with the widow.

Matt took a deep drink of his ale as he thought of CC. She was a beautiful woman, and he'd found her company most delightful. He had been pleased when he'd found out that she was not promised to Robinson, and he had even considered paying court to her himself until the memory of Faith's delicate beauty had intruded. Faith had been in the back of his mind all night, and though he'd tried to put the thought of her from him, he'd been unable to dismiss her completely, even amidst the splendor of the ball.

As he finished off his drink and signaled for the barmaid to bring another, Matt pondered again all that had happened during the last few days. The attitudes of Winthrop and Thornhill had shaken the foundation of his respect and love for his homeland, and he now found himself questioning the very tenets of his life.

He firmly believed that the colonists were true Englishmen, and since they were, they deserved every benefit of the laws of the land. He thought it completely outrageous that the two officers considered their men blameless. They'd claimed that the attack had not been reported, yet Matt couldn't help but wonder if it had been reported and then arrogantly dismissed, just as they had dismissed his outrage.

Matt was seething in frustration. He had to learn the truth.

The sound of the door opening drew his attention, and he glanced up to find Noah striding into the room, a black scowl marring his handsome features. Matt thought it odd that there had been no sound of a carriage drawing up, and he wondered how his brother had gotten back to the inn.

"Noah . . ." he called out.

Noah noticed Matt sitting alone at a table, and he made his way across the sparsely populated room to join him.

"You're back early," Matt noted with some interest as Noah sat down opposite him. "I hadn't expected to see you until morning."

Noah's gaze turned glacial at his teasing, but he didn't respond right away as Polly approached the table to serve Matt his fresh mug of ale.

"Can I get you anything, Lord Kincade?" Polly offered. The last night she'd spent with him had been even better than the first, surpassing even her most ardent dreams, and she was eager to be available to him whenever he wanted her.

"No. Nothing, Polly," he answered brusquely to deliberately discourage her. "Thank you."

Disappointed, but having no other recourse, Polly retreated to allow them their privacy.

"Well?" Matt prodded, sensing there was much he wasn't telling.

"Well, what?" Noah ground out.

"What happened with Eve Woodham? I didn't hear a carriage. I—"

"I chose to walk back," he answered.

177

"You chose to walk?" Matt quirked one dark brow in disbelief.

Noah glared at him. He did not want to discuss any of what had happened this night; not with Matthew, not with anyone.

"Walking is a mode of transportation," he drawled. "Now, if you've finished trying to pry into my private affairs . . . my intention in returning was to retire for the night. . . ."

"All right." Matt hid his grin by taking a drink. Noah was being as stoic as ever, and no matter how intriguing the circumstances, he knew that his closemouthed brother would not reveal a thing.

"You returned early from the ball yourself," Noah pointed out as he leaned back, relaxing a bit now that Matt's inquisition was at an end.

Matt's previously bemused expression turned serious as he replied, "I had things I needed to think about."

"Such as?"

He eyed Noah levelly before answering. "I had a slightly unsettling discussion with Winthrop and Thornhill."

"The military officers? Why?" His curiosity was piqued.

"I had overheard them talking about the quality of troops stationed here, and I commented to them on the lack of discipline."

"Yes . . ."

"I related all that had happened with Faith the other night and they were singularly unimpressed. It seems to me that they care very little about the plight of colonials. Some of their remarks were most disturbing and led me to believe that there might actually be a good reason for all the unrest."

Noah's lips quirked as he asked sarcastically, "Are you saying you're not nearly so furious with me now for my traitorous ways in betraying our country?"

"I'm saying that if Winthrop's and Thornhill's attitudes are pervasive among those representing our government, then it's no wonder that there is vast potential for a revolt."

"And just whose side would you be on, Matthew, if it came to that?" His question was pointed and gave the younger man pause.

"I don't know," Matt answered honestly. "Before tonight, even with the attack on Faith, I still was ardently against revolt, but now . . ."

"Now, nothing!" Noah was suddenly sitting stiffly in his chair. "Don't give it another thought."

The sharpness of his tone drew a puzzled look from Matt. "But . . ."

"You are Lord Matthew Kincade and you will not become involved in any of this." The last was a command. "Do you understand me?"

"I may be Lord Matthew Kincade, but I am a man, and I will make up my own mind," Matt countered with dignity.

"The hell you will! You insolent pup!" Noah ground out in low tones. "Don't be a fool. This entire situation could get very bloody, very fast."

"If it gets bloody, then I can be assured that you had a hand in it!" he snapped.

"My involvement is strictly business—profit and loss. What you're talking about is your life. I won't stand by and watch you get caught up in something that could be dangerous . . . possibly even deadly."

"It's not your decision to make, Noah," Matt said with slow intent. "It's mine."

"Matthew . . ." Noah sounded ominous, but Matt faced him with equanimity.

"I will do whatever it is I have to do . . . whatever I feel is right."

"But you're an English lord!"

Matt shrugged expressively. "And so are you, but you're doing what you feel is necessary. Right?"

Noah found himself frustrated at the willfulness his brother was displaying again, and he ordered in the tone that had always worked in the past, "We will be returning to

England in the spring, Matthew."

His movements tense, Matt got to his feet. Staring down at his older brother, he said only, "We shall see, Noah. We shall see."

Leaving his half-full mug of ale on the table, he stalked from the room, disappearing up the stairs.

Noah stared after him for a long moment before snatching up the tankard and drinking down the remaining contents. The different liquor hit him hard, but caught up in emotional turmoil as he was, he barely noticed. Tossing a coin on the tabletop for Polly, he followed in Matt's direction, seeking what he hoped would be serenity in his own chamber.

The rented room was cold and unwelcoming as Noah entered, and he remembered with regret the warmth and comfort of Kincade Hall. Suppressing the melancholy that threatened, he locked the door behind him and negligently began to discard his clothing. Clad only in breeches, he stretched out across the bed, resting a forearm heavily across his brow as he closed his eyes. His rest was short-lived, however, as the heavy fragrance of Eve's perfume seemed to surround him even there in his own room. Getting up, Noah moved to the washstand to scrub away the sweet cloying essence.

Eve . . . He should have known better, but for some reason, at the time he had felt driven to accept her advances. Certainly she was a beautiful woman, but it was a cold beauty that had reminded him, once they'd left the ball, of Andrea Broadmoor. From the moment they'd gotten into her private carriage, Eve had made it plain to him that she wanted him, kissing him full and flaming on the mouth and practically climbing onto his lap in her passion. Noah had never refused an offer so boldly put, but when they reached her home and were alone in the dark seclusion of the house, he suddenly felt no desire for a consummation with her. That had been an awkward enough situation for him to deal with, but what had made it even worse was that he found himself continually comparing Eve to CC.

He gritted his teeth even now as he thought of CC. Cecelia Demorest was a paradox. She was outspoken in her dislike for English noblemen; she was completely opposed to her own father's views on colonial relations; she'd masqueraded as a boy in her determination to help her secret cause; and she'd surrendered herself to him in hopes of maneuvering him into a more agreeable frame of mind toward her rebel group.

The realization that she had been untouched when he'd taken her struck a chord of emotion within him, and Noah frowned. How could it have been? Though she had denied during their argument that she and John Robinson were affianced, they had certainly seemed loverlike throughout the evening. Obviously, Noah realized now, he'd been wrong in that assumption, but why, if she cared so deeply for the other man, had she given her virginity to him?

Noah shook his head as if to clear it of unwelcome thoughts of CC, but it did no good as visions of the evening clouded his mind. Eve—blond and aggressive; CC—fiery but reluctant . . . Eve had known what she was about; CC had been untried.

Noah almost regretted that he had initiated her in such an abrupt manner. He forced himself to remember that CC had been the one using him and that she had not hesitated to return to her boyfriend as soon as she'd finished with him. Perhaps she was even with Robinson now. . . . He pictured CC making love to the other man and knew a moment of unexpected fury.

Suddenly angry with himself for even thinking about the wench, Noah stalked to the bed and lay back down, seeking rest. The ale along with the champagne he'd imbibed all night had numbed his senses more than he'd been aware, and he soon succumbed to a blissful, dreamless sleep.

*　　*　　*

Eve tore the artificial bird from her hair and threw it angrily across the room. Damn! Her body had been on fire with need for Kincade and he had left her! Just like that! She muttered a curse that would have done many a man proud as she stomped to her dressing table and sat down.

Eve stared at her reflection, trying to understand what she'd done wrong, but none of it made sense. The possibility that Lord Kincade might not prefer women occurred to her, but she quickly discarded it. He had seemed most receptive to her in the beginning, and everything she had heard about him had emphasized that he was quite the playboy. She could only conclude, with some embarrassment, that she had come on too strongly for his tastes. Judging from his aloof demeanor once they'd reached the house, Eve supposed that he had to be the type of man who liked to be completely in charge of a relationship.

With a snort of irritation, Eve got up and wandered restlessly about her bedroom. She wanted Noah Kincade in a most desperate way. His kisses in the carriage had been nothing short of rapturous, and she could hardly wait to be with him again. Still, she realized now that she would have to be more subtle in her approach the next time. He might have been put off tonight by her aggressiveness, but with any luck, perhaps she hadn't done any lasting damage. Brightening somewhat at the thought, she was almost smiling when Peggy knocked and entered the bedroom to help her undress.

"How did the evening go?" the maid asked cautiously. She had known that Lord Kincade had accompanied her mistress home, and she wondered why he was not there now.

"It was an absolutely marvelous ball," Eve lied, not about to admit to a mere servant that things had not turned out exactly as she'd hoped.

"And Lord Kincade?" Peggy ventured as she helped Eve don her dressing gown once she had completely disrobed.

"Lord Kincade was perfect, Peggy. Just as I'd expected

him to be," she assured her as she returned to the dressing table to allow her to brush out her hair.

"He accompanied you home, didn't he, ma'am?" She was accustomed to Lord Geoffrey spending the night and thought it unusual that Kincade hadn't elected to remain. Surely her mistress hadn't played coy . . . or had she?

"Yes . . ." She faked an ecstatic sigh as her thoughts turned sour. He'd accompanied her home, all right, and then had turned around and left!

"Will you be seeing him again?"

"I'm sure," Eve answered deceptively. She didn't doubt that she would see him again, but she had to wonder exactly when and where.

"I'm happy for you." Peggy smiled enthusiastically. "He sounded absolutely divine when you spoke of him earlier, and now to know that the reality matches the dream . . ."

"The reality was better than the dream," Eve's answer this time was definite and honest. "I'm more determined than ever that he is the man for me."

And indeed she was, for no man had ever treated her with such indifference. Kincade's distant attitude had aroused her desire for him to a fever pitch. Eve would have him. It would only take her a little longer to figure out how to go about it. When at last Peggy had departed, Eve climbed into the vast emptiness of her bed and began to plot. Somehow, very soon, she was determined that she would be sharing its wide comfort with Kincade.

Geoffrey sat in the darkness of his own study, half-full tumbler of bourbon in hand. Jealousy was eating him alive as he stared unseeingly into the surrounding blackness. Eve was with Kincade. . . . And knowing Eve as well as he did, he had no doubts that the other man was gracing her most comfortable bed. Infuriated and filled with more hatred than he'd ever felt in his life, Geoffrey threw the glass across the

183

room, listening as it shattered against the opposite wall.

"Lord Radcliffe?" The door to the study opened, and a glow of golden light permeated the room as his butler entered carrying a lamp. "Is something wrong?"

"Most definitely, Bartley," he told him rigidly.

"Can I be of service?"

"Not tonight, but by morning, I should think so."

"Very good, sir. I shall check with you then. Shall I clean up?"

"Leave it," Geoffrey ordered. "I need to be alone right now."

"Yes, sir."

When the servant had backed from the room and he was once again enveloped in darkness, Geoffrey smiled thinly. Somehow, some way, he was going to destroy Noah Kincade. He wasn't sure how just yet, but he knew he would. No one took what was his and got away with it. No one. And Geoffrey firmly believed that Eve was his.

Chapter Eleven

"Lord Kincade . . ." The sound of Polly's voice and her sharp knock at his door woke Noah to the blinding brilliance of the early-morning, and he almost groaned aloud as he struggled to sit up.

"What is it, Polly?" he growled.

"A note, m'lord," she replied hastily. "The gent who dropped it off said it was important you get it right away."

"A note?" Noah ran a hand through his dark, tousled hair as he stared blankly at the closed door. "Just slip it under the door, Polly."

Polly had been hoping to see him this morning, but she did as she was bid. "Yes, m'lord."

After a moment Noah made his way to where the sealed envelope lay just within his room and bent down to pick it up. The motion aggravated the throbbing in his temples, and he returned to the bed to sit back down, tearing open the envelope and drawing out the missive within.

Lord Kincade,

Would like to meet with you at nine o'clock this morning at the Green Dragon Inn. Have important news for you.

Graves

185

Despite his self-inflicted state of misery, Noah felt a surge of excitement. This was the contact he'd been waiting for. Graves had told him after the first meeting that he would be in touch as soon as they'd reached an agreement. Evidently they finally had.

Hastily Noah selected fresh clothing and set about getting ready to leave. He thought of asking Matt to accompany him, but remembering their conversation of the night before, he decided against it. As ardent as Matt had been, Noah knew it might be a devastating mistake to introduce him to any of the rebels. He did not want him getting involved.

Within the hour Noah had dressed, breakfasted alone in his room, and was ready to leave for his rendezvous. As he descended the stairs, he caught sight of Polly and motioned for her to join him.

"Yes, Lord Kincade?" Her eyes were sparkling as she hurried to his side.

"I'd like you to relay a message to my brother when he arises."

"Yes, m'lord?"

"Tell him that I was called away on business this morning and that I have a luncheon appointment with Edward Demorest at noon. I shall be returning here after lunch."

"I'll tell him," she promised, staring up at him with open adoration.

"Thank you, Polly. This is for your trouble." He handed her a coin.

"Oh, m'lord, it's no trouble at all. . . ." Polly was thrilled. "But thank you, just the same."

"You're welcome."

Eagerly anticipating the news he was about to receive, Noah left the inn and hired a conveyance to take him the distance to the Green Dragon.

Only a few men were gathered at the Green Dragon Inn on

Union Street that morning. Looking as unkempt as always, Sam Adams sat with his ardent supporter Ryan Graves, discussing what was for them the burning issue of the day— the decision to purchase the arms from Lord Kincade.

"You're prepared to meet his price then, Ryan?" Sam asked, his interest in the matter keen. Though Sam would never take an active part in any of the unrest, he was a great orator and would be a main motivating factor behind it.

"We're going to do our best to meet it," Ryan answered somewhat grimly.

Sam nodded. "That's all you can do."

"I just hope we have enough time to raise the funds." He looked up as the door opened and Noah entered the tavern. "Lord Kincade . . ."

Noah recognized Graves and Adams right away and moved purposefully in their direction.

"Good morning, gentlemen." He shook both their hands as they stood to greet him.

"Good morning." They were businesslike in purpose and wasted no time on pleasantries.

"I presume you have an answer for me regarding the shipment?" Noah began immediately.

"Indeed I do," Ryan said. "And I hope you will find it acceptable."

Noah nodded slightly as he glanced about the sparsely populated room. "Is this a safe place to discuss our dealings?"

"It is," Adams put in with assurance. The Green Dragon had long been the central meeting place of their cause and he knew everyone in the room. It was safe.

"Go on."

"We do not have the entire amount you've demanded. . . ." Ryan began.

"Then there is no point in our continuing this discussion," Noah said coldly as he rose to his feet. He was annoyed at having come all this way for nothing. Surely Graves could have just sent a message to that point and saved him the trip across town.

"Lord Kincade, please, sit down. I haven't finished."

Noah eyed him disdainfully. "I am a busy man, sir. If you cannot meet my terms, then we have no further business to discuss. I told you in the beginning that my price was firm."

Ryan held on to his temper with an effort. "If you will allow me to finish . . ."

Noah stiffly resumed his seat, wondering what else the man could have to say.

"While we have not yet raised the entire amount you're asking, we do have a substantial portion of it. If it is agreeable to you, we would be willing to pay you half now and half when the shipment arrives."

"How can I be sure that you will have the other half of the money by the time the materials reach port?"

"We only need a few more weeks."

Noah considered him silently. He had had no word of any sightings of the *Pride,* and he estimated that it could be as long as a month before the merchant ship made landfall.

"All right."

"I appreciate your understanding in this matter."

"You can contact me at the Red Lion regarding delivery of the sum you indicated. I expect to hear from you within the next few days."

"There will be no problem, I assure you."

"Good."

"An ale, or perhaps a glass of rum?" Ryan offered.

"Ale, please. It's a little early for anything stronger."

"Sam, can I get you anything?"

"No, Ryan, but I'm afraid I must leave now. I have to speak with the gentlemen who just came in. If you'll both excuse me?" Adams left the table and crossed the room to where the two newly arrived men stood as Ryan went to get their ales.

When Ryan returned with the tankards, they spoke of

inconsequential things until the sound of Sam's sharp protest interrupted them.

"You mean they still aren't willing to come around to our way of thinking?"

"No, Sam, I'm sorry."

"But we told them several weeks ago how important this was. . . . Why, we even sent out committees to impress upon them the strength of our convictions. . . ."

"It doesn't make any difference. They're refusing to go along with us."

Noah looked at Ryan questioningly. "There's trouble?"

"It's as we were saying at the meeting you attended. We are a nation of shopkeepers, and the British tea that is due in port soon represents a devastating attack against our own merchants. That tea cannot be allowed to come ashore and be sold only through British agents."

"Why is Adams so upset?"

"We've sent out committees to the agents to try to convince them of the error of their ways and to stop the tea from being delivered, but they've all refused to listen. I'm afraid something terrible may happen soon if any of the tea makes port and an attempt is made to unload it."

Noah listened intently. He was slowly coming to understand the legitimacy of the colonists' complaints, but was still determined not to become involved. It was none of his business what the government did with the tea. He was no colonist. He had no ties to this city. He was only concerned with his own affairs, and right now they were complicated enough.

"Perhaps things will be coming to a head sooner than we think. . . ."

"Regrettable, but it looks unavoidable."

It was near noon when Matt made his way through the winding maze of streets that was Boston, and his expression was serious as he debated the wisdom of the decision he'd made that morning. The night just passed had been a restless one as he'd tried to sort out his feelings. As dawn had repossessed the city, he'd felt a driving need to see Faith again. Matt tried to convince himself that he was only going to find out if she'd reported the attack to the proper authorities, but in truth—a truth he was trying to avoid acknowledging—he really wanted to see her one more time.

Finally arriving at the address he knew to be Faith's, Matt stood hesitantly before the modest wooden home. He was convinced that she despised him and he didn't blame her, for he knew he'd been completely out of line when he'd kissed her. It had been an impulsive gesture on his part, but after the trauma she'd suffered at the hands of the soldiers, he realized that it had been the worst possible thing he could have done. He had frightened her, and that had been the last thing he'd wanted to do.

Girding himself to face her now after all this time, Matt finally, grudgingly, acknowledged to himself that he was only using the report of the attack as an excuse to see her again. Faith had been in his thoughts almost continually since she'd raced from his room that day. The fact that her memory had haunted him during the Demorests' fancy ball last night had shown him just how much he truly cared about Faith. She had made an indelible impression on him, and he had to be with her one more time to apologize for his boldness and to ask her forgiveness. Ready at last, he approached the door and knocked, then stepped slightly back as he waited for someone to answer.

Concentrating on her stitchery, Faith sat by the window at the back of the house to take advantage of the brightness of the day. Her father's death had left her mother with only a small monthly stipend, and so it was necessary for them to take in sewing in order to supplement their income and keep food on the table.

Faith had been working doubly hard lately, for she felt

that she owed Lord Kincade the money for the doctor's visit to care for her mother. Thanks to him, her mother was back to good health again and she was determined to repay him for his timely help.

She sighed as she thought of the handsome young lord who'd rescued her from a fate worse than death. He had been kind and considerate even when he'd kissed her. Mesmerized by the memory, a faraway look shadowed her eyes, and Faith paused in her work, touching a hand to the softness of her lips. Matthew Kincade had been so perfect . . . her knight in shining armor. . . .

Tears stung her eyes as she realized that it was all a silly dream. Their meeting had been a quirk of destiny. They lived in two very different, very separate worlds, and they would never meet again. Irritated by her girlish fantasies, Faith began to sew again in earnest, deliberately forcing all thoughts of Matthew from her mind. It wasn't smart to moon over things you could never have, for she understood all too well that there was much in the world beyond her reach. Usually Faith could accept that and be happy, but somehow those few hours in Matthew's company had disturbed her serenity. She needed to completely erase even the slightest thought of him if she was ever going to be inwardly content again.

The knock at the door surprised her but did not frighten her. It was not unusual for garments to be dropped off at their little house at all hours of the day, and so she set aside her work and quickly went to answer it.

"Yes?" She opened the door wide, expecting to find someone delivering sewing, and instead was faced with Lord Matthew Kincade in the flesh. Her aquamarine eyes widened, and she swallowed convulsively as she stared up at him.

To Matt she looked more beautiful than he remembered, but when he noticed her stunned expression, his spirits fell. He immediately assumed that he'd made a big mistake in

191

coming. She looked so shocked that he wanted to quickly put her fears to rest.

"Faith . . . Miss Hammond," he quickly corrected. "I know you weren't expecting to see me again, but I thought it was important that I come to you and apologize."

"Apologize?" Faith blinked in confusion as she wondered why he thought he owed her an apology. She should be the one apologizing to him. He had done so much for her, and she had run away.

"I wanted to tell you that I was sorry, and I also wanted to check to make sure you were doing all right."

"I'm fine, thanks to you, and so is Mother. Please, won't you come in?" she invited, still trying to figure out why he was sorry. He had saved her, fed her, cared for her. He'd been wonderful!

Her unexpected invitation was more than he'd hoped for, and he quickly agreed, "I'd like that."

Faith led the way into the small sitting room. Sparsely furnished, it contained only a threadbare sofa and chair and two mismatched tables. Faith realized it was hardly what an English nobleman was used to, but at this moment she didn't care. He was here! She didn't know why he had come, but she wasn't about to question her good fortune. She was just thrilled to see him.

"Have a seat. Would you like some tea?"

"No, thank you," he declined as he sat down on the worn but comfortable sofa. "Is your mother here? I'd like to meet her."

"She had to go out for a little while, but I expect her back soon." Faith knew it wasn't quite proper to entertain a gentleman totally unchaperoned, but she couldn't send Matthew away.

"Good. Perhaps I'll still be here when she returns." His cool smile was at distinct odds with his nervousness.

"Mother would like that. I've spoken of you and—"

"You did?" He was surprised. He had expected that she

would only want to forget him.

Faith wondered why he sounded so amazed. "Of course. I told her how wonderful you were when you rescued me and how . . ." She suddenly realized she was revealing too much about her feelings for him, and she blushed deeply, beautifully.

Matt knew a spark of hope that maybe he'd been completely wrong about all that had happened between them. "You mean you weren't angry with me?"

"Angry?" Her aquamarine eyes were wide and questioning. "I don't understand. Angry about what?"

"I came here today to apologize for upsetting you the way I did. . . ."

"Upsetting me?" Her puzzlement was real as she drank in the glorious sight of him. He was every bit as gorgeous as she'd remembered him to be . . . tall and broad-shouldered with black hair and the most extraordinary blue eyes she'd ever seen. Faith was having difficulty keeping her expression from reflecting her joy at seeing him again.

Matt had known this wasn't going to be easy, and it wasn't. "I shouldn't have taken advantage of you as I did."

"How could you think you'd taken advantage of me? You were the one who saved me."

"I shouldn't have kissed you, Faith. I should have realized how the whole ordeal had upset you. After all that had happened to you, it was outrageous of me to be so forward. I only hope you'll accept my apology and forgive me for my momentary indiscretion. It won't happen again," he assured her.

Faith was torn between laughing and crying. He thought she had run from him because he had kissed her and she'd hated it! Inwardly she smiled. She hadn't run from him because she'd hated his kiss; she had run from him because she'd loved it. But then he was also saying, most seriously, that the kiss would never happen again, and her heart lurched at the thought. Faith knew realistically that there could be no future for them, but she also knew that she wanted to kiss Matthew Kincade. It had been the most exciting moment of her young life, and if she could, she wanted to repeat it. Her only problem was . . . how? If Matthew was not interested in kissing her again, then there was no hope. She certainly couldn't very well throw herself at him.

Faith understood with agonizing pain that it was wonderful that he'd come to apologize for something he had thought he'd done wrong, but in reality nothing had changed. Matthew Kincade was a titled aristocrat, and she was a lowly seamstress relying on her own handiwork to support herself.

"Lord Kincade . . ."

"Please, Faith." His gaze darkened as he reached out to take her hand. "Call me Matthew."

The touch of his hand on hers was electric. Startled by the sensations that flooded through her, she looked up, her eyes unexpectedly meeting his.

"Matthew, I . . ." She started to speak, but something in his expression stopped her and she held her breath in painful expectation as he bent slowly to her.

Matt was caught completely off guard by his reaction to the simple touch of her hand. Fiery excitement pulsed through his veins, and he was nearly overwhelmed by the need to take her in his arms. Faith was so lovely, every bit as beautiful as he remembered, and he longed to crush her to him, to keep her safe, forever. It was a new, powerful emotion for Matt, and he almost gave in to the desire to hold her. Only a sudden stroke of common sense stopped him from repeating his earlier mistake with her, and he drew back abruptly, shaking himself mentally as he released her hand.

The breathtaking moment of intimacy they'd shared was lost, shattered into jagged shards of disappointment, and Faith felt chilled by the change in him. Shifting slightly farther back on the sofa, she distanced herself from him. "Your apology is accepted, although there really was no need."

Matt was relieved at her response, but he, too, sensed the change in the mood between them. Not knowing what else to say, he hurried to ask her about her dealings with the authorities.

"There is one other thing I need to ask you about." In truth, there were a million things he wanted to know about her, but Matt knew he had to go slowly and win her trust before he could hope that anything else could develop between them. His gaze dropped to her lips, and he wondered if they had really been as soft and exciting as he'd remembered from the brief kiss they shared.

Faith could not imagine what he was leading up to. "Yes?"

"Did you follow through on the report to the authorities regarding the attack?" Matt directed his attention away from her loveliness and back to thoughts of his original purpose in coming here. He had to find out if the report of her assault had been dealt with fairly or if it had been disregarded as inconsequential.

"I did," she told him, and then added tersely, "although it was really pointless."

He frowned at her statement. "Why do you say that? You would have been able to identify your assailants, wouldn't you?"

"Possibly, but in the end it wouldn't have made any difference." Her tone was flat in resignation.

"Now I'm the one who doesn't understand." Matt scowled as he recognized that his worst fears about the soldiers' presence and the loyalists' attitudes were coming true.

"No matter if I could identify them or not, the two soldiers would never be brought to justice." Faith unknowingly affirmed his suspicions and, as she spoke, was unable to keep the bitterness from her voice.

"Are you saying that even if you had been able to

positively identify the men who attacked you, nothing would be done about it?"

Faith gave a curt nod as she met his piercing blue gaze. "Mother and I dealt with them once before. . . ."

"Something like this has happened to you before?" Matt was astounded.

"Not to me," she explained slowly, glancing down at her hands folded in her lap, "to my father. He was killed by a British regular several years ago."

"What happened?"

"Have you heard anyone talk of what is commonly called the Boston Massacre?" Faith asked.

"No, I'm afraid I haven't," he admitted.

"Well, several years ago there was a confrontation between a group of unarmed colonists and some British soldiers. The soldiers fired into the crowd and several men were killed. It was terrible. . . ."

"Were the soldiers prosecuted?"

Faith sighed as she remembered all the pain and confusion of the time. "Oh yes, they were tried, but nothing happened. They were let go . . . and they had committed murder! Don't you see! I knew even as I was reporting it that those two soldiers would never be punished for what they did to me. I only did it because you had insisted."

"And you've heard nothing?"

"No one cares." She shook her head. "I'm only a simple colonial without influence. It's been this way for a long time, and I don't suppose things will ever get any better." Faith sighed, "At least, not unless Sam Adams has his way."

"Sam Adams?"

"He's one of the most outspoken colonists opposing British rule. He thinks the colonies deserve independence, and frankly, I'm to the point of agreeing with him."

"You mean you support the rebels?"

Her eyes were flashing with an inner fire as she looked up at him. Faith knew he was a nobleman, but at this moment it didn't matter. "Yes, and sometimes I wish I was a man so I could join them."

While it was true that Matt was astonished by her declaration, all that she'd related to him had only reinforced his own disgust with the way things were being handled here in the colonies. The discovery that her father had been killed in cold blood by the British soldiers only hastened his complete conversion from loyal British subject to supporter of the colonists' grievances.

"Parliament has been taxing us unfairly for ages," Faith was saying. "The injustice of it all was one of the reasons why my father died. He'd been so infuriated by the abuses that he began attending the dissidents' rallies. One thing led to another. . . ." Her voice faded off. "I'm sorry. I shouldn't have gone into all of this. I'm certain as a member of the aristocracy, you're in complete disagreement with all I've said." She felt a moment of uncertainty, wondering how he was going to react to her outburst.

"On the contrary, Faith," Matt told her gently. "I admit when I arrived here in Boston a short time ago I was not aware of the injustices being perpetrated here, but since then I've become more involved. I find that I'm quite in agreement with you."

"You are?" She was taken by surprise by his answer.

Matthew nodded. "The handling of your situation, for instance, is shameful, but from all I've learned, it seems that it's not uncommon for such matters to be ignored. This time, however, is going to be different, for I intend to do something about it!"

"Matthew! No! You can't!"

"What do you mean?"

"It will only make matters worse! Please, just let it go. For my sake, please . . ."

"But when I think of what might have happened to you if I hadn't come along when I did." He was earnest.

"I know, and to this day I thank God for your help," Faith

197

told him with open honesty.

"Faith . . . I'm so glad I was there that night."

"I am, too."

Her eyes shone with a brilliance that mesmerized him and overruled his vows not to press her. Later he would remember this moment and wonder why she hadn't resisted. Now he only knew the need to hold her close and soothe away all her fears.

Faith was thrilled that he wanted to hold her, and she couldn't suppress a shiver of delight as she went into his arms. He was so strong and solid that she felt she would be safe as long as she was with him. It happened then. . . . Matthew kissed her. A sweet-soft exploration that was every bit as glorious as she'd remembered. This time, she didn't want it to ever end.

The willing surrender of her lips filled Matt with a driving need to deepen the kiss, and he possessed her mouth fully, his tongue searching out and dueling excitedly with hers. When she responded to his kiss and met him fully in that flaming exchange, he crushed her to his chest, relishing the feel of her breasts pressed tightly to him.

"Faith . . ." Matt was breathing heavily as he broke off the kiss and moved slightly apart from her to steady himself. Though not as worldly as his brother, Matt was not without experience. He knew better than to allow himself the ecstasy of having her in his arms. The way he was feeling, things could easily get out of hand too quickly.

Faith had been totally lost in the rapture of his embrace. She was hurt when he stopped kissing her, and she wondered if she had done something to offend him. Had she responded too fully? Had she acted the wanton? A dull flush of embarrassment stained her cheeks as she worried over her actions, and she looked up quickly when Matt gently reached out and cupped her cheek with a warm hand.

"There's no need to be ashamed, Faith. I feel it, too." His voice was gruff as his gaze met hers.

"You do?" she whispered in surprise as she saw the flame of passion he was keeping carefully under control reflected in his eyes. A shiver of expectancy quivered through her as she tried to imagine what it would be like to be possessed by him. Faith wanted Matthew Kincade more than she'd wanted anything in her entire life.

"I do. I have from the first," he admitted rather ruefully as he gave her a lopsided grin, "but I stayed away from you until now because I thought you hated me. . . ."

"Hated you?" This stunned Faith. "I could never hate you, Matthew."

"That's good to know now. When you ran from the inn that morning after I'd kissed you, it was the only conclusion I could come to."

She suddenly wanted him to know the full truth. "I ran away that day because I was afraid."

"I know. I frightened you. I never should have—"

"No!" she interrupted him sharply, and he glanced at her curiously. "I wasn't afraid of you."

"I don't understand."

"I was afraid of what I was feeling." It was difficult for her to blurt out her innermost feelings, but she knew she had to explain. "You had been so kind, and then when you kissed me . . ." She sighed. "It was almost a dream come true."

"So why did you run from me?" Matt was totally confused now.

"I ran because I knew there could be nothing between us. You're a titled gentleman and I'm—"

"You're the most beautiful woman I've ever met," he finished ardently.

Without another word, Matt brought her back into his embrace. His very touch was her heaven, and she melted lovingly against the hard width of his chest. They both silently marveled at how right it felt to be wrapped in each other's arms.

The exquisite scent that was Faith, a delicate essence of

199

roses and spice, surrounded Matt, stoking his already fiery desire, and he fought against surrendering to the mindless ecstasy that threatened. It would have been easy to give in to the power of his passion, but Matt knew he would have no peace if he actually made love to her now. If he abused this fragile closeness they'd established, he would be little better than the soldiers who'd so callously tried to abuse her. Slowly and with infinite care he set her from him, caressing the softness of her cheek with a tender touch.

"Faith, I've never had a woman complain about my title before," he told her wryly.

"I wasn't complaining," Faith said hastily. "It's just that we're from such different backgrounds. I couldn't believe that you really . . ."

"That I really cared for you?" At her nod, he answered huskily, "Well, believe it. You've haunted my thoughts since you disappeared from my room that morning. Faith . . ."

Their lips met in a soft, tentative kiss, but Matt hesitated to take her into his arms. When at last they drew apart, he stood taking her hand and pulling her up to him.

"I'd better leave now." Matt smiled faintly down at her.

"Do you have to?" Faith wanted him to stay with her forever.

Logically he knew it was the only way, but his heart and body longed to stay with her, to hold her and love her.

"I'm afraid so."

"Would you like to come to dinner one night? I know Mother would be happy to have you."

"I'd love to, thank you."

His acceptance brought a lighthearted smile to her face, and Matt realized then that he had never seen her happy before. It filled him with an unexpected warmth.

"Would tomorrow night be all right?"

"Tomorrow night would be wonderful," he assured her as he started to leave. "Until then?"

Faith watched until he had disappeared out of sight down

the street before going back inside. Once she was alone, she hugged herself excitedly. Matthew had come to her! He had kissed her and told her that he wanted to see her again! Faith couldn't wait for her mother to return so she could tell her all that had happened. She was so filled with joy that she almost danced as she made her way back to the rigors of her sewing, the task no longer seeming so wearisome.

Chapter Twelve

Margaret Kingsley took the cup of tea CC was offering and sat back with a contented sigh. "Thank you, CC."

"You're welcome, Margaret," CC responded as she handed a cup to Caroline Chadwick, too. "I'm so glad you had time to stop by this morning."

Usually CC was glad to see her friends, but today it was an effort just to remain pleasant. What little sleep she'd gotten had been less than refreshing, and she'd awakened this morning more tense than ever. She had been looking forward to a quiet morning alone with her thoughts, but all hopes of privacy had been shattered when Margaret and Caroline had shown up unannounced just to chat about the ball.

"Your ball was simply wonderful. Everything went so well," Caroline complimented.

"So you had a good time?"

"Of course we did," Margaret chided easily before adding in her most gossipy tone, "And so did quite a few others . . . Eve Woodham, for one."

CC groaned inwardly as she realized what was about to come.

"It was just disgusting the way Eve made a fool of herself over Lord Kincade last night," Caroline condemned. "She followed him around all evening long."

"And they even left together—early," Margaret offered in her usual busybody way. "I wonder how Lord Radcliffe felt about that. . . ."

"I saw him later with several young ladies gushing all over him, and he didn't look particularly upset by Eve's behavior," Caroline provided.

"We shall see." Margaret gave them a knowing nod as she drank her tea.

"I wonder how long Lord Kincade stayed with Eve after they departed? We all know that since her husband's death Eve has had the morals of an alley cat, so it's not hard to imagine what did go on once they were alone," Caroline sniffed judgmentally.

"You'd think the man would have better taste." Margaret's caustic comment brought a delighted peal of laughter from Caroline. "After all, every rumor I heard about him emphasized what a popular figure he was on the London social scene. With his vast experience, I can't understand what he could possibly find appealing in Eve."

"I know what Eve saw in him," Caroline pointed out with a wide smile, her gaze on CC.

"Ummm," Margaret agreed as she took a sip of tea. "He's unbelievably handsome, and titled on top of it all. I found him simply devastating."

Though she wanted to deny her feeling, CC found herself growing increasingly jealous as she listened to their conversation. She hadn't wanted to think about Noah and Eve, but now there was no avoiding it, and she was miserable. She realized Lord Kincade had been the center of attention last night. It seemed that everyone had been watching him, and she wondered if they had been aware of her time with him in the garden. Certainly they had been alone in the darkness far longer than was truly acceptable.

"Didn't you, CC?" Caroline asked, her question cutting into CC's thoughts.

CC tried to keep her expression bland as she faced her friend. "I don't know what you mean."

"I mean, darling, I saw you go outside with his brother Matthew, and then he followed shortly thereafter." Dying to know more, Caroline dropped all effort at pretense. "Matthew returned, but the two of you didn't . . . at least not right away."

"CC!" Margaret was avidly intrigued by this new tidbit of information and she set her cup aside, leaning forward to hear more. "Do you mean to tell me that you spent some time alone with that devilishly good-looking man?"

CC managed a small shrug. "Yes, but there isn't that much to tell. I had gone outside for a breath of fresh air, and he joined me on the terrace." She tried to sound unaffected. "He was very courteous." *A LIE.* "And we talked for a while." *NOT ENTIRELY A LIE.* "And then we came back inside." *SEPARATELY.* "He is a business acquaintance of my father, you know." *AND A TURNCOAT DOUBLE-DEALER.*

"What a disappointment that something didn't develop between you," Margaret grumbled good-naturedly. "You're so much more attractive than Eve, and you have so much more to offer a man."

CC breathed a deep sigh of relief that she'd managed the awkward situation so well. CC knew that if she could convince her friends of her disinterest in the man, she could convince anybody.

"Well, I thank you for the compliments, Margaret, but Lord Kincade is really not my type." CC wanted to scream the last in denial.

"And John is?" Caroline was quick to ask. "I noticed you spent a lot of time together last night. Are you becoming more serious about him? He is a wonderful young man."

"John is very dear to me." She kept her reply deliberately vague. "But surely you both must know by now that I have absolutely no intention of marrying anyone, any time soon."

204

"Of course." They sighed, disheartened that they hadn't learned any exciting news from CC.

"More tea?" CC offered.

"We'd love to stay on and visit some more, dear, but we do have to be going. We're meeting Marianna for luncheon. Would you like to join us?"

"I appreciate the invitation, but I'm still a little tired from last night. I think I'll just stay home today and rest." She accompanied them to the front door, carefully disguising her relief that they were finally going. Caroline and Margaret were her good friends, but they were very discerning, and it wasn't always easy to keep one's feelings from them. She was glad that she had managed to this time, for it wouldn't do for anyone to suspect that something had happened with Noah last night.

"Maybe next time."

"I wouldn't miss it," CC assured them. "Tell Marianna I said hello."

"We will."

When they had gone, CC made her way back to the quiet of the parlor and closed the double doors behind her. CC moved slowly across the room to stare out the wide, heavily draped window that overlooked the gardens. She could see the summerhouse in the distance, and her heart lurched agonizingly as she remembered all that had passed there.

Shaking herself mentally, she knew she had to get a grip on herself. Caroline and Margaret's idle chatter had hurt more than she cared to admit, and she wanted nothing more than to put all thoughts of Noah Kincade and Eve Woodham from her. What did it matter if he, after having had his way with her, went home with Eve? Why should she care if he'd bedded her, too? Kincade meant nothing to her. What had happened between them had been an accident that would not be repeated. As Margaret had said, he was a rake and a womanizer, and last night he'd certainly lived up to his reputation.

A shiver of disgust wracked her as she thought of Eve wrapped in Noah's arms, sharing his passion and being totally possessed by his hard, driving body. The vision was devastating to CC even as it angered her. Kincade might be a nobleman, but there was absolutely nothing noble about him.

Gilbert answered Noah's knock at the front door. "Lord Kincade, come in!" he greeted enthusiastically, ushering him inside. "It's a pleasure to see you again, sir."

"Thank you."

"Mr. Demorest was called away for an unexpected meeting this morning, but he told me to be certain that you were made comfortable if you arrived before his return. He was positive that he would be here by the noon hour, and it's almost that now," the butler quickly explained as he guided him toward the parlor. "Would you care for a drink while you wait?"

"No, thank you. I'll be fine," Noah declined.

"Please make yourself at home here in the parlor," Gilbert told him as he opened one of the parlor doors to admit Noah to the room. He thought it odd that the doors were closed but dismissed it as unimportant, for he knew that Miss CC's company had left a short time before.

"I shall. Thank you." Noah strode easily into the seemingly empty room.

"Yes, sir." The butler withdrew, closing the door after him as he went.

At the sound of someone opening the door, CC had turned from her tormented vigil by the window to stare aghast as Noah came striding into the room. For a brief instant CC was frozen into immobility by the sight of him, but the moment soon passed, and she found herself totally, irrationally infuriated. Kincade! In her home! How dare he! She couldn't prevent herself from venting her outrage.

"You!" she hissed venomously as she glared at him. "What are you doing here! I thought I told you to stay away from me!"

Noah was caught off guard by her presence, and the atmosphere in the room was suddenly charged as their gazes met. At the sight of her, a flicker of an unidentified emotion flared in his eyes, but Noah was quick to mask his feelings. Though his senses came alive at her very nearness, and the wildfire of desire that had possessed him the night before threatened to rekindle, Noah kept his expression cool as he fought against his disturbing reaction to her.

"Why, CC . . . what a pleasant surprise," he drawled, his lips curving into a mocking smile. "How nice to see you again."

"Get out of my home!" CC stalked across the room toward him, her hands resting belligerently on her hips.

Noah ignored her obvious upset and sat down on the sofa with an easy male grace. "I'm afraid that's not quite possible, my dear."

"Why, you! I'll call Gilbert and have him throw you out!" she declared, his arrogant, commanding attitude pushing her past control.

In a huff, CC started toward the doors to get the butler. She had to get away from him. He was so very attractive, and her reaction to him was so strong. Why, just the sight of him and the sound of his voice had set her pulse racing.

There was no doubt in her mind that she hated him and never wanted to see him again; yet from the moment he'd entered the parlor, she'd been flooded with memories of the heat of his mouth on hers and the rapture that had come when he'd taken her to the peak of pleasure. The realization of the power of her response to him only served to make her more desperate.

"I wouldn't do that if I were you," Noah remarked, and his words halted her flight toward the door.

"And just why is that?" she demanded.

207

"Because it just might prove embarrassing for you." Noah casually adjusted his cuff as he covertly watched the betraying play of emotions that crossed her face.

"I don't see how my asking Gilbert to escort you from the house would embarrass me."

"Personally, it doesn't matter to me what you do." Noah's smile was feral. "Go ahead and have me thrown out if you wish, but since your father invited me here today—"

"My father did what?" She couldn't believe it.

"Your father invited me for luncheon today, and I'm sure he would find it most strange if I were to depart so unexpectedly. Certainly he would want to know my reason, wouldn't he?"

CC gritted her teeth in frustration as she glowered at him, her expression stormy. "If my father knew what kind of traitor you were . . ."

"And just who is going to tell him? *You?*" he challenged, leaving her momentarily at the disadvantage. "I don't think I've ever met anyone as free with condemning labels as you are, my dear," Noah said harshly as he came to his feet and walked toward her. "You brand me ten times the lowlife, and yet you are no better. Isn't it rather like the pot calling the kettle black? I find it highly hypocritical of you to call me a traitor for dealing with the rebels while you continue your secret support to the very same group. How can there be any difference?"

"The difference is motive, Kincade!" she seethed. "I support them because of the injustices I've seen and lived with, while you're dealing with them purely out of greed. You don't care about the very real problems here in the colonies. All you care about is making money."

"You're right." His gaze was glittering as he stood before her. "That is *all* I care about—making money, and making it as quickly as I can."

"You're despicable," she whispered, and there was a tremor in her voice as she gazed up at him. She suddenly felt as if she was seeing the real Noah Kincade for the first time.

"I don't care what you think of me, CC, and what difference does it make as long as we can use each other to achieve our mutual ends?" Noah asked, reaching out to touch her cheek.

CC slapped his hand away, "I hate you, Kincade!"

"You didn't hate me last night," he taunted.

"Last night was a horrible mistake!"

"I didn't notice that you thought it was so horrible at the time." Noah found himself suddenly compelled to force her to admit that she'd enjoyed their encounter.

"You bastard! You're cold and unfeeling. Nothing like your brother. Matthew would never have forced me the way that you did."

The urge to throttle her was great, but Noah curbed it. His laugh was a sharp, derisive bark. "Force you? My dear, I've never had to force a woman in my life, least of all you. You wanted me, and you can't deny it!"

"I couldn't stand your touch!" she lied.

Her words provoked him, and Noah suddenly needed to prove her wrong.

Before she could react, he reached out and grasped her arm, dragging her forcefully against him. Excitement, hard and powerful, surged through him.

"Tell me how you can't stand my caresses, CC," he snarled as his mouth moved to claim hers.

Noah seemed so angry that CC had expected him to be rough, but the play of his lips across hers was soft and subtly seductive. CC was torn. She wanted to get away from him, but her body was responding to his kiss despite all her logic. Like a flower blossoming before the warmth of the sun, her senses craved more of this man. When he wanted to deepen the exchange, she could not deny him. A low moan escaped her as her will was vanquished.

Noah smiled to himself as he felt her resistance weaken. She wanted him. In spite of all her previous denials, there was no way she could disguise the depth of her attraction for him. He knew a moment of triumph as he realized that he could take her, right then and there, and she would not fight him. The fire of his passion flamed anew, and he brought her full-length against him as the wildfire of his desire threatened to burn out of control.

Only the sound of Edward's carriage drawing up in front of the house stopped Noah. His body was demanding more, yet reality dictated that he release her, and quickly. With an abruptness that shocked CC, Noah dropped his arms and stepped away, turning his back on her as he struggled to bring his surging needs under control.

For a moment CC felt cold, almost lost, and in her heart she cried out for him to take her back into his embrace. It was only when she heard Gilbert in the hall greeting her father that she understood his action. She wanted to speak but could think of nothing to say. CC was embarrassed. Noah had known all along that her denials were ridiculous, and he had just proven it. She could not deny it.

His runaway passion at last manageable, Noah turned back to face her. He immediately read the distress in her expression. "For a woman who deals so much in intrigue, it amazes me that you haven't yet learned to disguise your emotions."

His caustic words sliced through her, and her embarrassment turned to anger. "My emotions are none of your business!"

"Ordinarily I would agree with you completely. However, in this case, your father is about to join us, and you're still looking at me with eyes that are begging me to—"

"Shut up!" In a flurry of skirts, she marched away from him and threw the door open wide to go forth and meet her father.

Noah found himself smiling as he watched her go, and it took him a moment to realize the reason for it. . . . CC had

210

not denied his claim. Feeling strangely elated, he started out to greet his host.

Geoffrey Radcliffe sat in his study, sipping a glass of wine. "Bartley, I have a job for you."

"A job, m'lord?" his servant looked puzzled.

"Yes. It's rather out of the ordinary . . . something that only you and I should know about."

"Of course, Lord Radcliffe, you know I am the soul of discretion." Bartley's reply was stiff. He resented his employer's unspoken suggestion that he might have discussed his affairs with others.

"Yes, yes . . ." Geoffrey waved away his mood. "What I need is confidential information about someone else."

"Oh, I see. Please tell me how I can be of service to you," he asked earnestly, always eager to do his bidding.

"I need to know everything there is to know about Lord Noah Kincade," he explained in deadly tones.

"Lord Kincade, sir?" Bartley raised his eyebrows in surprise.

"Lord Kincade," he answered grimly. "I don't care what it costs. Just do it."

"Shall I undertake the endeavor myself or hire others to do the footwork?"

"Do as you wish. Just remember that I want no one, absolutely no one, to know that I am connected with this. Do you understand?" There was an underlying menace to his words.

"Of course, m'lord." Bartley nodded firmly as a shiver of fright skittered up his spine. "Will there be anything else?"

"No. Just be sure that you get this for me as quickly as possible. I have plans to make."

"I shall do my best." The servant left the room, wondering at Radcliffe's interest in the other nobleman.

When Bartley had gone, Geoffrey smiled thinly. Soon, very soon, he would find something about Kincade that was damaging, and when he did, he was going to use it to destroy the man. He thought of Eve and Kincade, and his fury increased. There was no way he would allow the other man to take what was his. No way.

Chapter Thirteen

As Faith and Ruth looked on, Ben Hardwick, their faithful longtime friend, agitatedly paced the length of the parlor. At well over six foot, Ben was a bear of a man. Though many found his size intimidating, the Hammond women did not. If anything, they found his presence comforting, for, since Robert Hammond's death, he had been their one stable connection with a far more pleasant past.

A sworn bachelor because the woman he loved had married another, Ben had been Robert's friend from childhood, and he had even been with him the night of his murder at the hands of the British soldiers. Before that night, Ben had been less than fully committed to the colonial cause. After that devastating, deadly encounter, he'd become an active member in the Sons of Liberty and a very outspoken supporter of Sam Adams's call for independence from England. His hatred of the English ran deep, and he trusted very few of them.

A middle-aged tradesman of limited means, Ben helped Ruth and Faith when he could and often took advantage of their standing invitation to join them for Sunday dinner. Unbeknownst to anyone, Ben cherished the time he spent with them. He enjoyed those sparse, yet tasty meals in their company more than he would have the finest of gourmet fare with anyone else.

"I can't believe you invited an English lord to dinner." He stopped his pacing to look at Faith, his shaggy dark brows arching in disbelief.

"I owe Matthew my life, Ben," Faith said with quiet assurance.

"I'm not arguing that," he replied, looking to Ruth. "I just don't know how you can accept him into your home."

Faith gave her mother no time to enter into the conversation. "Matthew's been perfectly wonderful to me . . . to us. When he came to see me yesterday and discovered that I had reported the assault, but that no action had been taken, he was outraged. He admitted that he hadn't understood the reasons for all the unrest when he'd first arrived in Boston, but that he did now and he was on the colonial side. I find your questioning him very insulting."

Ben was caught by surprise by her spirited defense of the nobleman. He knew for a fact that she harbored no great love of the English, and he found himself growing more and more intrigued by this Lord Matthew Kincade. The man had certainly managed to make a favorable impression on Faith. That being the case, it stood to reason that he certainly had to be someone special.

"You expect me to believe that your Lord Kincade is interested in the colonial cause—a cause that goes against everything he, as a nobleman, stands for?" The expression on Ben's broad face was skeptical.

"Yes." Faith's answer was firm as she looked from Ben to her mother, Ruth. "Matthew is a very exceptional man."

Ben scowled at her words, for he thought Faith too much the innocent and far too trusting a woman to be a good judge of this man's true character. True, Kincade had saved her from the soldiers. While the action had been a brave and heroic one, it did not necessarily recommend him for sainthood or win him automatic acceptance in his confidence. When all was said and done, Matthew Kincade was still an Englishman, born and bred. Faith had probably just been overly impressed by his title and timely kindness.

"But how can you be so sure that he isn't working for the Crown?" he challenged.

His suspicion angered her. "That's ridiculous! Matthew helped me when I needed help the most. How dare you accuse him of such dastardly behavior?"

"Darling, now don't get so upset. You know Ben is only trying to look out for our best interests." Ruth spoke softly to her daughter.

"That may be true, but his charge is totally unfounded. There was no way that attack could have been premeditated. No one knew I would be going out at that time of night." She turned to Ben.

"That's true enough," her mother agreed.

"And apart from our friendship with Ben, there is absolutely no reason why anyone would think that mother and I have any continuing connections with the rebels."

"Except for your father . . ." Ben added gravely.

"That was years ago and—" Faith was interrupted by a knock at the door, and she got up quickly and hurried to answer it. "This must be Matthew now. Once you meet him, you'll both understand why I feel as strongly as I do about him."

Matt stood just outside the front door of the Hammond house, anxiously waiting for Faith to answer. Though he had been constantly busy working with Noah and Lyle aboard the *Lorelei* since leaving her the day before, the time had passed slowly for him. Faith had been in his thoughts continually and, he found himself slightly bewildered by the strength of his emotions for her. Her kiss had been heavenly and he had not wanted to leave her. Matt knew that the frustration and anger he was feeling over his inability to right the wrongs that had been committed against Faith were justified, yet he also knew he could do no less than to heed her plea and let it pass. The necessity of accepting this mockery of justice did not sit well with him, but he vowed in his unspoken fury to see that she would never come to any harm again. That was one promise he fully intended to keep.

As the door opened, he looked up eagerly. "Faith . . ."

Faith felt her cheeks pinken as she met his avid regard. How handsome he was! She thought him even more so today, if that was possible. "Matthew, I'm so glad you're here. Please, come in."

Matt wanted nothing more than to pull her into his arms and kiss her, but he knew it was not the time or the place, for her mother was undoubtedly just inside. Instead he allowed his hungry gaze to feast upon Faith's delicate beauty, taking in her slim yet womanly curves beneath the worn, but attractive, deep green day gown. No woman clad in the richest of silks and satins and bedecked in the most exquisite of expensive jewels had ever looked more lovely to him. She was the woman of his dreams, the woman he wanted above all others. He stepped indoors and was forced to turn his full attention to the lovely older woman and the tall, burly man standing in the door to the parlor.

"Hello." He smiled as he moved to meet them.

"Lord Matthew Kincade, this is my mother, Ruth, and Ben Hardwick, an old family friend. Mother, Ben, this is Matthew." Faith made the introductions quickly after closing the front door behind Matt.

"It's a pleasure to meet you, Lord Kincade," Ruth began, but Matt quickly interrupted her.

"Please, Mrs. Hammond, I'd appreciate it if you'd call me Matthew." He bent over her hand in a courtly fashion as he flashed her his most engaging smile.

"Matthew . . ." Ruth was won over in that moment, and she returned his smile. No wonder her daughter had thought Matthew Kincade so wonderful; he was. His dress was exemplary, his style quiet, yet manly. It would be a hard-hearted woman who could resist his charming ways.

216

"Mr. Hardwick." Matt turned to shake Ben's hand, meeting his penetrating gaze squarely, with no reluctance. "I'd be pleased if you'd call me Matthew, too."

"And I'm Ben," Ben replied, feeling that possibly Faith just might have been right in her estimation of this man. He certainly was unlike any nobleman he'd ever encountered.

Matt glanced from Faith to her mother and knew that there could be no doubt as to her parentage. Both women were petite and delicately beautiful, with the same striking eaven hair. Ruth had drawn hers back into a sedate bun, but not Faith. She had only pinned up the sides of hers, drawing the thick, lustrous tresses away from her face and allowing the shining waves to fall about her shoulders in a gleaming cascade. Matt knew a sudden urge to run his hands through its silken glory, and he was forced to stifle the impulse with an effort.

"We're honored by your presence, Matthew. I'm so glad you could join us," Ruth told Matthew sincerely.

It had come as quite a surprise to her when she'd returned home from her errand the day before and discovered that Faith had invited Lord Kincade to dinner. At the time she'd argued with her daughter over the wisdom of her invitation, but Faith had been adamant, insisting that it was the very least she could do for the man who had saved her life.

Though she had acquiesced to her logic, Ruth had been expecting Matthew Kincade to be the typical English aristocrat and had prepared herself to deal with him as such. She was more than pleased to discover now that he was a gentleman above all else. She found, too, that Faith had been hedging a bit when she'd described Matthew merely as being handsome. Handsome wasn't the word for Lord Matthew Kincade. The nobleman was devastating. Staring up at him now, Ruth allowed herself to dream of a match between Faith and Matthew, for she could think of nothing that would please her more than to see her daughter betrothed to such a wonderful man.

"I'm glad to be here, Mrs. Hammond," he replied respectfully, his eyes lingering on Faith even as he spoke with her mother, "and I thank both you and Faith for the invitation."

Still unable to believe her good fortune, Faith smiled dreamily as she met his steady regard. As her gaze dropped to the firm line of his chiseled lips, turned up now slightly in the barest of smiles, her breath caught in her throat. Had the touch of his mouth upon hers really been that exciting? The memory of his kiss affirmed the thought, and she wondered if he would kiss her tonight should the opportunity present itself. The possibility thrilled her.

"Dinner is ready. Shall we go in?" Ruth suggested, directing the way into the small dining room.

The surroundings were not fancy; there were no servants to wait on them; the dishes were not of the finest china and the wine not the best, but Matt found himself enjoying the simple, yet perfectly prepared, fare more than any other meal he'd ever had. The conversation was pleasant, the mood convivial, and Matt felt perfectly content.

He put all troublesome thoughts from him during the dinner as he relaxed and enjoyed himself. At no time did he allow disturbing thoughts of the attack on Faith or of the state of his life in general to intrude. This was the moment he'd been waiting for, and he fully intended to make the most of it.

Occasionally as they dined, his gaze would lock with Faith's. All else would fade into the background as the image of their embraces the day before flooded through him in heated remembrance, and sent his blood racing through his veins. At those times it was only sheer willpower that enabled him to break off the contact and turn his attention back to the general conversation.

"How do you find life in Boston, Matthew?" Ben asked as they lingered at the table, the meal finished. He found his suspicions being slowly laid to rest, for he'd found nothing in

218

the younger man's manner to indicate that he was being anything less than forthright with them.

At the question, Matt's gaze automatically swung back to Faith and he answered, "I've found I've fallen quite in love with Boston, Ben."

His words sent Faith's hopes soaring. Was there hope that Matthew might stay here and forsake returning to England?

"You find Boston more appealing than London?" Ben wondered, a bit amazed by his statement.

"Boston is fresh and vital," he explained, mentally comparing Faith with the city. "There's a sense of excitement here that I've never experienced before, not even in London."

"Indeed, there is that," Ben agreed.

"Matthew, I have never really thanked you for saving Faith from the soldiers or for summoning the doctor for me," Ruth put in appreciatively.

"I wish I could have done more." Matt's answer was rigid as unwanted thoughts of the culprits going free and unpunished assailed him. "Especially where the attack was concerned. If I'd been able to catch the two men, things would have turned out differently. They would have been brought to justice, as they deserved."

Ben snorted in derision. "Don't fool yourself, Matthew. It wouldn't have mattered. Nothing would have been done, regardless."

Matt's tone hardened as he thought of his helplessness in the situation. "I know. Faith explained it all to me, but mark my words, someday, somehow, I'm going to see justice done."

"Matthew . . ." Faith interrupted worriedly as she sensed the sudden anger in him.

Ben, too, saw the undisguised outrage and determination in his expression. "Do you know much about the protests that are going on?"

"Not too much. Faith has mentioned a man named Sam

Adams as being one of the chief leaders of the group calling for complete independence, but beyond that I know very little about it."

"Would you like to learn more?" Ben asked, feeling that Matthew could possibly be an asset to their cause.

"I would," he answered firmly. "From what little I do know, I find myself quite in sympathy with them. It was hard for me to believe at first. . . ." Matt shook his head sadly. "And I ended up questioning my entire life prior to this. It took some time, but I'm now firmly convinced that certain powers have been, and are continuing to be, abused here. There have been some serious errors in judgment regarding the governing of the colonies, and it seems quite obvious to me that the colonists are not being treated with the same respect as other full English citizens. It's no wonder some of them are angry and are calling for a separate nation."

"You're right." Ben was quick to agree. "Feelings are running hot and high over this tea thing right now."

"And well they should be. The imposing of the monopoly may prove to be the biggest tactical blunder of all."

"There's a meeting of protest scheduled for later this week. It seems some of the ships carrying the tea are nearing port, and we're trying to determine exactly what to do about it. If you'd be interested in attending . . ."

Matt was instantly attentive, for he wanted to learn all he could. "I most certainly would be."

Faith felt a momentary chill as she remembered her father's fate. She suddenly found herself worried over Matthew's involvement with the rebels.

"Matthew . . . are you sure?" She hated herself for asking, but she didn't want him doing it unless he was certain.

"Yes, Faith, I'm sure," he replied with conviction.

Faith nodded in acceptance as her heart swelled with emotions. Just when she thought she'd discovered every wonderful thing about Matthew, she was surprised by another facet of his character. No longer was he just the fascinating, handsome nobleman who'd rescued her. Now she knew that he was definitely more deep than that. He had very real concerns, and he was willing to act upon them.

"I feel that my future is here in Boston, and I want to do whatever I can to make life better," he told her, a tender note of understanding in his voice.

A thrill rushed through her as she considered his statement. He claimed openly that *his future was here in Boston,* and Faith hoped she was a part of that future.

"It will be better all around if I make contact with you directly and leave Faith and Ruth out of it," Ben said.

"All right, but is there truly that much danger involved?" Matt wondered.

"There's really no way of knowing. There have been no overt actions against individuals yet, but who can say it will remain that way? With things just now reaching the fever pitch that they are, anything could happen, and at any time. I just want to be cautious so Ruth and Faith aren't put at risk. It's common knowledge that I visit here regularly. Though it's doubtful that anyone could make a connection between us simply because of the coincidence, I don't want to chance it."

"I agree," he replied seriously, "and I'll be waiting to hear from you. I'm staying at the Red Lion Inn."

It was over an hour later when Matthew took his leave. He stood with Faith in the front hall, just out of sight of Ruth and Ben, who had discreetly remained in the parlor to give them a moment to themselves.

"Dinner was wonderful, Faith. Thank you for the invitation." Matt knew he should go, but his need to kiss her had become almost overpowering. He had been anticipating this moment all evening. Now that they were ostensibly alone, he wanted to take advantage of the moment.

"I'm glad you were able to come, Matthew." Her voice was soft, her lips moist and parted, and her turquoise eyes were sparkling in unspoken invitation.

"So am I." His voice was husky as, at last, he gave in to the desire to hold her close.

Faith went into his arms without pause and, looping her arms about his neck, accepted his kiss with open pleasure. Matt, feeling her willingness, tightened his arms about her, bringing her even closer. The encounter was bliss-filled paradise for them both as they surrendered to the beauty of what was happening between them.

The perfect wonder of it was almost painful, and when they broke apart, they were each stunned by the power of their own feelings. It was then that Faith knew without a doubt that she loved Matthew, for there could be no other name for the emotion that throbbed so vibrantly and demandingly within her. Matt, too, realized the depth of the emotion that filled him. He stared down at Faith in silent, cherishing awe, realizing that his entire future happiness rested with this small woman he still held in his arms.

"When can I see you again?" Matt asked, his eyes dark with passion's denied intent.

"I don't know. . . ." she responded, still slightly breathless from the ardency of their kiss. "Tomorrow?"

"Tomorrow," he repeated, before bending to kiss her once more. This time, mindful of his own surging desire and Ben and her mother in the other room, Matt kept the embrace quick and sweet. "I'll see you then," he told her, and then he was gone, leaving Faith spellbound in his wake.

As Matt made his way on foot through the narrow streets of Boston on his way back to the inn, he was totally unaware of the furtive figure who'd emerged from hiding near Faith's house to follow him.

Ben and Ruth looked up as Faith reentered the parlor.

"Has Matthew gone, Faith?" Ruth asked.

"Yes Mother. He just left, but he said he'd be back to see me tomorrow," she told her dreamily.

"That's wonderful, dear. He's a very nice young man. I like him," her mother told her.

222

"I like him, too, Mother," she replied. "And I was right about him, wasn't I, Ben?"

"I believe you were, Faith. He seems everything you thought him to be. I wouldn't have been so open with him about the meeting this week if I hadn't thought he was truly interested."

"Good. Well, I think I'll go to my room." Faith was pleased that Matt had passed Ben's scrutiny. Ben had become a sort of surrogate father figure for her since her own father's death, and his approval of Matt meant a lot to her. "Good night, Ben. Good night, Mother."

"Good night."

When she'd gone Ben glanced to where Ruth was sitting. He had to take extra care not to let the depth of his emotions reflect in his expression. He had loved Ruth Hammond for as long as he could remember. His love for her had been born when he was a young and bashful lad, and it had endured unflaggingly through her subsequent marriage to his best friend.

Not that Ruth had ever had a choice in the matter. She had never known of Ben's true feelings for her because he had always been too insecure to profess them to her. He had silently suffered through the years, worshiping her from afar.

Ben had been struck by a terrible guilt when Robert had died so violently and so unexpectedly, for, though he mourned his best friend, he could not deny that he still coveted Robert's wife. The resulting misery had left him trapped in his world of unrequited love and had seen him devoting himself to Ruth in friendship only, never offering her the treasured love he kept locked privately within him.

"I guess I'd better be going, too," he said a bit edgily as he fought down the need to tell her everything.

"I'm glad you were able to join us tonight, Ben. You know how Faith and I look forward to your visits," Ruth told him pleasantly.

Inwardly, Ben groaned at her statement—*Faith and I look forward to your visits*. Despondently he wondered if she would ever come to think of him as more than a good friend. He gritted his teeth as he answered, "I'll be in touch with you during the week."

"That'll be fine," she said simply, and then added, "Matthew seemed quite smitten with Faith, don't you think?"

"He certainly did, but I just wonder if it will ever come to anything. Even though he seems personable enough, he is still a nobleman," he offered in the way of counsel.

"I know," Ruth sighed a little unhappily. "I think they'd make a most handsome couple, and I can tell Faith cares deeply for him, but you're right. Matthew Kincade is an English lord, and the differences between them are great."

Ben wanted to take Ruth in his arms and tell her not to worry, that everything would turn out for the best, but he knew he didn't have the right. Instead he merely reached out and patted her hand.

"I'm sure if they're meant to be together, things will work out."

"I hope so," she agreed as they both stood and started out of the room.

"I'll be in touch," he told her as they paused by the front door. He struggled with the urge to tell her the truth of his feelings for her for a long moment. Then he finally gave up the attempt and said rather awkwardly, "Well, good night, Ruth."

"Good night, Ben."

Ruth watched him from the doorway until he was out of sight down the street and then turned quietly back into the house, her expression slightly forlorn. Somehow, when Ben was there with them, life seemed real again, but when he left . . . it was almost like the warmth went out of the day. She wondered what her life would be like if he never had to leave. Irritated for thinking such foolish thoughts, Ruth scolded herself for even imagining that Ben might want to be more than just their friend, and she busied herself with tidying the house.

Matt was in a fine mood as he entered the inn, and he directed Polly to send up a hot bath and a bottle of wine to his room. So great was his excitement over his newly discovered love that he bypassed his own chambers and sought out Noah in his. Things had not been comfortable between them since they'd argued after the ball, and he wanted to tell him now all that had happened in hopes that they could come to an understanding.

"Yes, what is it?" Noah's voice rang out sharply in answer to his knock.

"It's Matt, Noah."

"Come on in," he called out, and Matt entered the room to find his brother and Lyle involved in a game of cards.

"Would you like to join us, Matthew?" Lyle invited, his eyes alive with good humor.

"Yes, how about it, Matt? It would be a relief to let this harbor rat pick your pockets for a while. He's already taken me for well over ten pounds."

"So I'm picking your pockets, am I?" the sea captain challenged with mock outrage.

"I wish it were true," Noah grumbled easily. "I've known for years that I was no match for you at the tables, but I'd hoped that my luck had changed."

"It's not luck, it's talent," Lyle explained pridefully with a wide smile as he counted the money before him. "What'll it be, Matthew?"

"I think I'll pass on the game," Matt wisely declined, and he smiled at their disappointment.

"Then I'll have to find some other pockets to pilfer," the captain jested, and took his leave of the brothers.

After a pause, Noah turned to Matthew. "Was there something you wanted to see me about?" he prompted.

Though he and Matt had worked closely together on

225

board the *Lorelei* the day before, they'd had little to say to each other. Noah had known that it was unusual for him to be so quiet, but he had assumed that Matt was just having trouble accepting that he had laid the law down about their returning to England. Now, since Matt had made the first move in initiating conversation between them again, he felt it was time to work at drawing him out.

"By the way, where've you been? We were looking for you earlier," Noah asked.

"That's all a part of what I wanted to speak with you about," he replied, moving to stand by Noah's window. Parting the drapes and glancing out across the darkened city in the direction of Faith's house, he hesitated in what he was about to say.

"Yes, what is it?" Noah sensed that what Matt had to tell him was of some import and turned his full attention to him.

"I've made my decision, Noah." Firm in his resolve, Matt turned away from the window to face his brother.

"Decision?" He was instantly tense as he recognized more than a little of the legendary Kincade determination reflected in Matt's unyielding expression.

Unconsciously, Matt squared his shoulders as he prepared for what he knew was about to come. "Yes, about returning to England . . . I'm not going, Noah. My future is here, in Boston, and this is where I want to stay."

"What!" Noah exploded. He had thought the matter settled, and now . . . "How can you even conceive of such an idiotic idea?" he demanded in his most imperious tone.

No longer an impressionable youth to be cowed by such a display from his big brother, Matt gave no ground. "I can conceive of such an 'idiotic' idea because the woman I love is here."

"The woman you love?" Noah was incredulous.

"Yes. I love Faith Hammond and I intend to marry her; if she'll have me, that is."

"You what?"

226

"You heard me, Noah. I don't think it's necessary to repeat myself. As to where I've been today, I've been at the Hammond home dining with Faith and her mother, Ruth."

"How can you even think of marrying Faith Hammond? She's the chit you rescued off the streets. . . ."

"I resent your implication." Matt stiffened.

"Have you proposed to her yet?" he challenged quickly.

"No, not yet, but—"

"No 'buts' about it. You can just forget any plans you had for marriage, young man. You won't be marrying any wench from the colonies. I'll see to that!" He was almost bellowing as he came to his feet, nearly upsetting the card table he was sitting at.

"Like hell you will!" Matt countered, not about to allow Noah to bully him.

"What did you say?" Noah's eyes narrowed in anger and his fury was barely leashed as he regarded him.

With cold precision, he answered, "I am going to marry Faith Hammond, and there is nothing you or anyone else can do to stop me. I had hoped you would understand, but . . ."

Noah felt the breach between them widening, and he suddenly feared losing his brother altogether. Matt was the only person he had left in the world. They were family. He'd had their future planned. . . . They were going to work together to reclaim the family fortunes . . . and now . . .

"Matt, what about our plans? What about Kincade Hall? Don't you want to go back home and set things to rights?" He changed his tactics, knowing that to argue further would only serve to make him more stubborn and resentful.

"I know that it's important to you, Noah, and I respect your desire to do it, but I've found that there are other things more essential to my happiness than money or possessions."

"You won't be able to live long without them, little boy," he snapped, but Matt was unfazed.

"I've told you before how I felt about the colonies. . . ."

Everything is so fresh and new here. We still own two ships. We could make a decent living from the *Lorelei* and the *Pride*. Let's rebuild our heritage, but let's do it here in the Americas. The opportunities for growth and development are endless."

Noah scowled, not wanting to listen to anything he was saying. "We will rebuild our heritage where it belongs! At Kincade Hall."

"If you choose to do so, that's your decision and not mine. I've made my choice—it's Boston," he answered grimly as he strode to the door.

"You know I control the purse strings until you're twenty-one." It was Noah's last hope for controlling his unruly, defiant sibling, and one he had not wanted to use.

Drawing himself up to his full height, Matt replied with dignity, "Blackmail will not work. If the money means so much to you, then keep it. I want no part of it."

"The wench means that much to you?"

"Faith is her name, and yes, she does mean that much to me. Now, if you will excuse me? I believe I'll retire for the night." Abruptly he quit the room, his happy mood dampened by his brother's response.

Alone, Noah stood in silent confusion, trying to understand the changes in Matthew and trying to make some sense out of all that had happened. He had thought that he'd had their future planned out. They were going to work together to rebuild all that had been lost, to reclaim their lands and reestablish their name as one to be respected among the peerage. Now it seemed that Matt wanted no part of it. He had even refused his rightful share of what money they did have, if it meant giving up his own plan to remain in the colonies and marry the young woman he loved.

Love. The word hammered through Noah and brought a cynical twist to his lips. It was an emotion that had eluded him through the years, and one he seriously doubted truly existed. There was lust and greed, and that was it. Probably, he thought cynically, since the Hammond girl knew of Matt's title, she thought she was latching on to a rich aristocrat. He gave a sharp, sarcastic laugh that echoed painfully in the silent room. A year ago that would have been true, but no longer.

Frustrated, Noah moved to the bed to lie down. Folding his arms beneath his head, he stared up at the ceiling with unseeing eyes. Unbidden memories of the ugliness of Radcliffe's insult and the resulting duel came screeching through his thoughts, disturbing him deeply. In a rare moment of weariness, he considered how easy it would be to turn his back on the past and never go back. As quickly as it entered his mind, he pushed the thought from him, disturbed that he could even think of such a thing. He had to go back to England. . . . He had to restore the Kincade family's place and honor in society.

Yet even as Noah reaffirmed to himself what he had to do, he couldn't help but wonder as to the purpose of it all if Matthew wasn't going to be there to share it with him. Feeling betrayed and very alone, he lay awake long into the night.

Chapter Fourteen

"I'm so pleased you agreed to come to dinner," Eve cooed as she sat opposite Noah at her dining room table.

"I was delighted with your invitation, Eve," he replied, and at that moment he meant it.

Noah had passed the last few days trying to decide how to deal with Matthew. He had approached his brother several times in an effort to discuss his plans with him further. However, Matt had been adamant about his decision, even though he had not yet proposed to Faith or been accepted. Despite his threat to the contrary, Noah had no intention of forbidding Matt his funds and so, finally, had let the matter drop. It pained him greatly that they had come to this, and yet he knew of no other way to reconcile their differences. Matt was as firmly determined to stay in the colonies as Noah was to return to England.

It was the need for distraction from his concern for Matt that had finally led him to accept Eve's invitation to dinner. He needed someone uncomplicated, someone who would help him forget all the conflict in his life, and he felt certain Eve was the one. He understood her. He knew that she wanted him, and if he found that she could be content with a strictly pleasure-giving relationship, he would be more than willing to oblige.

There had been a time after he'd received Eve's invitation when he had thought briefly of seeking out CC again. The memory of her heated kiss and the excitement of her sweet young body had continued to plague him. Several times he'd been in the midst of business discussions when the thought of her had entered his mind, momentarily diverting his attention from the important matters at hand. Even so, despite the mutual physical attraction they seemed to share, Noah had discarded the idea. CC had made it quite plain every time they'd been together that she hated him, and because he had no reason to believe that any future meetings between them would be any different from those of the past, he had pursued it no further. He was in no mood for a battle of wills with her, for he had had enough of irrational obstinance in dealing with Matt's defiance. He wanted a woman who was willing and who wanted him in return, not a woman he had to force to admit her passion.

"How have your business dealings been going?" Eve asked just to make conversation. She had no real interest in his business affairs. All she cared about was getting Noah into her bed. With any other man, she would have dispensed with the small talk, but Noah's reaction to her advances when he'd accompanied her home after the ball had tempered her aggressiveness. She knew she would have to bide her time, play the hostess and allow him to make the first move.

"Everything's been going quite well," Noah answered easily. "The *Lorelei* will be leaving Boston soon for a run to the islands."

"You aren't planning on sailing with the *Lorelei,* are you?" Eve asked quickly.

"No. I have another ship due in port soon, and I have to be here to handle the business transactions," he informed her casually.

"I'm glad," she told him in a sultry voice as she took a sip of her wine, her eyes meeting his over the rim of the crystal glass.

231

Noah's smile was sensual as he read the open hunger in her gaze. "I'll be staying in Boston until the spring."

"Good. That gives us plenty of time to become better acquainted." Her meaning was clear, yet she did not press.

"Indeed it does," he responded, lifting his glass in a silent toast as his eyes raked over her. She was a beautiful woman. Her curves were alluring, her eyes upon him were heated in invitation, and her mouth, full and pouting, promised untold delights. Noah knew that Eve Woodham would not fight off his advances; if anything, she would welcome them. Eve would make a very sensual mistress.

Eve saw the flame of desire in his gaze, and she began to tremble in excitement. Never before in her life had she wanted a man so badly. Lord Noah Kincade was her dream. She stared at him in the flickering of the candlelight, admiring his devilish good looks. His dark hair was unpowdered, and his refusal to follow the style only convinced her all the more that he was a man of his own convictions. He was not like Goeffrey, who constantly strove to stay abreast of the most current fads. Noah Kincade needed no artifice to prove his manhood. His shoulders beneath his perfectly tailored coat looked broad and strong, and she longed to caress his hard-muscled chest. The crisp whiteness of his shirt and artfully arranged cravat enhanced the darkness of his tanned, lean features. Eve knew a desperate longing to touch him and kiss him and take him deep within her.

Noah smiled at her then, and the slightly mocking smile sent Eve's pulses racing as she imagined that he'd read her thoughts.

"Shall we go into the parlor?" she suggested, still not confident enough to be more forward with him and hoping the more comfortable setting of the sitting room would encourage him to be more bold.

"As you wish." Noah maintained his aloofness as he followed her lead into the fashionably furnished parlor.

"Please, sit down. Would you care for a brandy?" Eve gestured toward the comfortable-looking sofa as she moved to a small liquor cabinet. At his nod, she poured him a generous amount in a snifter.

"Thank you." He accepted the glass as she sat down beside him.

"My pleasure," she purred, leaning comfortably back as she savored her own drink.

Noah's eyes were dark upon Eve as he raised the snifter to his lips to drink of the potent liquor, but as he tasted of the brandy he was reminded of the last time he'd partaken of it . . . and of the woman he'd met that night . . . CC.

Annoyance grew within him as the auburn-haired beauty drifted through his thoughts, and he wondered why he was thinking of CC when he wanted nothing more than to relax and enjoy the evening with Eve. As deceitful as he knew CC to be, he felt certain that she was probably out somewhere with John right now using her body to further their revolutionary cause. The thought of her sharing the secrets of her lovely body with another man enraged him, and Noah silently cursed himself for having agreed to Ryan Graves's terms so quickly. Perhaps if he'd played his cards right, he might have had CC at his beck and call—willingly—until the *Pride* finally arrived. As it was, now that he had come to an understanding with the rebels, there would be no real reason for him to have any contact with CC again. He found the prospect unsettling but didn't have time to dwell on it as Eve interrupted his thoughts.

"Is something wrong?" Eve was asking as she noticed the sudden, unexplained fierceness in his expression.

"No," he denied, not even wanting to consider that memories of CC's lovemaking might have the power to ruin a night of carnal desire in Eve's arms. "Nothing is wrong. Absolutely nothing."

Taking her glass, he placed it along with his on a nearby table and then wasted no time in pulling her into his arms.

Eve was elated. He wanted her! Surrendering to his demanding kiss, she met him in that passionate exchange, forbidding him nothing as his lips parted hers and his tongue delved within her mouth to tangle erotically with her own.

Sensually she pressed herself against him, and her hands were never still as they took the opportunity to explore the width and strength of his shoulders. The solid, taut feel of his hard, masculine body beneath her hands thrilled her, and she could hardly control her need to be free of her clothing and naked in his arms.

Noah had thought he would be able to lose himself in Eve's embrace, that a night of wild, undemanding passion was what he needed, but he realized now as he felt Eve's hands boldly exploring him that she was not what he wanted . . . not what he needed.

The realization that he really did not want to make love to Eve came as quite a shock to him. A short time ago in England any woman would have done as long as she was comely and clean, but now all that had changed, and he was confused. Even the sweet Polly at the inn, who was as eager for his favors as the aggressive Eve, had not appealed to him since the night of the ball. He wondered what had happened in that brief, yet enthralling interlude with CC in the summerhouse that could have affected him so deeply.

As Eve melted against him, her body alive and throbbing with barely leashed passion, she was totally unaware that another woman—a woman she thought little of—held Noah's thoughts. Hungrily she kissed him, moaning his name in a desire-drugged voice.

"Noah . . . I want you. . . ."

The sound of her voice jerked him completely back to reality, and he took her by her upper arms and tightened his grip to hold her away from him. Eve was stunned by his halting of their embrace, and she stared at him in bewilderment for a moment before speaking.

"Noah?" Her voice was throaty and suggestive. "Don't

you want me?"

The answer was obvious to Noah, but he knew he could hardly tell her the truth—that he didn't want her . . . that there seemed to be only one woman who could satisfy him right now, and that woman was CC Demorest.

"You're a beautiful woman, Eve, and I find you very desirable. . . ."

"Yes . . ." She was hopeful.

"But I am not in a position to make any commitments at this time, and I feel you deserve more than I can give you right now." The lie was a smooth one, and he felt certain that by his telling it, Eve would be left feeling good about herself.

"Noah . . ." Her heart swelled with even more love for him. He respected her! It was more than she'd ever hoped for, and she firmly believed that there was a very real chance for a marriage between them now. "You are such a wonderful man. . . ."

She leaned forward to kiss him tenderly. It was a kiss that Noah accepted without active participation.

"But I understand . . ."

"You do?"

"Yes, and it doesn't matter. The way I feel about you is so special. . . . I want you very much, Noah." Her meaning was clear.

"I don't want to use you, Eve," he said firmly as he got to his feet. "It would be best if I left now."

Eve reluctantly admitted that the night was lost. "All right, but Noah . . . ?" When he glanced down at her, she continued, "I'll be here, should you change your mind."

Noah bent to her then and kissed her one last time before letting himself out of the room.

The immense crowd assembled at Faneuil Hall was a noisy, vocal one, and Matthew stood at Ben's side listening with avid interest to all that was being discussed. When they had first arrived some time before, he'd been surprised by the size of the gathering. Though he had known from all he had heard that the revolutionary theory was growing in popularity, he'd had no idea that there were this many of them willing to stand up and be counted in their discontent.

Matt found the meeting fascinating. Men of all ages and walks of life were there expressing their opinions of what should be done now that the *Dartmouth,* one of the English ships carrying tea for the British East Indian Company, had docked at Griffin's Wharf. Everyone was in an uproar at the thought of the hated tea being unloaded, and a plan of action had to be formulated. The discussion was heated as opposing factions argued over the best way to deal with the situation.

It was during a particularly long-winded speech when Matt took the opportunity to glance around him that he caught sight of John Robinson standing with a younger man a short distance away. He was surprised by his presence, and he tried to imagine why Robinson would be interested in any of this. Curious, he told Ben that he would be right back and then edged his way through the boisterous throng in his direction.

"John!" he called out as he drew near.

"Kincade . . ." There was open disbelief in his tone.

CC, who had donned her boyish disguise in order to attend the meeting, felt her heart sink at John's greeting, and she paled as she tried to decide what to do.

"Just turn slightly away and don't say anything," John murmured under his breath.

"Right." CC had never in her wildest dreams expected to run into anyone with connections to her father at the meeting, and she was nervous. She had told her father that she was going to Marianna Lord's home for the evening, and if word got back to him somehow of her attendance here tonight . . .

"Good evening, John," Matt greeted as he came to stand

with them.

"What are you doing here?" John asked as he tried to position himself to block Matt's view of CC.

"I should be asking you the same thing. I thought you were an ardent loyalist." His comment drew unwelcome stares from a few of those nearby. "Who's your friend?"

John and CC were caught, and the moment was a tense one. There was no way to avoid the revelation without creating havoc, and the one thing they didn't want was to draw undue attention to themselves.

Bravely, CC made the decision herself. She turned quickly to face Matthew, watching in tense expectation as his expression turned from cordial to stunned disbelief.

"CC?" Matt could not believe his eyes. The young man was no man at all, but beautiful CC Demorest in disguise.

"Yes, Matthew, it's me."

"But, CC . . ." His surprise did not abate as he stared down at her. She was a gorgeous woman, the daughter of a wealthy British agent, and yet she was wearing nondescript, baggy boy's garments and attending a meeting of the dissident colonists.

Before Matt could say any more, CC motioned for him to follow her through the crowd to a more private spot near the back of the hall.

John was worried, and he stayed protectively by CC's side. He found Matthew Kincade's presence completely unsettling. As far as John knew, Matthew had taken no active part in his brother's negotiations with their group. John couldn't help but wonder what, if anything, Matthew knew about the situation. If he'd been told all that had happened, then they were in no danger, but what if he hadn't been told all the details and had merely come to the meeting for sport? Mentally, John prepared himself for the worst.

"CC, I don't understand. . . . What are you doing here, dressed like that?"

As John realized his worst fears were coming true, he

tensed, ready to do whatever was necessary to protect CC from disclosure. Although she was frightened, CC knew it was too outrageous a situation for her to try to lie about. She liked Matthew; she had from their first meeting, and she felt reasonably sure that she could trust him. She decided to tell Matt the truth and hope for the best. Certainly, since Noah was in the middle of negotiating an arms sale to the rebels, Matt couldn't very well threaten her with any kind of exposé.

"I came because I wanted to know what was going on," she answered simply, "and I dressed like this so I wouldn't be recognized."

Her blatant honesty surprised him. "But isn't it dangerous for you? You're the daughter of an important British agent. . . . Your father's a loyalist. . . ."

She gave a little shrug, "Much to my father's distress, we have long held different political views."

"Does he know about this?" He was incredulous.

"No, and Matthew . . ."—her gaze met his, open yet pleading for understanding—"I hope it stays that way."

"Your secret is safe with me," he promised. He had thought CC quite a lady when he'd met her at the ball, and he was now even more impressed. Not only was she lovely, but she was educated and an independent thinker, too.

"But what about you, Matt? I don't understand why you're here."

"Yes," John challenged, not at all sure of CC's decision to be honest with this man. "Why would a titled Englishman like yourself be interested in the complaints of the colonists?"

"I've found myself growing more and more intrigued with life here in Boston, and I wanted to learn more about the problems that are causing all the trouble."

"I'm surprised," CC put in, "although I don't suppose I should be."

"I don't understand." Matt gave her a puzzled look. "Why

238

do you find my interest so remarkable?"

"For a moment I was thinking that you were more like your brother," she remarked scathingly. "I have to remember that the two of you are nothing alike."

"I'm not sure if that's a compliment or not. . . ." Matt frowned.

"Oh, it is," CC told him hastily, leaving Matt to wonder what Noah had done to leave her with such a bad opinion of him. "You're much more approachable than he is and, I believe, far less opinionated. I mean, at least you're willing to take the time to listen, whereas Noah couldn't care less. I'm sure he thinks any complaints we colonists might have are not in the realm of his vital interests and therefore not of importance."

John stiffened imperceptibly at her use of the nobleman's first name. His gaze narrowed as he wondered just when she'd started referring to him so intimately.

"Indeed you're right. Many of my countrymen feel that way," Matt agreed. "I'm sure they would find my interest in such matters offensive, but I assure you that I am most serious in my intent. Since first arriving here I have discovered that the authorities are very selective about how and for whom they wield their power."

"You have?" CC was amazed at his answer.

"Yes." There was a blaze of emotion reflected in his eyes as he answered. "It was a lesson well learned, and I intend to help rectify the situation if I can."

"And Noah doesn't share your interest?" CC found that she had to know.

John's curiosity turned to jealousy as she used his first name again, and he tried to imagine what reason she might have for being interested in Lord Kincade's plans.

"No." Matt's answer was abrupt, reflecting the tension between them. "Noah has no real interest in any of this."

"I know," she replied a little too bitterly.

The sound of her tone drew a curious look from Matt and

he wondered how she could possibly know of Noah's affiliation. Then he remembered Noah's manipulations to be alone with CC in the garden the night of the ball and speculated that maybe there had been more to the moment, as he'd originally suspected. After all, her flight into the music room that night had coordinated with Noah's departure with Eve. . . .

"I didn't know that you and Noah had become so well acquainted," he ventured easily.

CC realized her mistake and hastened to try to cover it. "Oh, we're not."

But Matt was far too perceptive for her and he knew she was trying to hide something. Something had happened between them, for he knew his brother, and he knew that Noah did not discuss any of his personal affairs with anyone.

He glanced up then and saw Ben looking around in the crowd for him, his expression worried. "If you'll excuse me . . . I came with someone and I'd better get back."

"Of course."

Matt met her gaze squarely and told her, "I always keep my promises, CC." With that, he moved off through the crowd.

CC started to follow Matthew, but John grabbed her by the arm and halted her progress.

"John?" She turned to look at him quizzically.

"I want to talk with you. . . ." he said through gritted teeth.

"What? Why, of course . . ."

She went along unresisting as he pulled her back into an even more secluded corner.

"What is it? Are you worried about Matthew?"

"No, I'm not worried about him," he dismissed quickly, having believed Matthew Kincade to be totally honest. "He's the least of my worries. . . ."

"Then what?"

"I want to know what's going on with you and Kincade."

"Matthew and me?" She was confused. "There's nothing between—"

"I know that, CC. Don't play stupid. I don't mean Matthew, I mean the older one . . . Noah."

"Nothing," she denied as firmly as she could.

"I don't believe that, CC. I want to know how you came to be calling Lord Kincade by his *first* name!"

It was only then that she realized her mistake, and she hurried to try to cover her slip.

"He asked me to call him by his first name. . . ." she managed.

"When, CC?" he demanded, his hold on her tightening. John had heard rumors that CC had been out in the garden with Lord Kincade the night of the ball, but she had been so attentive to him that night that he had dismissed them as unimportant. Now, though, they had taken on a whole new meaning for him, and he was consumed with jealousy. "When you were in the garden alone together?"

CC felt herself flush, and she jerked free of his bruising grip. "It's none of your business, John! You have no hold on me!"

"Oh yes I do!" He tried to grab her again, but she eluded him and raced away outside into the night.

Her running out drew only a minimum of attention, but John knew all would be watching if he pursued her. Frustrated, angry, and seething with jealousy, he tried to bring his emotions under control as he turned his attention back to the speakers.

Noah's mood was black as he sat alone in the plush interior of his hired coach. Nothing was turning out as he'd planned. Nothing.

The shambles that was his life seemed to be growing even more complicated, if that was possible. The differences between Matt and himself were pronounced, and it troubled him that they had little common ground anymore since their last fight.

Noah knew that he had been hard on Matt at the time, but he'd truly felt that he was making a mistake in deciding to marry Faith and stay on in Boston, and he'd wanted to convince him of the error of his ways. Noah sighed heavily as he admitted to himself that all he'd managed to do was to alienate Matt even more. Now, whenever their paths crossed, they spoke briefly, but not of anything of importance. The encounters always left him feeling oddly bereft.

Noah had hoped a return to his old devil-may-care ways would cheer him, and for that reason he had accepted Eve's invitation to dinner. He scowled sullenly into the darkness as he thought of the past few hours. The evening had been a complete fiasco. He wondered again why he hadn't been able to banish the emerald-eyed vixen, CC, from his thoughts when he had been holding the lush, willing Eve in his arms. He could have taken Eve. She would have reveled in it.

What the hell was the matter with him that he didn't want a voluptuous, wanton, willing woman? A woman was a woman. . . . Weren't they all alike? The answer that forced its way into his consciousness left him completely stunned, and he immediately denied it as ridiculous. There was no way that CC Demorest meant anything to him. He knew what kind of woman she was. She was a deceitful, cunning witch, and he wanted no part of her.

As the image of CC making love with John Robinson flashed through his thoughts and tormented him, Noah cursed out loud at the vicious flare of jealousy that ignited within him, but he still refused to admit that he cared anything for her. The reason she was affecting him so, he decided with as much logic as he could muster, was because she'd been a virgin when he'd taken her. That was the only reason. There was nothing more to it than that.

The carriage was moving along at a goodly clip when

suddenly it lurched to an abrupt, unexpected halt that threw Noah roughly against the wall.

"What the . . ." Swearing loudly, he thrust open the coach door and yelled out to his driver, "What's happened?"

"A young boy, sir . . . run right out in front of me!" the driver told him as he jumped to the ground from his perch.

"Where? Is he injured?"

"I don't know yet. He's layin' there kind of still. . . ."

Concerned, Noah climbed out and hurried with the driver to see to the youth. The darkness hid the boy's identity until Noah got close enough to recognize her. He stood in shock for a moment, staring down at CC's inert form.

"CC . . . dear God . . ." He felt as if someone had torn his heart from his chest.

"You know 'im, sir?" The driver gave him a curious look as he wondered how such a fine gentleman could be acquainted with such an urchin.

"Yes, I know him," Noah growled, kneeling beside her and touching his fingers to the delicate pulse point in her throat. The steady rhythm of her heartbeat sent blessed relief through him, and he was grateful when she opened her eyes and looked up at him.

"Noah . . ." Her voice was soft and confused.

"Yes," he replied gruffly as he quickly disguised the feelings of joy that possessed him.

CC saw a flicker of some unknown emotion in his gaze but had little strength then to question it. "Noah . . ." It was a helpless sigh that wreaked havoc on his emotions, and with a muttered curse, he swept her up into his arms and strode back toward the carriage.

"Sir?" the driver asked, not knowing what to do as the gentleman placed the young boy in the carriage and then climbed in after him.

"Just drive for now. I'll give you directions in a moment. . . ." Noah instructed as he pulled the door shut.

The coachman stared at the closed door for a moment

before returning to his seat and once again taking up the reins.

CC sat quietly in the comfort of the coach, her heart, her mind, her soul filled with Noah's overpowering presence. When she'd opened her eyes after the accident and had seen Noah's handsome face hovering above her in the darkness, it had seemed for just a moment that she had been dreaming . . . that there had been no one else in the world but the two of them. The feeling had been rapturous.

Ever since their encounter in the parlor the other day, he'd been constantly in her thoughts. CC didn't understand why his touch and kiss could affect her so, but she knew that there was something about Noah Kincade that left her weak-willed and hungry for his touch. It worried her even as it fascinated her. She knew him. She knew what he was about and what he valued. He was not a man she could love, and yet she found herself irresistibly drawn to him.

CC sighed as the reality of the situation intruded on her. Running away from John, as she had, had been stupid. She shivered as she imagined the repercussions of anyone discovering her true identity. She was glad that she'd taken the time to anchor her tricorn so firmly, for that extra care had prevented it from being dislodged during the accident and had saved her from possible recognition.

Wearily she reached up to remove the pins that held the hat so securely. As she removed the tricorn and unpinned her hair, Noah turned to her. The relief he was feeling over the fact that she had suffered no lasting harm in the accident was quickly forgotten as his eyes met hers, and he read there what he thought to be her usual dislike of him. The thought infuriated him. He had just saved her from who-knows-what, and she had the gall to glare at him as if he were some kind of monster.

CC was trying to decipher the strained look on Noah's face when suddenly he erupted in fury, his eyes narrowing to the forbidding silver expression she knew so well.

"Just what the hell do you think you were doing running around the streets like that?" Noah snapped harshly, staring at her garb.

"It's none of your business what I was doing!" she countered, the last sweet fragments of her imaginings disappearing as wisps of fog before a cold, devastating winter wind.

"When you ran out in front of my coach, you made it my business!" he argued, not sure whether he wanted to shake her until she admitted the foolishness of her act or kiss her until she understood how frightened he'd been.

"Then I beg your pardon, Lord Kincade. Believe me, I had no wish to intrude on your evening, and I hope my untimely arrival didn't ruin any of your plans. . . ." she bit out ungratefully as she shook her head and allowed her hair to tumble free.

"I'm afraid you did ruin my plans . . . all of them. . . ." he muttered softly, more to himself than to her as he stared at her in the dimness of the coach light. Even Noah's anger, which was substantial, could not dampen the thrill of excitement he felt at having her so near, so unexpectedly.

Her upset was such that, even though his answer surprised her, it did not stop her from replying brashly, "Again, my apologies, although I fail to see how a moment's delay in your busy schedule could ruin anything. Just stop the carriage and let me out. You can then be on your merry way."

"Why? So you can try to kill yourself again?"

Wondering why he should even care, she glanced at him, puzzled, and time hung suspended as their gazes met and locked. They studied each other warily in the softness of the night shadows, his eyes, smoke-gray now, challenging and questioning hers as each dared to probe the other's thoughts and emotions. Slowly, as if mesmerized by the gentle rocking and sweet privacy of the carriage, Noah leaned closer and, without touching her in any other way, let his lips meet hers.

The moment was explosively enthralling as the gentlest of caresses sent shock waves of awareness through both of them. Noah moved back slightly to stare down at her in wonder, and he lifted one hand to tenderly touch her cheek.

"You're very beautiful, CC . . . very beautiful. . . ." His voice was low and filled with husky male desire.

CC felt as if she were drifting. The rough velvet sound of his deep voice and the tingling caress of his hand left her breathless and weak. All thoughts of hatred and distrust were banished. Languidly, as if she'd known for all her life that this moment would happen, she went into his embrace, whispering only "Noah . . ."

Noah gloried in her seeming willingness, and he wrapped his arms about her in a fiercely possessive hold as his mouth moved to claim hers, tasting and testing the joy to be found in that passionate exchange. Feverishly they broke apart for an instant and then melded again, the impassioned kiss a mere imitation of the mating their bodies so longed for.

CC felt Noah's hands upon the buttons of her shirt, and she shivered in expectation. She remembered well the ecstasy of his hands upon her bare flesh, and a low moan of excitement escaped her.

Until that moment Noah had been holding a part of himself back, refusing with that one last shred of resistance to believe that she was coming to him without a fight, but the sound of her eager need cast the last of his doubts aside. Boldly he parted the soft material and slipped a hand within to push aside her bindings and cup the round fullness of one breast. Tantalizingly, he teased the nipple to hardness as his lips left hers to explore the sensitive cords of her throat.

CC clung to Noah desperately as his hands and lips worked their magic upon her silken flesh, and when he guided her down to lie upon the comfort of the leather seat, she did not protest. His caresses were intoxicating, and she was drugged with desire. There was nothing she wanted more than to be one with him, and she looped her arms about his neck and pulled him down to her.

"Please, Noah . . ."

"Ah, CC . . ." he groaned as his lips moved lower to seek out the taut crests of her breasts.

CC whimpered her need as Noah suckled there, the erotic drawing arousing her to a fever pitch. For the first time in her life, CC knew a desire to touch as well as to be touched. She reached out to Noah in her excitement, caressing his hard-muscled form with eager hands. His response to her aggressiveness was immediate and exhilarating and she found herself enjoying the feeling of power it gave her to know that she was able to please him.

With trembling fingers CC unbuttoned his shirt and then embraced him fully, exploring his chest and stomach with a restless, heated touch, coming near but never quite touching that most intimate part of him. Her teasing caresses were driving Noah to distraction. Desperate to feel the softness of her hand upon him, he finally grasped her wrist and forced her to touch the hardness of his need for her.

CC gasped at his slightly rough maneuver, but when she saw reflected on his face the sheer rapture her caress gave him, she no longer needed to be forced. She wanted to please him. She wanted him to experience the same ecstasy that she felt whenever he touched her. More brazenly now, she traced patterns of fire upon his body, and Noah groaned in passionate need.

"CC . . . ah, love . . . I need you so. . . ."

"Yes, Noah . . . please, now . . ." she pleaded as he shifted his body away from hers to give him room to unfasten the breeches she wore.

"I've never made love to anyone wearing breeches before. . . ." he murmured with just a touch of humor as he slipped the offensive garment down her sleek legs, baring her womanhood to his questing caress.

"I wish you'd never made love to anyone before me. . . ." she told him almost fiercely as she felt jealousy surge within

247

her at the thought of him with another woman.

He did not miss the possessiveness of her tone as he gathered her near, and he told her huskily, "More importantly, CC, there will be no one after you. . . ."

The memory of Eve threatened the moment as she responded vaguely, "I wish I could believe that. . . ."

Noah did not answer, kissing her instead as proof of his desire, and CC put it from her as she surrendered to his masterful expertise. There was no more time for talk then as he moved between her thighs, and after freeing himself from his own breeches, he fitted himself to her in love's most intimate caress. CC gasped as she felt the magnificence of him slide deep within her, and Noah shuddered in excitement as he felt the wet, satiny heat of her close around him and hold him tightly. Wanting her aroused and ready, he began to fondle her again, pressing kisses to her silken flesh as he began his rhythm. When she started to move with him, matching his thrusts, he reached down to cup her hips and press her more closely to him.

That single demanding action sent waves of throbbing pleasure pulsing through her, and she cried out his name in her ecstasy. Noah felt her peak as he continued his driving possession, branding her as his own for all time. As his own pinnacle of love neared, he clasped her to him, rocking powerfully against her in the age-old dance of delight that soon had him spiraling mindlessly out of control in the rapture of his release.

They came back to reality, not softly as lovers should, but quickly and harshly when the driver shouted down.

"Sir, I've been driving for ages now. . . . Do you know where you want to go yet?" He thought the whole situation odd and wondered what was going on in his carriage.

His loud, demanding call shattered what beauty there was of the moment and left them chilled and suddenly cautious of each other. A confusing tumble of emotions assailed them both. Neither found the strength to speak of their thoughts

**A FREE ZEBRA
HISTORICAL
ROMANCE
WORTH**

$3.95

BUSINESS REPLY MAIL
FIRST CLASS   PERMIT NO. 276   CLIFTON, NJ

POSTAGE WILL BE PAID BY ADDRESSEE

ZEBRA HOME SUBSCRIPTION SERVICE
P.O. Box 5214
120 Brighton Road
Clifton, New Jersey 07015

or to look the other in the eye as they quickly moved apart. Noah swiftly rearranged his own clothing and shifted away to the opposite side of the coach while CC scrambled to pull on her breeches.

"Head for the Common," Noah ordered brusquely, buying them time.

"Yes, sir," came the reply as the carriage turned a corner, changing directions.

Noah watched CC surreptitiously as she worked at fastening the buttons of her shirt. When she seemed to be making little progress, he leaned forward and brushed her hands aside to do it himself. CC submitted to his assistance only because she was too nervous to do it herself.

As he performed the task, his knuckles pressed ever so lightly against the still sensitive tips of her breasts, and her body responded wildly to that simple stimulation. Nervously, wishing he would finish so she would be free of her torment, she held herself stiffly and tried to control her breathing so he would not know, but Noah sensed the change in her. He looked up at her questioningly, girding himself as he expected to face her fury.

Her expression was unguarded in that moment, and what he saw reflected on her flushed features sent a surge of disquieting emotion through him. Her emerald eyes were wide and soft as she tried to deal with her passion, and as she met his gaze, her tongue darted out to wet her lips . . . inviting without inviting.

Ensnared by the haunting beauty of her gaze, Noah paused in his endeavor and let his regard drop from her face to the still-exposed loveliness of her breasts. The shirt was gaping open, revealing their swelling, hard-tipped perfection, and he knew a commanding desire to press heated, arousing kisses upon that, her most erotic, flesh. At just the thought of claiming her once more his loins came alive, throbbing with maddening intensity. It was only the lurching of the carriage as it rounded yet another corner that tore his

249

thoughts away from his runaway desires and back to reality.

The reality was, he realized with a jolt, that this attraction between them had to be fought. His need for her was becoming almost an obsession, and he had to conquer it. He could not allow any woman to become that important to him. She was a female just like all the others; there was nothing different about CC.

The hidden thought taunted him that there was something special about CC, but he ignored it. He had come to Boston with only one goal, and he had almost accomplished that goal. He had no intention of allowing CC, a mere colonial chit, to interfere with his plans. He was going to reestablish the Kincade name in England. Nothing else mattered—not CC, not the damned revolutionary cause, not anything. Firmly he hardened himself against her, focusing on his goals.

As CC stared up at Noah, watching his expression turn aloof and slightly arrogant, her emotions were in a turmoil. She was aching with the need to be touched by him again, to feel the thrill of his lips upon her bosom and the strength of him buried deep within her, but her thoughts were at odds with her body, demanding that she control herself and deny her passion.

Logic was coldly dictating to her that she was a fool to have given herself to him. Noah was amoral, used people to his own benefit, and loved money above all else. If those reasons weren't enough to discourage her interest, he had every intention of leaving Boston and returning to England just as soon as he could.

Still, and this came as a devastating revelation, CC could not deny that she wanted him. She knew every bad thing about him, and yet, the moment he touched her, her body betrayed her and she could only surrender.

No one else had ever had the power to excite her as he did, and distraughtly, she wondered for a moment if she could possibly be in love with him. The thought frightened her and drained her desire as she fought to keep from even considering it. She could not, would not love Noah Kincade! Defiantly, in victory over her wayward emotions, she shuttered her own expression.

"I'll have the driver drop you near the Common," he said coolly, his gaze resting impersonally upon her now.

CC didn't know what she'd expected him to say and she was glad it was something unrelated to what had passed between them. "Yes. That'll be good."

"I think it's important that we make certain to avoid each other from now on." Noah spoke first with cool purpose.

"I didn't exactly plan this 'rendezvous,' you know!" Though CC logically agreed with his statement, her heart shattered in agony. She busied herself with fastening the rest of her buttons and cramming her hair back up under her hat.

He gave an exasperated sigh as he replied with disdain, "Please, there's no reason for us to belabor the point."

"There's nothing to belabor, Kincade." She girded herself against the need she had to go back into his arms and stay there as long as he would have her. "What happens between us defies sensibleness. I don't even like you. . . ." Her expression reflected the loathing she felt for both her own weakness and for him.

"What a relief," he remarked drolly, covering the odd hurt he felt at her declaration.

CC glared at him. "You just stay away from me, and I'll make every effort to avoid you."

"I shall do my best," he nodded.

The driver called down as he pulled the coach to a stop. "We're at the Common. Now what?"

Without another word CC opened the door and jumped out into the concealing Boston night, the sting of tears pressing her to hurry away before Noah could witness her upset. Noah found himself peering out the door after her, feeling suddenly as if he'd lost something very precious as he listened to the fading sound of her footfalls.

Chapter Fifteen

Geoffrey leaned his elbows on his desk as he stared at his servant in interest. "What you're telling me is that Kincade may have some connection with the dissidents, but that we can't prove it?"

"We can't prove it, *yet,* m'lord," Bartley answered with reassurance and respect.

"So since your first report to me the day after the Demorest ball about his meeting at the Green Dragon with this Ryan Graves and Sam Adams, he's done nothing? He's had no contact with anyone?" Geoffrey demanded sarcastically.

"Well, sir . . ." he hedged.

"What is it, man? Tell me everything!" Geoffrey slammed a hand on the desktop.

"He did have an assignation. . . ."

Geoffrey paled and then flushed with fury as he realized who the woman was. "With whom?"

"The Widow Woodham, sir," he answered tentatively.

"When?" he snarled.

"Last evening. The man I hired to follow him said that he went there early in the evening and remained for several hours."

"I see." His tone was icy as his resolve to destroy Noah

became more implacable. "What about his brother? Or the captain of his ship? Anything there?"

"The brother's activities show some promise. . . ."

"Oh?"

"Yes, m'lord. Matthew Kincade has been paying frequent visits to the home of the Widow Ruth Hammond and her young daughter, Faith. Hammond's husband, as you will recall, was one of the colonists killed during that shooting some years ago," Bartley offered helpfully.

"Hammond . . ." Geoffrey frowned. "No, I don't remember. I don't concern myself with that trivia."

"Anyway," the servant continued, "Hammond had been one of the troublemakers. We don't know for certain if his widow or his daughter is still involved with the rebels, but we have found out that they do keep company with Ben Hardwick."

"And just who is this Ben Hardwick?"

"Well, according to my sources, he's one of the most ardent supporters of Adams and Hancock, m'lord." He provided the information with a smile.

"Ah . . . the connection deepens. . . . Noah Kincade had a meeting with Sam Adams and Ryan Graves, and his brother is involved with one of Adams's staunchest supporters . . . to what purpose, I wonder." His eyes narrowed as he considered all the possibilities.

"I have heard that a romance is developing between the Hammond girl and the younger Kincade."

"Interesting, but hardly newsworthy," he scoffed. "He may be dallying with the girl, but I doubt there will be any more to it than that."

"I had thought the connection an odd one, too." He agreed with his master's assessment. "Also, there is one other piece of information."

"Yes?"

"Matthew Kincade attended the meeting about the tea shipments that was held at Faneuil Hall with Ben Hardwick."

Geoffrey nodded and then directed, "We have to discover just what they're up to. Do you have anyone involved with Adams and his followers who might be able to give us a clue as to the Kincades' purpose?"

"Not yet, but I'm working on it."

"Good. Pay whatever price is necessary, but find out. I need the information as quickly as possible."

"Yes, m'lord."

"You may go," he dismissed. As the servant reached the door, he ordered, "Have my carriage brought around. I suddenly feel the need to visit the Widow Woodham."

"Right away, sir."

When Bartley had gone to do his bidding, Geoffrey sat back in his chair, deep in thought. He was furious that things were taking so long, but he knew that some things were worth waiting for. Somewhere in Noah Kincade's activities there had to be something he could use against him. When he found it, he was going to destroy him completely. Eve Woodham was his. He knew it, and as soon as the carriage was brought around and he made the trip to her home, she was going to know it.

Matt sat with Faith in the parlor of her home. Ruth had just stepped into the other room, and at last he found himself alone with her. He'd been trying to get up his courage to propose to Faith for several days now. Each time he'd thought he was ready, he'd hesitated and the moment had been lost. Now he decided it was time. He loved her with a love that grew more potent every day, and he didn't want to waste another moment of time being apart. He wanted them to be married as soon as they could.

"Faith . . ." Matt's tone was a bit choked, and she looked at him curiously, noticing his serious expression.

"Yes, Matthew? Is something wrong?" Faith knew a moment of terrible fear. She loved Matt with all her heart, and the joy she experienced when she was with him was unlike anything else she'd ever known in her short life. Matt had become her whole world, and his solemn manner frightened her.

"No, Faith. Nothing's wrong," he answered, his blue eyes darkening to mirror the seriousness of his intent.

"Then what is it? You look so . . . I don't know . . . worried?" she ventured hesitantly.

Matt managed to flash her a grin that at once both thrilled her and relieved her as he reached out to take her hand. "I am worried. . . ."

"But you just said that nothing was wrong. . . ." He was confusing her.

"And I hope I still feel that way after I get through with what I have to say to you."

"I don't understand."

"Let me finish." He lifted her hand to his lips, his eyes sparkling now as they met hers. "Faith, there's something I've wanted to say to you for a long time, and I think it's time I said it."

"Yes? What?" she was totally mystified.

"Faith." His tone was suddenly deep with meaning. "Faith, I love you."

Matt was so pleased and relieved that he'd finally managed to say it that he smiled widely, quite proud of himself. His gaze searched Faith's as he said the words for some sign of her reaction, and what he saw reflected there sent his heart soaring.

"Matthew . . . do you really mean it?" Faith couldn't believe that he'd actually professed to love her. He was Matthew Kincade . . . nobleman . . . and yet he was claiming to love her! The thought filled her with rapture and she realized that maybe, sometimes in life, dreams really did come true.

"More than anything, Faith. I love you, darling. I have from the first moment I saw you, and I want you to do me the honor of being my wife."

The last came as a total shock to Faith, and she looked away from him. For all that she had allowed herself to fantasize about having his love, she had never, ever, even her most wild imaginings, thought that he would propose marriage! She was speechless.

"Faith?" Matt was suddenly very nervous. He had hoped that she would respond without pause, but she'd gone silent on him and he felt a terrible sinking feeling. What if she didn't love him? What if she didn't want to marry him? "Faith, I love you. I want to marry you."

Her turquoise eyes, when they lifted to his, were luminous and filled with tears. Matt wasn't sure if they were tears of misery or tears of joy.

"Faith?" He put his arms around her and drew her close.

"Oh, Matthew . . ." she cried. "Can you really mean it? You love me and you want to marry me?"

"I mean it, love. I've never felt this way before, and I know I'll never feel this way again. I love you, darling. I will forever." He murmured the last against the softness of her hair, and he felt the tension drain from him at her answer.

"I love you, too, Matthew, and there's nothing I'd like more than to be your wife."

Matt held her slightly away from him to look down at her. Never in his life had anyone possessed his devotion more completely. Faith was the woman of his dreams . . . the woman some men would search their entire lives for and never find. Matt had found her, and he never intended to let her go.

They came together in a rush of passion, their mouths meeting and blending, their hearts beating as one. Only the sound of Ruth clearing her throat in the doorway forced them apart.

"Faith . . . Matthew . . ." Her tone was reprimanding, and Matt jumped to his feet, embarrassed at having forgotten in his joy where they were and what they were about.

"Mrs. Hammond, my apologies. "I . . . we . . . well, I have just proposed to Faith and she's accepted, and I suppose, in the moment, we forgot ourselves."

"What?" Ruth was completely dumbstruck. She had hoped from the beginning that there might be a future for these two, but she had not planned on it. If there was anything she'd learned from life, it was to take what happiness you could while you could.

Faith came to her feet, too, and she took Matt's hand. "Yes, Mother, Matthew has proposed and I've accepted."

Ruth looked from one to the other, reading the love and happiness in their faces, and she smiled, moving into the room to kiss her daughter and hug Matt. "That's wonderful."

"I had hoped you would feel that way, Mrs. Hammond," Matt told her as he looked down at his future bride, his eyes alight with the depth of love he felt for her.

"Why wouldn't I?" Ruth was glowing. "I think you're a wonderful man, and I also think you love my daughter very much."

"Indeed I do, ma'am," he replied.

"Have you discussed the wedding yet?"

"No, Mother. Matthew had only just proposed when you came in," Faith answered, and then blushed as she remembered the kiss her mother had witnessed. "Matthew?"

"As soon as possible," he told them enthusiastically.

"Will you be wanting a big wedding?" Ruth asked cautiously. She expected that Matt might be wanting a splendid wedding and reception befitting his status in life, and the thought troubled her. There was no way she could afford more than the simplest of celebrations.

"I think that's something we have to talk about. There are things I have to tell you that need to be discussed," he told

257

them seriously.

Again Faith was puzzled by his tone and she drew him back down on the sofa beside her. "What do you have to tell us, Matt? It sounds important."

"I'm afraid it is, but it's not going to stop us."

"What?" Both women were attentive.

"As you both know, I am here with my brother, Noah."

"Yes, you told us about him. . . ." Faith urged him on.

"Well, Noah and I have had a falling out, and I'm not completely sure what my status is right now."

"I don't understand. What did you have a fight about?"

Matt sighed as his expression grew troubled. "It's a long story that began in England many months ago. You know that my father died recently."

"Yes . . ."

"When he died he left enormous debts that had to be settled against the estate."

"Oh no . . ." Faith was immediately sympathetic. "Did you lose everything?"

He smiled weakly. "Not everything, but almost. We still have two good vessels left and a small inheritance from our mother's estate."

"Your mother is dead also?"

"Yes, she died some years ago. Anyway, Noah was more affected by the losses than I was. It devastated him to see our family's holdings stripped away." He shook his head sadly. "Noah changed."

"How so?"

"We got along marvelously until this happened. The loss of all he held dear seemed to destroy him, and he suddenly became almost obsessed with the need to reclaim our heritage."

"I can understand his feelings," Faith said with empathy.

"I can, too, but there comes a time when maybe it would be better to start anew, start over fresh—throw out the past and look to the future. That's what I want to do. I like the colonies. I like Boston. I can see how a man with drive and ambition can make a comfortable living for himself."

"And Noah?"

"Noah wants to make as much money as he can, as quickly as he can, and then return to England."

"Have you told him how you feel?"

"Yes, and that's when we argued. He doesn't want me to stay behind. He wants me to go back with him, but that's when I told him that his dreams were his, not mine."

"I'm sorry." Faith's eyes were upon him with love and understanding.

Matt tried to shrug, as if it meant nothing to him, but he wasn't convincing. The pain in his eyes was too evident. "I've tried to talk with him about staying here, but he refused to even consider it."

"Matthew, why don't you invite him here to dinner for a small celebration?" Faith offered, looking to her mother for support for the invitation.

"We would love to meet him," Ruth agreed, "and this is the perfect opportunity."

"I would like that, and I think he would, too," Matt responded.

"Then it's settled. Why don't we plan on next Sunday? That way Ben can join us, too."

"It sounds wonderful . . . and the wedding?" Matt turned again to Faith.

"In two weeks?" she suggested eagerly, not wanting to delay their marriage any longer than necessary.

"Two weeks . . ." Matt agreed.

"Lord Radcliffe?" Knowing how her mistress felt about him, Peggy was surprised to see Geoffrey, and her voice reflected her reaction.

"May I come in?" Geoffrey asked in his most arrogant manner as he strode past the diminutive maid and glanced up the staircase in the direction of Eve's chamber. "Is Eve here?"

"Well . . . um . . ."

"Is she at home or isn't she?" he demanded, his gaze frosty upon her.

"If you'll wait in the sitting room, I'll get her for you." Peggy directed him toward the parlor and then raced up the back steps to her mistress's room.

Eve was sitting at her dressing table brushing out her hair when Peggy knocked at the door. She found the intrusion annoying, for she had given orders earlier that she didn't want to be bothered so she could spend the day totally wrapped up in her thoughts of Noah and the future she believed they had together.

"What is it?" Her tone was sharp with irritation.

"It's me, ma'am, Peggy. . . ." Aware that Eve had wanted to be undisturbed, she opened the door only a crack and peeked inside.

"Yes, I gathered that. What do you want?"

"It's Lord Radcliffe, ma'am. He's downstairs, and he wants to see you."

"Geoffrey . . ." Eve remarked more to herself than to Peggy. "All right. Tell him I'll be down shortly. Give him a drink or something."

"Yes, ma'am. I will."

When Peggy had gone, Eve quickly styled her hair back into a sedate bun and then stood up to straighten her skirts. Originally, after setting her sights on Kincade, Eve had sought to end all intimacies with Geoffrey, but she was now thinking better of the idea. Kincade's refusal to bed her had pleased her emotionally but left her decidedly hungry for a man. While she wanted no future with Geoffrey, she certainly wasn't going to pass up the opportunity to enjoy his sensual company, if he was so disposed. A small, cunning smile curved her perfect lips as she thought of how easy it would be to seduce Geoffrey, and she started downstairs with just that goal in mind.

"Geoffrey, darling . . ." Eve swept into the parlor with all her usual aplomb, and she was thrilled to see the spark of desire in his eyes as he came to his feet.

"Eve . . ." Geoffrey's cool tone belied the heat of his gaze as he greeted her.

"I'm so glad you dropped by," she told him with saccharine sweetness as they both sat down on the sofa.

"Really?" he drawled in mocking disbelief. "Somehow I hadn't thought you would be."

"Come now, Geoffrey." Eve tapped his arm in a light, flirtatious manner. "Whatever can you mean?"

Geoffrey knew Eve very well, and he did not appreciate her using her artful, manipulative ways on him. It tested his already sore temper, and he grabbed her hand in a vicelike grip.

"I believe you know what I mean, Eve." His words were a low, threatening growl as his hold on her tightened.

"Geoffrey . . . what do you want?" Eve's eyes widened slightly as his grip became painful. She struggled to pull free, but her efforts were to no avail.

His gaze raked over her lasciviously before he answered in a deceptively casual tone, "I've merely stopped by for a visit." He released her abruptly.

Eve eyed him cautiously as she rubbed her wrist. She had never seen this unpredictable side of Geoffrey before, and she was startled by it. Always in the past he'd been malleable and quite easy to influence, but today . . . today there was something very ominous about him. In a strange way, it excited her even as it frightened her.

"Would you care for another drink?" she offered, seeing his half-filled glass on the table.

"No. I didn't come here to drink, Eve, and you know it. Why do you feel it necessary to play coy with me?"

"I'm hardly playing coy with you, Geoffrey," Eve answered with as much indignation as she could muster.

261

"I wish that were true, my sweet, but I've seen and heard enough for myself lately to know exactly where your interests now *lie*. . . ." He stressed the last word with snide meaning.

"I'm sure I don't know what you mean." She was deliberately evasive.

"Your portrayal of innocence is not amusing, Eve." His gaze was hooded as he regarded her. "You made every effort to avoid me at the Demorests' ball, and then you left with Noah Kincade. The two of you have also shared a dinner assignation here just the other evening. I may be many things, darling, but I am no fool."

"I never thought you were." Eve was finding his manner far too overbearing.

He laughed harshly at her answer. "Come now, my dear, you tried to make a fool of me, and I'm here to let you know that you've failed. If I want you, Eve, I'll take you, and if I decide I don't want you anymore, then I'll be the one to end it. Do you understand me?"

She stared at him in silent wonder. Could this be the same Geoffrey who only several weeks ago had scurried to do whatever she asked? Had her flirtation with Kincade changed him so?

"I take it by your silence that you do understand." He put an arm about her waist and drew her closer.

Eve was mesmerized by his more forceful personality, and she did not try to resist him.

"I think it's important that you know I don't share what is mine with anyone, and you, my precious Eve, are mine!"

His mouth ground down on hers in a brutal assault that left no doubt in her mind as to his emotions. He was furious with her, and he was here to prove to himself and to her that she was still his.

A short time before Eve would have fought his domination, but she found this new, assertive Geoffrey much more appealing. Since she knew Kincade wouldn't be coming to her bed any time soon, she hungrily accepted his kiss, her arms slipping around his neck to entice him even closer.

Geoffrey was caught totally off guard by her response. He had expected her to fight . . . to argue . . . to refuse his advances, but instead she was submitting to him almost eagerly. Having temporarily lost his element of anger and vengeance in the face of her surrender, he softened his kiss to a more coaxing, tantalizing exchange.

"Geoffrey . . . it's been so long. . . ." Eve invited when they broke apart for a moment. "Let's go up to my room, where we won't run the risk of being interrupted."

She took his hand, and together they left the room with one thing and one thing only on both of their minds.

It was a long time later that they lay together, limbs intertwined on the wide softness of her bed. Sex between them had always been inventive and satisfying, but today there had been a new element to their coming together . . . the element of provocation.

Despite his deceptively calm demeanor, once Geoffrey had gotten her into bed, he'd been completely determined to control her. She had taunted him with her interest in Kincade, and Geoffrey was now resolved to prove to her that he was the better man. He knew her body as well as he knew his own, and he'd played upon her senses until she'd been crying out for him to satisfy her needs. Even then he'd refrained from giving her what she had so craved and had teased her with his body until she nearly fainted from the power of her desire. Only when she had completely surrendered to his will did he finally take her to the heights of ecstasy.

The moment of domination had given Geoffrey a supreme sense of power more stimulating than any sexual adventure they had ever shared. He'd held himself in restraint until the last possible second, enjoying the thrill of conquering her body as long as he could before seeking his own release.

Eve lay sated and relaxed beneath Geoffrey. They had

always gone on well together, but what had happened between them just now had been different from anything she'd ever experienced, and she wasn't quite sure if she'd truly enjoyed it or not. Geoffrey had mastered her. There was no other way she could describe it, and even as his caress had aroused, it had also degraded. His demanding, insistent touch had left her with no will of her own. She had been mindless in her need, and the discovery that he could reduce her to that left her unsure of herself. She was the one used to being in control.

Geoffrey braced himself above her on his elbows and smiled down at her in triumph as he began to move within her.

"Geoffrey?" Eve was amazed to find that he was ready for her again.

"Ah, yes, my dear. We have a lot of time to make up for and a lot of things to talk about. . . ."

"We do?" The question was a gasp as he rolled, bringing her above him, his hands commandingly on her hips as he guided her movements.

"Most assuredly," Geoffrey answered, his eyes glittering as he thought of her in this same position with Kincade. "Did you know how dangerous it is for you to be involved with Kincade?"

"I'm not involved with Kincade." She tried to deny her desire for the other man, but he wasn't believing it.

"Don't lie to me, Eve. I've known you far too long. I'm sure he's been in your bed, sharing your favors. . . ." His hands on her tightened painfully and she cried out.

"You're hurting me. . . ."

"Good," he snarled, his mouth twisting into a hate-filled smile. "You deserve far worse. . . . And perhaps I shouldn't tell you what I know, but I am not finished with you yet."

His hands swept up from her hips to squeeze and knead her breasts. When he could tell that she was beginning to enjoy his caresses, he stopped.

"This time, you please me, Eve. . . ." he ordered, and Eve, eager for more, started to move excitedly.

Her hands were everywhere upon him, fondling, caressing, touching, and Geoffrey responded in kind when his desires grew to a fever pitch. Pivoting again, he brought her beneath him and thrust powerfully into her until together they reached the pinnacle of delight. They drifted slowly back to reality, aware of little save the heat of their bodies and the harsh rasping of their breathing as the excitement waned.

Exhausted and weak, Eve lay quietly against Geoffrey, wondering at the strength of her response to his torrid lovemaking. Never before in all the time they'd been together had he been so overwhelmingly sensual, and she smiled in satisfaction.

"Eve." He rose above her to stare down at her, his features cold and remote.

The warmth she had been feeling died as she met his gaze. "Yes?" Her tone was soft and unsure, and it pleased Geoffrey to know that she was disquieted.

"You will not see Kincade anymore," he ordered.

It was a command that angered her. Who did he think he was? True, he might share her bed, but he was not her husband and had no claim on her.

She responded stiffly as she tried to move away from him. "You don't own me, Geoffrey, and I can see whomever I want!"

"I had never thought you to be stupid, Eve," he remarked derogatorily as he watched her climb from the bed to stand glaring at him, her hands on her hips. He studied her with an almost clinical detachment, his eyes visually caressing the pale beauty of her breasts and thighs. Eve was a vitally beautiful woman, and he knew he had to have her for his very own.

"You dare to call me stupid?" she gasped, and he gave a careless lift of his shoulders.

"It would seem so, if you insist on continuing to see Kincade. You see, I have some very private information about him that, once revealed, might ruin him forever." He watched Eve's expression as he spoke. "I'm certain that you wouldn't want to be caught up in all the ugliness once it comes out."

"What kind of information?" she asked skeptically.

Geoffrey chuckled evilly. "Do you think that I would reveal all to you? Surely you give me credit for more intelligence than that! Why, if I told you now, I have no doubt that you would run to your other lover with the news just as soon as I leave you."

That had been Eve's original intention, but now she hesitated. Supposing Geoffrey was right. . . . What if Noah was involved in something terrible? Did she dare risk everything to continue to pursue him, or did she give him up now, while she was still safe? Her dilemma was very real, for she wanted Noah very badly, but she knew she could not let Geoffrey know the truth of her feelings. Her eyes narrowed slightly as she considered all the angles.

"Despite what you may think, Geoffrey, I have never made love to Noah Kincade." Though it was not from a lack of trying on her part, she felt positive that she could use that bit of information now to her advantage. Slowly she moved sinuously back toward the bed, aware that his eyes were upon her.

"Really?" He wasn't quite sure whether to believe her or not.

"Since you're so well informed about my activities, I'm sure your informants must have told you that he never spent the night. They did report that to you, didn't they?" She sat on the edge of the bed and rested a teasing hand upon his chest.

"Yes, but . . ."

"There are no 'but's' to the situation, Geoffrey," she told him huskily. "Kincade has never spent the night with me. No

266

one has since my husband died except you, Geoffrey. You're the only one. . . ." she purred as she traced her hand lower, nearer to his manhood.

Geoffrey found her touch disorienting, and he had to force himself to concentrate on what she was saying. "You want me to believe that you haven't slept with Kincade?"

"It's the truth and I wanted you to know it." Her hand caressed him boldly. Knowing that his power to resist her was weakening as she deliberately sought to arouse him and then seduce him, she smiled seductively. "You're so wonderful, Geoffrey. . . ." She let her gaze drift over his body before returning to meet his passion-darkened eyes. "So strong and virile. I can't tell you how grateful I am that you care enough about me to warn me about Kincade."

"I care about you, all right." His voice was husky as his desires flamed.

Geoffrey's earlier anger and jealousy had slowly dissolved upon her confession of never having bedded Kincade. Now, caught up in the web of her skillful charms, he was once again totally enamored with her. She had struck any doubts he'd had about her from his mind, and he knew now that she would be his, and his alone. Pulling her into his arms, he pressed fervent kisses upon her waiting lips.

"You're mine, Eve, only mine," he growled between kisses.

"Yes, Geoffrey . . ." She managed to make her words sound like a sigh, but in reality she was celebrating her victory.

While she was giving him the outward appearance of being his, and his alone, Eve had already decided that she could not give up her dream of becoming Lady Kincade. She was firmly convinced that Noah was her destiny, and she knew what she had to do to fulfill that future. She would play Geoffrey along and encourage his complete trust and devotion until she could maneuver him into revealing to her the damning evidence he had against Noah. Once she was in possession of that information, she would go to Noah with it and thus win not only his unending appreciation, but also his love.

Until then, though, she knew she would have to be very careful as to how she handled the situation, for she could not risk Geoffrey catching on to her plan. The time to begin convincing him of her desire for him was now, and she arched herself against him in total sensual abandon, aggressively seeking to make him once again her willing sensual slave.

Chapter Sixteen

Noah's expression was wooden as he sat tensely in the hired carriage across from Matthew that following Sunday. He knew he would have to be his most cordial during the upcoming evening, but he was finding it difficult to control the anger he was still feeling over the complications in his life and the way things were turning out.

When Matt had come to him several days before with the invitation to join Faith and her mother for dinner, his first instinctive response had been to refuse. It had only been the realization that if he cut Faith and Ruth Hammond, he would be losing Matthew for all time that had forced him to accept.

Noah did not want to socialize with these colonials. He did not want to become personally involved with any of them. He only wanted to complete the arms sale and return to England, but fate seemed to be intervening at every turn, wreaking havoc on all his plans. Matt had fallen in love with Faith and proposed to her against his expressed wishes. That had been distressing enough, but it also turned out that her father, though now dead, had at one time been a member of the dissidents. Through Faith, Matt had now made contact with the rebels and is in the process of becoming more and more active in supporting their cause. Matt had truly become his own man, and Noah was helpless to deal with it in the logical ways he thought best, for he loved his brother too much to forbid him his heart's desire.

When Matt had told him of Faith's acceptance of his proposal that night, Noah had pointedly asked him how he planned to make a living to support his wife. He had expected Matt to relent on his claim that he didn't want any of the money Noah controlled and pleaded with him to release his share. But Matt had remained steadfast to his principles, and it had been Noah who had backed down, telling his brother in the end that he would not withhold his fifty percent of the profits from their shipping ventures.

The moment had been perfect for a complete reconciliation between them, but Noah had refused to give any more ground or to show any happiness over Matt's choice. He had kept his manner aloof and disapproving, never allowing Matt the chance to get close.

"Noah?" Matt's voice cut through his thoughts as he stared out the window at the passing city.

"Yes?"

"There's going to be another meeting at Faneuil Hall tomorrow night. Would you like to—" Matt got no further in his effort to interest Noah in the current colonial trouble.

"No." His tone was flat and adamant. "You know I have no desire to become embroiled in any of this."

"I had hoped that you might be seeing things differently now. . . ."

"No, dear brother, I haven't changed. From the very beginning I've wanted no part of the trouble here, and I still feel that way. My regret is that I haven't been able to convince you of the insanity of the course you've set for yourself, but I will not try to stop you," Noah told him, and Matt fell silent for the remainder of the trip to the Hammond house.

The coach drew to a stop outside the small home, and Matt descended first, leaving Noah to follow. Faith had been eagerly anticipating their arrival, and the moment he knocked, the door flew open and she was in his arms.

"I'm so glad you finally arrived!" she told him excitedly as she gave him a quick welcoming kiss on the lips before drawing away to greet Noah. "And you must be Noah. . . ." Faith turned to him, and though she was very nervous at meeting him for the first time, she didn't show it. "I'm Faith. Welcome to my home."

Noah was caught totally off guard then when she stood on tiptoes to press a gentle kiss on his cheek. He found himself engulfed in the fragrant sweetness of her perfume and the warmth of her welcome. As he had watched her kiss Matt, Noah had felt a bit out of place witnessing their brief intimacy, but now he suddenly had found himself included in that special openheartedness. It was an awkward moment for him even as he found a part of himself responding to her.

"Thank you," he returned a bit gruffly, not quite sure how to take this enthusiastic young woman. Faith was even more lovely than he remembered with her shining, ebony tresses and sparkling blue eyes. He found himself understanding much more clearly how his brother had happened to fall completely under her spell. She was enchanting.

"Please, come inside and meet my mother and Ben Hardwick. Ben's a longtime family friend," she confided as she took his arm and drew him into the house, giving Matt a quick, special smile over her shoulder as she did so. Matt followed along, closing the door behind them.

Matt was worried about how this first meeting between Noah and his future bride would go, and he was puzzled by Noah's lack of animation, wondering if his brother was deliberately going to remain aloof to express his disapproval of the situation. Concerned that Noah in his disparagement might hurt Faith in some way, his nerves stretched taut. He would not allow anyone to harm the woman he loved, not even his brother.

"Matthew . . . you're here. . . ." Ruth came out of the

parlor with Ben trailing behind her to find Faith surrounded by the two Kincade men. "And you must be Lord Kincade. . . ." She addressed Noah, her gaze widening as she considered what a strikingly handsome man he was, so tall and regal.

"Noah, may I present Ruth Hammond and Ben Hardwick. Ruth and Ben, this is my brother, Noah." Matt made the introductions quickly.

"Lord Kincade, I'm honored," Ruth and Ben said, and Ruth flushed a little in excitement as Noah bent politely over her hand.

"My pleasure," he replied, and while he smiled at them cordially, it was not a smile that reached his eyes. His gaze was guarded, as were his emotions. He did not want to find anything here that he liked. He did not want to think that Matthew would be able to find happiness without him. Logically, he knew his reactions were less than fair, but he didn't care.

"Come in and let's have a glass of wine before dinner," Ruth said, ushering everyone into the sitting room. The money for the wine had been gleaned from the hard-earned savings she'd kept hidden away for just such a special occasion.

When they had settled into the small parlor and the wine had been served, Ben proposed a toast. "To Faith and Matthew; may they find the complete and lasting happiness they deserve."

Noah stood near the mantel slightly apart from everyone as they drank to their future happiness. His intense regard was fathomless as he watched Matt with Faith. They sat together on the sofa seemingly oblivious to the world, their gazes locked, their expressions rapturous.

Though he was careful to keep his thoughts masked, Noah couldn't help but feel left out of the entire situation. He had always anticipated that Matt would marry well and settle down on the lands at Kincade Hall, but now . . . the memory of the past and the frustration of the present filled Noah with the urge to throw the empty wineglass he held with all his might against the wall and watch it shatter into a million splintering pieces.

"Matthew's told me so much about you, Noah, that I feel as if I know you already." Faith spoke up boldly once she'd managed to tear her attention away from Matt. She had noticed that he was holding himself slightly aloof, and she wanted to make him feel welcome.

"Oh, really?" Noah arched a dark brow in consideration of her remark, and he wondered just how much Matt had told his fiancée about their business.

Faith studied the tall nobleman with open interest as she tried to engage him in conversation. She found Noah to be a very handsome, slightly taller, older version of Matthew, but that was where she felt the resemblance ended. Matthew was warm and open and honest, whereas Noah Kincade struck her as being a very private person, not given to revealing anything about himself to anyone. She wondered if he had always been like this or if their more recent difficulties had forced him to become so hardened.

"Yes, Matt tells me that you're planning to return to England in the spring."

Noah let his gaze slide to his brother and then back to Faith as he wondered just how much she knew about the state of their financial affairs.

"Yes, I'll be returning as soon as the weather breaks in the spring," he answered with polite indifference.

"Do you miss England?" Ruth asked, wanting to keep the conversation flowing.

"Yes" came his curt reply as his thoughts drifted back to his more carefree days when the pursuit of money was not a major factor in his life. "Yes, I do miss it. It will be good to return. I had hoped that Matthew would be coming with me, but he tells me that he's decided to remain here in Boston."

"This is where my future lies, Noah," Matt answered

273

firmly, defensively.

"The opportunities are unlimited for shipping and transport here in the colonies," Ben joined in. "What with the rum trade and all . . ."

"Noah and I haven't discussed the details of just how we'll be handling the business from now on, but I'm certain we'll have it worked out before he departs in the spring," Matt put in. Then, addressing his brother directly, he added the idea he had been considering since he'd first decided to remain in Boston. "I see no reason why I couldn't handle our business contracts on this end, since you're choosing to return to England and remain there permanently."

"It seems you've been giving this a lot of thought," Noah remarked.

"Well, the wedding does take place in less than two weeks, and I wanted to have some idea of what my prospects are going to be before then," he said simply.

"Have you two decided where you're going to live after you're married?" Ben asked.

"We've discussed it," Faith answered, "and we thought it would be best if Matt moved in here with Mother and me for the time being. We'll have our own room and enough privacy, I'm sure."

Noah was astounded by the news. His brother, living here? The house was clean and neat, but atrociously small, and he wondered how Matt would possibly be able to contend with such limited living space. True, they had suffered through the weeks of living in cramped quarters on board the *Lorelei* and at the inn, but only because there had been no other alternative. Now Matt was deliberately choosing to live under such conditions for possibly a lengthy period of time, and Noah was mystified. What had possessed his brother?

The lilting sound of Faith's laughter drew Noah's attention then, and as he glanced at her, he knew the answer to his own question. Love had possessed his brother in the form of this lovely wisp of a woman whose devotion to

Matthew was obvious. Her voice softened when she spoke to him and her eyes reflected the depth of her love for him.

A pang of envy seared Noah as he watched the open affection between Matt and Faith, and he suddenly felt very alone. Even calling upon his resolve to return to England to set things right did nothing for his somber mood. The goal he had been driven to achieve for so long now seemed somehow insignificant, and Noah willed himself to believe that this feeling of purposelessness was merely transitory. Surely, as soon as he got things settled with the *Pride* and was on his way back to London, he would be more himself.

His thoughts were interrupted as Ruth suggested they dine. While the dinner was not elegant, the food was certainly well prepared and plentiful.

"We're going to be married at our church," Faith explained as she spoke of the wedding preparations to Noah and Ben, "and then return here for a small party . . . just family and a few friends." Her eyes were upon Noah as she spoke, for she was trying to judge his reaction to their plans. She felt certain that the Kincades were used to far more elegant fare than anything she and her mother could provide, and she was fearful of drawing his disapproval.

Noah met her gaze and sensed her fears. Though he had always hoped for the very best for his brother, he couldn't help but feel that maybe, this time, the very best for Matt did not necessarily have to be the most expensive. Matt loved Faith. Why else would he have risked all . . . his livelihood . . . his inheritance . . . his future . . . to remain here with her? That knowledge was enough for Noah. His brother had grown up into a strong-willed, determined man who knew what he wanted and let nothing stand in his way. Noah realized with a bit of a start that he was proud of him for having stood firm in the face of his own opposition.

"It sounds fine," he told Faith, giving her his first real, heartfelt smile of the night, "and as long as the two of you are happy, that's all that matters."

His words stunned Matt even as they pleased him, but he said nothing, not wanting Faith to be aware of the discord that had existed between them before regarding the wedding.

With all the arrangements made, the talk drifted to other subjects, and it was Ben who brought up the subject of the tea.

"I hope nothing further develops with the tea situation."

"What's happened?" Matt was instantly curious.

Ben was ready to answer openly when he realized that Noah might not share their beliefs, and he glanced in his direction questioningly.

"It's all right, Ben. You can talk freely," Matt assured him.

"Well . . . if you're certain . . ."

"I am."

"What my brother is trying to tell you, Ben, is that while I have no desire to become involved with your causes, I have no reason to run to the authorities with anything I might hear here tonight. Your opinions are safe with me."

Ben gave a curt nod and continued. "There are two more ships due in port any day, and both are carrying more of the English tea! You know the uproar the *Dartmouth*'s arrival caused. . . . Well, if the other two ships dock and the authorities try to unload, then there could be violence."

"Things have gone that far?" Faith asked worriedly, concerned for both Ben's and Matthew's safety should they find themselves caught up in the protest.

"They have. I've heard talk that they might even try to dump it, should word come that it's to be unloaded."

"Dump it?" The others were amazed.

"That's right. The Sons are willing to do whatever it takes to prevent the tea from being landed and sold. Emotions are running wild over the issue and I'm sure popular support would be with us."

"But what about the authorities? Aren't you concerned about what might happen? Certainly if you take such actions, there could be repercussions," Noah pointed out.

"We are ready to fight, if it must come to that," Ben answered stiffly.

Noah's feelings were divided. He worried that Matt might somehow get involved in the fighting, and yet the news that the colonials were ready to take up arms for their cause gave him hope for the success of any future arms deals he might arrange. It was an emotional dilemma that left him troubled.

"What plans have been made?" Matt asked with great interest.

"From what I understand, they've petitioned the governor to send the ships back without unloading their cargo. If they leave, there will be no problem, but if Hutchinson insists that they stay and unload . . . well, there are some ideas as to how to go about it, but nothing definite yet."

"I want to be involved," Matt told him firmly. "You'll keep me informed?"

"Of course," Ben promised. "You know how much your support is needed. We need everyone's help." He looked to Noah, wondering at his loyalties. "Noah? Are you interested in attending any of the meetings?"

Matt glanced at Noah then, wishing that there were some way he could convince him to become involved. With the two ships they owned, they had the capability to do much good for the cause, but Noah had shown absolutely no sign of wavering in his pursuit of his original goal . . . to make a profit.

"I think not, Ben," Noah declined, refusing to elaborate, but knowing that it would bode ill for him if any kind of open connection was made between himself and the rebels. All his dealings with them until this time had been accomplished with the utmost secrecy with only the innermost circle of the rebel group knowing of his part in the arms sale, and he wanted to keep it that way. The fewer people who knew about his business, the less likely he was to get into any kind of trouble with the Crown, and trouble was the one thing he wanted to avoid.

"That's a pity. The opinion of an accomplished gentleman like yourself would carry a lot of weight," Ben encouraged.

"That may be, but my brother seems to be the only one in the family with a mind for rebellion," he drawled, his tone giving a double meaning to his words that only he and Matt understood.

"Well, perhaps with time I can change your mind." Matt picked up on his response immediately.

Noah shrugged off any hope that Matt had that he would be converted. "Perhaps, but I doubt it. I have my own course set, and I do not see any reason to alter my plans."

Frustrated, Matt let the topic drop, for he knew his brother well enough to realize that it would do no good to push it. Noah had already made far more concessions than Matt had ever imagined he would. He would allow himself to be satisfied with the way things were, at least for now.

The conversation strayed away from the troubles of the times then and on to other things. It was some time later when Noah found himself on his way back to the inn alone, Matt having elected to stay with Faith a little longer.

As the carriage rumbled over the uneven streets of Boston, Noah thought of the glowing love that existed in the Hammond house. There was a bond of unity there that no person or circumstance could shatter. Faith and Ruth had experienced the worst of times and yet were still close and happy.

Noah supposed it was the fact of their obviously contented happiness that gave him so much pause. Always in his life, his own happiness had been related to, not his family, but the unending quest for good times. His father had seemed to be completely wrapped up in the business and Matthew had been away at school, so he had primarily been alone and left at loose ends with well-lined pockets. He had enjoyed without thought the best that society had to offer ... women, food, horses. He had assumed that that was what his life was supposed to be. Now, after having seen the Hammonds' and Matthew's utter contentment with their lifestyle, he was growing more confused.

Was happiness what he had believed it to be all along . . . unending funds and friends who wanted only the best things in life? Or was he seeing a new side of life previously hidden from him by that veneer of great wealth? Was happiness having money and spending it, or was happiness the inner peace that comes from knowing that you're loved and accepted no matter what terrible things destiny may throw your way?

Noah scowled into the darkness. Being the man of firm resolve that he was, he did not like to question himself once he'd set himself upon a course of action, but the doubts that were arising within him refused to be dismissed. He had been wrong in his original estimation of Faith's reasons for wanting Matthew, and it bothered him to consider that he might be wrong now.

A sudden, rough, jolting of the carriage that sent him almost tumbling from the seat reminded him, much to his disconcertion, of his encounter with CC, and his mood only grew more black. He had tried not to think of her since that fateful night, but she was always there in the back of his mind, stirring a mixture of emotions within him that defied understanding.

CC had caused him nothing but aggravation from the moment of their first meeting, first with her opinionated views on life, and then again when he'd discovered her involvement in political affairs that were directly related to his plans. He cursed himself silently for having given in to the impulse to sample her charms, but damn, she had been so tempting and had seemed, at the time, to know what she was about.

Still, if he had not allowed himself to take her there in the summerhouse, she would never have become such a fire in his blood. Noah realized to his dismay that he was unable to put the remembrance of her sleek supple body from him. Never before had any woman had such a hold on his thoughts. Something had happened between them that night that had left him confused and angered. He was haunted by CC . . . her loveliness . . . her scent . . . the brightness of her smile. . . .

He frowned at that last thought, for it was seldom that she had ever smiled in his company. Their every encounter had seemed to be a confrontation, and Noah was still stunned to think that they had made love so spontaneously in the coach that night. True, it had ended with angry words, but the memory of her, willing for once, in his arms had the power to stir him even now.

Noah shifted uncomfortably in his seat and suddenly wished himself away from the blasted colonies and back in England. Even as he made that wish, he realized how very lonely a life it was going to be once he did return.

CC stared at Anna in disbelief. "John's downstairs?"

"Yes, ma'am, and he asked to see you."

She shook her head slightly in amazement, for she could not fathom what John could possibly have to say to her. It seemed their discussion during the meeting had said it all, and she was determined to have nothing more to do with him. His unexpected and unwanted visit, however, was forcing her to have to tell him the truth of her feelings.

Sighing slightly, she finally answered in reply to Anna's summons, "Tell John that I'll be down shortly."

"Yes, Miss CC." Anna headed from the bedroom.

Alone again, CC girded herself for the upcoming confrontation. She knew the depth of John's feelings for her. Though she felt sympathy for him, she knew she could no longer tolerate his behavior. Checking in the mirror to be certain that she looked presentable, she took a deep breath and started from the room, anxious to get the entire scene over with.

John was standing at the window staring out at the night. He had been angry with CC after the way she had acted the night of the meeting and so had stayed away from her as long as he could, but today the need to see her had been so strong that he had thrown caution to the wind. Nerves on edge, he now waited to see her for the first time since she'd fled his company, and he wasn't quite sure what to expect.

"Good evening, John." CC came into the room and stood with formal intent just inside the parlor door, refusing to let him think that things were all right between them.

"CC . . ." John turned quickly to face her, his gaze searching her face for some sign of her mood.

"To what do I owe the honor of your visit?" she asked coolly, remaining where she was.

John's heart sank at the standoffishness of her position and her tone. "I felt the need to see you. . . . I wanted to explain about the other night. . . ."

"I really don't think there's any explanation needed, John. We've been through this before and I thought you understood my feelings in the matter."

"I . . ." John wasn't sure what to say next. He had known that CC didn't love him, but her behavior at their ball had given him hope that all that was changing. "I had thought that perhaps you had changed in your feelings for me."

CC was surprised and answered firmly, "I told you how I felt about you, John. Ours was a friendship."

"But at the ball . . . you were with me most of the night. . . . We were together, as I'd always hoped we'd be. . . ."

"You were my escort, nothing more," she supplied, squashing all of his fragile hopes.

"I see," he said in a low voice as his gaze riveted on her, "and you took advantage of my friendship to disguise your tryst with the Englishman, is that it?"

Though she had not planned for what had happened with

Noah the night of the ball, John's words aptly described the situation she'd found herself in. CC felt a stain of color pinken her cheeks.

John swore violently under his breath. "When did you first meet him, CC? Here with your father? And the night of the meeting, when Kincade showed up to present his arms deal . . . you didn't sneak out because you were afraid you'd be recognized, did you? You left to see him, alone, outside . . . didn't you?" he charged furiously.

"You're wrong, John," she finally defended herself. He had guessed the bare facts, but he didn't know the truth behind them.

He snorted in derision. "So you say, but everything I've seen tells me that I'm right."

"I see no need why I should have to explain myself to you. As I told you before, you have no claim on me. No man does."

"I bet you wouldn't say that to your dear Lord Noah Kincade, would you?"

"You have pushed our friendship beyond its bounds, John. I see no reason to continue this discussion. Please leave," she told him curtly.

John's manner immediately changed as he realized that she was ready to cut him completely. "CC . . ." he pleaded, striding toward her, his arms outstretched in supplication. "CC, don't you understand?"

"John . . ." She tried to warn him away, but he was too emotionally overwrought to listen.

"CC, darling, I love you. You've known that forever, it seems." He took both of her hands in his even though she resisted his effort at first. "I came here to apologize for my behavior the other night, not to argue with you." When he saw no lessening of her determination in her expression, he went on, "Don't you understand what I'm feeling? Don't you understand what it did to me to discover your involvement with Kincade? I love you. I want to make you my wife, and

282

yet you spurn me at every turn."

"John, I've told you before that I didn't love you. Why do you continue to believe that I'll change in my feelings for you? I like you as a friend, but obviously that's not enough for you. For both of our sakes, I'm ending our association now. After tonight I think it would be best if we don't see each other again."

CC's words pierced his heart in the most painful of ways. Unable to stop himself from one last, desperate effort to win her love, he swept her into his arms and kissed her.

CC stood perfectly still in his madly passionate embrace. She knew there was no point in struggling against him and that soon he would realize she wasn't responding and release her.

Her prediction came true as John thrust CC from him in disgust. "So that's the end of it. . . ." His eyes bored into her, the agony of her final rejection mingling there with his anger at his own weakness for her.

"It has to be, John. There's no other way. I'm sorry."

In that moment in a flash of revelation CC saw her own situation mirrored in John's emotions. He loved her just as she loved Noah . . . hopelessly, without a chance for any kind of future together.

"Goodby, CC. I hope someday you find your true happiness." With that he left the room, the closing of the front door giving testimony to his complete departure from her life.

CC lifted a trembling hand to her lips as she drew an unsteady breath. It was over. John was gone. The relief she felt was immense, but the sympathy she felt for him ran deep. How terrible it was to care for someone who could never return your feelings. . . .

Noah had made it plain to her from the beginning that he had only been 'taking what she was offering.' Instead of fighting him the other night in the carriage and insisting that his opinion of her was wrong, she had fallen into his arms without protest like a fool. She shook her head in despair as she realized that, like John, there could be no happy ending for her either. Lord Noah Kincade had used her, and she had allowed him to do it. He had felt no emotion for her but lust. When the spring came he would return to England, and she would never see him again.

The pain that that last thought brought was devastating and she sank down on the sofa, lost in a haze of loneliness that was so powerful it frightened her. She recognized now, as the agony of the truth of her feelings engulfed her, that she loved Noah. She hadn't wanted to. She had fought it with all her might, but sometimes the heart just refused to follow the dictates of the mind.

"Miss CC?" Anna's voice interrupted her thoughts.

"What?" She looked up, a bit startled to find her maid standing in the parlor doorway.

"Are you all right? You look a bit pale. . . . Is there anything I can get for you?"

"I'll be fine, Anna," she answered, thinking that the one thing she really needed, she would never have . . . Noah Kincade's love.

"If you're sure, miss . . ."

"Yes, I'm sure." Her tone was melancholy, and Anna could only guess at the cause as she left her mistress alone with her thoughts.

Chapter Seventeen

CC stared aghast at Ryan Graves. "Surely you aren't serious. There must be someone else who can do this. . . ."

"I'm sorry, CC. Both Joshua and I are willing to make the trip," he replied, gesturing to Joshua Smith and himself, "but you're the only one who could go in there without drawing attention to yourself."

She shook her head quickly. "No. I can't do it, Ryan."

The rebel leader was stunned by her refusal. "CC, we have to get this money to Lord Kincade. We promised him over a week ago that he would have it soon, and I'm sure he's wondering at the delay in the initial payment. If I try to deliver it . . ." Ryan hesitated, glancing poignantly at Joshua. "There's no telling what might happen."

"I don't understand. What could possibly happen if you give it to him?"

Ryan's expression hardened. "We have it from a reliable source that Lord Kincade's movements about town are being monitored. We don't know if he's aware of the surveillance or not, and we can't take any chances. The deal is too close to fruition. We have to see it through. It has to be you, CC. You're the only one who is not regularly known."

CC vacillated, tormented by the decision she had to make. She did not want to see Noah again, yet if the entire arms deal was to fall through because of her refusal to take the money to him at the inn ... she hesitated to answer, knowing that she couldn't tell them the real reason why.

Joshua Smith sighed in very real exasperation as his gaze rested coldly upon her. "I told you we shouldn't allow a woman to be included in any of this, disguise or no disguise. This is men's business, and females shouldn't have a part in it."

Joshua's words stung her pride, as he'd hoped they would, and she stiffened as she answered, "I'll do it."

"Thank you, CC." Ryan slanted Joshua a triumphant look as he handed her the wrapped parcel that contained the first of the two payments they'd agreed upon for the shipment.

"Does Kincade know I'm coming?"

"No. We didn't even want to risk sending a message."

"I see." She frowned slightly at the thought of arriving unannounced. "What if he isn't at the inn?"

"He should be," Ryan answered, noting the time, "but if for some reason he isn't, just keep the package with you until you can make contact with him. Then report back to me to let me know how everything went. I'll be here until midnight tonight. If you have any problems and don't get the money to him until tomorrow, you can send word to me at home."

"Fine."

"Also, I've enclosed a letter with the money explaining the situation to him, so you won't have to. The less time you spend with him, the better off you'll be. We don't want to put you in danger either."

"I appreciate that."

"Good. I'll be expecting to hear from you within the next eighteen hours," Ryan told her seriously. "And remember, caution is the word of the day. Be as inconspicuous as you can."

"I'll be careful," she promised.

"Good luck."

Carrying the parcel under her arm as if it were of little importance, CC strode from the room in her practiced boyish style. She left the safety of the Green Dragon and went out into the dark of the early Boston night, all the while pensively wondering who it could be who was so interested in Noah that they would be having him watched.

Joshua looked at Ryan, his expression worried. "Do you think she'll be all right?"

"I hope so," Ryan replied tensely. "We have a lot riding on this deal and I don't want anything to go wrong."

"Why do you think she refused at first? Do you think she was too afraid?"

Ryan frowned thoughtfully. "No. I think I know CC fairly well and she doesn't frighten easily. I'm not sure why she didn't want to have any contact with Kincade. Maybe she thought that he might discover her true identity. After all, he does do some business with her father."

"That's true," Joshua nodded. "But I'm sure she'll do fine. All she's got to do is to make sure he gets the package. Minimal contact. Nothing else. It shouldn't prove too difficult."

Noah sat in the taproom drinking a mug of ale and listening with little interest to the conversations flowing about him. Though it was early evening, he was already thinking of retiring to his chamber for the night, not so much because he was tired as because he was bored. The day had passed relatively quickly for him as he'd worked with Lyle on board the *Lorelei* in preparation for the ship's departure on the short trip to the islands, but now the night stretched out before him in endless monotony. Matt had gone to visit Faith, and he was alone.

"Can I get you another drink, m'lord?" Polly sidled up to his table and brushed slightly against him.

"Yes, Polly, I do believe I'll have one more." Noah smiled

with cool politeness, taking care that she read no invitation in his expression.

Polly's expectant look faded as she noted his lack of interest. "I'll be right back with your ale."

"Thanks."

She was as good as her word and he accepted the tankard, tipping her generously as he stood up.

"Should my brother come in in the next hour or so, tell him to come on up to my room, will you, Polly?"

"Yes, Lord Kincade. I'll tell him," she promised before she moved away to see to her other customers.

Noah paid little attention to his surroundings as he took up his fresh mug of ale and started upstairs. He did not notice the door to the taproom opening or the youth who slipped undetected inside.

CC's nerves were stretched taut as she entered the taproom of the Red Lion Inn. Though it was true that she was a bit nervous because this was the first time she'd gone anywhere in her disguise save the meetings and rallies, the real cause of her upset was the prospect of seeing Noah again. She dreaded the moment. Her feelings for him were like a wildfire raging within her soul. She was afraid that if he touched her, all would be lost again, just as it had been in the carriage the other night.

She was surprised when she caught sight of Noah on the staircase. Without drawing attention to herself, she picked up her pace in hopes of catching up with him before he entered his room. Noah was unaware that CC was coming up behind him. When she reached out to grab his arm, he was startled and immediately spun around to see who it was.

"CC?!" he croaked in astonishment as he stared down at her in the dim light of the hallway. "What the hell are you doing here?"

"Be quiet," she warned him with a glare as she glanced around to be sure no one else had heard.

Noah realized his mistake in blurting out her name.

Shaking off the hold she had on his arm, he snared her wrist and dragged her with him the rest of the way down the hall to his room. As quickly as he could, he unlocked the door and then unceremoniously drew her inside. He released her to close the door behind them and light a lamp.

"You didn't have to be so rough!" she snapped as she rubbed her wrist.

Noah stood halfway across the room glowering at her as he tried to figure out why she had come. One part of him was ecstatic to see her again, but the other, harder part of him wondered at the reason for her unexpected visit. They had agreed in the carriage to stay away from each other, and yet here she was. . . .

"I thought we'd agreed to avoid each other?" he charged.

"We did, and believe me, this was not my idea," CC returned, scowling mutinously.

"Then why, my dear Miss Demorest, are you here?" Even while he was taunting her, though, Noah thrilled to her presence. His gaze went over her hungrily, memorizing every detail of her appearance and reviving every memory of her carefully concealed womanly curves.

CC answered in low, nervous tones, "I'm here because Ryan Graves sent me to you."

Noah's blood began to race at her words as both passion and fury flamed within him. So Robinson hadn't been the one directing her at all. It had been Graves all along. . . . Yet, even as he was angry, Noah knew that he wanted her as he'd never wanted another. He stepped closer, looming over CC threateningly.

"Oh, he did, did he?" Noah's predatory smile revealed his thoughts all too clearly, and CC, feeling nearly overwhelmed by his nearness, took a step back.

"Yes . . . I have something for you. . . ." she began.

"I'm sure you do." He reached out for her, but she neatly sidestepped his attempt to touch her.

"Here. Take this so I can go. . . ." Her hands trembled as

she held out the parcel.

Noah frowned as he glanced from the package to CC. "What is it?"

"The payment due you from Graves."

"What? He sent you to me by yourself with all that money?" Noah was enraged that the revolutionary would have sent CC on such a hazardous errand. Didn't they care that something might have happened to her?

"It was necessary," she explained.

"Why was it necessary?" he challenged.

"Nothing happened." CC tried to dismiss his concern.

"You were only lucky," he scoffed.

"That's beside the point."

"Maybe, but you didn't answer my original question. Why did they feel it was necessary to send you on this trip? Any of the men could have done it."

"That's true, but it doesn't matter. They sent me and I did it. There's a letter inside the package that explains everything. Here." CC held out the money again. "Take this so I can leave. It wouldn't do for anyone to get suspicious of me."

As Noah accepted the payment, his hand accidentally touched CC's and the contact was electric. Their gazes met then, and all thoughts of danger and intrigue were swept from their minds as the memory of their passion for each other surged to the forefront. There was no denying it for either of them. Noah silently placed the parcel on the bedside table before drawing her to him.

CC knew she should run.

"Noah . . . I have to go. . . . Please, let me . . . we shouldn't . . ." Her protests were feeble, and Noah overruled them with but a single kiss.

She knew she should not allow this to happen, but the touch of his hand and the warmth of his closeness drove all thoughts of flight from her. She loved him and soon he would be gone. There could be no tomorrow for them, but at least she could have tonight. . . .

Hungrily she returned his kiss, her lips parting beneath his, her heart pounding erratically in her breast. She had not thought she would have the opportunity to be with Noah ever again, and yet here they were, locked in each other's arms, lost in the splendor of their mutual need. It was her longed-for paradise.

She wound her arms around his neck, hugging him to her as she molded herself to his hard-muscled strength. Every fiber of her being longed for oneness with him, and she clung to him, weak with desire.

Noah was enthralled as his mouth sought to press kiss after heated kiss upon her waiting lips. No nectar had ever tasted so sweet or filled him with such rapturous joy. Exhilarated, he felt the need to be joined with her, to clasp her to him and merge their bodies into one perfect unity. His hands moved restlessly to the soft curve of her hips and pressed her full against his throbbing desire. Noah and CC were so absorbed in the excitement of the embrace that they did not hear the door open or close.

Matt had entered the taproom shortly after Noah had headed for his room with CC in pursuit, and Polly had intercepted him at once with Noah's message to come right up. Matt had hoped to have a long talk with Noah this evening about their plans for the future and so he hurried on upstairs to speak with him. Since Noah was expecting him and the door was unlocked, Matt did not bother to knock but simply opened the door, walked in, and pushed the door shut behind him.

The sight that greeted him shocked and disgusted him. There in the middle of the room stood Noah locked in an embrace with what looked to be a young boy. It was something he had never suspected of his brother, not even in his wildest imaginings, and he could only gape in outrage.

"Noah!?" Dear God!" His voice was a hoarse croak and he backed toward the door in an effort to escape the tawdry scene.

Reality did not intrude upon CC and Noah until the sound of Matt's voice so very near and so very filled with loathing pierced their Elysian interlude and shattered the moment of bliss. Jolted out of his reverie, Noah suddenly realized that in his overwhelming need to possess CC again, he'd forgotten the message he'd left for Matthew, and more important, he'd forgotten to lock the door.

"Matt . . ." Noah's voice was sharp as he tried to stop his brother from leaving. When CC would have turned to face Matt and relieve Noah of the necessity to explain a most embarrassing situation, Noah held her tightly to him and murmured, "Keep your face averted."

"I'm leaving. . . ." Matt ground out, his tone terse with condemnation. "I hadn't meant to intrude. Polly just said that—"

CC could almost feel the violent emotions that were being barely held in check by both brothers, and with a supreme effort she twisted quickly in Noah's shielding embrace.

"Matthew . . . wait. . . . It's all right . . . really. . . ."

"CC, damn it!" Noah swore. He had wanted to protect her from recognition and yet she had openly and willingly given away her identity.

"CC?"

A kaleidoscope of comical emotions ranging from censure to understanding to humorous crossed Matt's face as he stared at CC dressed in her boy's disguise.

"CC . . . Miss Demorest, I presume." The jarring tension that had seared him when he'd first entered the room faded quickly away, leaving him feeling slightly foolish, and he grinned in self-derision. "Thank heaven it's you; I should have remembered. . . ."

"What?" Noah looked questioningly from CC to his brother. "What should you have remembered?"

"CC's disguise, of course," Matt answered easily.

"You knew about the disguise?" Noah was astonished.

"Yes, CC and I ran into each other at the meeting at Faneuil Hall and I vowed to keep her secret." Matt suddenly looked thoughtful. "That explains *my knowing*, but just how did *you* find out?"

"He discovered my involvement the night of his first rendezvous with Graves," CC supplied, moving out of the circle of Noah's arms the moment he loosened his grip. "You do know about all that, don't you?"

"Yes, he knows about it," Noah snapped, suddenly irritated and not quite sure why.

"You're a member of that group?" Matt was astounded to find out that she belonged to the innermost decision-making group.

"Yes," she answered with pride. "I have been almost since the beginning."

Everything quickly came together for Matt now that he better understood the relationship that existed between Noah and CC. No wonder she'd sounded slightly embittered when they'd spoken of Noah the other night. If she cared for him, as she obviously did or she wouldn't have just been in his arms, his refusal to become involved in the revolutionary movement and his determination to return to England had no doubt hurt her terribly.

"So that's how you knew so much about—" Matt began, and CC flashed him a warning look.

"Knew so much about what?" Noah demanded, wanting to know everything about Matt and CC's acquaintance.

"Oh, nothing. Listen, I can speak with you any time, Noah. I'll just—" He started for the door to allow them time together, but CC spoke up quickly, halting his progress.

"No! I'll go. . . . I must. . . ." She rushed to the door. "Goodby, Noah." Her eyes were filled with sadness as they met his across the room, and without another word she fled the room.

"CC . . ." Noah started after her, but when he emerged into the hall she had already disappeared down the steps, and he knew it would not do for him to race from the inn in hot pursuit of a messenger boy. Slowly, unaccountably miserable, he turned back inside and closed the door.

"Noah . . . what was that all about?" Matt was frowning, not understanding CC's haste to be gone.

"CC was sent by Ryan Graves to deliver the first half of our payment for the arms." He gestured toward the table, where the money lay untouched.

"Oh." Matt was disappointed, for he had hoped that there might be more to her visit than that. "I thought she might have had another reason—"

"There was no other reason for her visit, Matt." Noah cut off his insinuation.

"That's too bad. CC is a very special woman." Matt admired her very much, and he let his feelings for her show in his tone. "A man could do far worse."

"Perhaps." Noah refused to reveal anything of his feelings for CC, and Matt finally let the matter rest.

As Matt considered the whole scenario for a moment in silence, he thought it odd that a woman had been sent on such a potentially dangerous mission, and he asked, "Why in the world would the leaders send CC to you with the money? Wasn't that slightly dangerous? One woman . . . alone . . . unprotected?"

"I asked her the same thing, and all she would tell me was that there was a letter in the packet that would explain everything." Noah quickly unwrapped the parcel and, with little interest, set the money aside in favor of the envelope enclosed. "Let's see here. . . ."

Silently he read the missive, and his jaw tensed in explosive anger. "I don't believe this. . . ." He looked up at Matt, stunned.

"What?" Matt took the letter.

*Lord Kincade—It has come to our attention that your
every move about town is being watched. We have no
idea why, but certain precautions must be taken from
now on in our dealings, and I will no longer be able to
meet with you personally. Please understand, and if
you can explain the surveillance, send word. Graves.*

"Damn! We're being watched, Matt . . . or at least I am,"
Noah snarled, striding to the window and staring out at the
seemingly deserted street below.

"But why? Who would want to know your movements?"

Noah's mind was racing, and his expression was etched
with anger as he paced furiously about the room. "Who
indeed? I have no enemies here. Except for my one brief
meeting with Graves and Adams at the Green Dragon Inn
some time ago, there's been no other open contact between
us."

Matt felt the sudden weight of his own actions.

"Noah . . ." His tone was solemn.

"What?"

"I wonder if it could be because of me."

Noah frowned at the thought. As much as he didn't want
to lay that guilt on Matthew, it fit. Matt had argued with
Winthrop, Matt had been seeing Faith regularly, Matt had
attended the meetings at Faneuil Hall, and he was definitely
involved in the growing unrest.

"Damn!" he swore, his once-softening feelings toward
Matt's relationship with Faith suddenly hardening. If
anything happened to his arms deal . . . "I told you not to get
involved with the rebels! I warned you about what could
happen, but you refused to listen! And now . . ."

"Noah, I—"

"Stay away from Faith and stay away from the meetings!"
He was livid that his plans might be ruined.

"Faith and I are going to be married shortly, in case you've

295

forgotten, and I will not let anything interfere with that."

"Not even the possibility that you might be jeopardizing our entire future?" Noah countered.

"We can protect ourselves now that we know about the surveillance."

"It's not that simple, Matthew."

Matt was not about to give quarter. "Noah, it most certainly is. So far we've done nothing that could be considered illegal. I've attended a few public meetings. So what? There's no way they could have any proof that we're involved in any wrongdoing. The only way they could prove anything would be to get hold of the *Pride*'s manifests and make a connection between the payment you just received and the rebels taking delivery of the arms."

"Maybe so, but we can't be sure. Until we are, I want you to steer clear of anything controversial," he ordered.

Matt's eyes were aglow with an inner fire as he glared at his brother. "Noah, I will do nothing to endanger your plans, but you cannot ask me to stay away from the woman I love."

"I most certainly can if our lives depend on it!"

"Then I'm afraid there can be only one solution." Matt stiffened as he prepared to do the one thing he'd never wanted to do. "I will move out of the inn tonight and sever our relationship. You should then be freed from any further surveillance."

"What!?" His statement caught Noah totally off guard. "You can't mean that."

"I do," he answered grimly. "You're forcing me to choose, Noah, and there can be only one choice."

"I didn't mean that you would have to give up Faith permanently," he argued.

"I don't have the control over my emotions that you do. I can't turn them off and on at will. I love her. She deserves my protection, and I intend to give it to her. If it means sacrificing everything else in my life to be with her . . . then I'll do it."

Noah was stunned. Matt loved Faith so much that he was willing to give up everything for her. Everything.

CC glimmered unbidden into his thoughts, and he compared what he felt for her to what Matt professed to feel for Faith. The result was total confusion, and he got a grip on his own runaway thoughts only by telling himself that his relationship with CC was far different from what Matt and Faith shared. There was no future for CC and him. Attracted as she might be to him physically, she hated him now just as much as she had in the beginning. She didn't love him. No words of love had ever been spoken between them. What they'd shared had been lust.

Matt took Noah's silence to mean that there was no need for further discussion between them, that he was willing to make the break for the sake of the shipment and the profit to be made.

"If you'll excuse me, I'll see to packing my things."

"Matt . . ." Noah started to protest, but it was too late. Matt had already gone from the room. Noah followed him and knocked loudly on his door. "Matt! We need to talk more about this."

The door was pulled almost violently open and Matt stood there, tall and proud before him. "There's nothing more to say, Noah. Not really. You have your priorities, and I have mine. I will be very careful from now on, and I will make certain that my activities are never connected to yours."

"Where will you go? What are you going to do?"

"What am I going to do?" Matt smiled faintly. "I'm going to marry Faith and live happily ever after. You might do well to ask yourself the same questions."

"What do you mean? I know what I'm about."

"Are you still so sure, Noah? Are you still so positive that your future is in England?"

"Of course!" he replied a bit too quickly.

"What about CC?"

297

"What about her?"

Matt shrugged, suddenly weary of trying to convince Noah to see things more clearly. "I'd better finish my packing. I'll be in touch, and if you should need to get a message to me, leave word at Faith's."

With that Matt slowly closed the door, and Noah stood silently in the hall, lost deep in his thoughts.

CC nimbly climbed the tree's supportive branches and with amazing agility levered herself into her bedroom through the unlocked window. As quickly as she could, she stripped off her disguise and hid it in the armoire before donning her dressing gown and sitting down at the dressing table to brush out her tangled locks.

She had thought that she would be calmer by the time she reached home, but even after stopping long enough to report back to Ryan, her emotions were still reeling from her contact with Noah. Though the memory of what had almost happened between them sent chills of excitement up her spine, she thanked heaven that Matthew had shown up when he had. If they hadn't been interrupted, they no doubt would have made love, and CC knew that she could never let that happen again.

Drained by the strain of the night, she didn't even bother to put on a gown, but curled up on the bed just as she was. Sighing, she hugged a pillow near and pulled the counterpane over her for warmth. Gradually she grew warm and the tension eased from her. In that last half-awake, half-asleep moment when her defenses were totally down just before sleep claimed her, CC whispered his name with the softness of a sigh. "Noah."

Noah was awake. Try as he might, sleep would not come, and so he stood now at the window in the concealing darkness of his room, staring out at the star-studded night sky. The evening had been a total disaster. His unexpected encounter with CC, the discovery that they were being watched, and his subsequent fight with Matthew had left his nerves raw and on edge.

Noah bitterly resented Matt's timing in walking in when he had, for he had been on fire with the need to make love to CC again. She was gone now, perhaps this time for good. Even though he knew that his desire for her had not lessened, his body still burned with passion for her and he was helpless to do anything about it. He could not go to her and seek her out, for he felt without a doubt that she would refuse his advances. With the heat of his loins throbbing in an almost painful reminder of the sweetness of her body curved so perfectly to his, he made his way back to the bed and lay down, trying to turn his thoughts to other things . . . to Matthew. . . .

Matthew. A lurching emptiness filled him at the memory of his brother's steely determination. He knew it had been pushing to ask him to stay away from Faith and the rebels for a time, but wasn't the ultimate success of their venture worth the sacrifice? Even as Noah thought the question, he knew what Matt's answer to it would be. There was no sacrifice too great for love. None.

Miserably, Noah closed his eyes and rested a forearm across his brow as he gave a low, defeated laugh. He had thought love was his purpose in restoring the Kincade name. He had grown up being tutored in the importance of family history and family traditions. He had been indoctrinated with the importance of carrying on the Kincade name, of maintaining the many estates and houses and, above all, of doing nothing that would detract from the honor of the Kincade family. He had been taught that his pride in being a Kincade went before all else.

His entire life until just recently had been directed by those teachings. Then the changes had come—first with his father's death and then the discovery of his father's betrayal of all that Noah had been told was important. The losses had been so vast that they had raped the Kincade fortunes and rendered the heirs near paupers. Noah, trapped by the cruel twist of fate that had stripped him of everything else, was left with only his pride intact. It was that pride that drove him on, relentlessly, to reclaim all that had been lost.

Still, as he lay alone in the silent blackness of his rented chamber, Noah could not help but wonder at the price he was going to have to pay to achieve the goal he had set for himself. His pride had already cost him Matthew, and he wondered if the final end would be worth it. He might very well restore the Kincade name, honor, and riches, but when he finally did, would anyone care?

The thought echoed hollowly through him, and he muttered a curse into the darkness. It had to be worth it. Just because his father had been weak didn't mean that he was. He would not deviate from the course he'd set for himself. He would do what he set out to do. He would concentrate on business and rebuild it all. But even as he vowed to himself again to continue, his fervor was gone; instead, suddenly, it all seemed an uphill battle with little real reward at the end.

Troubled, Noah sighed deeply, seeking sleep but knowing that his thoughts were too confused to court real rest this night. When at long last sleep finally did come, he dreamed of England and Kincade Hall in the frigid, barren, lonely months of winter.

Chapter Eighteen

Matt swung down from the carriage as it drew to a stop before Faith's house. Though he had just left her a short time before, he felt a driving need to see her again. His encounter with Noah had left him feeling jaded and slightly embittered, and he needed the warm, healing sweetness that only Faith could provide.

"You be wanting your trunk, sir?" the driver called down.

"No. I won't be staying here. Wait for me. I shouldn't be too long."

Knowing that at this time of night there was little call for his services, the driver readily agreed to the delay.

Faith and Ruth were surprised by the knock at the door. Faith hurried to answer it, thinking that there must be an emergency of some kind for them to be getting a visitor at this time of night.

"Matthew?" Her surprise was as real as her delight to see him again so soon after they'd parted. "Come in. . . . Is something wrong? You look worried." She took his arm and drew him into the welcoming glow of her small home.

"Faith? Did I hear you say that . . . Why, Matthew, it is you. . . ." Ruth was puzzled as she greeted her future son-in-law.

"I'm sorry to bother you again so late in the evening, but I wanted to let Faith know that I'll be changing residences."

"What?" Both women were astonished and confused. "But why?"

"Noah and I had a disagreement of sorts, and I decided to sever my connections with him. I've moved out of the Red Lion, and I'll be taking a room at the inn near here," he tried to explain.

"Your argument with Noah must have been very serious for you to take such drastic measures," Faith said softly as she took Matt's arm and guided him into the parlor. The muscles in his arm tensed beneath her hand at her words. Though he said nothing else immediately, she quickly perceived the gravity of the situation. "You and Noah are very close, aren't you?"

"We used to be," he supplied grimly.

"Can you tell me about it?" she urged, wanting him to be open and honest so she could somehow help to ease the distress he was obviously feeling.

Matt raked a hand nervously through the thickness of his dark hair. "There isn't much to tell. We had a major falling out over something, and I decided that it would be better for us to part."

A pain seared through Faith as she thought she knew the reason for their separation.

"It's because of me, isn't it?" she asked, her eyes trapping his and forcing the truth from him.

"Only indirectly," Matt managed, glancing toward Ruth and then back to Faith. He knew he owed her the complete truth, for only then would she be able to understand everything.

"I don't understand. . . ."

"You know how I explained to you about Noah's and my situation." He waited until she nodded. "Before we left England Noah was determined to make as much money as he could very quickly. He discovered while making inquiries into the most profitable goods to ship that some of the

302

groups supporting revolution here would buy arms at a premium price."

"Yes, so?"

"I need your secrecy on what I'm about to tell you."

"Yes, of course. You know we'd do nothing to harm you or your brother."

Matt knew he could trust them implicitly and told them, "Noah has contracted to sell the *Sea Pride*'s arms shipment to the rebels here."

The news pleased both the women. "But that's good news, Matt. He's not as averse to our cause as you led us to believe," responded Faith.

Matt couldn't prevent a weary laugh. "I'm afraid you're reading nobility into this where there is none, love. Noah didn't do it because he cared, he did it to make money. Period. He'd sell the damned weapons to the devil himself if there was a profit to be made."

The pleasure of the moment faded before his explanation.

"Anyway," Matt continued, "Noah just found out that someone has been following him, keeping track of his movements about town."

"But why? Did someone find out?"

"We don't know, but logically it fits since I am getting involved in things with Ben and we are engaged. . . ."

"You think they're watching Noah because of you?"

"It's the only possibility that makes sense," he sighed. "The arms are due in at any time now. Noah wanted me to stop seeing you and to stop attending the meetings until all the business transactions had been completed. I refused."

Faith's expression was troubled as she met his gaze. "I do not want to come between you and your brother."

"You didn't, Faith," Matt told her firmly. "There was no reason for me to stop seeing you. Though your father was involved in the movement, you're not in any way. I told him it was ridiculous to ask that of me, especially since we are to be married so soon, but all he was concerned with was the arms deal." He shook his head slowly in remembrance of their conversation. "So in an effort to help him, I told him I would sever all connections between us. That way whoever was watching him would know he was not in any way involved with my activities."

"And he didn't argue the point?" Faith was amazed that Noah would let Matthew do this.

"I didn't want to argue. He was trying to force me to do things his way, and while his way may work for him, it isn't always the right way for me." He leaned forward and pressed a soft kiss on Faith's cheek. "Don't worry. Everything's going to be fine."

Tears filled her eyes as she realized that he had just sacrificed his own brother for the love of her. "Matthew . . . I don't want you to do this. You love your brother. . . ."

"It's done, Faith, and I'll hear no more about it." He stood up. "Now I'd better be going. The carriage I hired is waiting outside. I'll get in touch with you in the morning and let you know where I'm staying. Good night, Ruth."

"Good night, Matthew. I'm sorry things have turned out so badly for you."

"Things haven't turned out badly," he denied, looking down at Faith with his love for her clearly reflecting in his eyes. "Things have turned out perfectly. I love your daughter, Ruth, and she will soon be my wife. Nothing could make me happier."

"Matthew, wait. . . ." Faith tugged on his arm when he would have started from the room.

"What?" He frowned, wondering at her anxiety.

"There's no reason for you to go to another inn," she insisted, her eyes glistening with tears of love and admiration for him.

"Of course there is, and it's getting late."

"No. Matthew, marry me tonight. Then you can stay here with us."

A lopsided grin quirked his lips. "Tonight?" The thought

was not without appeal, for the long days until the wedding had seemed to stretch endlessly before him, barren and empty.

"Mother?" Faith turned quickly to her mother as she still clutched at Matt's arm, refusing to let him go. "Will you care? We could go to a minister tonight and everything would be perfect. . . ."

"But the wedding?" Ruth was bewildered by her daughter's sudden plea.

"We could still have the party here, Mother." She looked hopefully to her.

Understanding the poignancy of the moment, Ruth agreed with a light chuckle. "If Matthew has no objection to accepting your brazen proposal, neither do I."

The idea, so unexpected and so welcome, filled Matt with a glow of joy. He swept Faith into his arms and spun her quickly about.

"I'd be delighted to marry you tonight, Miss Hammond," he pledged as he gave her a quick kiss, and Faith laughed delightedly at his play.

"Mother? Do you know . . . ?"

"Yes, dear, and I'll give Matthew directions for the driver while you go gather up a few things to take with you," Ruth answered in anticipation of her question.

When Faith returned to the room a short time later with a small bag packed, Matthew had already instructed the driver to bring his trunk inside and had given him the necessary directions to the minister in the country Ruth had suggested.

"We're ready if you are, Faith," Matthew told her.

Faith hugged her mother quickly. "Thank you."

"Your happiness means everything to me. Now, go and be with your man," Ruth whispered.

With stars in her eyes, Faith gave her mother one last kiss and then flew to Matt's side.

"We'll be back sometime tomorrow," Matt told Ruth as he helped Faith with her cloak and then ushered her from the room.

"God bless you both," she called out as they climbed into the waiting carriage, and she watched as the coach rumbled off down the street.

Candles flickered mellowly, casting unsteady shadows upon the walls, as the words being spoken in hushed adoration echoed in the unheated chamber. Matthew and Faith were unaware of the chill in the room, though, for they were wrapped in the fire of their love. Standing slightly apart, they repeated their vows. Their gazes were solemn upon each other, and their hearts were pounding in excited anticipation as Matt slid his signet ring upon her finger, claiming her as his for all eternity.

At that moment, for the first time, Matthew regretted the fate of the Kincade fortunes, for he would have loved to present Faith with his mother's diamond-studded wedding band on this, their wedding night. The band, which had been in the family for generations, was to have come to him as part of his inheritance. It hurt him now that it had had to be sold to pay his father's debts. How proud he would have been to be able to present Faith with such a fabulous token of his love. . . .

Matthew focused on his beloved then, and though she wasn't wearing a white lace gown or carrying a bouquet of fragrant flowers, he knew Faith had never looked lovelier to him. Her hair was down, framing her face in a soft torrent of raven curls and emphasizing the wide glory of her sparkling eyes. It was from his heart that he had pledged his life and his love to her. He longed to take her in his arms and never let her go.

Faith smiled as they were pronounced man and wife. She had never quite believed that this moment would ever happen, and she felt as if she were in a dream from which she hoped that she'd never awaken. With Matthew as her husband, her life was perfect.

As she gazed up at him, her pulse quickened. He was now and forever her husband. They were bound to each other for the rest of their lives. The thought brought comfort as well as excitement. He was so strong and so handsome, and she loved him so much. Surely, as long as they had each other, they would be happy.

Tenderly, unable to resist another moment, Matthew bent to Faith and kissed her with gentle promise as he murmured in a low tone just for her, "I love you. . . ."

The thrill of knowing that they would soon be man and wife in more than name only left Faith breathless. It seemed an eternity to her before the papers were all signed and their business finally concluded. When at last Matt whisked her from the small chapel and back into the coach, he drew her across his lap and held her close.

"We'll be at the inn soon," he promised, kissing her softly.

"I know," Faith returned, looping her arms about his neck and hugging him tightly.

Suddenly serious, Matt loosened the loving grip she had on him and held her slightly away. "Faith?"

"What?" She was surprised by his move.

"You're not sorry, are you?" His eyes were dark with the worry that was besieging him.

"Sorry? About what?"

"Sorry about not having a proper wedding . . . sorry about having to run off like this . . ." His gaze searched hers for the answer.

"Matthew!" she scolded lovingly, reaching up to caress the leanness of his cheek. "If you'll remember, this was my idea. I was the one who proposed it. I love you, and I couldn't bear for us to be apart another minute."

"Ah, Faith!" He turned to press a kiss to the palm of her hand and then growled as he crushed her to him. "I love you so much."

His lips sought the sweetness of hers in a fervent kiss of

love and need, and Faith gave a low purr of satisfaction deep in her throat in knowing that he did love her. That was all that mattered.

It was long after midnight when at last they drew up in front of an inn. After one last heart-stirring embrace, Matt tore himself away from Faith to secure them lodging for the night, leaving her safely ensconced in the carriage while he tended to it. At first the innkeeper, a bony scarecrow of a man named Carson, was not overly pleased to be roused at such a late hour, but when he discovered that his customer was an English lord, he immediately hurried to see to his needs. While not the fanciest of inns, it was clean, and Matthew chose the best room the tavern had to offer. He directed that a hot meal be sent up to them as soon as possible, along with a bath for his wife. After paying for the room, he went back out to escort Faith inside.

The room on the second floor was spacious. By the time Matt and Faith entered, a small fire had already been set in the fireplace and several lamps lighted for their convenience. Brightly colored scatter rugs adorned the dark, highly polished hardwood floor, and the bed had been turned down, its wide softness beckoning the lovers to test of its comfort.

"Matthew, the room . . . It's lovely." Faith murmured her approval of the cozy interior. A faint blush pinkened her cheeks as her gaze lingered on the bed and she tried to imagine the intimacy of sharing it with Matthew this night.

Matt smiled warmly as he noticed the direction of her gaze and read her thoughts. He was about to take her into his arms for a passionate kiss when a knock at the door interrupted him. His smile twisted to a wry grin as he called out, "What is it?"

"Your meal, m'lord" came the innkeeper's answer, and Matt regretfully moved away from Faith to open the door to admit him.

A table was set for them, and the finest fare the tavern had to offer was served along with a bottle of its best wine.

"I'll have the bath up directly," Carson related as he scurried from the room.

"That will be fine." Matthew couldn't wait for him to be gone, and he closed and locked the door with great relish. "Now, my sweet . . ."

Faith saw the flame of desire in Matt's eyes, and she didn't hesitate to go to him, wrapping her arms about him and nestling against the warm width of his chest. "I love you, Matthew Kincade. I always have and I always will."

Matt stood still, cradling her against him, content for the time to just cherish the closeness and rightness of the embrace.

"Let's dine before the food grows cold," he suggested as he felt his senses begin to stir. There was nothing Matt wanted more than to make love to Faith, but he wanted their first time to be perfect. He deliberately postponed the ultimate, knowing that anticipation always heightened the satisfaction.

With all the gallantry of a gentleman at court, Matt seated her at the table and poured a glass of wine for her before taking his own chair. They said little as they sampled of the inn's fare, each eating sparingly, for their thoughts were far from food. It was not food they craved, but a far more important nourishment—the nourishment of the soul from love's embrace. Across the narrow width of the small table their eyes met and held, and Matthew lifted his wineglass in toast to his bride.

"May we be this happy always." He spoke in a low, intimate tone that sent a shiver of expectation through Faith. There was something innately sensual about the way Matthew lifted the glass to his lips. Faith suddenly wished his lips were tasting of hers instead of the full-bodied wine.

Faith remembered every touch and kiss they'd ever shared, and she longed to experience the fullness of his passion. His body was a mystery to her, and she was eager to

309

learn everything she could about pleasing him. Her mother had told her very little of what to expect on her wedding night beyond that there might be some pain. In spite of that, she was to submit completely to her husband's will. Faith smiled to herself, for submitting was hardly the word to describe what she was feeling in giving herself to Matthew. She wanted him. Her body craved closeness with him in the instinctive way that had existed since the beginning of time. Her need was a deep, heart-stirring drive for possession that eclipsed every other emotion she'd ever experienced.

Again Carson's knock at the door shattered the mood. They exchanged heated, knowing smiles as they silently acknowledged that this would be their very last interruption.

"Your bath awaits, my lady," he told her with flourish when at last they were alone again, the bath having been readied behind a privacy screen.

"You truly thought of everything, Matthew." She regarded him with open enchantment. "Thank you . . ."

"I only wish it could have been more, love." Matt grew solemn again as he thought of the past and the beauty of Kincade Hall.

Faith rose from the table and slipped her arms about his waist, resting her head against his heart. "I don't want more, Matthew. I have everything I could possibly want right now. I have you." Her gaze lifted to his and he could see the truth of her words. "Nothing else is important . . . not the past, not the future. . . . Only this moment matters."

Overcome by the heartfelt sentiment, Matt could not reply; instead, he lifted her into his arms. Their lips met in a gentle exploration as Matt slowly made his way to the bed and lowered her to its comfort, the bath suddenly completely forgotten.

"Matthew . . ." She whispered his name in a worshipful whisper as he broke off the kiss.

With impatience, Matt tugged off his coat. Turning slightly away, he tossed it negligently aside as he quickly untied his cravat. Faith watched his movements in sensual fascination, noticing how perfectly his snowy white shirt fit across his broad shoulders and how his dark pants clung like a second skin to his slim hips. It was as he turned back toward her that she noticed the unmistakable evidence of his growing desire, and she lifted her arms to him in ready welcome.

Matt could delay no longer and he lay down beside her, drawing her full-length against him, his hips pressing with breathtaking familiarity to hers. "It seems I've waited forever for this moment."

"We don't have to wait any longer. . . ." Faith drew his head down to her for an ardent kiss that told him of her own needs.

The quiet privacy of the moment, the intimacy of their position, and the heady sweetness of the wine they'd drunk all enhanced their senses. What began as only a kiss spiraled into a whirlwind of no longer forbidden desire. Their mouths met and parted only to meet again, as if unable to taste enough of the nectar of each other.

With tempered boldness, Matt worked at the buttons of her bodice. He remembered the sight of her naked loveliness, and he longed to touch those silken orbs. The memory of her bared breasts had haunted him all this time. When he finally pushed the material of her gown aside and unlaced her chemise, he lowered his lips to caress the satiny splendor of their creamy fullness.

Faith had never experienced the ecstasy of a lover's knowing touch before. Her breath caught in her throat at the rapture that flooded through her as Matthew pressed kiss after heated kiss upon her sensitive flesh. Waves of heat pulsed in her veins as his lips explored the peaks and valleys of her bosom. Her eyes widened in a mixture of delight and fear at the feverish feeling that was overpowering her.

"Matthew . . ." she gasped, frightened by the strength of her newly discovered desire.

311

Hearing the edge of panic in her voice and afraid that he might have hurt her in some way, Matt drew back. His eyes were dark with concern as he gazed down at her flushed features. "Faith? Did I hurt you?"

"Hurt me . . . ? Oh no, Matthew. You didn't hurt me. . . . It's just that I . . . I . . ." She was suddenly too shy to put all she was feeling into words. "I'm sorry."

"You're sorry?" He frowned, growing even more perplexed.

Knowing that she was botching the whole moment, she caressed his cheek. "It just felt so strange . . . so wonderful . . . I was almost frightened of the beauty of it all."

The tension that had been building within him drained away at her words and he smiled tenderly. "I'm the one who's sorry. I'll go more slowly for you. It's just that I've wanted this for so long."

"So have I, love," she told him seriously. "Shall we start again?"

"There's no reason to start again." He took her hand and held it over his heart so she could feel the heavy pounding of its excited rhythm beneath her palm.

"But . . ." Faith started to protest, for she thought he meant not to make love to her that night.

Matt saw her confusion and smiled tenderly. "There's no reason to start over, because we never quit. Our talking is just as important as our touching. I want to know that I please you in more ways than just the physical, sweetheart."

"Oh, you do, Matthew. You do." She took his hand then and drew it to her breast. "Please . . ."

His gaze was filled with adoration as he cupped one pale mound and teased the pink tip to pertness. "Did you like it when I kissed you there?"

Again Faith blushed, but she didn't hesitate to answer, "I think I must have, for I've never felt anything so . . . so . . ."

He bent to her breast and kissed the peak before lifting his head to supply the word. "Exciting?"

312

"Ummm . . ." she murmured, her eyes closing as he laved the taut crest with maddeningly arousing caresses.

With the utmost of care, he initiated her to the ecstasy of his touch, fondling and teasing her until she was clinging to him, weak with desire. Needing to be nearer, he left her embrace to strip off his shirt, and Faith looked up at him accusingly when he moved away.

"I want us to be closer. . . ." he explained quickly as he tore at the buttons on his shirt in his eagerness to shed his clothing.

"I do, too," she agreed, surprising him as she sat up and pushed her gown off her shoulders. "Help me?"

The invitation was innocently put, yet Matt knew the urge that sometimes drove men to rip gowns from women's bodies. There was nothing he wanted more than Faith naked beneath him, and had she an ample wardrobe, he might just have given in to his most primitive urge. As it was, he contained himself with an effort, and after divesting himself of everything save his pants, he hurried to help her remove her gown. Taking her hand, he helped her up from the bed. With as much restraint as he could manage, he finished loosening the gown and slipped it completely off her.

Faith had been quietly observing Matthew's expression as he helped her undress. When at last she stood before him clad only in her chemise, stockings, and shoes, she knew the ultimate glory of being a woman. His concentration on her was complete, and reflected in his expression was all his driving male need for her. It filled her with a sense of feminine power and emboldened her to bend forward and seductively remove her stockings and shoes. She had never fancied herself to be particularly sexy or beautiful, but the look on Matt's face made her feel that way, and she wanted to do all she could to heighten his pleasure in the moment.

"Will you help me with the chemise?" she asked softly.

Matt swallowed nervously at the thought that one last gesture would remove the final barrier protecting her and

313

make her his . . . totally. Then, as if in a trance, he took a step forward and pushed the chemise down her arms. He had untied the garment earlier in their play, and it had been gaping open, revealing just the swelling curve of the sides of her breasts as she stood there. Now, as the soft material slid lower, it clung with tantalizing distraction to the taut peaks. Forced to touch her again in order to free the chemise so it could complete it's descent, Matthew reached out with shaking hands and parted the garment. It fell the rest of the way to the floor unnoticed as he remained unmoving before her, his blue-eyed gaze aflame as he stared at her unclad loveliness.

Faith was more beautiful than he had remembered, and Matt hesitated for only an instant before crushing her to him in his most possessive embrace. She was his! Never before in his life had he experienced such a depth of emotion. He held her tightly in his arms, feeling how perfectly she fit against him. They had been made for each other. No one and nothing else mattered—only their love and need existed.

Together, without speaking, they moved to the bed and lay upon it, mindless to all but their desire to be one in love's most binding caress. Hands sought, lips met, and limbs intertwined as they explored the limits of pleasure together. With infinite care, he sought her most secret place. Though Faith balked at his first careful, questing touch, she soon gave herself over to his expertise, learning more of her body from Matthew than she had ever known before. His hands gentled her, readying her for his fullest possession. Faith felt herself growing more and more alive with his every rhythmic touch, and she could only wonder at the wonderful tension he was building deep within her.

It was when his lips sought her breasts again that the answer became known to her. She went rigid with delight as his knowing caress took her to unexpected heights of ecstasy. She cried out her rapture as the exhilarating sensations washed through her. Faith was so caught up in the throbbing pleasure of it all that she barely noticed when Matt shifted slightly away to shed his pants.

It seemed the most natural, most perfect thing in the world for Matthew to fit himself so intimately between her thighs. She welcomed him with a languid, sensual smile, wrapping her arms about him and pulling him down. The pain of their consummate melding was brief, but not blinding, and Faith went stiff only because of the newness of it as he first breached her virginal tightness.

"Oh, love," Matthew groaned, locked in the heat of her body; his instincts were screaming at him to move, to seek his own release, but he held himself back, unwilling to lose the soul-stirring enthrallment of the moment. "You are so perfect."

"We're perfect together, Matthew," she whispered, her hands drifting down his back toward his hips in a slow exploration that was silently driving him out of his mind.

"I always knew it would be this way," he told her as he kissed her deeply. "You feel so wonderful to me. . . ."

As her hands reached lower, innocently trailing fire wherever she touched, he could no longer control the driving urge to take her, and he began to move.

"Matthew?" Faith was surprised, having had no idea quite what to expect.

"Move with me, Faith," he urged, thrusting hungrily within her.

Faith moved experimentally at first, unsure of how best to please him. Matthew sensed her hesitancy, and he slipped his hands beneath her hips to help guide and instruct her movements. She understood then as he tutored her and she matched his motion excitedly, wanting to give to him as much joy as he'd given to her.

Matt had wanted to hold back, to prevent his passions from running away with him, but her eager sweetness drove him beyond all control and he sought his release deep in the hot velvet center of her body. He gasped her name as he

315

peaked in triumphant splendor, and he clasped her to him as he collapsed against her.

Faith sensed that she had pleased him and she pressed a gentle kiss to his shoulder as she lay beneath him. He was her husband and she had satisfied him. She felt very content.

Together they drifted in the soft silence of love's aftermath. Their joining had been everything they'd expected and more. They were perfect together and they knew without question that the future could hold nothing but happiness for them. Sleep stole over them as they lay still joined in that most intimate embrace, and they rested, filled with peace and love.

Chapter Nineteen

"Ben . . . what a wonderful surprise. Come in." Ruth's expression was at first surprised and then welcoming as she opened the door wide for him to enter.

"Thank you, Ruth." His gaze was warm upon her as he followed her inside.

"Is something wrong? Is that why you've come?" She was concerned, for Ben rarely paid a visit except for their traditional Sunday afternoons.

"No, absolutely nothing is wrong. I was just trying to get in contact with Matthew. I stopped at the Red Lion and spoke with his brother. He told me Matthew might be here. . . ."

"He's not here right now, but I hope he and Faith will be back soon," she told him as they sat down in the parlor.

"Oh? Where did they go?"

"Oh, Ben, I have the most fabulous news!" she began excitedly, wanting to share her joy with him.

Her smile was so bright that Ben thought she suddenly looked years younger, much like she had when he'd first fallen in love with her all those years ago. There was a painful tightness in his chest and his smile faded at the memory.

"What news?" He could not imagine what had happened

to make her so happy.

"Matthew and Faith eloped last night. I expect them back any time now."

"They eloped?" He was confused. "But why? I thought the plans were already made. . . ."

"Things changed." She tried to explain as simply as she could. "Matthew had a falling out with his brother. He was moving out of the Red Lion and into another inn. He stopped here to tell Faith, and she suggested that they just forget all the plans and elope."

Ben knew a true moment of jealousy over the younger couple's happiness, and he wondered in a moment of bitterness why things couldn't work out that way for him.

"Isn't it wonderful?" Ruth was still talking.

"Yes . . . yes, it's wonderful," he replied gruffly.

"You're not happy about it?" She perceptively sensed that something was troubling him.

"Of course I am. There's nothing I want more than Faith's happiness," Ben said earnestly.

"Then why do I get the feeling that something is bothering you?"

"It's nothing," he denied.

Ruth lay her hand upon his arm as she leaned toward him to meet his gaze. "Ben?"

Their eyes met, and he quickly looked away. The motion seemed almost guilt-ridden and intrigued Ruth even more.

"Ben Hardwick, what is troubling you?" she pressed.

"I said nothing." He shrugged off her touch and hurriedly got to his feet. He knew if he allowed himself even the briefest of seconds to enjoy the closeness, all would be lost. "I came by to find Matthew. If he shows up early enough, tell him that I'm going to be at a meeting at the Green Dragon this afternoon around four and that he can meet me there."

"And if he's late?"

"If he gets back after that, tell him I'm pretty sure there's going to be a big rally tonight at the hall."

"Ben . . ." Ruth clutched at his arm as she rose to stand by him. "You don't think there's going to be trouble, do you?"

Instinctively, without conscious thought, he pressed his hand over hers reassuringly. "I hope not, Ruth. I hope not." As he realized what he was doing, he moved quickly away, breaking off the contact. "I've got to go."

She followed him to the door, and as he started outside, she said, "If you ever need me for anything, Ben, you know I'm here."

He nodded tersely, and then, shoving his hands in the pockets of his coat, he strode off down the street.

Geoffrey eyed Bartley skeptically. "You say there has been no further contact between Eve and Kincade?"

"No, m'lord," the servant replied quickly. "We have been watching them both very carefully. Mrs. Woodham has been seeing no one but you."

"Good," he replied with a self-satisfied grin. "Perhaps the rest of our work will prove unnecessary. . . ."

"Shall I stop the surveillance of Lord Kincade and his brother, sir?"

Geoffrey was silent for a long moment. Even though Bartley had just reported to him that Eve had not been seeing Kincade, he was still not completely convinced that nothing existed between the two of them.

"No," he finally answered, "don't cut it off yet."

"Yes, m'lord."

"What have you learned about the Kincades lately? Anything more regarding the possible connection with the dissidents?"

"Nothing directly," he reported less than enthusiastically. "However, Lord Noah Kincade did make a large cash deposit at the bank."

"Large? How large?" Geoffrey was instantly alert, and when Bartley quoted the sum, he was impressed. "Obviously they've just sold something or received a down payment of some kind. . . ." He frowned as he considered the news.

"Also, sir, it appears that the brother has moved permanently out of the Red Lion."

"He moved out?" This puzzled Geoffrey. "But why?"

"I don't know too much, sir. All I do know is that yesterday evening he hired a conveyance, had his trunks loaded, and went to the Hammond girl's house. She joined him then and they left town."

Geoffrey chuckled. "Ah, a tryst . . . Where did they go?"

Bartley looked a bit uncomfortable. "It seems to be more than a mere tryst, m'lord. My man just reported back to me this morning that he followed them last night to a small village church, where they were married."

"What?! He actually married the wench?"

"Yes, sir, and they spent the night at a small inn out in the country."

"So the rumor about a romance between Lord Matthew Kincade and this Hammond wench was true."

"Indeed."

"I find it totally appalling that a nobleman of his stature would feel the need to marry the chit. It's just amazing the depths to which some men sink in search of pleasure," Geoffrey scoffed.

"Indeed, m'lord," Bartley replied in dignified agreement with his master.

Geoffrey frowned. "It's a bit odd, don't you think, that a wealthy man like Matthew Kincade would elope with someone like this Hammond girl?"

"Odd, sir?"

"It had always been my feeling that the Kincade brothers were quite close. Why do you suppose the younger one felt the need to sneak off into the night to wed?"

"I'm sure I have no idea."

"The damned fool could have had her just for the taking. She's only a colonial. See what more you can find out about that. It intrigues me."

"I'll do that, sir."

"Anything else pertinent? No meetings with Graves or Adams to report? No secret rendezvous?"

"No, nothing."

"Fine. Continue to have them watched. Perhaps there is more to all this than we're discerning right now."

"As you wish, m'lord."

Faith leaned contentedly on Matthew's shoulder, a small smile playing about her lips. "You know, we never did make use of that bathwater. . . ."

Matt chuckled as he tightened his arm about her. "I don't know about you, but by the time I thought of it, the water was far too cold for my liking."

"I never gave the water a thought. I had other things of interest on my mind. . . ." She leaned closer and kissed his cheek.

"I did, too," he told her huskily, meeting her lips for a long, sensual exchange.

The fires of desire flamed to life anew, and Matt released Faith regretfully. He was still amazed by the power of his passion for her, and he knew it would not do to allow himself too many liberties with her here in the carriage.

"Matthew?" she asked. Her expression was petulant as she looked up at him, and her lips were pursed in an adorable pout, begging to be kissed.

"What?" He tried to ignore the stirring in his loins, and the voice inside him that urged him to kiss her again.

"Why did you stop kissing me?" she asked. She had come to thoroughly enjoy his lovemaking and could see no reason to deny themselves whatever intimacy they could share in the carriage. After all, they were married.

"Because it isn't proper," he managed in a strangled voice.

"But we are married, Matthew," she countered, pressing

321

against him.

"That's true, but . . ."

"Don't you want me anymore?" Her eyes were aglow with her own need for him, and he tore his gaze away from hers.

"Of course I want you."

"Then kiss me." Brazenly she shifted from her sitting position to lean across his lap facing him. "Please?"

"Oh, Faith . . ." He gave up his fight and kissed her.

In victory, Faith smiled to herself as she unbuttoned his coat and slipped her hands within to touch his chest.

"Faith! Don't . . . stop that. . . ." Matt came up gasping for air as he tried to remove her hands from beneath his coat.

"I thought you liked me to touch you. . . ." she challenged.

"You know I do." His answer was a growl.

"We have lots of time. . . ." She glanced out the window at the passing countryside.

"We do?"

She nodded, and the coy look she gave him broke down his last barrier of resistance. Hungrily, his mouth sought hers and he quickly busied himself with unbuttoning her cloak. Faith gave a low-throated purr as his hands caressed her through the fabric of her gown.

"I never knew being married could be so delightful, husband," she told him huskily as she linked her arms about his neck.

"I didn't either," Matt replied.

When the carriage finally rolled to a stop in front of the Hammond house a long time later, they were resting most happily in each other's arms.

"We're here, love," Matt told her as he brushed her hair aside and pressed a soft, thrilling kiss to her neck.

"I know," she murmured almost sadly. She had wanted this time of enchantment to last forever, and she was afraid that returning to the reality of life would ruin what they had.

Matt descended from the carriage as soon as the driver opened the door for them. After paying him the substantial amount he owed, Matt helped Faith down and escorted her inside, leaving the driver to follow with their things.

"Mother? We're back. . . ." Faith called out, her happiness evident in her voice as they entered the house.

"Faith? Matthew? You're back already. . . ." Ruth came forth from the parlor eagerly to greet them. After kissing and hugging them both, she asked, "Did everything go well?"

"Perfectly, Mother. Matthew and I are now married."

At that, Ruth hugged her again as her gaze met Matthew's with love and respect. "I'm so happy for the both of you."

"Thank you."

The driver came in then laden with their things, and while Faith showed him where to put everything, Ruth drew Matt aside.

"Ben came by looking for you earlier today."

"Ben?" Matthew frowned. He had managed for the past twelve hours to put all thoughts of the growing unrest from his mind, but now he was back and nothing had changed. "Has something happened? Did he say?"

"He wanted you to know that there's an important meeting of some kind at the Green Dragon Inn at four o'clock this afternoon. I was supposed to tell you that you could meet him there."

"I'd better go." Matt was reluctant to leave Faith so soon.

"Go where?" Faith asked as she rejoined them after showing the driver out.

"Ben sent word that there's a meeting this afternoon at four," he explained.

"Don't you want to go?" She noticed his lack of enthusiasm.

"It's not so much a matter of not wanting to go as it's a matter of not wanting to leave you."

"You're only going to a meeting, Matthew." Faith came to him and put her arms around him. "I'm sure you'll be back in time for dinner. Go on. It's almost three already. You know they need you."

323

He lifted her chin and kissed her quickly, uncaring that Ruth looked on. "I'll go, but believe me, there's no place I'd rather be than here with you."

She smiled up at him warmly. "I know."

It was near dusk as Noah grimly approached the Hammond house. He had spent the better part of the day on board the *Lorelei,* but even as he'd busied himself there, his thoughts had been of Matthew and their bitter parting the night before. Logically, he knew it was probably the best thing. For his business's sake, he could risk no overt connection to the rebels. Still, it troubled him that Matthew had left without taking his share of the money, and Noah was determined that he should have sufficient funds. He had deposited half of the rebel advance in a reputable bank in Matthew's name and was on his way to the Hammonds now to leave word that the money was available for him.

"Noah!" Faith was surprised to find her new brother-in-law standing on her doorstep when she opened the door.

"Hello, Faith." Noah was unsure of his welcome and so kept his tone cool.

"Please, come in," she invited warmly, holding the door wider for him to enter.

"No. Really, that's not necessary. I just came by to leave a message for Matthew. I don't know where he's taken up residence yet and—"

Before he could say any more, Faith cut him off. "He's taken up residence here, Noah. Please, come in. You can give him the message yourself, for he got home a short while ago."

Noah looked decidedly uncomfortable to learn that Matthew had moved in with Faith and her mother, and he hesitated to take her up on her invitation.

"Noah, Matthew and I were married last night."

"What?"

"Please come in and we'll explain everything." At her continued insistence, Noah entered the house. "He's in our bedroom. Make yourself comfortable in the parlor while I go tell him that you're here."

Faith hurried down the short hall to her room at the back of the house.

"Matthew . . ." She entered their room without knocking and stopped dead still.

"What do you think?" he asked with a lopsided grin as he turned to face her from the washstand where he stood.

His face was covered with a mixture of soot and red Indian war paint, and about his head he wore a headband adorned with several feathers that stuck up at a rather rakish angle. He wore dark, nondescript clothing and had a blanket thrown about his shoulders.

"Dear Lord, what are you doing?" Faith demanded after she regained her composure.

"It's part of a plan."

"What plan?"

"The leaders have sent one last demand to the governor requesting that he send the ships back without unloading the tea. If he agrees, there will be no problem, but if he refuses . . ."

"If he refuses, what?" Faith was growing worried. She had no desire to lose her husband as she had lost her father.

"If he refuses, then we will take care of the tea ourselves."

"Matthew . . . couldn't this be dangerous?"

He shrugged, and then, understanding her fears, he came to her to take her in his arms. "Don't worry. Nothing is going to happen to me. Who knows? If the governor comes to his senses, we may not even have to act. Now, what was it you wanted when you came into the room? You seemed rather excited about something."

"Oh . . . I almost forgot." She drew back. "Noah is here to see you."

"Noah?" Now it was Matt's turn to be surprised. "I hadn't

thought. . . . He's actually here?" At her answering nod, he strode quickly from the room in search of his brother. "Noah?"

Noah was standing near the window when he heard Matthew approaching. As he turned to greet him, he was totally unprepared for the sight of Matthew dressed as an Indian, and the shock was evident on his face.

"What the . . ." Only Faith's presence behind him stopped him from swearing.

"Faith said you wanted to see me?" Matt asked, his expression guarded. He was not sure why Noah had come, and he was not about to act as though nothing had happened between them.

"Yes, I have something of importance to tell you, but first, what are you doing dressed like that?"

"Since you desire no further contact with the rebels, I suggest you not ask." As his brother scowled, Matt asked again, "Now, you were saying?"

Off balance and decidedly uncomfortable, Noah replied tersely, "Yes. Here." He handed him the small portfolio.

"What are these?" Matt glanced from Noah to the papers.

"I deposited your share of the funds in your name. Those are the papers."

"I told you how I felt about the money, Noah," Matt said flatly.

"I know, but I would never refuse you what's rightfully yours," he answered.

Matthew regarded him solemnly. "Thank you."

Noah could only nod. "I understand that congratulations are in order?"

"Yes, Faith and I decided that there was no point in waiting any longer. We were married last night."

"I'm sorry that I missed the ceremony, but I want you to know that I wish you the best."

"Thank you, Noah." Faith went to him. "I know that means a lot to Matthew." She looked from brother to brother. "I think I'll leave you two alone now. Noah, it was good to see you again. Please, come back."

When she had gone Noah glanced at Matt again. "You're not getting caught up in anything foolish, are you? I don't want you taking unnecessary chances. We both know that things could get violent at any time now."

"As I said—"

"I know what you said," Noah exploded, "and you know how I feel about you risking your life and limb. For God's sake, man, you have a wife now!"

"I'm very aware of that," Matt replied heatedly, "but this is something that has to be done. Even CC feels that way."

"CC?" Noah froze at the mention of her name. "What has CC got to do with this?"

"She's involved, just as I am."

"Involved in what?"

Matt closed the distance between them. "There's going to be a rally tonight at six o'clock at Faneuil Hall. Word has been sent to the governor that we want the three ships returned to England with their cargo intact. If he agrees to ship the tea back, then everyone goes home, but . . ."

"But what?" Noah ground out in annoyance. He wasn't quite sure why he felt a driving need to know what was going to happen; he just knew that he had to find out.

Matthew hesitated only briefly before telling him all of what was planned. "If word comes back that the governor has refused, then we're going to take care of the tea ourselves."

"What do you mean?"

"I mean, we're going to go on board the ship and dump it in the harbor."

"That's outrageous!"

"Yes, it is, isn't it?" Matthew smiled quixotically. "But when we get done, Parliament will know that we're serious."

"Matthew . . ." He wanted to convince his brother that it was foolhardy to try such a stunt.

"Don't say it, Noah. This is my decision. This is something I have to do."

"But there are troops everywhere. . . . There might be trouble. . . ."

"We have to take a stand. It's time to let them know that we will no longer tolerate their continued interference in our business."

"And CC is in on this?" The thought that CC might get caught up in a potentially dangerous situation left him rigid with sudden fear for her safety.

Matt read his concern for CC and was inwardly pleased. "She was at the meeting and seemed most determined to participate."

"Didn't Graves try to stop her?"

"Why? Are you worried about her?" he probed.

"She's a woman, damn it!" he snapped as his brother touched a nerve.

"A very capable woman," Matt supplied. "She's proven herself before; there was no reason to doubt her now. Besides, nothing bad is going to happen."

"I wish I had your confidence. . . ." Noah muttered, troubled.

"Join us, Noah," Matt suddenly implored. "You know we're right about things. Come with me."

"No," he snapped, striding toward the door. "You know how I feel about this."

"And you know how I feel." They faced each other one last time before Noah slammed from the house.

"Matthew?" Faith called. "Did Noah leave?"

"Yes." His answer was curt, and she felt disheartened to know that they had come to no reconciliation.

"Did you talk?"

"It did no good. I should have known. . . ." Matt looked down at her and his sadness was evident.

"I'm sorry." She touched his arm sympathetically.

"So am I, love. So am I."

Noah was furious and frustrated as he entered the

taproom of the Red Lion. Even Polly was surprised by his surly mood, and she hastened to do his bidding lest she feel the bite of his jagged temper.

Bound to inaction by decisions of his own choosing, Noah sat alone as he downed his ale in a few deep drinks and then called for another. The next heady brew followed its predecessor as Noah's thoughts churned with anxiety over what might happen this night. He was concerned about Matt, but he knew Matt was a man, and most capable of taking care of himself. What concerned him most was CC's safety, and just the fact that he found himself worrying about her infuriated him. What did it matter if she got herself killed? Why should he care that she was doing something so potentially dangerous? The questions bombarded him endlessly as he consumed ale after ale, and still Noah refused to examine his true feelings to find the answers. He didn't want to worry about CC or care about her, yet there could be no denying that he did.

The conflict built within him until the sound of the clock striking six—the scheduled time of the meeting—drove him to his feet. Enraged, knowing that he could not sit idly by and let CC possibly come to harm, he drained the last of his brew and sought out Polly.

"I need a horse," he told her brusquely. "Who should I see?"

"A horse, m'lord? Wouldn't you prefer a carriage? The weather's not the best, you know." She was surprised by his unorthodox request.

Noah glanced outside and noticed that a light rain was falling. Still, despite the miserable weather, he insisted, "No. Tonight I need a mount."

"Then Jack's the one to see, sir. He's out back in the stable," Polly answered.

"Thanks."

Without another word Noah quit the room, his pace rushed as he feared he might be too late.

Chapter Twenty

The colonists, now over seven thousand strong, were crowded together in the Old South Meeting Hall. Their number had proved far too great for them to remain at Faneuil Hall, and they had been forced to relocate to the larger building. Eagerly now, they listened to the speeches calling for justice as they awaited the governor's answer to their request that the tea be returned to England.

Out of sight of the main assembly, the selected group of patriot "Indians" waited patiently for the secret signal they knew would be given if it became necessary for them to take action this night. Their spirits were high even though they were well aware that violence might result if a confrontation with the redcoats occurred. It was time to take a stand against the abuses of the Crown, and they knew it.

Matthew and Ben, both in their Indian garb, were near the rear of the group when Matt caught sight of CC standing alone off to the side. The camouflage of her costume was so good that at first he wasn't certain it was her. Hesitantly he left Ben's side and maneuvered closer, breaking into a wide smile as he finally recognized her beneath the heavily applied soot and paint.

"CC!" Matthew made his way to her side.

"Hello, Matthew." CC had known that he was to be

involved and was not surprised to see him.

"I must say, my dear, that you make the best-looking warrior I've ever seen," he told her in good humor as he noted her long braids and the single feather stuck in her headband.

"You're looking rather savage yourself," she returned with a tight laugh, the seriousness of what they were about to be involved in leaving her slightly on edge.

"Are you nervous?" Matt asked, hearing the tautness in her tone. Noah's concern had somehow become his concern.

"Just a bit," she replied honestly. "With so many warships in the harbor, you can't help but wonder what will happen if we do make the attempt. . . ."

"Perhaps you should stay behind. . . ." He was hoping that he might be able to convince her to stay back where it was safe, but as soon as he uttered the words, he knew he'd made a mistake.

Fire flashing from the emerald depths of her eyes, she turned on him. "Matthew, I had thought you were different . . . that you understood. Don't you realize how long and how hard I've fought for just this moment? I have to be a part of this!"

He was about to respond when a sudden hush fell over their group, and they caught sight of Sam Adams climbing atop a bench at the front of the hall. The crowd went silent as everyone waited breathlessly to hear his announcement.

"This meeting can do nothing more to save the country."

Adams's phrase was the signal they'd been waiting for, and the response was wild as the crowd poured forth from the hall, heading in the direction of Griffin's Wharf and the three tea-laden British ships.

Captain Pitt assumed direction of the "Indians" and divided them into three distinct groups, each one being responsible for a different ship. Caught up in the excitement of the moment, there was no time for CC and Matthew to talk further as the eager disguised patriots started off toward the wharf.

Riding as quickly as conditions would permit, Noah raced over the narrow, winding, rainslick streets on the mount he'd gotten at the inn. The considerable amount of liquor he'd consumed had erased his usual stoic control over his emotions, and he was frantic to find CC. Noah's thoughts were only of her sweetness and the possible danger she was facing. He knew he had to do something to protect her, if not from the troops, then from herself. When at last he rounded the corner and spied Faneuil Hall ahead, he was surprised to discover that it was deserted.

"Where's the rally?" Noah called to a small group of men still lingering near the entrance as he sawed on the reins to bring his horse under better control.

"Moved to the Old South Meeting," one returned.

"Thanks." Putting his heels to the horse's flanks and giving it full head, he was off again.

The light, chilling drizzle had ceased, and the moonlight, pale and bright, broke through the remaining low cloud cover as Noah finally reached his destination. The crowd was streaming out into the street, and it was only with great difficulty that he managed to keep his mount under control. Desperately searching for some sign of CC, he attempted to wind his way through the crush of bodies. His expression was thunderous as he scanned the huge crowd.

"The Indians . . . where are the Indians?" Noah knew he was taking a chance to ask.

"They're up ahead," someone shouted back.

With iron-handed control, Noah urged the horse forward, paying little heed to the people who were forced aside to make room for him to pass. His quest seemed endless as he fought his way through the crowd, his silver gaze combing the multitude for CC's slender form. He moved ever onward, oblivious to anything but the driving need to find her. Griffin's Wharf came into distant view, and the fear that he might not reach her in time filled him. It was then, just as his

332

frustration reached its zenith, that he spotted the Indians emerging from a side street slightly ahead of him.

"CC!" He roared, kneeing his mount on at a more hurried pace.

CC had stayed close to her group through the entire trek to the wharf, but when she heard someone call her name, she stopped to look back. The sight of a horseman charging her way through the mass of people paralyzed her with fear. Who knew she was here besides those directly involved? No one, she thought, unless her father had decided to check up on her story of being at Marianna's house tonight for dinner. The knowledge that her hesitation had revealed her true identity sent her on a run back down the side street in hopes of eluding her unknown pursuer.

For one heart-stopping moment Noah lost sight of her, and he was forced to rein in near the intersection to search the crowd for her again. It was through sheer luck that he glanced back the way the Indians had come and saw her fleeing through the shadows of the narrow side street. Furious with CC for involving herself in something so potentially dangerous, he gave a vicious curse and wheeled his mount around. Leaving the excitement of the wharf behind, he galloped after her down the nearly deserted lane.

CC had hoped to escape the man who was following her, but the thundering of horse's hooves coming in her direction made her realize that he was still behind her. Dread filled her. The blanket she'd worn was slowing her movements, so CC threw it off as she ran desperately on, blindly seeking refuge down another, more narrow, alleyway. Her ragged breath scalding her throat, her limbs quaking under the strain of her flight, she darted through the darkness.

Any other horseman might have had difficulty following her, but Noah was an experienced equestrian who'd spent many hours riding to the hounds in England. Compared to the chase given a fox across the open countryside, CC presented little challenge to him. Swooping down the alleyway, he charged up beside CC. Without slowing his pace, Noah leaned to the side and scooped her up with one arm, pinning her effectively against his side. Only then did he pull back on the reins and slow his horse's breakneck pace. Panicked, CC fought with all her might against the steely strength that held her.

"Let me go!" Wriggling and kicking, she struggled to be free. When one of her kicks struck the horse the wrong way, causing him to move skittishly, she froze, thinking she was about to be thrown. In the tense moment, the strong arm about her waist tightened threateningly.

"I wouldn't do that again if I were you, CC," Noah growled in her ear. "I'm not all that familiar with this horse, and if he decides to bolt, we both might find ourselves in the mud."

"Noah!!" she exclaimed in fury and surprise as she finally recognized his voice. Quieting, she twisted partially around to look at him. "What are you doing?!"

"Right now?" He raised one dark brow mockingly. "Well, right now, my dear, I'm rescuing you before you get yourself involved in something you might not be able to handle."

His arrogant, self-assured words infuriated her. "How dare you!? Just who do you think you are?" Her temper was seething.

Noah didn't bother to reply as he grasped her more firmly and shifted her to sit in front of him. To hide her costume from any possible prying eyes, he pulled her close and wrapped his greatcoat around her. The feel of her slight weight resting against him filled Noah with an odd sense of rightness, and a small smile curved his mouth for just an instant before her next sharp words penetrated his liquor-induced haze.

"What do you think you're doing? Let me down!" CC tried to push free of his grip.

"Shut up, CC," he told her in an emotionless tone as he fought down the warm feelings that had stirred to life. He could tell by her outrage that it would do little good to try to explain his motives in coming for her. She hated him now, just as she always had, and he had no doubt that his behavior had only hardened her already firm resolve not to have anything to do with him.

"I will not!" She struggled against Noah's overpowering strength with all her might and almost succeeded in getting herself dumped from the horse as it shifted nervously beneath them.

"CC!" He said her name threateningly through gritted teeth as he fought to keep his hold on her and to bring the horse under control.

Knowing that she could not break free, CC suddenly found herself panicking for a different reason as his hand slid familiarly about her midriff to pinion her protectively against his chest. Excitement, burning and breathless, streaked through her at his touch. It shocked her that her senses were responding so wantonly, for this was no sensual embrace. Noah was not trying to arouse her. CC was determined that he would not learn of her weakness, and she responded with false bravado.

"I don't want to go anywhere with you, Kincade. If you don't let me down this instant, I'll scream!" she hissed as she glared up at him.

Warning Noah of her intent was CC's biggest mistake, for he reacted quickly, clamping a hand over her mouth and stifling even the smallest of her objections.

"I am in no mood to listen to your viperish tongue," he ground out as he guided the horse through the maze of streets, heading in the opposite direction of the wharf. "I'm getting us both out of here before the trouble starts."

CC was humiliated by his move, and her fury knew no bounds and she began to fight him again. Still, his superior strength prevailed and he held her immobile. Realizing that it was impossible to free herself, CC gave up her efforts.

As they continued to ride on into the night, CC tried to

control the wild emotions that were plaguing her. She loved Noah. She wanted to relax comfortably against him and enjoy riding within the warm circle of his arms. She longed to press herself intimately against the solid heat of his chest and listen to the strong, reassuring beat of his heart. Romantically, CC realized that Noah had come for her, that he had swept her up on his steed and had carried her off . . . just like Anna had imagined all those weeks ago.

It was the thought of her maid that brought CC back to the present, and she found herself amazed by the direction of her thoughts. Mentally she berated herself for being ridiculous. She understood and had accepted that Noah didn't really care about her. CC knew it would do no good for her to pretend otherwise. He desired her as he desired any woman, and being the virile man that he was, he would take her if the occasion presented itself. Beyond that, she was certain Noah harbored no deep-seated affection for her. When they had argued that night in the carriage after having made love, Noah had seemed quite relieved when she'd declared that she felt no attachment to him. CC could still remember his mocking response to her statement that she didn't even like him, and even now the memory of his disdainful attitude hurt.

The few kisses they'd shared the night she'd taken him the payment from Graves had been nothing more than a momentary slip of willpower on her part. He had made the overture and she had not denied him. CC knew that she had no one to blame but herself for that encounter, and she was still thankful that Matthew had interrupted them in time. The only way she could save herself from another intimate encounter with him was to get away as quickly as she could. Holding herself rigid, she strove to keep herself aloof from Noah and from the feelings of desire that were surging through her.

When Noah felt CC stop struggling, he knew it was a partial surrender. He was used to her fighting him every inch of the way, and in his drunken haze, he felt inordinately pleased with himself that he had at least mastered her that much.

"If you promise not to scream, I'll take my hand away," he told her in a low voice. "Nod if you agree to be quiet."

Quickly CC nodded, and she sighed in relief as he took his hand away from her mouth. "Where are you taking me?"

"Out of harm's way," Noah answered shortly, not really having an answer. He had not considered before *where* he would take her once he had her away from the scene. He had only known that he had to find her. Now, faced with the dilemma, he glanced about, trying to gauge their location. Finding that they were near the Green Dragon Inn, he headed in that direction. He felt relatively certain that it would be deserted now, for most of its patrons were probably involved in all the excitement at the wharf.

They rode on in strained silence to the inn. Noah guided the horse around to the stables at the back and halted near the stable door. As he had suspected, there was no one in attendance. Reluctantly releasing his hold on CC, Noah swung down from the saddle and quickly helped her to dismount. His hand at her waist, he aided her descent, her body sliding intimately against his as he lowered her to the ground.

The damp, sweet scent of hay and the cloaking darkness of the night poignantly brought to mind the last time they'd been here. Noah felt his blood quicken at the memory. He had not expected his reaction to the thought to be so powerful and so exciting, and he kept his gaze hooded as he looked down at her, his hands still possessively at her slim waist.

Even though he guarded his emotions from her, CC could feel the heat of his regard, and she knew she had to get away before she succumbed to her own desire for oneness with him. Her heart was pounding as she stared up at him. She wished frantically that he would release her, for the heat of their touch seemed to burn right through her clothing, stirring to life a brilliant wildfire of desire.

"I want to go," CC insisted, trying to move away from him.

"No." Refusing to free her, Noah tightened his grip, his fingers biting into the tender flesh.

"Why not?!" she hissed in frustration.

"Because I don't want you going back there and possibly endangering yourself. If violence should break out . . ." Noah's gray-eyed gaze glittered dangerously at the thought of her being caught up in the mass confusion of a riot and of how helpless she would be to defend herself.

"Your brother's there," she challenged, "and you didn't bother to rescue him!"

"Matthew's a man," Noah snapped. "He's perfectly capable of taking care of himself if things happen to get out of hand."

"And I'm not?"

"For God's sake, CC. You're a woman!"

"And just what is that supposed to mean?!" CC argued. Though her temper was hot, she was suddenly, sickeningly weary of constantly battling the male prejudice of her father and John and Noah.

"It means exactly what you think it means." Noah found himself growing furious with her again. "You're a woman, so why don't you take pride in the fact and act like one?!"

"I do act like a woman!" CC retorted, stung by his insinuation. But even as she protested, she was aware of the boy's clothing she wore, the feathers in her hair, and the paint and soot smeared upon her face.

"When? What day? What hour? I must have missed it." He was brutal in his angry assessment of her. Didn't she realize what could happen to her?

"How dare you say such things to me! And what business is it of yours anyway?"

"I dare because I believe in telling the truth," Noah told

her. Her words reminded him of the last time they'd argued over his interest in her business. It had been that night in the carriage . . . the night of their chance encounter. She'd been warm and willing then, if only for a short period of time.

"The truth as you see it!" CC countered quickly. Suddenly it no longer mattered to her that he didn't want her involved in political intrigue. What did matter was that he thought her less than feminine, and she was devastated by his bluntness. How could he say such a thing, when he, of all people, knew the true depth of her womanhood? Self-doubt assailed her. Had her lovemaking been so terrible? Had her inexperience bored him? Did he really think her mannish?

Her fragile femininity, under attack now by his brusque outspokenness, urged her to prove him wrong, to show him just how mistaken he was. Just because she didn't totally conform to the day's standards for females didn't mean that she was lacking in any way. She was a woman in all ways, and she was going to confirm it in Noah's mind right now. Never again would he doubt her.

Determined, she put the hurt aside and concentrated on changing his mind and bringing him to his knees. So he thought her less than feminine, did he? He wouldn't for long. A wicked gleam glinted in her emerald eyes. She knew enough about the tricks females employed to woo their men. Hadn't she listened to Marianna, Margaret, and Caroline? And hadn't she seen Eve Woodham in action at the various parties and balls? CC slanted him a steamy look from beneath half-lowered lashes.

"Noah . . . do you remember the last time we were here?" She made sure to add a sultry touch to her tone, and as she'd planned, her change of mood caught him by surprise.

"What? Yes, of course I do." Noah grew wary, wondering at her purpose. He had expected her to keep arguing, not change the subject.

CC knew how effective it was to keep a man slightly confused from having used the same technique on her father numerous times. "Do you remember how untimely our interruption was?" She purred the question as she edged closer to him, leaning lightly against his chest.

Desire, sweet and hot, burst into flame deep within his vitals as she slowly lifted her arms and linked them behind his neck. Noah was not quite sure what CC was about, and he wasn't going to ask. He remained unmoving.

CC moved fully against him then, wanting to tease him to action. "What would have happened, Noah, if we hadn't been interrupted the first night? Did you want me as badly as I wanted you?" Her voice was a throaty whisper as she rose up on tiptoes to press her lips to his, and she felt him stiffen in surprise. CC wasn't sure if it was the kiss or her words that had affected him, and she didn't care. All she wanted was to prove to him that she was woman . . . all woman.

His last remaining shred of control shattered as her small tongue darted between his lips, seeking his in a deeply seductive kiss. A low groan escaped him as he gave in to his desires, his hands slipping from her waist to move restlessly across her hips and spine. His lips met hers time and again as CC aggressively sought his mouth. Past and present blended in his mind as she taunted him with her heady love, moving her lips in restless invitation against his.

Noah realized distractedly that CC was his heaven and his hell. She had caused him more worry and aggravation than any other woman in his entire life. She had involved herself in his business, declared her dislike for him more times than he could remember, and then made love to him with passionate abandon. He was obsessed with her . . . with the glory of her touch, the taste of her intoxicating kisses, and the unbelievable rapture that came with making love to her. Nothing had ever affected him more deeply than being one with her. Noah longed to know that joy again, to be sheathed within the hot, silken core of her body.

The thought that one day he would have to leave her threatened, but he banished it from his thoughts. Suddenly there was no tomorrow, no revolution, and no Kincade Hall awaiting his reclamation. There was only the moment and CC, at last desiring him as much as he desired her.

When he had made the cruel remark to CC about her lack of womanhood, he had done it, not to hurt her, but in hopes of discouraging any more unorthodox behavior on her part. Tonight he had been running around Boston like a madman, trying to find her and save her from possible danger. Noah didn't know precisely why he'd done it, he only knew that he had. He did not regret it, for, at moments like this when she was in his arms willingly, the drugging wine of her kisses was worth any price he had to pay.

"Noah . . . I didn't want that first night to end as it did." CC whispered his name in between kisses, teasing him with memories of that first passionate encounter they'd shared there in the barn. "Noah . . . please . . ."

Hungrily, she rose up and kissed him full and flaming on the mouth again as she slipped her hands beneath his greatcoat to begin unbuttoning his shirt. The buttons disposed of, she spread the material wide and caressed the bared strength of his chest, tangling her fingers through the coarse, dark curls that grew there and teasing his flat male nipples until he drew a sharp breath at the unexpected sensation.

"CC." Her name was a husky groan as the need to taste of her pleasure ignited to full-blown passion. Without conscious thought, he tightened his arms around her, relishing the sensation of having her crushed so tightly to him.

"Touch me, Noah. Know that I'm woman, as I know you're man." As she said it, she let her hands trail lower to trace the outline of his surging manhood through his breeches.

He tensed in sensual agony at her touch, his desire urging him to take her then, quickly and strongly. CC felt his reaction and smiled to herself. So he thought she was not feminine, did he? The realization that her one simple touch

341

could stir him so completely filled her wtih a great sense of her womanly power, and she was determined to exploit it to its fullest. She broke off the embrace, despite Noah's initial reluctance to end the kiss, and took his hand.

"Let's go inside, shall we?" There was nothing subtle about her invitation, and when she led the way into the empty, shadowed darkness of the stable, he followed without protest. CC glanced quickly about to make certain they were completely alone and then guided him to a pile of fresh hay. Feeling sure that they would not be interrupted, she dropped his hand and began to brazenly unbutton her own shirt.

Noah stood, enthralled, watching her disrobe. Never in his wildest imaginings had he expected such of CC. He found himself totally mesmerized by her movements as she shrugged the baggy boy's shirt off her shoulders and tossed it thoughtlessly aside. Suddenly CC was standing before him nude from the waist up, and his gaze riveted on the pale, creamy perfection of her breasts. He remembered how sensitive the pink-tipped mounds were, and he longed to caress their fullness, to weigh their softness in his palms and tease the rosy crests to peaks of excitement.

CC noted the direction of his heated regard, and she gave a small, languid stretch, running her hands up her rib cage to cup her breasts enticingly. All else faded into oblivion as Noah stared in fascination at her alluring posture. No mistress before her had ever done anything so completely erotic, and Noah was captivated as he watched her. Only when her hands moved lower again did he manage to tear his gaze away from her breasts.

CC knew that she was in control of the situation, and she gloried in her mastery. Loosening her breeches, she let them slide slowly, enticingly down over her rounded hips. When at last she stood before Noah completely nude, she lifted her eyes to his and read there in his devouring gaze all she wanted, and needed, to know. He desired her.

"You look like an Indian maiden," Noah managed hoarsely.

CC gave a husky laugh and asked lightly. "Not an Indian warrior?"

"Never an Indian warrior," he swore as he took the last step that separated them and swept her into his embrace. "You're woman, CC. All woman. And you're mine."

He said the last most fiercely, and CC was both stunned and thrilled by the declaration. When his mouth claimed hers in a deep exchange, she melted against him. Her body was on fire with the need to know him again, and she felt bereft when Noah released her briefly to remove his greatcoat. He spread the garment out on the pile of fresh hay and then lifted her into his arms to lay her upon it. CC found the sensation of her nakedness next to his still-clothed form highly erotic. He seemed so strong, so masculine. . . . She wanted to remain in his arms forever.

"Love me, Noah. Please, love me." For the first time, she voiced her own needs.

Noah's gaze was dark with passion as he moved slightly away to undress, and he regretted the time it took him to shed his clothing. CC watched hungrily as he stripped off his shirt. She longed to run her hands over his hard-muscled back and shoulders. The rest of his clothes soon followed, and her gaze was eagerly upon him . . . the slim line of his hips, the long, straight power of his legs, and the surging proof of his desire for her.

"Noah . . ." CC breathed his name as she lifted her arms to him in invitation.

He didn't speak but went into her arms without hesitation, clasping her slim, silken softness to his hard male frame. CC gasped at the sensation as his lean strength seemed to brand her with its searing heat.

Everywhere they touched they were different. Where she was smooth, he was hair-roughened; where he was muscle,

343

firm and powerful, she was soft and yielding. Yet, even as they were not alike, they complemented each other. His every masculine angle seemed to fit perfectly to her tempting feminine curves.

His mouth sought hers in a heated exchange as his hands began a restless exploration of her most secret pleasure points. CC was not about to let him take complete control of their lovemaking, though. Aggressively, she sought to please him. Remembering Noah's excited reaction to her earlier caress, she reached between them to fondle him boldly, stroking his throbbing hardness with knowing intent.

"Ah, CC . . ." Noah shuddered as she caressed him, and fearful that he might embarrass himself if he let her continue, he reached down to grasp her wrist and move her hand away. "Enough . . . I want to love you, sweet."

"Yes . . . oh, yes."

CC was ready for him—she had been almost since the beginning. She parted her thighs to his questing touch, knowing the joy his caress could bring and wanting to experience that joy again. She shuddered in ecstasy as his hand explored her pleasure point with a knowing rhythm, bringing her close, ever so close, yet denying her that last thrilling release.

"Noah . . . please . . . I need you now . . ." she begged, pulling him closer.

Noah understood her desperation, for his own desires were running wild as he felt the wet heat of her need. Positioning himself between her legs, he sought her womanly delights, moving slowly forward until he was buried within the silken heart of her. Her velvet flesh held him tightly, and the sensation almost sent his desire spiraling completely out of control.

Noah wanted to wait, to enjoy the feeling of just being a part of her, but CC's own passion would not be denied. Knowingly, she moved her hips against his, urging him to begin, and he could no longer hold back. He thrust within her avidly as he continued to caress and kiss her. CC clasped him to her heart, wrapping her legs about his driving hips and holding him ever closer. His hands were everywhere, cupping, molding, teasing, and she grew mindlessly enraptured. She was his, body and soul.

"Noah . . . oh, love . . . I need you so. . . ." CC cried as ecstasy of her excitement peaked in a blaze of throbbing desire.

CC tensed exquisitely as the waves of rapture pulsed through her. Moments later, when she felt Noah shudder in his own ultimate pleasure, she held him close, feeling triumphant in knowing that she had been able to satisfy him as completely as he'd satisfied her.

They lay together in peaceful serenity, savoring the bliss of their closeness. What had begun as a taunting seduction on CC's part had ended in enchantment for both of them. Noah had never known lovemaking so beautiful, so giving, and he wanted to cling to the preciousness of the moment, to capture it and save it forever.

Slowly Noah raised up above her, and bracing himself on his forearms, he stared down at her. How could it be that this woman had such a hold on his emotions? He didn't understand it, and right now he didn't even want to think about it.

"CC . . ." he said softly, "you feel so perfect to me. . . ."

"Oh, Noah . . ." She blushed at his description and looped her arms about his neck to pull him down for a sweet, gentle kiss. "You feel good to me, too."

His lips left hers to explore the sensitive flesh of her throat, and CC felt shivers of delight course through her.

"You know, we could stay like this all night. . . ." he murmured. Moving even lower, he caught the taut crest of one breast gently between his teeth and nipped at it in a pain-pleasure caress that left her clutching weakly at his shoulders.

"Noah . . . don't . . . oh, Noah . . ." CC threw her head

back, arching her breasts to him, wanting more even as she was frightened by her abandoned response to his sensual punishment.

What slight pain there had been turned to ecstasy as he drew the tender bud into his mouth and sucked gently.

"There's nothing I want more than to hold you and please you. . . ." he swore against the soft flesh of her breast.

His lips and tongue were doing such marvelous things to her that she began to move restlessly beneath him. He stoked the glowing embers of her need to life again, creating a whirlpool of desire that swept her up in its power. CC hadn't meant to say it, had never wanted to reveal the truth of her need for him, but in a moment of mindless delight, she cried out to him, "Please, Noah . . . don't ever leave me. . . ."

Noah stiffened at her words, and though he wanted to promise that he would stay with her forever, he knew it would be a lie. No matter how much he wanted her, no matter how much he craved the ecstasy of her lovemaking, he could not stay. Everything that was important to him was in England, and that was where he belonged.

When the heights of her ecstasy had passed, CC lay sobbing in his arms. His mastering of her senses had been complete, and she felt weak and well loved.

"Oh, Noah." Gazing up at him, she sighed, the love she felt for him shining in the emerald depths of her eyes. "Being with you is so wonderful, I wish we never had to part."

"I'm afraid that's not possible, my dear." His tone was almost aloof as he shifted away from her.

The moment of true intimacy was shattered by his coolness, and CC stiffened, suddenly wary of him.

"You don't want me?" she challenged.

"Of course I want you," Noah replied quickly, his gaze raking with scalding intent over her slender, supple form. He knew that it would be senseless to try to deny it after the passion they'd just shared.

"Then I don't understand," she frowned, trying to figure

out exactly what he meant.

Noah suddenly realized that the rest of his life seemed empty without CC, and he knew he couldn't possibly leave her when it came time for him to sail. He wanted her. He needed her. Noah thought of what a beautiful Lady Kincade she would make and how she would grace Kincade Hall, and he knew then that he wanted her to be his wife. CC would be perfect at his side. She was gorgeous, far more attractive than any of the women about the *ton*. She would do the Kincade name justice, and her father's reputation would put her in good stead with his peers, colonial or not.

"CC, you know that I'll be going back to England in the spring." He met her gaze seriously. "Marry me and return with me."

CC stared at him for a long moment in speechless disbelief. He had just proposed. It was what she had dreamed of, and yet, even as he had offered her marriage, he had made no mention of loving her. She had seen marriages undertaken without love, and they had seemed torturous for all parties involved. As much as she loved him, she knew it would be useless.

"No, Noah, I can't." It broke her heart to refuse.

Her refusal stunned him. He had never proposed to a woman before, and he had never expected her to turn him down. Anger surged through him.

"Why not? Is it this damned cause you're so involved in? Walk away and leave it! As Lady Kincade, you would take London by storm. . . ." he offered, not imagining the real reason for her rejection.

"Noah . . ." She spoke his name miserably as she waited for him to say the words that would win her heart and her undying love, but they never came.

"I could give you everything you've ever wanted. . . ." Noah went on, thinking that the promise of riches would win her.

"I have everything I've ever wanted, thank you!" CC grew

livid. He was making her sound just like a kept woman!

"But, CC, I could take care of you and protect you. . . ." He was, after all, Lord Kincade, Noah thought with more than a little pomposity.

Her fury knew no bounds! So he wanted to take care of her and protect her, did he?! He was just like John, only worse! John at least had professed to love her! Noah had told her only that he wanted her, nothing more. No doubt he wanted her only to be an ornament for him to put on display . . . to grace his life, to decorate his hall, and to warm his bed. He wanted her to become a mindless, simpering nothing, just like all the other aristocrats she'd ever met, and she wouldn't do it.

"I don't need you or anyone else to take care of me!" CC was seething as she moved jerkily away, standing up and beginning to pull on her clothing.

Her abrupt anger startled him and he stared at her in confusion, trying to understand her reaction to his words. "It's certain that you need *someone* to take care of you!"

CC regarded him sadly. His command of her senses had been total. His possession of her body had been powerful and exciting. Still, for all the wonder of having shared the delights of loving him, there had been no meeting of their hearts. It had only been their bodies that had touched, and CC found, to her despair, that she could not separate the two. What touched her physically also touched her emotionally. If she loved with her body, she also loved with her mind.

Noah, she understood painfully, made no such distinction. While their passionate mating had only succeeded in deepening what she already felt for him, it had only been another sexual encounter for him. She had thrown herself at him, and he had taken what she offered. The thought thoroughly distressed her, and she knew she had to get away from him.

"Since it's obvious that you hold such a low opinion of

me, I see no reason for us to have any further contact," she told him coldly as she quickly tugged on her breeches. "From now on, stay completely away from me."

Noah, still dumbstruck by her manner, could only stare at her in mute surprise. Mistaking his silence as threatening, CC wheeled about to glare at him.

"I mean it, Noah. I don't ever want to speak with you or see you again if we can avoid it; do you understand? Whatever it was we shared, and I hesitate to call what happened between us a love affair, it's over. . . . You've always known how I felt about you. Why did you think I'd changed?"

"I didn't know that it was normal for a woman to make love to a man she despises." Noah's gaze turned steely as he regarded her.

"As I said a long time ago, what happens between us defies explanation. That's precisely why I want you to stay away from me."

"Believe me, my dear Miss Demorest, it will be my pleasure to avoid your chaotic company."

CC slipped into her shirt and quickly buttoned it as Noah began pulling on his own breeches. He was still only partially dressed when she started from the stable.

"CC . . . where are you going?"

Her gaze glittered in furious defiance. "I told you before, Kincade, I don't need or want your protection!"

With that she disappeared out of the building and into the chill of the December night.

Chapter Twenty-One

Noah was shrugging into his frock coat when the knock came at his door. "Who is it?"

"It's Marty from the *Lorelei,* m'lord," the young cabin boy answered respectfully. "I've got a message for you from Captain Russell. He says it's important."

"Come in, Marty," Noah called out, glancing toward the door as the youngster came inside.

"Thank you, Lord Kincade." Marty, a small, skinny lad raised in the slums of England, was in awe of Noah, and he bobbed a nervous nod in his direction. He found the fact that he was even speaking to the nobleman amazing, and he was determined to do a good job of it.

"What is it Captain Russell felt was so important?" he asked, picking up his greatcoat, ready to depart as soon as their conversation was at an end.

"He said to tell you that the *Sea Pride* has been sighted and that she should make port within three days."

Noah smiled widely in confident satisfaction. "That's excellent news, and I appreciate your delivering it to me, Marty."

"Yes, m'lord."

"Take this for your trouble and tell your good captain that I will be speaking with him very soon." Noah handed the boy a coin and then saw him to the door.

"I'll do that, sir, and thank you."

When the young man had gone, Noah moved back to the washstand to check his appearance one last time in the small mirror there. Satisfied that he looked his best, he donned his greatcoat and started on his way to the Hammond house. Noah had been invited to dinner tonight in honor of Matt's birthday, and now it looked as if they had even more to celebrate. Within a matter of days his negotiations would be completed, and he'd be well on his way to rebuilding their lost fortune.

Noah's spirits were high when he arrived at their home, and he was welcomed warmly by Faith, Matthew, and Ruth. The meal was enjoyable and the conversation flowed easily as he and Matt both chose to avoid the issues that caused problems between them.

"I have news that will be of interest to you, Matthew," Noah finally told him as they retired, alone, to the parlor after dinner.

"Oh?"

"Just as I was leaving the inn to come here tonight I received word that the *Pride* has been sighted and is within three days of port."

Matthew was pleased but solemn as he answered, "It's not a moment too soon, considering what's probably going to happen."

"What do you mean?"

"Since the 'tea party' last week, rumors have been flying that there definitely will be reprisals against us. Dispatches carrying the news of our actions are already on their way back to Parliament."

"Do you have any idea what might be done?"

"It's hard to say. Whatever happens, the colonists . . ." Matthew paused, realizing that he could no longer talk about the revolutionaries from an outsider's standpoint, for he was one of them now. *"We're* not going to stand for it."

A sardonic smile curved Noah's mouth. "That's quite a change from the argument you gave me in the beginning about how I was betraying my country by selling war supplies to the insurgents."

Matt knew he should be angered by his brother's sarcastic comment, but he chose to ignore it. "Yes, I suppose it is," he agreed, "but I've learned a lot since then."

"Such as?" Noah had thought Matt might argue with him, and his brother's capitulation surprised him.

"Such as, a man must have justice if he is to survive."

"How noble," he replied.

"I'm not being noble, Noah," Matt stated sharply. "I'm being realistic. It's not fair for Parliament to try to keep such strict control over the growth and activities of the colonies. If the Crown decides to punish us for our attempts to put things to rights, then there will be trouble."

"And you're now willing to take up arms for that cause?"

"Yes. I am," he answered with firm conviction.

"I find it totally contradictory that you condemned me for selling the arms to the colonists, and yet now you're willing to make use of them yourself."

"I am willing to fight, because I truly believe in what I am fighting for." Matthew fixed him with a penetrating regard. "You, on the other hand, are making the sale out of a pure love of money, not for any finer moral principle. You profess to be loyal to the Crown, yet you show no hesitation in making a fast profit dealing in goods that will most assuredly be used against representatives of the very government you say holds your devotion. That was what I found distressing originally, and now that I know the truth of things here . . ."

Noah's gaze turned cold as he shrugged. "What is there about this movement that everyone is so ardent in its defense?"

"It's a matter of justice, Noah," Matt replied slowly.

"For you maybe, but not for me," he replied bluntly when Matt had finished speaking. "You know my only reason for coming to this Godforsaken land was to recoup our losses. I am not interested in your cause. My goal has not changed, and I see no point in discussing this. We have agreed to disagree. We each have different goals in our lives. I have come to accept yours. I would expect the same consideration from you."

"I don't like feeling that we're at odds with each other. I thought if you came to understand my . . . our point of view, it might help you to decide. . . ."

"Decide?" Noah looked at him in amazement.

Matt looked him straight in the eye as he answered, "Decide to join with me and work for the revolution."

"My life is in England, Matthew. You know that."

"But it doesn't have to be! You could live here. We could continue Kincade Shipping on a small scale and work right here, out of Boston."

"No."

"Don't you care about anything except reclaiming our 'lost' heritage? What about CC?"

"What about her?" He was suddenly on the defensive. He did not want to think about her or talk about her.

"I had thought that there was something between the two of you."

"You thought wrong," he answered harshly. "CC means nothing to me." Even as he said it, he knew it was a lie, for CC was the first and only woman he'd ever actually asked to become his wife. The memory of her refusal still had the power to hurt him. "Nor do the colonies."

His determined response quelled any hope Matt had of encouraging him to his own way of thinking, and he sighed deeply to himself, feeling more discouraged than ever.

"Now, back to the subject of business." Noah quickly dismissed the other discussion, not wanting to dwell any further on their differences. "Since it's not safe for me to make direct contact with Graves or Smith, I want you to send word to them that the shipment will be here probably by the week's end. I expect the balance due me delivered before I turn over the supplies."

"I'll tell him. Do you want CC to be the one to bring the payment to you at the inn again?"

"No!" Noah's answer was abrupt. He wanted to stay as far away from CC as he could. She was the last person in the world he wanted to see.

"No? Is there a problem?" Matt asked, wondering at his reaction.

Noah glowered at him. "No, there's no problem. I just think it's too dangerous for her to be involved. Have them think of another way to get the money to me, but I want to have it in hand before we go any further with this deal."

"All right," he answered, finding his brother's protectiveness of CC curious if, as he said, she meant nothing to him. "How do you plan to get the arms to them? Are you going to have them smuggled in?"

"Smuggling's no good. Demorest already knows that the *Pride* is due in port at any time and that she's carrying arms. I thought it would be more convincing if the goods were to be stolen off the ship while it's in the harbor. If the rebels were brazen enough to dump the tea, certainly they'd be willing to board a merchant ship carrying arms, don't you think?"

Matt nodded thoughtfully. "We'll just have to be very careful. Violence was avoided when we dumped the tea, and I want to make sure there's not any trouble when the arms are taken."

"I don't foresee any problems." Noah was confident that his idea would work. When all was said and done, he and Matthew would come out of it looking the innocent victims. "Just tell them to get the money to me, and I'll take care of the rest."

The women rejoined them then, and the conversation drifted to other things. Noah brought up the subject of the party to be held the following evening at Major Winthrop's home.

354

"We received the invitation before your elopement. Do you plan on attending?" Noah asked.

Matthew stiffened perceptibly at the thought of attending a ball in the home of the man who'd made so light of the attack on Faith. "Please extend our regrets."

"You won't be going?"

"I wouldn't grace Winthrop's funeral with my presence," Matt disdained. "I have little use for the man. He's an ass."

"I find your assessment most accurate," Noah commented dryly, "and would prefer to beg off myself, but image is everything at this point. I must show my loyalty to the Crown at every opportunity if the arrangement with the rebels is to come off smoothly. I certainly can't give the authorities any reason to doubt me, especially since we still don't know who it is who's having me followed."

"I'm sure you haven't given them any reason to worry. I can't help but wish you had."

Sensing another confrontation, Noah cut him off curtly. "Matthew!"

"Think about all I've said, Noah. My life will be here now." He gazed fondly at Faith before looking back up at his brother. "I'd like yours to be, too."

Noah stood up, "You know my plans. I don't intend to change them. If you'll excuse me? It's getting late."

"Of course." Matt realized that he had pushed him too far.

"I'll bid you all good night. Ladies . . ."

Matt did not regret his attempt to reconcile Noah to his own way of thinking, but he knew that he should say no more at this time. He walked with him to the door and watched as his brother pulled on his greatcoat.

"I'm glad you came to dinner, Noah." It was a heartfelt statement.

"Thank you for the invitation." His answer was brusque, the pressure he'd felt at Matt's effort to convert him from his own goals having taken the comfortable glow from the evening. "You'll be in touch?"

Matt nodded. "I'll give Graves the information as soon as possible and then get back to you with his reply."

"I'll be waiting. Be sure he understands that time is of the essence. We have to work this right or all could be lost."

"I'll tell him."

Ryan Graves looked at Joshua Smith, his expression strained. "There's no way we can do it."

Smith stared blankly at the closed door through which Matthew had just exited. "I know. I had thought there would be more time. . . . What can we do?"

"There's only one thing we can do, and that's ask him to let us take delivery on the arms and then trust us to come up with the rest of the money later." Graves was desperate.

"Kincade's a hard one," Smith observed. "He's not going to give a damn about our motives or our promises. He's already threatened to sell to the redcoats, and I don't doubt for a minute that he would."

"If he does, we've lost everything . . . including the first half of our payment."

"It was a dangerous agreement from the start."

"I know, but I was so positive that we'd have the funds by the time the materials arrived."

"What are you going to do?"

"There's only one thing I can do. I've got to go to him and ask him for an extension in the payback."

"And if he says no?"

Graves looked defeated. "I'll worry about that when it happens."

It was late, and the taproom of the Green Dragon Inn was almost deserted. Seated at a table in a secluded, dark corner, Noah faced Ryan Graves. His expression was stony as he regarded the rebel leader.

"Graves." His tone was deadly. "We had an agreement. The balance was to be due and payable upon the delivery of the merchandise."

"Yes, we did, Lord Kincade," Graves agreed miserably.

"And now you're telling me that you can't meet those terms?"

"Not exactly . . ." he hedged.

"What, then, are you telling me *exactly?*"

"When we made the agreement, I thought there would be more time to get the money together."

Noah was cold and indifferent to his problems. He wanted the cash due him, and he wanted it now. He had made the deal in good faith. "I'm sorry if I'm not particularly sympathetic to your problem, Graves."

Graves paled at his statement. "Lord Kincade," he began earnestly, "we will pay you the full amount due. You have my word on it."

"I had your word before that you would have the money by the time the merchandise arrived," Noah told him. "I'm afraid there isn't any reason to continue our discussion. The *Pride* will probably make port late tomorrow or Sunday. Have the money to me by then, or the deal is off."

"But Lord Kincade . . . !"

Noah got to his feet, his gaze dispassionate upon the other man. "I expect to be hearing from you soon."

Girding himself, Graves looked up. His eyes locked with Kincade's silver ones and he thought the nobleman's eyes the coldest he'd ever seen. "I'll do my best."

With a curt nod, Noah left him.

Graves was a defeated man as he faced those gathered in the back room of the Green Dragon's stables the next day. "I have news for you, and I'm afraid it's not encouraging."

Everyone turned their attention to him, wondering what terrible thing had happened.

"What's wrong?" John asked worriedly.

"It looks as if our deal with Lord Kincade is going to fall through," he answered succinctly.

"Why?" CC couldn't stop herself from inquiring.

"The Kincade ship carrying the arms we needed is due in port in a matter of hours. According to our agreement, we were to pay him in full upon taking delivery of the goods."

"Yes. So?" another member wondered.

"So we're short. We don't have the full amount we agreed to, and Lord Kincade has threatened to call off the arrangement if he doesn't receive payment in time."

"Did you tell him we were good for it?" CC spoke up again.

"Of course, but he wasn't buying. It's cash before delivery or nothing. Does anyone have any ideas?"

CC's thoughts strayed from the conversation at hand. She could imagine Noah's mercenary attitude. He cared only for his own pleasure and profit. Obviously Noah wanted money, and just as obviously, he intended to get it. Nothing else mattered to him. Nothing else except . . . A shiver shook her as she remembered their last encounter. There was one thing Noah had wanted that he hadn't gotten. Her.

From the very beginning, he had accused her of trading her favors for the rebel cause. He had been wrong those times, but maybe this time it would be a risk worth taking. CC's mind was racing as she began to plan.

CC said no more as Graves continued to discuss the issue with those present. Tonight Noah would be at the Winthrop ball, as she would be, and she was going to make him an offer. It was an offer she felt reasonably confident that he wouldn't refuse. Surely, as much as Noah had said he wanted her, he would not turn her down.

Geoffrey Radcliffe stared at his servant, his expression one of outrage. "What do you mean, Kincade's managed to elude your man twice?"

"I'm sorry, my lord," Bartley was apologetic. "The best I can figure is that he's aware of the surveillance."

"How could that be?"

"I don't know. All I know is that he disappeared from the Red Lion the night of the disturbance at Griffin's Wharf. The man watching him didn't even realize he'd gone until he saw him returning late that night."

"And?"

"He disappeared yesterday for several hours."

"You have no idea where he went?"

"No, m'lord. I'm sorry."

"Well you should be!" Geoffrey raged as he imagined Kincade sharing Eve's bed, tasting of her passion. "I expected competence, Bartley!"

"I know." He was suitably humble. "I do have some new information on his brother, if that's of any consolation to you."

"Yes, what is it?"

"Young Matthew Kincade is deeply involved with the dissidents."

"He is, is he?" Geoffrey's eyes narrowed dangerously as he considered how he could use the information.

"Yes. I don't have positive identification on this, but my sources are reasonably certain that he was one of the 'Indians' at Griffin's Wharf."

"I see. . . . And that's the same night that Noah Kincade was gone from the inn, correct?"

"Yes, Lord Radcliffe."

"Did your informants indicate that Noah Kincade might have been one of the 'Indians,' too?"

"No. There was nothing said about that possibility."

Bartley's answer was not the one Geoffrey had wanted to hear, and his mood grew black. "Have the surveillance continued," he told him abruptly.

"Yes, m'lord."

"That will be all, Bartley," he dismissed.

When the servant had gone, Geoffrey settled back in his chair to ponder all he'd just learned. He had been seeing Eve regularly, yet he still did not trust her completely. She had capitulated to his way of thinking much too quickly for him to believe the validity of her professed change toward Kincade. Perhaps Eve was still interested in the other man and had warned him to take care when coming to see her. That possibility bore consideration.

The other possibility—that of Kincade being involved with the rebels in some illegal way and its resulting ramifications—would certain spell disaster for the arrogant nobleman, if only he could prove it. Geoffrey swore under his breath at his lack of vital information.

Tonight at the Winthrop's he would observe Kincade carefully and perhaps discover the real truth behind his "secretive" activities.

Chapter Twenty-Two

"CC, darling, whatever is the matter with you tonight?" Caroline asked sharply as she noticed her friend's lack of interest in their discussion.

"Yes, CC. Is something wrong?" Marianna pursued. The Winthrop's ball was certainly among the high points of the social season, and yet CC seemed to be distracted, as if her thoughts were elsewhere.

"Nothing's wrong," CC answered quickly, annoyed that she had let her disquiet show. "Why do you ask?"

"You seem rather vague this evening. It's almost like you're here, but your thoughts aren't," Margaret observed. "I noticed John isn't here yet. Is he coming later?"

"I wouldn't know," she replied flatly.

"CC! You're not telling us that you've thrown John over?"

"No, I'm not telling you that. You seemed to have guessed it all by yourselves," CC snapped.

Her friends looked genuinely perplexed by her manner.

"CC, we hadn't meant to pry. It's just so unusual for you to be so . . . oh, I don't know . . . quiet, I suppose." Marianna tried to make amends.

Instantly contrite for revealing too much of her own inner turmoil, CC turned a warm smile on the three women who'd been her closest friends for as long as she could remember.

"I'm sorry. I shouldn't have been so sharp with you."

"It's perfectly all right, dear," Caroline assured her. "We all have our days."

"Indeed we do," Margaret agreed, and then urged, "But tell us. What happened with John? You two had been so close for so long."

"I know." CC knew it would do no good to try to avoid telling them the truth, for one way or the other they would eventually find out. "I care for John very much, but he wanted to get married. I'm just not ready for marriage yet."

"You could have done far worse," Marianna said.

"That's true, Marianna, but I don't love John," she said with very real conviction. As much as she thought of John and had tried to love him, Noah Kincade was the only man who would ever hold her heart.

"I suppose we might as well drop the subject then," Caroline sighed, "although I was hoping for a spring wedding for the two of you."

"You're just going to have to wait a little longer," CC replied, making an effort to keep her tone teasing.

Margaret, who'd been keeping an eagle eye on the entryway to check on late arrivals, broke into the conversation in hushed tones. "Look! There's Eve. . . . And, well, my goodness . . . tonight she's with Lord Radcliffe! The way things had gone at your ball, CC, I would have expected her to show up with Lord Kincade."

All eyes turned in the widow's direction and watched her grand entrance into the ballroom.

"My goodness, she certainly does spread her favors around, doesn't she?" Caroline put in sarcastically as she gazed disdainfully in Eve's direction, critically assessing the other woman's low-cut, stylish gown of deep rose silk.

"I wish the woman would make up her mind!" Margaret sniped. "But, of course, as long as she's dallying with both of the Englishmen, the rest of our men are safe. I doubt she has time for more than two. . . ."

362

"I hadn't thought she could best her last gown for outrageousness, but she certainly gives it a try with that one," Caroline supplied, noting how dangerously close Eve's bosom came to being fully exposed.

"I hope she doesn't sneeze or bend over," Margaret added, giving the others a quick, mocking smile, and laughter rippled softly through their midst. "Of course, it might just be the highlight of the evening if she did."

CC watched Eve with Radcliffe and was greatly relieved to discover that she had not come with Noah. A knot of apprehension tightened in her stomach, though, as she regarded the slender beauty, her hair powdered and piled high in another stunning design, her hips swaying suggestively in her full-skirted gown. There was no doubt about Eve's attractiveness, and just because the other woman hadn't come with Noah didn't mean she wouldn't make a play for him once he arrived.

Nervously anticipating seeing Noah again, CC kept her eyes trained on the hall and wondered when he would finally get there. She knew it was going to be difficult approaching him. She had ended her involvement with him and had hoped never to speak with him again. Yet she knew she had to make the sacrifice for the sake of the revolution.

"Oh, look . . ." Marianna spoke up. "Lord Kincade's finally arrived, and he's come alone. Do you suppose he asked Eve and she turned him down for Geoffrey?"

"Hardly," CC remarked. "There's no comparison between them."

"Do I detect a note of interest in Lord Kincade on your part?" Caroline was quick to note her defense of the handsome Englishman.

"No," she denied. "I just find Geoffrey totally obnoxious."

"Ah, the lesser of two evils, CC?" Margaret questioned.

"Something like that." CC's reply was vague.

The subject was dropped, yet the other women couldn't help but notice that CC was watching Noah Kincade's every move. And indeed she was. He looked so magnificently attractive in his black velvet coat, dark breeches, and snowy white ruffled shirt and cravat that she couldn't tear her gaze away. She found it difficult to believe that she had actually shared Noah's passion, and she knew in that moment that she would never stop loving him. CC had hoped that by staying away from him her feelings for him would lessen, but now she knew her love for him was for all time and would never cease. Her going to him for the cause would not be a sacrifice of her body, but a sacrifice of her soul, for it would devastate her to love him again and then have to be parted from him.

CC wasn't quite certain of the best way to approach him, and she worried at what his reaction to her would be. Excusing herself from her friends, she moved to the refreshment table to sample the punch, hoping to fortify herself before the big encounter.

Eve was casually making the rounds of the ballroom on Geoffrey's arm, greeting and being greeted by the other guests, when she first saw Noah enter the room alone. Her heartbeat quickened at the sight of him. He was so darkly handsome, and his perfectly tailored clothing clung to his tall, masculine frame. She longed to be free of Geoffrey and in Noah's heated embrace, but she knew she had to be very cautious this evening. She had managed to convince Geoffrey of her devotion, and she could not risk revealing her true feelings to him. Not yet. Not until she had the information that could help Noah. Though she had been seeing Geoffrey regularly since the Demorest ball, she had not yet managed to secure even one thread of information from him about Noah's so-called dangerous activities. Eve felt trapped now by Geoffrey's manipulations and by the power of her own desire for Noah. There was nothing she wanted more than to become Noah's lover and, ultimately, his wife, and she was furious at her own inability to achieve that goal. When Geoffrey's arm slipped possessively about

Eve's waist, it took a major effort for her to maintain a politely civil demeanor and gaze up at him seemingly with affection.

Noah glanced about the crowded ballroom, his expression carefully schooled to reveal none of his displeasure at being there. Had it not been necessary for his business dealings, he would have remained at the inn to await word from the rebels. He had still not heard from Graves. With the *Pride* due in port at any time, he was growing concerned as to whether or not the deal would be concluded. Certainly he had a market with the government, but his profit would suffer considerably, and that was one thought that did not sit well with him. *Damn the rebels anyway!* he thought viciously.

Noah looked about, searching for a familiar face, and to his dismay, his gaze collided with CC's as she stood alone at the refreshment table. Anger surged through him as he felt his desire flare to life at the sight of her. He didn't want to care about CC. He didn't want to feel this unending need for her, yet he did. It annoyed Noah to no end that he had been unable to dismiss his feelings for her. She was only a woman. He'd had many before and, no doubt, would have many after her. He had proposed. She had refused him. That ended it. He had been a fool to offer her marriage, and he was thankful now that she'd turned him down. She had made her feelings for him perfectly clear, and they had both finally recognized that what had existed between them had been sheer animal lust. Surely, he reasoned as he turned coldly away from her direction, the passion he felt for her would fade with time.

"Lord Kincade! Good to see you."

At the sound of Edward Demorest's warm greeting, Noah faced the older man and shook his hand. "Edward, it's good to see you, too."

"Has Matthew come with you?" Edward glanced around, wondering at the younger nobleman's absence.

"No. He had other plans for the evening."

"Pity. I would have enjoyed seeing him again. He's a good lad. I like your brother."

"I'm sure he feels the same way about you, Edward," Noah replied honestly.

"Shall we join the others?" Edward suggested, drawing him toward a small group of guests.

"By all means," he agreed, hiding his displeasure at finding Eve and Radcliffe in the gathering, along with Percival Thornhill and his host, Harley Winthrop. "Good evening, Eve . . . Radcliffe."

"Kincade." Geoffrey returned his greeting.

Noah watched Geoffrey surreptitiously for a moment, wondering if news of his brother's death had reached him yet. He was relieved to discover that there was no change in the man's demeanor toward him.

"Good evening, Noah." Eve boldly used his first name as she fought to keep her desire for him from showing.

"Eve. You're looking lovely this evening." His gaze dropped to the tops of her lush breasts, so daringly exposed. He toyed with the idea of taking up with her. Certainly, after CC's erratic behavior, a warm and willing woman would be wonderful. The thought held some appeal.

"Thank you." She smiled faintly, aware of Geoffrey's presence at her side and knowing that it would not be wise to push things at this time.

Noah nodded his greeting to Winthrop and Thornhill. "Gentlemen. Thank you for the invitation, Major."

"It's an honor to have you," Winthrop replied. "Your brother didn't come?"

"No, but he sends his regrets."

"Give him my best."

"I shall."

"Harley . . . have you any more information about the raid on the ships?" Edward asked, resuming their earlier conversation. He was worried about the possible disruption of trade by the renegade colonists.

"We know who did it," Winthrop replied levelly, his tone deadly.

"Then why don't you prosecute?" Geoffrey demanded, puzzled by the government's lack of action in the case. It had been an outrage against England that these backwater "Americans," as they were beginning to call themselves, had dumped three shiploads of the finest tea in the harbor.

Harley's lips thinned into a smile that seemed more of a grimace. "We aren't prosecuting, Lord Radcliffe, because we can't find any witnesses willing to testify."

"That's ridiculous," Geoffrey sneered. "Surely you have some means of making them talk!"

"Are you suggesting violence?" Edward's eyes widened as he looked to the aristocrat.

"Whatever it takes. These rabble-rousers cannot be allowed to continue to run the city! Destroy them now, before they cause even more damage."

"Lord Radcliffe, while your suggestion is valid, I'm afraid we'd end up arresting most of the population of Boston. There were thousands of people at the wharf that night . . . thousands!"

"So you're not going to do anything?" Edward was dismayed.

"We are going to act, but not until we have direction from Parliament. Dispatches have already been sent."

"In the meantime, we sit and wait and hope the rebels don't riot again," Edward complained. "Mobs controlled this city once before, and I don't want to see that happen to us again."

"The colonials are so stupid," Geoffrey remarked disdainfully, hoping to prod Kincade into revealing something incriminating here before Winthrop and Thornhill.

"They can't be too stupid if they dumped the tea and managed to get away with it," Noah remarked dryly. He was surprised to find himself angered by Geoffrey's attitude and defending the dissidents.

"They haven't managed to get away with it!" Thornhill countered.

"Oh?" Noah quirked a brow questioningly at the officer. "It seems to me, from the tone of your conversation, that they have."

"They'll be punished for their outrage, mark my words," Harley put in seriously.

"Indeed they will be, eventually," Edward agreed, disappointed that action against the rebels wouldn't be immediately forthcoming, but knowing that certain channels had to be followed.

Noah looked at Edward and wondered what he would say if he knew of his daughter's involvement with the rebels. "As you say. But if you can't prove anyone's involvement, I don't see how you can exact retribution. Unless, of course, you decide to punish the entire city."

Winthrop and Thornhill nodded. "It will probably be our only alternative, considering our current situation.

"The entire city?" Noah was surprised.

"Indeed. If so many people were actually witnesses of the dumping of the tea and yet not one of them will come forth with information, then I think a general punishment is definitely in order. That is, if there's no way for the military to handle it," Geoffrey added as he opened his ornate snuffbox and took a pinch, enjoying that small vice to the fullest. "I think it's essential that we teach these insurgents a lesson, once and for all. They shouldn't be allowed to disrupt things."

"If a plan of that sort is enacted, I hardly think it's the colonists who are the stupid ones." Noah felt certain that any retribution against the town of Boston would inevitably lead to tragedy. There was much more involved here than just a few shiploads of tea. Still, he found himself wondering at his need to debate the point.

Geoffrey stiffened, his face growing pale in light of Noah's remark. "Kincade, perhaps your defense of the revolution-aries is because you're one of them!" he challenged. He had not meant to reveal any of what he knew, but his temper was flaring over Noah's remark.

"I beg your pardon." Noah arched one brow in question, his mocking look causing Radcliffe to flush.

"I said, perhaps you're one of them. You've certainly been most vocal in their defense tonight."

A collective gasp escaped those present. Eve was distressed as she realized that the damning evidence Geoffrey claimed to have against Noah must be proof of his involvement with the rebels.

Noah's smile was strained. "I don't think there's anyone here who could possibly question my loyalty to the Crown."

"I do," he snarled viciously, driven on by his embarrass-ment.

Noah's expression was stony as his gaze rested on the other nobleman. Before this night, he had had little feeling one way or the other toward the man. Now, however, after listening to him, Noah knew that Geoffrey personified everything he despised about the English ruling class. He was a fop and a spoiled bounder. Noah had met many men like him during his years on the *ton*. They were a useless, ornamental breed, dedicated solely to their own pleasure. . . .

The thought abruptly occurred to him that, in a way, not too long ago he had been one of them. The realization jarred him, and he knew an instant of true soul-searching as he tried to understand why he was suddenly so disdainful of British society. Hadn't his whole existence, up until now, centered on reclaiming his lost fortunes so he could return to their midst? He frowned slightly as he suddenly realized that he didn't care about being accepted by them any longer.

"Geoffrey." Eve noticed Noah's expression and thought that trouble was about to erupt. She tugged on his arm, hoping to draw him away from what was developing into an ugly confrontation. "I'd like a cup of punch now."

Radcliffe shook off her hand, his eyes glowing with an inner fervor. "Oh no, my dear. I'm not quite through yet."

"Geoffrey . . . please." Eve was suddenly very worried. She knew of Geoffrey's reputation as a swordsman and did not want to think that Noah might be hurt, or even killed, in a useless confrontation between them.

Her defense of Noah only served to infuriate Geoffrey more and revived all the earlier jealousy he'd felt toward the other man. "Shut up, Eve," he silenced her cruelly. "You can't protect him."

"I hardly need protection," Noah said sarcastically, "female or otherwise."

"Ah, but I say you do," Geoffrey sneered insultingly, suddenly wanting to force him into a duel. Before he'd left England, he had been renowned for his swordsmanship, and the thought of running Noah through gave him immense pleasure. With him dead, he would finally be sure of Eve's affections.

"Then that is your sadly mistaken judgment of my character," Noah answered smoothly, refusing to take his bait. After his bloody, deadly duel with Geoffrey's brother, James, months before in England, he had sworn never to cross swords over an insult again.

Fury gripped Geoffrey as Noah's evasive answer left him the fool before Demorest, Winthrop, and Thornhill, not to mention Eve. Out of control in his anger, desiring only to redeem himself before these colonists, he backhanded Noah viciously.

A sudden hush fell over the ball as all attention was riveted on them.

Noah flinched at the blow, and his eyes glittered dangerously at the direct challenge. Still he held himself in check, staring at Geoffrey in frigid silence. "As I said before, the dissident colonists are not the dullards here in Boston. If you will excuse me?" With a small, formal bow, he turned his back on Geoffrey and walked with dignity from the ballroom and the house, leaving the other nobleman red-faced and helpless in his outrage.

Edward looked to both Percival and Harley in confused disbelief over what had just happened as Geoffrey shook with rage.

"He refused my challenge!" Geoffrey bellowed in bewilderment. "You saw him! He's a cowardly—"

"You were goading him and trying to push him into it." Edward defended Noah. "He merely refused to be drawn into your deadly game."

"But he's involved with the rebels!" Geoffrey blustered, hoping to salvage something by besmirching Noah's reputation.

"Do you have proof of your accusation?" Harley asked quickly.

"Nothing positive, but I'm sure of it!"

"Thinking something is true is one thing; having definitive proof is another," Winthrop added.

"You shouldn't make statements you can't back up, Lord Radcliffe. Besides, I am certain that Lord Kincade would do no such thing. I personally will vouch for his integrity," Edward told them.

"You're wrong, Demorest!" Geoffrey countered heatedly as he found himself cornered. He longed to tell them about Matthew Kincade's connection, but he wasn't certain that he could produce any witnesses to back up the charge. The information Bartley provided, while it might be accurate, could not always be substantiated by reliable testimony.

Edward eyed him distastefully. "Speaking hypothetically, Lord Radcliffe, if what you say is true, then why would Lord Kincade be selling a shipment of war materials to the Crown?"

Geoffrey was left speechless by the news. *How could it be?* Everything he'd managed to find out about Noah had pointed to his being involved with the rebels. Yet Demorest was now saying that Noah's business interests were all legal and aboveboard. . . .

"Geoffrey, why don't we . . ." Eve broke in, wanting to distract him from his anger, but he would have none of it.

Embarrassed and feeling decidedly emasculated before those he'd lorded himself over, he glared at her malevolently, and then he, too, stalked from the house, vowing silently to himself to have revenge upon Noah.

Eve knew a moment of true consternation as she tried to understand what had just happened. One moment the conversation had been pleasant, and then the next, Geoffrey and Noah had been insulting each other. Her ego was such that she could only allow herself to believe that, beneath all the open exchanges about 'rebel involvement' and such, she was the true reason for their heated words. A small, self-satisfied smile curved her lips as she envisioned the two handsome noblemen vying for her favors.

"If you gentlemen will excuse me, I think I'll mingle a bit," Eve said sweetly as she moved away from the three remaining men.

"Of course, Eve," they answered with little real interest.

CC had been standing alone at the refreshment table when Geoffrey had slapped Noah. She had been unable to hear any of the conversation that had preceded it, and she wondered what had been said to precipitate the exchange. In dismay, she watched as Noah turned coolly from Geoffrey and strode purposefully from the house. Before she could hurry to her father's side to try to find out what had happened, Caroline joined her.

"Did you see that?" Caroline was in a dither as she touched CC's arm in barely concealed urgency.

"Didn't everyone?" CC replied a bit sarcastically as she noted all those present watching Geoffrey with open interest.

"What *were* they discussing that could have caused such trouble?"

"I can't imagine," she responded honestly, and then both women tried to keep from gaping as Geoffrey stormed off then, leaving Eve alone with the other men.

"You don't suppose they were quarreling over *her*, do you?" Caroline was obviously distressed at the thought. She thought Eve obnoxious enough without having the two aristocrats fighting over her.

CC's heart ached at the possibility, and she answered in a low voice, "Lord, I hope not."

"Me, too! Go find out from your father," Caroline urged as she glanced back to where Margaret and Marianna were still sitting. "We're just dying to know the truth of it."

"Yes . . . all right . . ." CC had not wanted to think that Noah might have been arguing with Geoffrey over Eve, but now that the question had been raised, she had to know the truth. Leaving Caroline at the refreshment table, she hurried to her father's side just as Eve moved off to mix with the other guests. "Father . . . what happened?"

Edward took his daughter's arm and guided her slightly away from the others. "I'm not sure." He was truly puzzled by Radcliffe's personal attack on Noah. "We were discussing the rebel movement, and then suddenly things got out of hand. . . ."

"What do you mean? Why would they argue about the revolutionaries? They're both loyal Englishmen. . . ."

"That's what's confusing. Radcliffe was incensed over the dumping of the tea, and he was calling for retribution against the entire city. Lord Kincade remarked, in so many words, that it would be a stupid thing to do. Radcliffe took exception to his statement, and one thing led to another. . . ."

"They weren't arguing over Eve then?"

Edward chuckled, "Eve was trying her best to prevent the argument, but Radcliffe would have none of it. In fact, her defense of Kincade only made him angrier."

CC sensed, in irritation, that Eve was the primary cause of the whole thing, even while nothing had been openly said. "Are they going to duel?" CC's eyes reflected her worry as she stared up at her father.

"Amazingly enough, no," her father informed her.

"He refused the challenge?" She was truly shocked, for such behavior was unheard of.

Edward nodded. "Lord Kincade walked away, even though Radcliffe had accused him of being involved with the rebels."

"Radcliffe accused him of that?" CC was stunned. Had Geoffrey been jealous of Eve and Noah and subsequently had Noah followed? "Is there any truth to it?" she asked with forced innocence.

Again Edward gave a confident, manly laugh. "No, my dear. I vouched for Lord Kincade myself. I imagine the closest he's come to being involved with the rebels was the discussion we had that first night he joined us for dinner."

CC felt her stomach lurch at that news. If the truth about Noah's double-dealing was ever found out, it was possible her father would be ruined. She forced a pleasant smile, even as her thoughts were troubled.

"Well, at least they're not coming to any violence."

"Radcliffe, I'm sure, wanted to fight him, but Lord Kincade would have none of it." Edward frowned. "It does seem rather odd, though, that a nobleman would 'turn the other cheek,' so to speak. Still, Kincade doesn't seem the cowardly type."

CC quickly found herself defending Noah. "I'm sure he's not."

"Well, whatever else, they've certainly given us something to talk about for the rest of the evening."

Harley looked at Percival, his expression troubled. "I've never seen anything like it. . . ."

"Neither have I," the other military man agreed. "If a man's challenged publicly, it seems he should take up the fight."

They both fell silent for a moment as they took deep

drinks of the bourbon they'd just procured from a passing servant.

"You don't suppose there's any truth to Radcliffe's accusations, do you?"

Harley shook his head in mild confusion. "Heavens, no! He's a peer of the realm, and with Edward's testimony to Lord Kincade's business dealings . . . well, I most certainly would think not. What bothers me is Lord Radcliffe's charges. Why in the world would he accuse him of such treasonous misdeeds?"

"Perhaps there's more to this than we'll ever know." Percival let his gaze drift pointedly in the direction of the beauteous widow as he remembered Eve's defense of Kincade, and Radcliffe's reaction to it. "If you get my meaning."

Harley gave a low laugh. "Indeed, you may very well be right."

Chapter Twenty-Three

CC lay upon her bed much later that night, frustrated and unable to sleep. Her plan to approach Noah at the ball had been foiled when he had departed early, and she was now desperately trying to decide what to do next. Time was of the essence where the arms deal was concerned. She knew the only way she could still accomplish her goal to help the cause was to go to Noah at the inn. A firm resolve took hold of her, even though she readily admitted to herself that she was frightened to face him so boldly. Girding herself, she threw off the blankets and hurried to her armoire to search for her boyish garments. Only a short time later, she was racing, unnoticed, through the night-shrouded streets of Boston on her way to the Red Lion Inn.

Noah sat alone at a secluded table in the taproom of the inn. His thoughts were troubled as he wondered what repercussions might result from his unsavory confrontation with Geoffrey this evening. Noah was glad now that Graves had insisted upon the extra precautions regarding their dealings. He felt reasonably sure that his business connections were still unknown. Certainly, if Geoffrey had had proof positive of his involvement, he would have used it tonight in the presence of the military officers. As it was, Geoffrey had ended up looking the fool for flinging "unfounded accusations" at Noah in an effort to goad him into a fight. Noah smiled grimly at the thought of having bested the other man with words, and he dismissed as unimportant any aspersions cast upon his character for refusing the challenge. His reasons for refusing were his, and his alone, and he truly didn't care what anyone thought about it.

The only good thing that had come out of the evening was the fact that he now knew who was responsible for his being followed. He had no doubt that it had been Geoffrey. The *why* of it was less than clear, yet he tended to believe it was all somehow related to Eve. Certainly Geoffrey had responded viciously when she'd tried to divert their clash, and he sensed that perhaps his slight flirtation with her had been the cause. Eve looked to be warm and willing, but he seriously doubted that she was worth dueling over.

Sighing, Noah drained his tumbler of bourbon and glanced up around the room. A good-size crowd still lingered despite the lateness of the hour, and though he was surrounded by people, he knew a moment of intense loneliness. He didn't like being so isolated . . . so alone.

Polly gave a throaty laugh as one of the other customers pulled her onto his lap, and Noah suddenly thought of CC. A scowl creased his brow. Damn, but the vixen haunted him! The memory of how lovely she'd looked at the ball flitted through his mind, and he wondered where she was right now. Was she with another man, making love, or home with her father, all safe and sound? He hoped for the latter, and then cursed himself for even caring. Calling out abruptly to Polly, he ordered another drink. His attention focused on the buxom barmaid. He did not notice as a youth entered the dimly lit taproom and crept undetected up the staircase to the second floor.

CC darted around the corner of the second-floor hall, out

of sight of the lower level, and drew a deep, ragged breath. She had not thought that many people would be belowstairs in the taproom at this time of night, and she hoped no one had noticed her. Her breathing steadied, she moved on silent tread down the hall to the room she knew to be Noah's.

All the way to the inn, she had debated with herself the best way to handle this, and she still had formulated no plan. Stiffening, she swallowed nervously and raised a hand to knock softly at the door. CC waited tensely for his answer to her summons, but none came. Inhaling deeply, she knocked again, this time with a little more force, but still there came no answering response. Annoyed, frustrated, and fearful of being discovered, CC knew she couldn't stand in the middle of the hall forever. Boldly, she reached down and tried the doorknob, and to her surprise, it opened. She thought Kincade the fool for leaving his room unlocked, but at the same time thanked her lucky stars that it had been. Quietly, she slipped into the room and closed the door behind her.

The glow of the low-burning fire in the fireplace cast heavy shadows in the chilly chamber. With her hands on her hips, CC stood in the middle of the room, pondering what to do next. Obviously Noah had not yet returned to his room from the ball, and she couldn't stop herself from wondering where he'd gone. Was it possible that he'd met Eve somewhere? The thought sent a shaft of pain through her heart, and she quickly put it from her, knowing it would do no good to dwell on such possibilities.

CC paced the room nervously like a caged beast as she tried to decide what to do. She had expected Noah to be here and now was at a loss as to her next move. What did a woman do when she was out to deliberately seduce a man? Should she approach it as a business arrangement or try a more subtle, more feminine tactic? Somehow, the feminine method seemed more likely to succeed. Noah had accused her the last time they were together of being less than

378

womanly, and he had responded excitedly when she'd let her feelings for him run wild. Tonight, again, she would set aside her inhibitions and go to him as a warm and willing woman . . . a woman who wanted him and no other. That part of her plan did not trouble her, for it was the truth. What bothered her was the part after they had made love . . . the part where she would agree to be his wife if he would sell the arms to the rebels at a lower price. She hoped she could be convincing, and she hoped he really wanted her enough to go along with it.

A shudder of nervousness left her slender limbs quaking, but driven by her determination not to fail, CC pushed all negative thoughts away. A man's lover, she decided, would no doubt greet him in bed. Hurriedly, she discarded her hat and stripped off her clothing. Pulling the pins from her hair, she combed her fingers through its silken length, letting it tumble to her shoulders in tousled disarray. The chill in the room was a frigid caress, and she was shivering as she slipped naked beneath the covers. CC was tense and more than a little frightened, for she wasn't sure just how she would be received. The blankets pulled up to her chin, she lay huddled there in the darkness awaiting Noah's return.

It was almost an hour later when CC heard the heavy sound of his footfalls in the hall, and she swallowed nervously at the sound of the door being opened. With all the bravado she could muster, she adjusted the blankets lower until they barely covered her bosom and then posed in what she hoped was a seductive position.

Noah had been drinking continually since he'd left the ball. He had hoped that the liquor would help him forget CC and all that had happened tonight, but instead of easing his worries, he'd become even more immersed in them. Angry with himself for still caring about the chit and missing Matthew more than he could ever admit, he entered his room in the lowest of moods, shutting and locking the door behind him.

"Noah . . . I'm so glad you're here. . . ." CC murmured seductively.

Her greeting stunned him, and he turned quickly from the door. Silence hung between them as he stared at her in disbelief. His mind reeled at the sight of her in his bed, willing. Mesmerized, a man possessed, he started toward her.

CC grew worried when Noah didn't respond to her greeting, and she wet her lips nervously as she watched him slowly cross the room in her direction. His expression was unreadable in the semidarkness of the room. "Noah . . . I've been waiting for you," she told him in a strained, husky voice.

Noah could not take his eyes off her as he moved ever closer. CC was here . . . in his bed . . . naked and obviously willing. She looked glorious. Her burnished hair was a cascade of caressing curls as it fell softly about her shoulders and lay teasingly against the curve of her blanket-covered bosom. Her expression was inviting, her lips moist and slightly parted as if ready to be possessed by his. . . .

As much as Noah would have liked to cast aside his doubts and take his fullest enjoyment of CC, the cynic in him wondered at the reason for her being there. It was pleasant to think she had wanted him so badly that she was willing to risk everything to come to him, but Noah knew better. When last they'd parted, CC had made no secret of how she felt about him. She had refused his proposal. Noah seriously doubted that her passion was the driving force in her coming here tonight. Though his body was commanding him to take her and not question his good fortune, Noah felt sure that she had to have an ulterior motive.

"Noah?" CC was sounding more nervous now as he drew nearer. Desperately, she was wondering if she'd made a drastic mistake. Did he hate her now since she'd refused his offer of marriage? Would he welcome her or throw her bodily from his room? The latter had not occurred to CC before, and she knew a moment of panic at the thought.

Noah stopped beside the bed and let his gaze roam over her. CC was the one woman he wanted. Still, skeptic that he was, he was not going to allow himself to have her until he knew the truth behind her presence. He would play along with her game for a little while, and then when the truth came out . . . Noah sat down and, without saying a word, took her in his arms and drew her near.

CC's nervousness eased at the discovery that Noah was not angry about her being there, and she went into his embrace almost eagerly in her relief.

CC's newfound submissiveness sent a shock of pure animal pleasure through Noah. He realized this response was what he had wanted from her since the beginning. He had wanted CC warm and willing and loving. His body responded heatedly to the difference, and his previous passion for her paled before the new emotion that surged through him. Noah recognized this emotion, yet fought against acknowledging it. He was shaken to the very core of his being by the unexpected discovery, and his mouth sought hers in a devastating exchange that left them both breathless and desiring more. With eager hands he pushed the blanket lower, baring the sweetness of her breasts to his gaze and caress. Noah pressed her back onto his bed, stripped the rest of the blanket from her, and followed her down onto the wide softness.

CC's arms encircled Noah's neck, drawing him to her, and she met him hungrily in another kiss, her small tongue darting boldly between his lips to duel erotically with his. As he lay fully upon her, the heat of his need pressed firmly against the soft flesh of her belly. She knew then that she had been fooling herself in thinking that she was doing this strictly for the revolution. She wanted Noah. She had never stopped wanting him and probably never would. He was the man she loved. She wanted to marry him and bear his children. The war supplies had merely been a justifiable reason to see him again, to love him and to share in the drugging glory of his passion.

As his lips left hers to trail fiery kisses down her throat and across her shoulders, her need overwhelmed her senses. CC didn't care about anything except Noah and the joy that came from pleasing him. Her nipples hardened as shivers of excitement coursed through her veins. She arched against the solidness of his chest, begging in mute testimony for the more intimate touch of his mouth upon her aching, throbbing breasts. When at last his lips sought out that tender flesh, CC cried out at the wonder of it and began to move beneath him as her hands caressed him in restless need.

"Noah . . . Oh, Noah, I love you. . . ." She said it before she realized, and yet her passion was such that she didn't even care.

Noah, however, was surprised by her declaration and he paused in his lovemaking, his moment of the mindless passion lost. *She loved him.* . . . Over and over she had declared her hatred for him, yet now, tonight, she was telling him she loved him? It didn't ring true. His desire drained from him as he realized her presence here really *was* a lie.

CC, caught up in the wonder of his ardor, didn't notice the change in him immediately.

"What is it you want, CC?" Noah asked, the cynicism of his tone muffled against the softness of her breasts. He was tense as he anticipated her answer.

"You, Noah . . . only you," she gasped, still in the throes of the feverish excitement he'd created within her.

It bothered Noah to discover that he wanted to believe it . . . that he wanted to be the one who held her heart, but he wouldn't allow himself even to pretend.

"CC . . . I want to know what it is you want." He repeated his question sharply as he braced himself above her on his elbows and glared down at her.

"Noah?" CC blinked in confusion, her passion-dilated emerald eyes gazing up at him questioningly. She knew a moment of true apprehension as the smoky depths of his eyes turned to the impenetrable, steely regard she knew so well and hated so much.

"I want to know the real reason you're here, CC," Noah demanded cuttingly. He watched the play of emotions on her face. She had never been adept at disguising her feelings, and Noah could read in her expression all the embarrassment that went with his calling her bluff. His heart sank as he realized that he had been right in his assessment. She was up to something. "Well?"

"I don't know what you mean. . . ."

"Spare me your innocence, darling," he mocked her as he moved away, needing to distance himself from her shapely unclad body. "I've told you before how bad you are at hiding your true emotions."

CC shivered involuntarily and she wondered if her reaction was from the chill in the room or the derision in his tone. She answered simply, "I'm here because I want to be." *The truth . . .*

Noah strode across the room and parted the drapes as he stood at the window. Keeping his back to her, he retorted, "CC . . . I find that very difficult to believe. The last time we were together you vowed your hatred for me and wanted me to stay away from you forever." When she started to speak, he cut her off and kept on talking. "I complied with your wishes. I stayed away from you as you asked. Yet now you show up here in my bed, and you tell me that you love me. Do you really expect me to believe it?" Noah faced her. "Or are you the type of woman who always wants what she can't have?" His gaze rested heatedly on her lush figure. "Cover yourself, woman!" Noah barked the order.

CC, seeing the desire revealed in his eyes, decided to make one last attempt at seduction. "Noah . . . Come to me, Noah. . . . I want you desperately. . . ." In an alluring movement, she rose from the bed and walked enticingly toward him.

Noah's passion taunted him to take her and be done with it, but his logic asserted itself over his baser needs. Though he found the sight of her captivating, he kept a tight rein on his desire.

CC came to stand before him and then lifted her arms about his neck. On tiptoes, she raised up to press her lips to his, hoping to distract him from his thoughts. Noah accepted her kiss with a minimum of participation. CC was puzzled by his lack of response. Wanting to break through his suddenly icy control, she began to rub herself sensually against him. Her sinuous motions did come very close to shattering his composure, but CC never knew it as Noah viciously gripped her by her forearms and pulled her arms from about his neck.

Holding her away from him, he ground out, "I want to know what's going on here, and I want to know it now."

CC was caught in a trap of her own making. She knew there was only one way to escape from the web in which she found herself entangled. The only solution was to tell him the complete truth from the very beginning.

"You're hurting me. . . ." she protested.

Abruptly he released her. "Get your clothes on."

No longer confident of her ability to seduce him, CC hurried to do as he'd commanded.

"Start talking, CC," Noah ordered as he tried not to watch her as she dressed. Desperate in his own way, he struggled to look anywhere but at her, for the sight of her tempting breasts and dark triangle of femininity at the junction of her thighs was all too appealing.

CC sighed as she conceded, "All right, Noah."

With jerky motions, she tugged on her shirt, quickly buttoned it across her breasts, and then pulled on the trousers. She felt decidedly unattractive and very vulnerable, but she was determined that he not know of her insecurities as she turned to face him. Schooling her expression not to reflect her nervousness, she glanced up at him. What she saw there caused her to grimace inwardly.

"Well? Why are you here? And what is it you want?" Noah folded his arms across his chest, the gesture making him seem even more unreachable, as his gaze bore unnervingly into hers.

CC wavered. . . . Should she just blurt it out or try something else? Finally, knowing she couldn't avoid it, she admitted, "I do love you, Noah. I have for a long time."

"Right," he drawled sarcastically.

"No, that is the truth." CC almost took a step toward him, but his ominous expression put her off. "I freely admit that I didn't want to love you, but . . . but sometimes we can't control our feelings." She gave a small, helpless shrug.

"So," Noah began somewhat bitterly, "you love me, and you came here tonight only because you couldn't bear to be parted from me any longer. Is that what you want me to think? Really, CC, sometimes you do astound me. You love me, but you refused to become my wife. . . ." His eyes were cold upon her. "Somehow, it just doesn't fit."

Suddenly CC was angry. She had just bared her soul to him and he was mocking her. "I wouldn't become your wife because you don't love me! Do you think I wanted to be married to a man who doesn't love me? You proposed, but you didn't profess any feeling for me at all! I know you're attracted to me physically, but beyond that, what do we have? You want to return to England, and I—"

Noah was stunned by her outburst. She had said that she loved him. His heart was swelling with joy at the thought as the recognition of his own feelings surged forth. The emotion he had refused to confront for so long was before him now, and he knew without doubt that he loved her, too. Before he could speak and declare himself, though, CC went on.

"And I want to help the revolution in any and every way I

can. That was the reason why I came to you tonight. I knew that you wanted me. I came here with the intention of offering to become your wife if you would sell the munitions to Ryan at a lower price." CC drew a deep, ragged breath as she paused.

Noah went from overjoyed at the news that she loved him to completely furious at her for her deception, and his voice reflected the heat of his wrath. "So you're making the ultimate sacrifice, are you?"

"No . . . it's not like that at all." CC tried to convince him that it was no sacrifice on her part, that she wanted him as much as he wanted her, but he was beyond listening to her.

"The hell it isn't, CC!" he snarled. "You didn't want to marry me before, but now that you need something from me, you're willing to barter your body to get it!"

"Noah! You don't understand!" she cried, wanting him to know that she loved him, and even if she didn't hold his love, she would marry him.

"Oh, but I do, Miss Demorest, all too well." Noah's eyes narrowed as he studied her. "There's one thing you haven't considered in your approach, though. What if I no longer wanted to marry you?"

His words were like a physical blow, and CC blanched. "Don't you?"

"I'm not sure. . . ." Noah took a step toward her and reached out to tangle one hand in the velvet curtain of her hair. "Perhaps I should sample of the merchandise you're trying to trade one more time before I firm up or dismiss the deal. . . ."

His hand tightened in her hair, and CC whimpered slightly as he pulled her to him. Noah's mouth ground savagely down on hers, raping the sweetness there, and CC felt her knees buckle at his cruelty. She struggled to get free then, knowing that her cause was a useless one.

"Noah . . . please . . ."

"What?" He quirked a brow in sardonic disbelief of her

protest as he drew back. "You aren't willing to let me taste of the charms you want me to 'purchase' for a lifetime? Come now, CC, be reasonable." His lips curled into a sneer as he jerked her tightly against him and ran his hands over her with insulting familiarity.

CC felt degraded and abused by his actions. "Noah . . . I do love you. Please don't do this. . . ."

"Do what? Take what you're offering? This time, my dear, there can be no dispute that you *are* offering, can there?"

Tears stung her eyes as she looked up at him, and for an instant Noah felt himself waver. Did she really love him? Had she been telling the truth, or was it a ploy? He was confused and angry, and he shoved her from him.

"Get out of here, CC," he told her brusquely, "and tell Ryan and all the others that my terms have to be met or I will sell the shipment to someone who has the money." With that, he stalked to the door and opened it for her.

CC stood in shock for a moment before snatching up the rest of her belongings and racing from the room. Noah closed the door quickly behind her, and when she heard him turn the lock, she could no longer prevent her tears from falling. In failure and misery, she leaned against the hallway wall as she pulled on the rest of her clothing. Disguised once again, she hurried from the now deserted inn.

Chapter Twenty-Four

When the loud knocking on his bedroom door did not abate, Geoffrey angrily struggled to sit up in bed, taking great care not to move too quickly, for his head was still pounding from the excess of liquor he'd imbibed after leaving the party the night before.

"Blast you, Bartley! What is it?" he shouted in irritation, and even the sound of his own voice pained him.

"I'm sorry, m'lord, but a letter has just arrived for you." Bartley's tone was suitably apologetic through the solidness of the closed chamber door. "The bearer said it was extremely important."

"Just who was this 'bearer'?" Geoffrey snarled as he climbed slowly from the comfort of his bed and began to pull on his red satin dressing gown.

"He was a seaman from a merchant ship, m'lord. The missive is from your family in England."

Geoffrey was halfway to the door when he stopped, a frown creasing his brow. Incredulous, he asked. "Did you say it was from my family?"

"Yes, Lord Radcliffe."

With great haste, Geoffrey unlocked the portal and took the letter from the servant. "Bring me a cup of hot tea," he directed. Then, staring down at the envelope and immediately recognizing the strong, slanted lines of his father's script, he changed his mind. "No . . . wait. Make that a generous portion of bourbon instead."

"Right away." Bartley scurried off to bring his suffering master the libation he'd requested.

Geoffrey closed the door and wandered back into the room, his mind racing as he tried to imagine what news could be in the letter. Since his "exile" to the colonies, his family had made little effort to keep in contact with him. His funds were deposited directly to his accounts, and they seldom sent any news. As he studied the envelope, he couldn't help but wonder what major event had occurred to merit sending him a letter. Curious, Geoffrey sat back down on his bed and tore it open.

Geoffrey—
   It is with the deepest of sorrows that I must send word to you of your brother James's untimely demise. You are now the next in line for the title, and it is imperative that you return home at your earliest convenience. Your mother and I await your arrival. . . .

Geoffrey paused in his reading to look up and stare about him in stunned amazement. His brother was dead! He smiled in cunning delight at the news. So old James was dead, was he? Geoffrey couldn't be more pleased. James had been a thorn in his side from the earliest days of their childhood, and he would not miss him. *And,* he thought with a real sense of triumph, *I will one day be the earl—not James!* Realizing then that there was more to the letter, he directed his attention back to the missive. . . .

James was killed in a duel by Lord Noah Kincade.

Geoffrey's eyes widened as he stared in utter disbelief at the news. Kincade had been responsible for his brother's death? The same Kincade who'd had the gall to face him at numerous social engagements? The same Kincade who'd refused his challenge last night? He read on. . . .

> *Knowing what an expert swordsman your brother was, I cannot help but believe that it was a less than fair fight. There can be no peace in our family until justice has been served. Kincade must be made to pay for this outrage.*
>
> *Come home as quickly as you can. We need you here. All the past is forgotten. We will welcome you with open arms.*
>
> *Your mother and father . . .*

Geoffrey's joy at the unexpected change in his fortunes was still there, but his hatred for Noah had intensified. Kincade had murdered his brother and had cowardly refused to accept his challenge last night. The man, if he could be called one, was a spineless fool who deserved what he got. No longer content with just proving Noah guilty of treason, Geoffrey was resolved to make him pay for his actions, and pay with his life.

The single knock at the door brought him back to the reality of the moment, and he bid his servant to enter.

"Your bourbon, sir." Bartley placed the silver tray on the bedside table.

"Thank you, Bartley." Geoffrey was still a bit distracted as he considered the best way to proceed. It was only as the servant turned to leave that he spoke up. "Bartley . . ."

"Yes, m'lord?"

"I have a most important job for you. . . ."

It was late afternoon as Matthew and Ben sat in the parlor of the Hammond house, their serious expressions reflecting their grim mood as they regarded each other.

"There's no other way?" Matt asked, his tone revealing his disturbance over the news that Ben had just given him.

"None. We've tried everything we know," Ben confided. "You're our only hope, Matthew."

Matt shifted uncomfortably at Ben's request. He had hoped it would never come to this—a complete showdown between Noah's goals and his own. When Noah had sent word to him earlier that morning that the *Sea Pride* had made port, Matt had notified the rebels immediately of the ship's arrival. He had just received word back from Ryan Graves, through Ben, that they could not meet the terms of their original agreement with Noah. According to the rebel leader, their funds were completely drained, and there was no way they could come up with the additional money needed by the time Noah had demanded.

"If you could just talk with your brother," Ben was saying hopefully. "We will pay him the amount agreed upon. It will just take us longer to get it, that's all."

"I know. I trust you, but . . ." Matt hedged, knowing what Noah's answer was going to be even before he asked.

"Matthew, we must have those supplies." Ben's gaze was earnest upon him.

"I know, Ben." Matt stood up, squaring his shoulders in an unconscious gesture against the battle of wills he knew was to come. "I'll do my best."

"That's all we ask, Matthew. That's all we ask." Ben shook his hand fervently.

"Faith," Matt called to his wife. The women had retired to the kitchen to give the men the privacy they'd needed for their political discussion.

Faith appeared in the parlor doorway with Ruth beside her. "Did you want me?"

"Always." Matthew gave her a warm grin as he moved toward her. "I must meet with Noah, so I'll be gone for a while."

"It's important?"

"Very, but I should be back before dark."

"We'll wait dinner for you then."

"Good." He bent to press a soft kiss on her lips before retrieving his greatcoat and heading from the house. "I'll be back."

When Matthew had gone, Faith returned to the kitchen while Ben and Ruth stood alone in the parlor.

"There are problems?" Ruth asked tentatively as she gazed up at him.

"Yes," he answered tersely, trying to come to face the fact that they might not get the supplies they so desperately needed.

"Is there anything I can do?" she offered sympathetically. She remembered how the injustices of the day had upset her husband, and she wanted to be of any help she could to Ben. He was such a dear man, and he had come to mean so much to her. . . .

Ben turned to Ruth, his eyes dark with unspoken emotion. "Just letting me be here with you helps."

She sensed the meaning behind his words and boldly took a step closer to Ben. "Really, Ben?" She touched his arm lightly, and there was an immediate feeling of real intimacy to the moment.

Ben found himself caught up in a situation he wasn't sure how to handle. Should he gruffly dismiss her question or confess to her his long-denied devotion? Frustrated by all aspects of his life at that instant and feeling that things could not possibly get any worse, Ben decided not to hide his true feelings any longer.

"Yes, Ruth. It helps. Your warmth and hospitality are the only sweetness in my life."

"Just my warmth and hospitality?" Ruth pressed the issue. The feelings she had for Ben had long since passed being strictly friendly. She had been out of mourning for her husband for quite a while now, and she knew it was time to begin life again. Ben was the man she wanted in her future.

Ben was trapped. He wanted to tell her that he had loved her forever. He wanted to sweep her into his arms and make love to her. Casting his fear of rejection aside, Ben gave in to the power of his wayward emotions and took her into his arms.

"Ruth, my darling . . . you are the one constant that makes my life worth living," he declared fervently just before his lips met hers. It was a soft, gentle exploration that sent shudders of excitement through him, and when Ruth molded herself willingly to him, he could hardly believe his luck. "Ruth?"

"Oh, Ben! I've wanted this for such a long time. . . ." She smiled up at him, her eyes alight with her true feelings for him.

"You have?"

"Oh yes," she sighed, kissing him again.

"I have, too," he finally admitted when they drew apart. "You're always in my thoughts. . . . I love you, Ruth. I always have."

"But, Ben, I never knew." Ruth was amazed as they moved to sit together on the sofa.

Ben shrugged almost guiltily. "I was afraid. I didn't know how you felt about me."

"Oh, Ben, I love you, too." She went into his arms again, thrilled at the joy of her newfound love.

He was surprised by the discovery, his blinding happiness dimming his worries about the war supplies and Matthew's confrontation with Noah. He gathered Ruth close, seeking out her lips for another cherishing embrace. He knew that from this moment on, no matter how dark the following days became, he would be happy. He had his love, and it was a love that would last forever.

Noah sat at the desk in the captain's cabin on board the *Sea Pride*, going over the contracts and manifests. At the sound of the door opening he looked up expectantly, thinking to find Captain Wells returning. He was surprised and pleased to find that it was his brother entering the room. Noah came to his feet and moved from behind the desk to greet him.

"Matthew, I'm glad you're here. I see you got my message this morning." He hoped that Matt was the bearer of good news regarding his deal with the dissidents.

"Yes, I received it." Matt's response was guarded.

"And have you notified Graves?" Now that the *Pride* was in port, Noah was anxious to conclude the business negotiations as quickly as possible.

"I did." Matt sat down in the chair before the desk as Noah returned to his seat behind it.

"And?"

Matthew had been dreading this moment since he'd left Ben. He knew his brother's loyalties, and he knew that there was very little real hope that he would change his mind. Still, he had to try.

"Graves has sent word that they do not have the funds to complete the deal at this time," Matt supplied levelly. "They do promise to make full restitution if you allow them to take delivery now and pay the balance due later."

"Damn!" Noah exploded. "I should have known they wouldn't be able to come up with the money!" Angrily he got up and began to pace the small cabin. His expression was thunderous as he mentally calculated the cut in profit he would have to take in selling directly to agents to the Crown. "Tell him the deal is off. I warned them."

"Noah . . . surely you don't want to cancel the whole thing," Matt began.

"The name of the game is profit, Matthew," Noah replied dispassionately. "I trusted them once. I can't afford to trust them again."

"What if I tell you I am willing to forgo my share of the profits if you will let Graves have the goods at the price they've now paid?" Matt considered this as the only solution for settling the problem to the benefit of both sides.

"What!?" His suggestion took Noah completely by surprise.

"I want you to conclude the transaction with Graves, and any monies that are not forthcoming can be taken out of my share of the profits."

"I can't let you do that!" he argued logically. "What are you going to live on? You have a wife now, and she's dependent upon you."

"I am fully aware of my obligations, Noah," Matt replied stiffly. "However, there are some things that take precedence. If the sanctions come, as they most certainly will, we have to be prepared. We need those supplies."

"Matthew," Noah said in his most earnest tone, "you can't be serious about this."

"I am."

"I can't let you do this. What will you live on? How will you exist?"

"If I have to, I will get a job. I'm not averse to hard work, Noah."

"That's ridiculous! You're a nobleman . . . a Kincade, for God's sake! I'll arrange a deal through Demorest. I should be able to clear enough to support us both for the time being," he conceded.

Matthew realized then that the change in his brother had been so complete, he was now sounding just like the avaricious English money dealers who'd gleefully claimed their possessions in payment of their father's debts. "I don't believe this. . . ." he remarked, stunned as he perceived the overall view of everything that had happened to them and the final results.

"What don't you believe?" Noah glanced at him quickly, wondering at his tone.

"I don't believe that you've changed so completely. You've actually become one of them."

"What are you talking about?" Noah demanded in annoyance.

"I'm talking about your obsession with money. Just now you sounded exactly like the bankers and debt collectors who scavenged our inheritance after father's death. Don't you remember how callous they were? Money was all that mattered to them. They didn't care about the lives that would be destroyed, or the traditions that would be broken—only the money mattered."

Matthew's analogy jolted Noah deeply. For the first time he saw clearly how very greatly he'd changed and what those changes had wrought in his life. He had followed the path he'd thought would bring him happiness. He had believed that reclaiming their lost wealth and status would make him happy again, but now he knew it wouldn't. Happiness was not related to things. Happiness came from within. In that silent moment of introspection, Noah accepted that he was not happy with himself.

He understood then that his quest to return triumphantly to England with his pockets well lined had carried with it a price far too great to bear. He had forfeited his closeness with Matthew. Not only that, but he had been so wrapped up in his pursuit of riches that he had discovered his love for CC too late to do anything about it. Now she was lost to him, too. The social life he had once thought he'd missed no longer held any appeal for him. He was alone, and he was miserable. Lost in a vortex of despairing, yet revealing, emotions, Noah could not reply for long moments as he stared at his brother.

Matthew, thinking Noah's silence reflected unspoken anger on his part, went on to defend his position. "Noah, I don't need money to be happy. I love Faith and the life we live here in Boston. All I want is to ensure that a free and open life will exist for our children and their children after them. It's for that reason that I support the revolution. I've seen the injustices and the high-handed ways of the government officials. I know the Crown is treating us as if we were ignorant children. We are educated men, Noah, who are only demanding rights that should be ours already!" He paused, his troubled gaze fixed on his brother's stony features. "Please, try to understand. I'm not alone in this. As you well know, the majority of those in Boston supported the dumping of the tea. Even CC Demorest—the daughter of one of the most important British agents in all the colonies—supports us without reservation. You know that."

"Yes, I know that," he replied hoarsely, thinking of CC. He loved her, and she was lost to him. So often they had loved and had not known it. She had confessed as much last night, and he'd refused to declare himself, taking umbrage at her effort to help the rebellion. Noah wondered how he could have been so blind not to have recognized what he was feeling, and he silently cursed the pride that was making it difficult for him to admit the truth even now. All this time he had been intent on only one thing—making the money in order to return to England. In the course of that single-mindedness, he had almost missed the very essence that would make his life worth living—CC . . . beautiful, loving CC. Noah knew a moment of very real anguish as he thought of how he'd humiliated her the night before, and he wondered if her profession of love had been true.

"I wish I could convince you to see things our way." Matt was becoming more and more dispirited as he talked, for he thought Noah was, once again, refusing to listen. "I hate the fact that this caused a rift between us. I want us to be close again, like we were before all the trouble started . . . before father died."

It occurred to Noah then that that was all he really wanted, too. "All right." Noah's reply was quick and brusque and left Matthew completely speechless.

"All right?" Matt finally managed as he stared at him in wonder.

"Yes, all right. You can have the goods."

"Are you serious?"

"Have you known me to jest lately?" Noah fixed him with a steady regard.

"Well . . . no . . ."

"Then you know my answer is serious," Noah said, suddenly feeling very relieved.

"You're selling us the goods, the payment doesn't need to be made until later?" Matt repeated dumbly.

"I'm selling you the goods for the money I've already collected. Tell Graves to forget the second payment. We've made enough profit just off the first half they've paid us to support us both for a while."

"Noah . . . I don't understand."

"Well, I do, at long last," Noah sighed. He raked a hand nervously through his dark hair as he glanced up at his younger brother, studying him with glowing eyes. Matt had become a man . . . a fine, intelligent man, and Noah knew he deserved the truth—all of it. "I've been wrong, about a lot of things. And you were very right about the money. . . . I have been obsessed with it, ever since that night. . . ."

"What night?"

"The night James Radcliffe and I quarreled." Noah looked away as the bitter memories flooded through him, and his hands clenched at his sides as he remembered the vileness of the other man's accusations.

Matt remained silent for a moment and then asked, "Do you want to talk about it?"

Noah faced him. "I've never wanted to before. It was something I believed better off forgotten, but I think it's long past time that you knew." Noah took a deep, steadying breath, dredging forth from the depths of his soul all the ugliness of that night. "James had never made a secret of his dislike for me, and when he heard of Father's death and our resultant losses, he seemed to take particular delight." Though long suppressed, the memory of James's sneering attitude and snide, underhanded comments still had the power to fill Noah with angry humiliation. It had been a painful time, and it was only with the greatest of willpower that he forced himself to continue relating all that had taken place. "I had been playing cards in the study with several friends, and he made a point of seeking me out. I had been aware of all the talk, but I was not prepared for such a vicious, open attack. . . ."

"What did he say?"

"James claimed that Father was not only a gambler, but a drunken coward as well. He accused him of committing suicide rather than face up to his losses, and he proclaimed that I was, no doubt, just as much a weakling as he was."

Matthew paled at the revelation. "Suicide? Father? Never!"

Noah nodded his agreement. "Up until that point, I had been managing to keep myself together. I had withstood the almost continual barrage of criticism and slights, but his insults pushed me beyond all reason. It had been bad enough that it had happened, but to have our family honor insulted was more than I could bear. No matter what else we are, the Kincades are not cowards."

"I'd always known that James's insult had to have been grievous to have evoked such hatred in you, but I'd had no idea just how despicable the man really was. No wonder you responded as you did. I'm sorry. . . ." Matt took a conciliatory step toward Noah, his heart aching as he understood finally his brother's torment.

"You have nothing to be sorry for." Noah shrugged off his concern.

"No, but I feel now that I should have been there for you. You've carried the burden all alone, all this time."

"It's better that you didn't know until now. You see, I've been too intent on what we lost. I'd lost sight of all that we had. I had forgotten what was really important in life."

Matt's gaze met and held his, and they embraced then, as brothers long parted but now reunited. When they moved apart, the warmth and affection that had long been missing between them for some time had returned.

"I'd better let Ben and Ryan know of your decision. Do you have a plan yet?"

Noah nodded, "I want this done tonight. The sooner it's over with, the better off we'll be."

"What do you want me to tell them?"

"Have them meet around midnight. As I estimate, the watch will be the lightest then, and there'll be less chance of being caught."

"I'll tell them. What about Captain Wells?"

"I'll take care of him," Noah assured Matt. "Just tell Graves to make sure his men know that they have to move quickly and quietly. And one more thing."

"What?"

"I don't want you to be involved with the actual 'stealing' of the merchandise. You and I have to come out of this looking innocent, or we could be arrested for treason."

Matthew nodded his understanding. "What are you going to be doing tonight while all this is taking place?"

"I hadn't thought about it."

"Why don't you return to the house with me now? You could stay with us, have dinner and spend the evening."

"Thank you, I appreciate the invitation, but perhaps it would be better if we all went to an inn for dinner tonight," Noah advised.

Matt frowned. "Why?"

"Lord Radcliffe and I had a slight run-in at Winthrop's, and in the heat of the unpleasant exchange he openly suggested that I was involved with the rebels."

"He did? Based on what proof?"

Noah nodded, grimacing. "He didn't have any definite proof, so his accusations were scoffed at by those listening, but I don't want to take any further chances. I'm firmly convinced that Radcliffe is the one who's having me followed."

"Lord Radcliffe?" Matthew was genuinely surprised. "But why?"

"I'm reasonably sure it all started because of my involvement with Eve Woodham."

"He's jealous?" A glimmer of understanding lit his eyes.

"Evidently so, and there was absolutely no reason for it."

"But I thought . . ."

"You thought wrong, Matthew," Noah cut him off sharply. "There's only one woman I care about, and that woman isn't the lovely widow Woodham."

"She isn't?" Matt asked, trying to subdue the lopsided grin that threatened.

Noah scowled blackly at his brother's amusement. "You've known all along what it took me until tonight to realize."

"You love CC?"

"Yes. I love CC," he answered flatly, "very much."

"That's wonderful! I'm sure she cares about you, too. Why don't you go to her and tell her how you feel?"

"I can't," Noah refused quickly.

"Why not?"

"The reason why I can't is none of your business. Just believe me when I say that things are finished between us." He remembered how terribly he'd humiliated her, and he knew he'd destroyed any chance they might have had for happiness.

"I'm sorry," Matt said earnestly.

"So am I . . . more than I can ever say."

There was a long, strained pause in the conversation before Matt brought up the subject of his encounter with Radcliffe again. "You didn't say, but I want to know what you and Radcliffe argued about at the ball. Did you have words over Eve?"

"No. We didn't openly argue over her." Noah gave Matt a measured look as he offered, "The general discussion had turned to the raid on the tea ships, and Radcliffe had made the remark that a show of force was needed to teach the dissidents here in Boston a lesson."

"He did?"

"Yes. He called the rebels fools, and I told him, in so many words, that the only fools were those who were so anxious to issue sanctions against the entire town of Boston."

"You defended us. . . . Thank you." Matt paused in amazement and then frowned. "I can't believe that Radcliffe didn't call you out for that remark."

"He did," Noah answered.

"He did?" Again Matt was astounded by all that had happened.

"Yes, but I refused to take up his challenge." Noah's eyes solemnly met his brother's as he searched there for understanding of his motive in turning down the duel.

"I'm glad." Vivid memories of the bloody clash in England still lingered in his thoughts.

"Yes, well . . . so am I." Noah was suddenly uncomfortable with all that he had revealed and he headed from the cabin. "Give me a few minutes to speak with Wells to make the arrangements for tonight, and then we can be on our way."

"I'll wait here for you."

The two scurrilous-looking men crouched low behind the stack of barrels near the waterfront, watching the two men approach.

"Is that him, Pete?"

"Aye, Mick, that's the bloke," Pete replied in low tones as he glanced down the dimly lit wharf.

"You sure? I don't want to go killin' the wrong fella," Mick told him nervously.

Pete gave him a derogatory look. "Whatsa matter with you? Ain't you never done this before?"

"I ain't never killed no one before . . . at least, not

402

deliberately, anyhow," Mick admitted.

"Well, just shut up and start swingin'. When they go past us, you take the one nearest you and hit him on the back of the head with your club. I'll take care of the other one. With any luck at all, we can drop 'em and rob 'em without drawin' any notice. We just gotta be fast. Remember, Mick . . . fast, quiet, and sure."

"We gonna rob 'em, too?"

"Why not? Just 'cause we're gettin' paid to kill 'em don't mean we can't make an extra pound on the side. They look pretty well lined in the pockets, you know what I mean?"

"Yeah . . . I know what you mean," Mick agreed, suddenly not feeling so skittish about the job they'd been hired to do. "But how come there's two of 'em? I thought we were only hired to kill the one."

Pete shrugged. "Who cares? One or two, makes no difference to me. All I want is the money that's due me when the job is done."

Noah and Matthew were deep in conversation as they strode along the street. They were completely unaware of the imminent threat until the two attackers launched themselves at them from behind.

"Matt! Watch out!" Noah shouted as he heard a stirring behind them and caught sight of their would-be assailants.

Matt was immediately alerted to the danger, and both brothers reacted much more quickly than the thugs had expected. The power of the killers' first blows was deflected and caused little real injury. The ensuing fight was bloody and vicious as the men grappled in the darkness. In the end, despite the hired men's dirty tactics, it was Noah and Matt who stood victoriously over their attackers' prone figures.

"Who? Why?" Matt gasped as he rubbed his jaw, sore and discoloring from a well-landed punch.

Noah wiped at the blood that trickled from the corner of his mouth as he stared down at the two. "I don't know, but I intend to find out." Kneeling down beside Mick, who was just beginning to stir, Noah grabbed him up by his shirtfront and gave him a rough shake.

"What?! Ouch! My head . . ."

"Your head's going to be hurting a lot worse if I don't get some answers out of you fast!" Noah snarled down at the shocked, battered cutthroat.

"What do you want to know?" Mick squealed in fright as he stared up at the man he'd tried to murder just moments before.

"I want to know why you attacked us?"

"We were hired . . ." he confessed hurriedly.

"Who hired you?"

"I don't know the gent's name, but Pete does! Pete'll tell you! I swear!"

In disgust, Noah turned his attention to his now-groaning companion. Angrily, he moved to the other man and snatched him up in the same manner as Matt stood guard over Mick. "I want to know who was behind this, and I want to know right now!" he demanded threateningly of the stunned Pete.

Pete had never expected two such fine-looking gentlemen to be able to fight back so brutally, and he was still recovering from the shock of having failed in the attack. "Will you let us go if I tell you?"

Noah smiled coldly. "If you don't tell me, I may not bother with the authorities at all."

Pete swallowed nervously as he glanced to where Mick lay. He realized then that there was no hope for their situation, and he quickly told him everything. "The man's name was Bartley, and he had an English accent, just like you."

"That tells me nothing." Noah spoke with little belief. "Does this Bartley work for someone else?"

"I don't know. . . ."

Noah tightened his grip on the thug, and the man squirmed nervously.

"But we can show you where he lives!" Pete continued. "We followed him home after we made the deal. We was wantin' to know who was behind wantin' you dead just in case they didn't pay up when the time came."

"Someone made a point of wanting me killed?"

Pete nodded. "The directions were to kill Lord Noah Kincade and to make no mistakes."

"Well, your first mistake was thinking you could do it." Noah stood and dragged the ruffian to his feet. "Bring that one along, Matt. We're going to find out right now who's behind all this."

They reached the side of the street opposite Radcliffe's home after a long trek through town, and Noah was not surprised. Glancing at Matt, he told him, "Either he's completely furious over my refusing his challenge, or he must have learned of my duel with James."

"I was afraid of something like this. What are you going to do, turn these two over to the authorities?"

Noah looked at Pete and Mick in disgust. "Yes, and then I'm going to meet with Radcliffe personally. Can you take care of our other business alone?"

"Yes," Matt assured him.

"Good. Let's find a constable. I'm most anxious to come back here and face him, man to man." There was grim determination reflected in Noah's voice as he headed away from the residential street with Pete in tow.

Chapter Twenty-Five

Eve drew slightly away from Geoffrey and gazed up at him with what she hoped was a good imitation of adoration. Since the ball at Winthrop's, she had been weighing her options between continuing with Geoffrey or pursuing Noah. After much deep thought, she had concluded it would be much wiser, for the time being, to stay with Geoffrey. She had made the decision, not because she desired Noah any less physically, but because his refusal to accept Geoffrey's challenge had lowered him in her estimation. That, coupled with the doubts she now had about his involvement with the dissidents, left her slightly leery of getting any more deeply entangled with him.

Eve wanted a man who was rich, handsome, and would marry her and take her back to England. In the beginning she had thought that Noah fit that bill, but now she was wondering. She had resolved that the best thing to do would be to bide her time. Certainly if Geoffrey's accusations were true, it would come out eventually. If they weren't, Noah would be vindicated, and she could continue her pursuit of him without the fear that she might be endangering her own status.

Now, smiling up at Geoffrey beguilingly, she asked, "What was it you were so eager to tell me, Geoffrey?"

Geoffrey's smile was confident. "I have some marvelous news, my darling."

"Oh?" Eve was growing more intrigued by the moment. "Tell me . . . do. Don't keep me in such suspense. I've been dying of curiosity ever since I received your note earlier today." She traced a single finger down the buttons of his waistcoat as she tried to coax the information from him.

"The news is that my brother James is dead."

Eve blinked in surprise as she stared up at him, trying to interpret his mood. "Geoffrey, I'm so sorry . . ." she began, thinking consolation was in order.

"Spare me the sorrow, Eve. I'm not in the least regretful of his passing."

"You're not? I don't understand. . . ." She frowned as she regarded him.

"James was my older brother, sweet, and I've hated him for as long as I can remember," he explained casually. "Now that he's dead, I'm the next in line. The title and all the family's holdings will come to me upon my father's demise."

"Geoffrey . . . how wonderful for you!" Eve began, and then knew a moment of consternation. Now that he was to inherit everything, would that mean he was going to have to return to England? "But, Geoffrey . . ." she pouted prettily, "does this mean you have to leave me?"

"My father has requested that I return to England as quickly as possible," he told her, making no effort to hide the smirk of satisfaction he was feeling over being asked to return home. He had never thought he would live to see the day when his father would welcome him back with open arms, but he knew it was about to happen. Not only that, but he would be returning with the good news that he had seen to it that Lord Noah Kincade had paid for the murder of James with his own life. How proud his father would be!

"Oh, Geoffrey . . ." Eve was devastated at the news. He would be leaving her! Now what was she going to do?!

"But don't worry, Eve. I couldn't leave you behind. You

shall come with me, and as the mistress of the future Earl of Radcliffe, you will want for nothing." Geoffrey thought he'd figured everything out. He wanted Eve for his own, but now that he was to be the earl, he knew she wouldn't make a suitable wife.

Eve was shocked into silence by his arrogant statement. He expected her to uproot herself and travel back to Britain with him as his *mistress!?* Outrage consumed her. *His mistress!* But before she could shriek her displeasure, the sound of a commotion in the hallway interrupted them.

"Lord Kincade! You can't just burst into Lord Radcliffe's home!" Bartley's loud protest warned Geoffrey of the imminent confrontation.

Geoffrey paled as he realized that the men Bartley had hired must have failed in their attempt, and he glanced around nervously. "Quick, Eve, go into the library and close the door. Wait there until I come for you."

"What is it, Geoffrey? Is something wrong? Why must I leave?" she asked anxiously as he steered her almost forcefully toward the connecting door to the library. "It's only Noah Kincade, isn't it?"

"No, nothing's wrong, but this is private business—something between Kincade and me. Just stay out of sight and be quiet." He closed the door behind Eve and rushed back to his desk. Searching desperately through his top drawer, he found the dueling pistol he kept there, primed and ready for possible danger. As Noah came crashing through the door, Geoffrey gripped the gun and held it down low so the other man wouldn't know of its existence, at least not yet.

Noah had noticed Bartley's quick, anxious glance toward the closed door at the back of the house when he'd first come charging into the hall. He had allowed himself to be detained by the servant for only an instant before pushing his way past as he'd headed for the room. Without pausing to knock, Noah had slammed through the door to find Geoffrey standing, almost casually, behind his desk.

"Lord Kincade, how nice of you to stop in." Geoffrey mocked, giving him a tight smile.

The cold deadliness of Noah's anger was apparent in his voice. "I turned down your challenge last night, but I am not refusing you now. I will take much satisfaction in meeting you face-to-face, as *men* should." The last was meant as a taunt, for he felt Radcliffe was lower than the lowest spineless creature for his hiring of the thugs to murder him.

"As you met my brother?" Geoffrey sneered.

"Yes, as I met your brother," Noah answered rigidly. "But I will take much more pleasure in seeing you dead. Your brother at least was a man. You are a cowardly fool!"

"Bartley," he directed sharply to the servant standing fearfully at the doorway, "send for the authorities. Lord Kincade has broken into my home and threatened my life."

"Yes, m'lord." Bartley rushed from the house.

"It was my life that was threatened, Radcliffe! Mine and my brother's! I had thought that we could settle this privately between us, but I shall be more than happy to tell the authorities about your hiring the assassins to kill me."

Geoffrey raised the gun and pointed it directly at Noah's chest as he smiled ferally. "You aren't going to be alive when they get here, so I have no worry on that account. You see, Kincade, what I shall tell the authorities is this. . . . You broke into my home, forced your way into my study, and then attacked me. I have Bartley for a witness, and upstanding citizen that I am, no one will doubt me." He stepped around the desk.

"Why, you . . . !" Noah's eyes narrowed as he sensed the danger, and his body went taut.

"You see," Geoffrey went on brazenly, "there were no aspersions cast upon my character the other night, whereas you . . . Well, your motivation would be quite clear. I had revealed to all your unsavory connections, and you wanted to silence me before any more damage could be done to your reputation." He cocked the pistol as he studied Noah mockingly. "Yes, that sounds most plausible. . . ."

"You're not serious?" Noah glanced from the gun to Geoffrey, trying to judge his intent.

"I have nothing to lose, and everything to gain," he sneered. "By killing you, I'll earn my parents' respect. They'll welcome me back with open arms. Decadent though I may have been in the past, no one would ever expect me of anything so unseemly as murder. And once I've assumed the title of the Earl of Radcliffe . . ." His smile was satanic as he moved closer to Noah, wanting to make sure that he didn't miss.

Noah read the crazed look in his eyes and knew that his moments were numbered. Desperate to save his own life, he launched himself at Geoffrey. Geoffrey had not expected Noah to attack, and he hesitated in surprise. It was that moment of hesitation that cost him his advantage. Knocked to the floor by the force of Noah's tackle, he barely managed to keep his hold on the gun, and they began to grapple savagely as each tried to gain control of the firearm.

Eve had been standing with her ear pressed to the connecting door, listening eagerly to their conversation. Geoffrey's declaration that he was going to kill Noah frightened her, and when she heard the sound of their struggle, she opened the door a crack to watch. There, in the middle of the study floor, she saw Noah and Geoffrey brutally fighting over the weapon. Horrified, she watched as they rolled violently about the room, each trying to get the advantage of the other.

Geoffrey, never one for physical violence, felt his strength fading as he continued to battle Noah. In a last grim effort, he tried to push him away with all his might and bring the gun to bear upon his chest, but Noah read his move and made a desperate grab for his wrist. Muscles straining, they fought on.

Eve found the sight of two grown men engaged in battle oddly exciting, and she watched, mesmerized. It was only at

410

the sound of the shot being fired that the deadly reality of the situation intruded. She gasped in stark terror as both men went rigid and then lay still upon the floor.

The gun still clutched in his hand, Noah was shaking as he drew back to stare down at Geoffrey's lifeless features. He didn't know how it had happened, but he didn't question his good fortune at being the one left alive. Wearily, he got to his feet.

It was in that position that Bartley and the law officer who'd accompanied him discovered Noah.

"He's in here. . . ." Bartley was saying as they rushed down the hall and into the room. The servant stopped dead in his tracks to stare at the scene before him in outrage. "He's murdered him! He's shot Lord Radcliffe!"

The constable hurried to take the gun from Noah as the servant bent over his dead master.

"It's like I was telling you! Lord Kincade forced his way into the house and threatened Lord Radcliffe! That was when Lord Radcliffe sent me to get you. . . . But it was no use! I was too late!"

Noah blanched at the servant's accusation and he turned to the law officer, wanting to give his side of what had happened. "I can explain everything. Radcliffe drew the gun on me, we fought for it, and it went off. It was self-defense."

"Not if what Mr. Bartley says here is the truth," the constable charged coldly. "You're under arrest for the murder of Lord Geoffrey Radcliffe."

"But I was defending myself!!" Noah protested. "If you'll check, you'll find that the weapon belonged to Lord Radcliffe. I came here unarmed."

"Let's go." The constable gave Noah a forceful push toward the door. "You can tell your side of it when you're arraigned. All I know is that we heard a shot, and I found you standing over the victim with the murder weapon in your hand."

"But—"

"Shut up." He turned to Bartley. "Shall I have help sent to you?"

"Yes," the servant requested, still stunned by all that had happened. "What are you going to do with him? He's guilty! He killed Lord Radcliffe!"

"I'll see that he's incarcerated, and he'll go to trial. Will you be willing to testify?"

"Of course! The man is a murderer, and I want to see him pay for what he's done!"

The realization that Noah had shot Geoffrey during the struggle had frightened Eve. Silently closing the connecting door, she'd given thanks that her presence hadn't been discovered. Upon hearing Bartley's charge that Noah had murdered Geoffrey, she'd grown fearful that she might be implicated in some way. As quietly as she could, she grabbed up her cloak in the hall and escaped from the house while Bartley and the constable were still in the study with Noah. Traveling on foot, she made her way as quickly as possible back to the safety of her own home.

"Miss Eve?" Peggy greeted her, a bit surprised to find her mistress returned so early and on foot. "I hadn't expected you to return until much later."

"Yes, well, Lord Radcliffe had some unexpected business come up, so I came home," she answered nervously.

Peggy took her cloak. "Can I get you anything this evening?"

"Yes. Have a hot bath brought up and a bottle of sherry," she told her, feeling definitely in need of a potent drink to steady her nerves.

"Right away, ma'am."

A short time later, glass of liquor in hand, Eve eased herself into the hot, scented water. Her thoughts were turbulent as she went over in her mind all that had happened. Geoffrey was dead. A few hours before, the news would have devastated her, but now she found she couldn't care less.

Geoffrey had been an ass. The man had thought she would be pleased with the news that he wanted to make her his mistress! She'd found his declaration highly insulting and thought he well deserved the end he'd met. Certainly, had they been able to continue their conversation without Noah's interruption, she might have shot him herself in her outraged indignation. Noah had merely saved her the trouble.

Noah . . . She smiled at the thought of him. He had been arrested for Geoffrey's murder. He had been accused by Bartley's testimony and convicted by his own stance when the law officer had entered the room. Only she could save him from a certain death sentence. Eve smiled even more widely as she imagined how grateful Noah would be for her timely rescue. Tomorrow she would go to the jail to see Noah. Perhaps, if she played this whole thing right, she might end up as Lady Kincade yet.

Draining the last of the sherry from her crystal glass, she refilled it again. Leaning back against the edge of the tub, Eve relaxed as the heat of the water and the potency of the liquor began to relieve her tensions. True, she had seen a man killed tonight, but she knew that it would all turn out to her advantage. Closing her eyes, she imagined herself married to Noah and returning to England as Lady Kincade. The dream appealed, and she grew determined to make it a reality.

Faith had been eagerly awaiting Matthew's return and she greeted him at the door when he finally made it back to the house. Her joy at seeing him was short-lived, however, when she noticed the rumpled condition of his clothing and the bruise already forming along his jaw.

"My darling, what's happened to you?" Faith ushered him quickly into the parlor, where her mother and Ben awaited him.

"Nothing important; I'm fine." Matt dismissed her worry

easily as he hurried forth to speak with Ben.

"How can you say it's not important when you look like you've been involved in a street brawl?" Faith followed him into the room.

"I have been involved in a street brawl, but that's not what matters right now. That's all been settled. What's important is"—he paused to draw her close to his side as his gaze met Ben's squarely—"that Noah has agreed to sell us the entire shipment for the amount already paid." His tone was triumphant as he happily revealed Noah's change of heart, and all thoughts of his unsavory encounter were wiped from the others' minds at the news.

"Noah agreed to that?" Faith was stunned but pleased, and Ben and Ruth exchanged puzzled looks.

"Yes." Matt nodded down at her. "We talked for quite some time. It was his decision . . . his offer."

"You told him of the arrangement Graves had suggested, didn't you?" Ben was totally dumbfounded by this change in Noah Kincade.

"Yes, I approached him with that offer," he explained, "but after we'd talked for a while, he told me to tell Graves that he would agree to deliver for the amount already paid."

"Matt, that's wonderful!" Ben was truly excited. "I'd better get back to Ryan right away with the news."

"I'll go with you. Noah explained to me how he wants the transfer to take place, and I think you'll be pleased with the plan he's devised."

"Let's go, then." Ben stood, glad to be the bearer of good news for a change.

"Wait up for me," Matt told Faith as they paused near the front door on their way out. "We're going to meet Noah later for dinner so no one suspects us."

"All right. You'll be safe now?" she asked, knowing that danger was always possible.

"Yes. I'm not going to participate in the actual moving of the goods. I'm just going along to help set everything up."

They shared a parting kiss.

"Be careful." Faith and Ruth both echoed the same sentiments as they watched the men they loved disappear into the darkness of the night.

"Ryan?" Ben's tone was hushed as he knocked on the door to the room in the Green Dragon's stable.

"Yes?"

"It's me, Ben Hardwick. Matthew Kincade is with me. . . . We have news."

"Just a minute . . ."

Ben and Matt could hear the murmur of voices and then footsteps approaching the door before the lock turned. When the door finally swung open, they moved inside immediately. Matt was surprised to find that several members of the group were still there, and that CC was one of them.

Ryan Graves regarded both men solemnly as he closed and locked the door behind them. He was filled with despair at his own failure to get the money for the war materials, and he was worried about how long their cause could exist without the necessary arms to defend themselves.

"Yes. What is it?" he asked dejectedly, expecting only bad news from these two men.

"Ryan, Noah Kincade has agreed to sell us the arms at the price already paid," Ben supplied quickly, anxious that everyone share in the good news.

Ryan stared at him in confusion. "He what?"

"I spoke with Noah just a short time ago, and he has agreed to sell you the shipment at no further cost," Matt told them.

"I don't understand. Why did he have this sudden change of heart?" Ryan couldn't help but be suspicious of the man who had been so coldly indifferent to his own plea just a short time before. "Is he setting us up? Has he planned something with the agents of the Crown in hopes of having us arrested when we take delivery?"

Matt was quick to defend his brother. "No! Absolutely not!"

Ryan eyed Matt skeptically. "I find it hard to believe that your brother's done a complete turnaround in his loyalties."

"Rest assured, Ryan, that Noah is a man of his word," Matt said in earnest. "He's also devised a plan that should work perfectly. I've already gone over it with him and am prepared to explain it to you now."

"And just what is this plan?" the leader asked.

Matt went on to outline in detail what Noah had arranged.

Ryan checked his pocket watch and then remarked, "We'll have to move, and move quickly; it's after eight already." Ryan had been convinced by Matt's firm testimony in his brother's defense, and he was now ready and willing to follow through on the nobleman's plan. Instructing the others in attendance to go out and notify those who could help, he ordered that they meet back there at the stables at eleven o'clock.

"What shall I do?" CC asked in annoyance when Ryan had failed to give her an assignment.

"I want you to wait here."

"Ryan—" she began, but he cut her off.

"I have no time to argue with you. Your disguise is an effective one, but we can't take the risk of possible discovery tonight. You may participate in the 'raid,' but the streets are too busy at this time of the evening for you to be running errands."

"You allowed me to take the initial payment to Kincade," she argued.

"That was a matter of necessity. This is not." He turned away, refusing to allow her any more discourse in the matter. "We'll meet back here at eleven. Any questions?" When none were forthcoming, he turned to Matthew. "I take it that it will be better for you not to help us tonight."

"That's right. Noah had insisted that we be as visible as possible to residents of town all evening."

Ryan nodded in accord with his thinking. "Wise decision."

He extended his hand to Matthew. "I thank you for all you've done for us, and if we can ever help you, you only have to say the word."

Matthew shook his hand in a firm, binding handshake. "Thank you. I appreciate it."

"Let's be off. Ben, you come with me. CC, are you going to wait here until we return?" Ryan asked as the others quickly dispersed to be about their business.

"Yes. I'll stay." CC was almost sullen in her agreement.

"Fine. We'll be back. Again, Matthew, our thanks."

The door closed behind them as they started off to help round up the other supporters they needed, and suddenly Matthew and CC were left alone in the privacy of the small room.

Matt knew a great sense of relief as he watched them leave, for he felt that everything was finally going to work out. All along he had hoped that Noah would come around to his way of thinking, and at last it had happened.

His mellow mood was interrupted, however, when CC turned on him and asked pointedly, "Did your brother really agree to those terms, or did you bribe him with your share of the profit?" CC's question was sharply put. After her disastrous encounter with Noah the other night, she thought it completely out of character for him to reverse himself and suspected that there had to be a more driving reason for him to alter his stance . . . a reason that probably had to do with money.

Matt's smile was easy as he replied, "Noah set those terms himself."

At his answer, CC's brows arched in surprise. "He did?"

Matt nodded, his pleasure evident in his calm expression. "Yes."

"I don't know what you said to him to make him change his mind, but I'm glad it worked. We needed those arms desperately. I know I tried everything I could think of . . ." Her tone was resigned and more than a little sad.

Matt was baffled by her statement and wondered exactly

417

what had gone on between his brother and CC. He knew for a fact that Noah cared deeply for her, and yet Noah had declared that there was no future for the two of them. Now he found that CC seemed as miserable in her own way as Noah was, and he wondered if talking to CC honestly would help.

"Noah's had a lot of things to work through lately, but I think he's finally getting everything back into the proper perspective," he offered, hoping to initiate a deeper conversation between them.

"It doesn't matter," she hastened to reply, not wanting to reveal too much of her own feelings. It didn't matter that she loved Noah. She knew that he did not love her and that he never would. "All that's important is that Ryan gets the materials he needs."

"The cause is all you care about?" he questioned probingly.

"Yes," she answered firmly, but her gaze shifted away from his.

"I'm sorry, CC, but I don't believe you. I've seen you and Noah together," Matt prodded, wanting to get to the bottom of the trouble between Noah and CC so he could help them, "and since I doubt seriously that you're the type who would try to influence Noah's decisions through less than honorable means . . ."—Matt was referring to the night she'd delivered the payment to Noah at the inn, and he'd walked into the room to find them heatedly embracing—"I think there might be more to your relationship with Noah than just business."

CC, however, had immediately thought of her most recent visit to his room, and she flushed guiltily. "I'm sure I don't know what you're talking about," she told him coolly.

"I'm talking about the embrace I witnessed between the two of you at the inn the night you brought him the first payment from Graves," he charged. "I'm talking about the fact that you two care for each other."

Glaring up at him defensively, she said, "You're wrong. I

418

don't care about him. Not at all. He has no soul, no feelings. He's cold and hard. All he really cares about is money."

Matthew was sure that she'd answered far too quickly and far too angrily. "CC, this change in Noah is real."

She snorted her disbelief.

"CC, there is a lot that you don't know about Noah . . . about the both of us."

"I know everything I need to know about him," she bit out.

"Do you know the reason for our coming to Boston in the first place?" Matt's gaze met hers, and she could read there pure honesty and openness.

"No, Matthew, and I don't want to. I've had enough dealings with Noah, and I think I understand him quite well. He is selfish, greedy, and amoral. He has no interest in our bid for independence. He just wants to make a fast profit off our grief and misery and then go back to England."

"I don't argue with your assessment of Noah. I'm sure from your point of view, that's the way he appears, but there's a reason for it."

"Please, spare me. . . ." she began frostily, but Matt refused to let it drop.

"Noah and I came to Boston because we had lost everything we owned in England," he started, and CC glanced up at him questioningly.

"You're rich. . . . Everyone knows that," she scoffed. "You own Kincade Shipping and—"

"We *were* rich," Matt emphasized. "You see, we discovered when our father died that he had been a gambler. His debts were so extensive that by the time the estate was straightened out, all Noah and I had left were the two ships, the *Lorelei* and the *Sea Pride*. Everything else was gone. Our money was gone. Our country estate and our London town house had to be sold to pay Father's outstanding debts. Our social position was forfeited. Noah was made a social pariah. Where once he'd been celebrated as a glorious member of the *bon ton,* he was suddenly an outcast. His pride suffered immeasurably, and he vowed that somehow, someway, he was going to reclaim it all. He became hardened to everything except his need to recoup our losses. He became a man possessed." Matt shrugged. "I didn't realize how much he had changed until the duel. . . ."

"Duel? What duel?"

Matt continued, "An insult was publicly issued by James Radcliffe, Geoffrey's older brother, and Noah challenged him to a duel. The whole ordeal was so painful that it's something we will never speak of again."

"What happened?" CC was caught up in his story.

"Noah killed Radcliffe."

CC gasped. Was this the reason why Noah had refused Geoffrey's challenge at the Winthrops'? And did Geoffrey know of the fateful duel?

Matthew went on, "It was a fair fight; there were witnesses to attest to it. But, CC, I'd never seen anything so brutal in my life, and I hope I never do again. It was then that I realized how deeply Noah had been affected by all that had happened. He was a changed man."

"I had no idea. . . ."

"I know. We've spoken of it to no one, yet I'm sure the news will be out soon. I'm positive that Radcliffe has now found out about Noah's connection to his brother's death."

"How do you know?"

"There was an attempt to murder Noah tonight." Matt's purpose in telling her was to gauge the depth of her feelings for Noah.

"What?!" CC paled and went still at the news.

"And Radcliffe was the one who hired the two men. They were given explicit instructions to see Noah dead."

CC's eyes widened in fear for the man she loved, and her hand was trembling as she reached out to clutch at Matt's sleeve. "Is Noah all right?"

Inwardly, Matt was pleased to see the truth of her emotions reflected so openly in her expression. "He's fine.

We managed to fight them off together."

"How do you know it was Geoffrey?"

"With a little applied persuasion, the men confessed as to who'd hired them," he explained.

"Where's Noah now? Is he safe?"

"After we turned the thugs over to the authorities, he told me to take care of working out the rest of the arms deal while he went on to Radcliffe's."

"He went to see Geoffrey? But why? Why didn't you just tell the authorities everything you knew and let them take care of it?"

"Noah wanted to handle it himself. He was going to face Geoffrey down with his knowledge of the planned attack, and then tell him that, rather than turn him in, he was going to accept the challenge he'd issued at the Winthrops'." Matt's tone was icy with hatred for the cowardly aristocrat.

CC had heard of Radcliffe's reputation with a sword. "Radcliffe is known for his expertise with a sword. . . ." Her emerald eyes darkened as she worried about Noah fighting him.

"Do I detect a note of concern in your voice, CC?" he asked, feeling most pleased with himself for having evoked such a response from her.

"Matthew! Don't toy with me!"

"You love Noah, don't you, CC? Why don't you tell him how you feel?"

"I have told him, and that's precisely why I know there's no future for us. Now tell me," she went on anxiously, "is Noah good enough with a sword to best Radcliffe?"

"Noah won't have any trouble handling Geoffrey," Matthew told her confidently, wanting to reassure her.

CC felt little relief at Matt's trust in Noah's ability. Instead she could only worry that something terrible might happen to Noah. All it took was just one mistake . . . one error in judgment . . . and he could be killed.

"You must let me know when the duel is to take place . . . I have to be there for him, even if he doesn't care. . . ."

CC insisted.

"Believe me, CC. He cares," Matt confided.

His declaration surprised her, and she glanced at him, puzzled. "How can you be so sure of Noah's feelings for me?"

"Because he told me." Matt read her shock at his revelation.

"Noah told you that he loves me?" Her heart was pounding, and she knew a moment of sublime joy.

Matt nodded. "He also told me that there could be no future for the two of you. Do you know why that was?"

CC looked away, embarrassed.

"CC?"

"I have to see him, Matthew. . . . I have to talk to him."

"He may be back at the Red Lion by now, but I don't think it would be wise for you to venture there dressed as you are."

"No. I'd better wait until tomorrow, when all of this is over. Matthew?"

"What?"

"Thank you for telling me." His confirmation of her longed-for dream filled her with joy, and tears stung her eyes as she gazed up at him.

"You're welcome," he grinned, feeling inordinately pleased with himself, and he touched her cheek with a gentle hand. "My brother is a very lucky man, whether he knows it or not." CC gave him a bright smile. "Now, I'd better get out of here. It's important that I let myself be seen about town tonight, so I won't be arrested for consorting with the rebels tomorrow when the theft of the arms shipment is discovered."

"Be careful, Matthew."

"I will," he answered as he started toward the door.

"You'll let me know about the duel?" she asked, stopping his progress from the room.

"Yes. I'll send you word as soon as I find out," he promised, and then he was gone, leaving CC alone with her thoughts of Noah.

Chapter Twenty-Six

Though Matthew appeared outwardly relaxed as he shared a late dinner with Faith and Ruth at the Red Lion, in actuality, he was nervous and on edge. When he and Noah had parted after turning in Radcliffe's hired thugs, they had agreed to meet at the inn by ten o'clock to dine. Now, however, it was well past midnight, and Noah had still not arrived.

Worries assailed Matthew. Had Noah encountered some kind of trouble with Radcliffe, or had something happened with the *Pride* that had demanded his immediate attention? Matt longed to know but realized it would be foolhardy for him to rush down to the wharf in search of him.

"Matthew?" Faith, intuitively aware of his very real distress, reached out to touch his hand.

Matt glanced up at her as he brought his thoughts to bear on the present. "Yes?"

"Shall we go now, or do you think we should wait for him a little longer?" she asked, her own concern for Noah reflecting in the depths of her blue-green eyes.

At her gentle prod, he realized that they had long since finished their meal and that there was no reason to linger any longer. "It is getting late. . . . I suppose we should be going. . . ." Matt began.

"I think so," Ruth agreed.

As Matthew rose from his seat and moved to assist Faith and Ruth with their wraps, a man came rushing into the taproom and hurried to join the men at the bar. He was welcomed warmly by his friends and immediately began to relate some bit of news to them that caused quite a furor among those gathered there. His thoughts still on Noah, Matt paid scant attention to the man until he heard Radcliffe's name being bandied about.

"That can't be true!" Someone doubted his story.

"It's true, I tell you!" the man declared vehemently to the others as the conversation grew excited at the bar. "I just heard it myself!"

"Come on, Gerald," another sneered. "I don't believe it!"

"Lord Geoffrey Radcliffe is dead! He was shot! Murdered tonight in his very own home!" the man insisted unwaveringly as he assumed a most pompous pose. He felt himself to be most consequential since he was bearing such important news, and he could hardly wait to relate the rest of the information he'd learned to his eager comrades.

Matt froze at the news, and his eyes suddenly glowed fervidly as his features grew strained and pale.

"Matthew?" Faith and Ruth, too, had overheard the conversation, and Faith glanced concernedly from her husband to the group of men.

He gave an abrupt shake of his head to silence them as he strained to hear all that was being said.

"Do they know who did it, Gerald?" someone else asked.

"They most certainly do. The authorities arrested him right on the spot. They caught him with the murder weapon in hand," Gerald informed them.

"Who was it?"

Gerald's expression reflected his delight in delivering the next bit of information. "The murderer is none other than Lord Noah Kincade."

"Lord Kincade?" A chorus of voices echoed the name in stunned surprise.

Matthew had almost sensed what Gerald's answer would be, and as he heard him pronounce Noah's name, a gut-wrenching pain seared through him. Without conscious thought, knowing only that he had to get away from the inn as quickly as possible without attracting any undue attention, he hurriedly escorted Faith and Ruth outside into the cold darkness of the December night. It wasn't until they were safely ensconced in a hired conveyance and on their way home that he spoke.

"As soon as I drop you at the house, I'm going to find Noah."

"Shall I send word to Ben?"

"There's no reason. What happened at Radcliffe's had nothing to do with Ben and the others. It was private and personal," he explained, and then suddenly a curse erupted from him as he felt close to violence. "Damn! What the hell happened between Noah and Geoffrey tonight?"

"The only way you'll find out is to go to him," Faith urged. "I'm sure he's innocent. Noah would never kill someone like that."

At her naive belief that Noah was incapable of savagery, the vivid, bitter memories of Noah's deadly duel with James Radcliffe surged into mind.

"I pray to God you're right," Matt ground out, hoping against hope that Noah was innocent, and believing deep in his heart that he was. For, though his brother had been discovered with the murder weapon in his hand, Matt knew for a fact that Noah had gone to Radcliffe's unarmed. If anyone had introduced guns into their confrontation, it had been Geoffrey.

"I know I am," Faith told him solemnly. "He'll probably be freed by morning. Just wait and see."

Despite Faith's hopeful encouragement, Matt felt that all was not as simple as it seemed. The situation must have looked very incriminating for Noah to have been arrested on the spot, and he wondered if there had been any witnesses to the shooting.

"Mother and I will be waiting up for you," Faith said supportively as the carriage drew to a stop in front of her small house.

"I don't know how long I'll be. . . ." he said distractedly as he climbed out and helped his wife and mother-in-law down.

"Don't worry about us. Just go to Noah and help him." Faith kissed him softly before going inside.

Matt strode back to the carriage and climbed in, ordering the driver, "To the jail, and fast."

"Yes, sir."

It was just after one in the morning when Matthew stormed into the jail and demanded to see Noah.

The jailer, a burly, mean-looking man, eyed Matthew disinterestedly before replying with only the barest essence of civility, "There's no visiting allowed this time of night."

"That's ridiculous! I'm Lord Matthew Kincade, and I've just received word that my brother has been arrested. I demand to see him so I can find out about all these trumped-up charges," Matt declared indignantly, calling upon his most imperious manner.

"Lord Kincade's brother, eh?" The guard sized him up more critically, judging his worth. "Well, I suppose I could bend the rules for a nobleman . . . for a price." He added the latter under his breath.

Disgustedly, Matthew tossed the man several coins and then watched as the jailer tested each coin for value.

"I don't suppose it would do much harm to let you in for a few minutes." He gave Matt a sly grin as he pocketed the money and then crossed the room to take the keys to the cells down from the hook on the wall.

"Thank you," Matthew replied stoically, wanting more than anything to knock the guard's smile right off his fat, smirking face.

After checking Matt for possible hidden weapons, the jailer took up a lamp and led him through a narrow passage to the back of the building. Unlocking a heavy barred door, he shoved it wide to allow Matt to pass through.

426

"Five minutes. No more. I'll be waiting right out here."

"You've been most kind." Matt gave him a pained smile as he stepped into Noah's private hell.

Noah was lying on the cot in his cell when he heard footsteps coming down the hall toward him. He knew the hour to be late and could only wonder at the reason for the disturbance, since the guard had told him that he would be allowed no contact with anyone until the following day. The sound of Matthew's voice filled him with hope, and when the door swung open, he rose quickly from the squalid bed to greet his brother.

"Matthew!" They regarded each other in stricken silence for just an instant before embracing.

"What happened?" Matt asked worriedly when they broke apart. He regarded his brother seriously and read in Noah's troubled gaze all the strain and anxiety he was keeping carefully under control. "We waited at the inn for hours. . . ."

"I know. I'm sorry, but they wouldn't allow me to send any messages tonight. How did you find out?"

"We accidentally overheard some men talking about Radcliffe's death and your arrest. Are you all right?"

"I'll be fine once I get out of here," Noah told him wearily as he began to pace the tiny cell. "I've demanded to be taken before the magistrate. If everything goes well, I'll plead my case tomorrow afternoon and then be released."

"I don't understand how any of this happened." Matt shook his head in confusion. "The rumor was that you had a gun . . . ?"

Noah nodded, his distress with the whole situation reflected in his expression. "I did, but it was Geoffrey's. He'd just gotten word of James's death and was convinced that I'd murdered him. He had the gun and was ready to use it. I fought him for it, and it went off while we were struggling."

"Weren't there any servants around?"

"Oh, yes. His faithful man, Bartley, was there. He'd refused to let me in initially, so I made the mistake of pushing

427

my way past him. Geoffrey sent him for the authorities, and by the time he got back, the fight was over. He told the constable that I'd broken into the house, and then when they found me holding the gun, standing over him . . ." Noah rubbed the back of his neck in a weary, almost defeated, motion.

"Did you tell the arresting officer that it was self-defense?"

"Yes, but with Bartley standing there claiming it was the opposite . . . well, my argument didn't seem very persuasive."

"You'll be out tomorrow." Matt tried to sound confident.

"I hope so. If not, the Radcliffes will certainly have had their revenge, won't they?"

"Time's up!" the guard shouted in an obnoxiously loud voice, abruptly interrupting their conversation.

"I'll be at your arraignment," Matt promised solemnly.

"I'll see you then."

The jailer was standing at the door grinning evilly as Matthew gave Noah one last reassuring look and then departed. Alone once again, Noah stretched out on the hardness of the cot and stared into the rank darkness of his cell. He'd been through many difficult times lately, but none had been as precarious as the position in which he now found himself. Still, he was Lord Noah Kincade, and that should count for something. Hopefully, justice would be served. Yet even as he tried to envision his own release, he knew the fact of Bartley's testimony weighed heavily against him. It would not be a simple matter to prove his innocence. Though Geoffrey hadn't planned his revenge this way, Noah wasn't at all sure he would be able to escape the dead man's devious clutches.

Miserably, he tossed on the hardness of the bed, seeking the blissful mindlessness of sleep, but the solace of rest would not come. Instead his thoughts were restless, dwelling first on Geoffrey's death, then the earlier attack upon himself and Matthew, and finally, on the conversation they'd had shortly before they'd left the *Pride*. Unbidden, CC slipped into his consciousness as he remembered Matt's point-blank questioning of his feelings for her. With a muttered curse, he swung his long legs off the uncomfortable cot and sat up. Bracing his elbows on his knees, he rested his head in his hands, his spirits sinking lower by the minute.

CC. Noah swore silently as his wayward thoughts centered on her. It was bad enough that he couldn't sleep for the memory of his encounter with Geoffrey, but to be tormented by images of CC was almost more than he could bear. Still, despite his desire not to think of her, her image floated through his mind—CC as he'd first seen her when she'd blushed so furiously, caught in the act of censuring English aristocrats . . . CC dressed in her boyish garb, and their first passionate encounter . . . CC in his arms in the gazebo, surrendering to the power of their mutual attraction for each other.

The memory of their lovemaking sent a surge of desire through him and drove him to his feet. In agitation, Noah began to pace the cell. He loved CC more than he'd ever loved another woman, but as he had told Matt earlier, he knew there was no hope for their future. Matt had declared that he was sure that she cared for him, but Noah knew that any affection she might have harbored for him had been killed by his blunt brutality to her when she'd come to him in his room.

Noah shook his head slowly in the sad acknowledgment that he had indeed lost her, and in that instant, all his other losses paled in significance. He had thought that money was what he needed to make him feel whole again, but he recognized now that CC's love was the only thing that would restore him. Determinedly, Noah vowed to himself that he would tell her how he felt once he was cleared of the charges against him. He knew she would be totally justified in laughing in his face, but he also knew he had to make the attempt, for the thought of a life without her was just too painful to even consider.

*　　*　　*

"Mr. Demorest?" Gilbert interrupted Edward and CC as they breakfasted together.

"Yes, Gilbert? What is it?" Edward asked.

"There's a boy here with a message for you. He says it's urgent, sir."

Edward gave his daughter a regretful glance as he lay his napkin beside his plate. "I'm sorry, my dear. I was looking forward to a leisurely breakfast with you this morning. I'll rejoin you just as quickly as I can."

"Of course, Father," CC replied, trying not to let her nervousness show as she wondered what news the messenger was bringing.

She glanced quickly at the clock on the mantelpiece. It was a little after 10:00 A.M., and CC knew that enough time had elapsed for the "theft" on board the *Sea Pride* to have been discovered and reported to the necessary port authorities, her father being one. With shaking hands, she lifted the delicate china cup and took a sip of the hot tea, hoping it would soothe her jangled nerves.

Thoughts of the excitement the night before returned, and CC drew a deep sigh of relief. The raid on the *Sea Pride* had come off successfully, and all involved had agreed that Noah's plan had been a stroke of genius.

A small smile curved her lips as she thought of Matthew's firm declaration that Noah did indeed love her. The smile soon faded, though, as she realized the possible danger Noah could be facing this very instant. Matthew had promised that he would relay any word of the duel to her, and the fact that she'd heard nothing from him left her slightly unnerved. Had they fought yet, or had they managed to avoid such a deadly confrontation? Determined to find out exactly what had happened, she vowed to seek out Noah as soon as she could and to tell him that she still loved him. She hoped that all Matthew had revealed about Noah's feelings for her was true. A faint doubt threatened, but she pushed it firmly aside. According to Matthew, Noah loved her, and she loved Noah—that was all that mattered.

The seeming resolution of her situation left her feeling oddly pleased, and she took another drink of her tea. It was then that CC realized she'd been so caught up in her thoughts that she hadn't sweetened the steaming brew. The bitterness of it caused her to grimace, and she was reaching for the sugar bowl just as the sound of her father's voice boomed through the house.

"Lord Kincade!?"

CC went immediately tense at his tone. Though she could make out no more of the conversation, she assumed that he had just been told of the rebels' actions the night before. Forcing herself to relax and assume an innocent demeanor, she waited for him to return. At the sound of the front door closing and footsteps coming back her way, she glanced up.

"Is there a problem with Lord Kincade? I heard you mention his name. . . ." CC asked coolly as she casually spooned a small amount of sugar into her tea. Expecting him to tell her of the outrageous rebel raid, CC was totally unprepared for his reply.

"Yes . . . I don't know how to tell you this delicately, but Noah Kincade has been arrested and charged with murder."

CC's spoon dropped from her benumbed fingers and clattered noisily against the china saucer. "What did you say?"

"The message I just received was from Winthrop. Noah Kincade was arrested late last night for the murder of Geoffrey Radcliffe."

"Oh my God!" she gasped, blanching at the news. How could this have happened? Noah would never have murdered Geoffrey in cold blood. It had to have been a fair fight!

Thinking her upset was due to the indelicacy of the news he'd just given her, Edward came to put a supportive arm about her shoulders. "Now, now, dear."

"I can't believe it, Father. What happened?" CC finally managed, struggling to bring her desperate fear for Noah under control.

"All I know from Harley's note is that Kincade broke into

431

Geoffrey's home and shot him. The constable found him with the murder weapon in his hand. There could be no mistake."

"But it's ridiculous! Noah Kincade is hardly the type to kill anyone so barbarically." CC wanted to protest his incarceration more vehemently, but she knew she had to temper her reaction lest she accidentally reveal too much.

"I don't know," Edward said thoughtfully as he moved to rejoin her at the table. "Considering all that happened at Winthrop's the other night . . . perhaps there was some truth to Geoffrey's charges after all, especially taking into account the one other piece of information Harley supplied that I think is particularly relevant."

"Oh? What?" CC struggled to keep her expression reflecting only mild interest.

"It seems that we've all been laboring under the wrong impression of the Kincades."

"How so?" She lifted her cup to her lips as casually as possible, hoping that her father wouldn't notice how badly she was trembling.

"Well, according to some new information Harley just received, the Kincade family has lost its fortune. It appears they're in dire financial straits."

CC pretended to be shocked by the news. "But, Father, how can that be?"

"It seems the family's fortune was lost to gambling debts incurred by the father," he supplied.

"That doesn't necessarily mean Noah and Matthew are doing anything illegal," CC pointed out.

"The fact that they've lost their money doesn't, it's true; however, it would make a connection with the dissidents much more plausible. The rebels, I'm sure, would pay a fine price for war materials, and that *is* what Kincade's shipping, you know. Maybe he is involved with them after all. Maybe Geoffrey was right in his accusations the other night, and maybe, just maybe, Kincade went there to silence him."

"What's going to happen to him?"

"I'm sure he'll be taken before the magistrate, probably sometime today."

"Will he be released then?"

"It's hard to say. It will depend on what kind of evidence there is against him."

"I see." CC sounded blasé in her interest, but in reality, she was in a panic at the thought of Noah in jail, accused of murder.

As calmly as she could, CC changed the subject to less important matters until, at meal's end, she excused herself from the table. Stifling the urge to race to Noah's side, she retired to the quiet of her room to think things through. CC wondered whether she could go to the jail and visit Noah without causing even more trouble. Certainly her heart insisted that she go to him right away, but logic dictated that trouble might ensue if her presence was reported to her father. How would she ever explain to her father her need to visit Noah, a man she'd professed to dislike, while he was in jail?

CC paced the room like a caged tigress for a long time, weighing the situation, until finally she knew she could delay no longer. Though her father might grow suspect of her activities if he found out about her visit, CC knew she had to take the risk. She loved Noah, and she had to let him know of her devotion, especially now when he was embroiled in such a dangerous situation

Hoping to draw as little attention to herself as possible, CC pinned her hair up into a sedate style and changed into her most nondescript day gown. After telling her father as coolly as possible that she was off on a shopping spree, she donned a dark cloak and concealing bonnet and hurried from the house.

The Honorable Millard Prescott, magistrate and an ardent king's man, sat on the high bench glaring down at Noah, his heavy-jowled face florid beneath his white, curled wig. "You presume too much, Lord Kincade!"

"I am an innocent man!" Noah protested furiously, feeling suddenly desperate. He had come into his arraignment believing that he would be vindicated, but he knew now that had been a foolish hope. The case against him was clear, and all the evidence indicated his guilt. "I was trying to wrestle the gun from Lord Radcliffe when it accidentally went off. The pistol belonged to Radcliffe! He was threatening me! Had I not fought him, Your Honor, I would be the dead man right now, not Lord Radcliffe!"

"We have a witness—Mr. Bartley—who, as you know, has testified to the fact that you forced your way into Lord Radcliffe's home and threatened His Lordship's life. This witness has declared in a sworn statement that Lord Radcliffe sent him to bring the authorities because he was afraid of you. We also have a sworn statement from the officer who returned to the house with Bartley. He states that they found Lord Radcliffe dead and you standing over him wtih the murder weapon in your hand."

"It was self-defense!"

"Lord Radcliffe is dead, while you are most alive, sir."

"Radcliffe was the one who introduced the gun to our argument! He—"

"Silence!" the judge's voice cut through Noah's attempt to explain.

Stricken, realizing that the truth was not going to come out, Noah fell silent.

"Lord Radcliffe has been murdered, and there is additional information that adds weight to the testimony already given against you. It appears that you and Lord Radcliffe had a major confrontation at a party at Major Winthrop's home. Is that true?"

"Yes," Noah ground out, feeling Radcliffe's trap closing more securely about him.

"And is it also true that this argument was over a supposed connection between yourself and the dissidents who are calling for independence for the colonies?" Judge Prescott demanded, his eyes narrowing accusingly as he regarded Noah. He thought it most revolting that a nobleman of Lord Kincade's status could possibly be involved with such rabble.

"Yes, there was an exchange of words between us regarding that subject, but—"

"Lord Kincade! I have not asked for a dissertation from you, merely an answer," the magistrate interrupted before he could say more. "Isn't it also true that your family is virtually penniless? That your fortunes are all but lost?"

"Yes." Noah answered tersely as he fought down the feelings of humiliation that threatened to engulf him. He had feared that such evidence would appear, and his fears had not been unfounded. He held himself proudly, mindful of who he was, and the dignity that went with that position.

"Is it not also a fact that your brother, Lord Matthew Kincade, has recently married one Faith Hammond, whose father was a known political troublemaker?"

"The fact of my brother's marriage is irrelevant to the case against me," Noah stated with dignity and righteousness.

"Lord Kincade, these other things may have substantial bearing on the case, and we must give careful consideration to all possibilities," the magistrate instructed harshly. "You're request for release is denied. From the facts I have before me, I think it would be ludicrous to even consider it. Trial will be in three weeks, and until that time, you will remain in custody."

Noah went white-faced at his pronouncement. He glanced back into the sea of faces of the spectators who'd watched his debacle of justice and caught sight of Matthew. His brother had risen to his feet at the judge's announcement, his fists clenched in frustrated fury, his expression anguished in his torment. Though Noah wished he could comfort and somehow reassure him, he knew it was impossible. He kept his own silver-eyed gaze inscrutable as their eyes locked in a silent exchange. At the guard's direction, Noah turned away from Matt. With what little control he had left, he allowed himself to be led from the courtroom, maintaining his calm demeanor even now in the face of his greatest travail.

Matthew watched Noah go, and he realized how humiliated his brother had been in having his bid for freedom denied, and their losses revealed publicly. Desperate and worried, Matt knew the evidence was damning, and he wondered if Noah had even the slightest chance to prove his case.

"If he's convicted of murder, as it seems he will be, they'll hang him!" a man who'd been sitting near Matthew proclaimed to a companion, and Matt couldn't help but overhear their conversation.

"You really think so? He is a nobleman. . . ." His friend expressed his doubt.

"Of course." The man nodded firmly. "It was Lord Radcliffe he killed, and they can't let that go unpunished. Kincade will face the gallows."

"But what about those other charges? Do you think he really is involved with the rebels? That would amount to treason!"

"Indeed it would, but who knows? Either way, if he's convicted, he's a dead man," the man concluded almost flippantly.

Matt fought with all his strength to keep his temper under control as he walked away with seeming casualness. In the opinion of the two men, Noah had already been proven guilty. Matt felt certain that a jury would probably react the same way. His mind was racing as he tried to decide what to do next. He could not sit idly by and watch his brother hang for an offense he was certain now Noah had committed in self-defense. It was then that he recalled Grave's open-ended offer of help, and he hurried from the chambers determined to seek him out.

Chapter Twenty-Seven

Eve was beside herself with delight as she descended from her carriage in front of the jail. Everything was working out far better than she could ever have hoped. Peggy had come to her just as she was leaving to pay Noah a visit with the "news" that Lord Kincade had been arrested for shooting Lord Radcliffe. She'd also related that he had already been arraigned and was not going to be released but would remain incarcerated until the date of his trial. Peggy had expected her mistress to be disturbed, and knowing this, Eve had obliged by pretending to be terribly upset by the news, not letting on that she had known most of it since the night before. Now, as she prepared to meet with Noah, Eve found the information that he had already been arraigned and denied release exciting, for it strengthened her position with him. Surely Noah would be amenable to whatever she suggested, considering his current circumstances.

"I'm here to see Lord Kincade, please." Eve smiled beguilingly at Frank Douglas, the young guard on duty.

As Douglas glanced up, his eyes widened at the sight of the gorgeous woman standing before him. She was a vision of loveliness, and he stared at her speechlessly for an instant, savoring the perfection of her pale tresses and beautiful features. Finally, realizing how ridiculous he was acting, he bolted to his feet and stammered, "Yes, ma'am . . . right this way, ma'am!" Hurrying to open the door that led to the cells, he unlocked it and held it open for her.

Eve started to walk past him. "Thank you so much."

"He's the last cell on the right," Douglas told her courteously, and she rewarded him with another bright smile. The delicate scent of her perfume teased his senses, and his heart began to beat erratically as she swept past. As he followed after her down the narrow hall, his gaze remained heatedly upon her, and he found himself mesmerized by the feminine sway of her hips. He thought her one of the most attractive women he'd ever seen, and he envied Lord Kincade her affections.

As Eve moved down the hall, she surveyed the interior of the jail with disdain. It was a dark, depressing place, and she couldn't wait to see Noah freed from its confines. How wonderful it was going to be—marrying him and having him in her bed! She could hardly wait! Her pulse was racing at the thought, and she was eager to see him again. Eve noted with relief that Noah was the only prisoner. She was glad that if the guard left them alone, they would have at least some modicum of privacy in which to talk.

"Kincade . . . you got company!" Douglas called out gruffly as they reached the cell, and he unlocked the heavy door.

Since returning from his arraignment, Noah had been prowling the small area of his confinement in a state of morose agitation. Consumed by the enormity of the charges against him and his seemingly hopeless position, he was desperate to come up with a way to prove his case.

He had not murdered Radcliffe! It had been strictly self-defense, and yet no one believed him. Was this to be his end? The absurdity of his current miserable state filled him with bitter emotion. Things had seemed so final at the hearing.

Even the judge had seemed convinced of his guilt. Was he to have no recourse?

The sound of voices came to him then, followed by the creak of the office door opening into the hallway. Noah stopped his incessant pacing to face whoever was coming to see him. He hoped it was Matthew returning with the best attorney in Boston.

"Noah?" Eve called his name tentatively as she stepped into his cell.

Noah was greatly disappointed when he discovered it was Eve, for she was one of the last people he wanted to see right now.

"I'm here, Eve," Noah responded flatly. Her pale beauty made the jail seem even more sordid than it was. He suddenly became aware of how disheveled he was after having spent the past twenty-four hours in the same set of clothing, and how his overnight growth of beard had left him looking more than a little disreputable.

"Oh, Noah . . . I came as quickly as I could," Eve gushed as she entered the cell to face him. He looked very tired, and she was pleased. The more hopeless he thought his situation to be, the greater power her testimony would have over him.

"I'll be right out front if you should have any trouble, ma'am," the jailer interrupted as he heard someone else entering the outer office.

"Yes, of course, but I'm sure we'll have no problems, sir," she answered courteously, never taking her eyes off Noah. How she longed to be held in his strong arms! How she wanted to be the one to soothe the worried look from his brow and comfort him in his time of desperation!

"It was kind of you to come," Noah said calmly as he watched the jailer disappear back down the hall.

"Well, I just couldn't stay away, especially after I heard that you weren't released after your arraignment." She gave him a measured look, wondering exactly how to broach the subject.

Noah thought her presence there odd. He wished she would say whatever it was she came to say and then leave. "Yes, it appears that I will be a *guest* here for some weeks."

"Yes, I know, and I think I may be able to help you." Her eyes were brilliant upon him as she moved a bit closer, ready to tell him her proposition.

"I appreciate the thought, Eve, but I doubt that that's possible," Noah told her.

"But that's where you're wrong." She smiled sweetly as she rested a hand lightly upon his chest. "You see, I have certain information. . . ."

Noah went tense at her taunting statement and wondered angrily what it was she knew. He gripped her wrist tightly as he demanded, "What information?"

"Suppose, just suppose, there was a witness to your struggle with Geoffrey last night," Eve said in a teasing voice.

"Eve . . ." Noah's tone was threatening, as her coy innuendos grated on his already frayed nerves. "If you know something, for God's sake, go to the authorities with it!"

"Ah, but darling." She moved closer, as if to share a confidence, and slipped her other about his neck. "Why should I do that unless there's something in it for me?"

"I don't know what you're talking about, Eve," he retorted, a muscle in his jaw tightening as he suppressed his rage. Did she, in truth, know something that could set him free? If she did, they why was she hesitating in going to the authorities with the information?

"I know you're the type of man who's not averse to making a profitable deal."

"Yes . . . so?"

"If you cooperate, I can arrange for you to be out of here before the day is done."

"What kind of deal are you planning? What is it you want?" Noah's eyes were cold upon her.

"Haven't you always known? I want you, Noah, only you." Brazenly she pressed herself fully against him and rose

440

up to kiss him passionately on the mouth.

CC was nervous as she approached the jail. She wasn't quite sure what kind of reception she was going to get from Noah, plus she was concerned that her father might discover her highly unorthodox visit and question her motives. She was so wrapped up in her own thoughts that she did not notice Eve's carriage waiting out in front as she entered. It surprised her to find the outer office deserted, but a guard soon appeared from the back of the building. She was glad that he was not one of her acquaintances and, forcing herself to remain calm, she crossed the room to speak with him.

"I'd like to visit Lord Kincade, please," CC requested demurely.

Douglas shook his head in amazement as he wondered just how many beautiful women Kincade knew.

CC, aware of his hestitation, worried that something had happened to Noah, and she quickly asked, "Is there a problem?"

"Oh no, ma'am. I don't have a problem." He grinned almost slyly as he made the statement. He had thought the blond woman good-looking, but this one was even prettier . . . and younger.

CC was puzzled by his attitude but dismissed it as unimportant. The only thing that mattered was that she see Noah and let him know how she felt.

"Then may I see him, please?" she pressed.

"Yes, ma'am. Just go right through this door." He held the door wide to admit her. "I'm sure you'll be able to find him without any trouble. He has someone with him already."

"Oh? Well, thank you." CC wanted to rush to Noah, but she moved with a calm deliberateness that belied her true feelings. She assumed that Matthew was the person he was seeing, and she was relieved to think that Matt would be there to take the edge off the first moments of their encounter.

The hall stretched long and narrow before her as she headed on her way. She was nearly to the end when the sound of a woman's voice—Eve's voice—came to her!

"I know you're the type of man who's not averse to making a profitable deal."

"Yes . . . so?"

"If you cooperate, I can arrange for you to be out of here before the day is done. . . ." Eve's tone was husky with sensuality.

The rest of the conversation blurred as CC froze, and her heart jolted painfully within her breast. Miserably, she realized that it was not Matthew who was visiting Noah, but Eve. Noticing that it had suddenly become quiet, she took that last fateful step forward to see Noah and Eve wrapped in a passionate embrace. CC was disconsolate as she backed away, and it took all of her willpower to muster the cool demeanor she possessed as she left the jail. She was so immersed in her own agony and so desperate to get away that she didn't notice she passed one of her father's business acquaintances on the street as she fled the scene.

When the kiss ended, Eve gazed at Noah longingly, the desire she felt for him plain to read upon her lovely features. "I've wanted you since the first moment I saw you. We were meant to be together."

Noah's expression was inscrutable as he stared down at her dispassionately, not speaking, only listening.

"It was just a quirk of fate that I happened to be at Geoffrey's last night, but I was." Eve smiled up at him confidently. "I saw everything. I know exactly what happened between the two of you. It was self-defense, Noah. I know that Geoffrey was planning to shoot you, and that you fought over the pistol. I was watching even when it went off during the struggle."

442

Noah went rigid in his anger. She had been there, yet she had allowed him to be arrested for Geoffrey's murder! What kind of vicious viper was she?

"What terms are you setting for your testimony?" he asked icily as his gaze was steely upon her.

"I want you to marry me, Noah," she told him archly.

"What?" He couldn't prevent the disbelief that entered his tone.

"Make me your wife. I'll be a good wife to you, and I'll make a lovely Lady Kincade." She preened knowingly, thinking her victory assured.

"No." There was no hesitation in Noah's reply, for the thought of spending a lifetime tied to this conniving witch filled him with revulsion. There was only one woman he cared about, one woman he wanted to marry—and she wasn't Eve.

Eve stared up at him in confused outrage, shocked by his quick reply. "You're refusing?"

"Yes, Eve. I'm refusing." His answer held a note of finality to it.

"But that's ridiculous!" she shrieked. "You'll hang for sure if I don't testify in your behalf!"

"That may well be, but I am Lord Noah Kincade, and I do still have my pride." He walked away from her and stood looking back at her with regal contempt. "As you well know, I am innocent of the charges against me. I will not prostitute myself, not even to gain my release from this hellhole."

"Are you saying that you find almost certain death preferable to a marriage to me?" Eve was furious and crushed at the same time.

Noah's silver eyes raked over her in disgust, and without his saying a word, she had her answer. Eve flushed painfully at his unspoken insult.

"You're a fool!" she hissed at him.

Noah shrugged.

"You'll be sorry!"

"I sincerely doubt it," Noah replied.

"I hope you rot in hell!" Eve snarled, wishing Geoffrey had shot him!

A faint, derisive half smile touched his lips at her remark. "That is a very definite possibility."

At his answer, Eve glared at Noah scathingly and then stormed from the cell. Slamming the barred door shut as she left, she never looked back. She had been defeated, and in a most personal way. Never before had Eve been rejected or denied something she'd really wanted. Ever the actress, she disguised her emotional turmoil as she bid the guard goodbye, then quit the building and climbed into her waiting carriage.

Her feeling for Noah had undergone a drastic change. The pain of his open rejection had pierced her heart and hardened her. What once she'd considered love was now converted to hatred. Filled with the desire to see him suffer, Eve vowed to herself never to reveal to anyone what she had seen and heard that night at Geoffrey's. If Noah didn't want her and preferred to die rather than marry her, so be it. He would face the gallows without her testimony, and she thought it a suitable end for him. Content that he would pay the ultimate price for his arrogance, Eve settled back on the seat in the coach and smiled as she envisioned Noah's execution.

CC returned home, raced upstairs to her room, locked herself in, and threw herself upon her bed. Only then, when she was certain she was alone, did she allow herself to cry. Noah and Eve . . . She had thought that there was nothing between them, but she'd been wrong. Obviously they were lovers. Why else would Eve have come to him at the jail?

The memory of their embrace and the snatch of the conversation she'd overheard thundered through her thoughts. *"I know you're the type of man who's not averse to making a profitable deal."*

444

"Yes . . . so?"

"If you cooperate, I can arrange for you to be out of here before the day is done. . . ." The conversation lingered hauntingly in her mind, and CC tried to think clearly for a moment. Eve had been promising to arrange Noah's release, and she wondered how that could be possible when he'd already been denied his freedom at his arraignment. Something wasn't right. Something didn't fit.

Sitting up in the middle of her bed, she frowned in concentration as she wiped angrily at the tears that still dampened her cheeks. How could Eve guarantee Noah would be freed? Did the other woman know something vital about the shooting, or did she have a connection with someone of influence? The latter thought sent a chill of fear through her as she considered the possibility that Eve was fronting for the authorities and perhaps trying to get information from Noah regarding the rebels in exchange for his release. Certainly, after hearing of Noah's arrest for Geoffrey's murder, her father had been convinced that he was involved with them. Were they the ones behind Eve's "deal"?

Suddenly realizing that Noah might reveal everything in order to save his own neck, CC charged off the bed. She had to warn Ryan and the others of Noah's possible treachery. After taking only a few moments to bathe her face in cool water so no one would know she'd been crying, CC started from her room, intent only on getting to Ryan as quickly as possible. She was just starting down the staircase when her father's study door opened, and he stepped out into the hall with Thomas Highland. CC backed away from the stairs and down the hall, waiting for Highland to leave. She had too many important things on her mind right now to waste any time making pleasant conversation with her father or one of his business associates.

"Thank you, Thomas. I appreciate your coming by and letting me know," Edward was saying as he accompanied him to the door.

"I thought it was something you should be informed of, so I came over as soon as I could."

"Again, my thanks."

CC heard the front door close behind the visitor as he left, and she started down again, eager to be gone. To her surprise, she came face-to-face with her father, who was on his way upstairs.

"Cecelia . . ." He stopped and stared at her, his expression quixotic.

The fact that he had used her full given name gave CC pause, and she smiled as brightly as she could at him as she continued on her way down. "Hello, Father."

"I thought I had heard you come in a bit earlier, and I was just on my way up to see you. Are you planning on leaving again?"

"As a matter of fact, I was," she replied easily. "Was there something important you had to discuss with me, or can it wait until this evening over dinner?"

"I think it's important enough to delay you. Were you planning on going shopping again?" he inquired.

"As a matter of fact, yes—" she began, but he cut her off.

"Get into my study right now!"

Her father had never spoken to her in such a furious tone of voice before, and CC's eyes widened in surprise as she tried to imagine what could have angered him so.

"Of course," she agreed, leading the way into the privacy of his personal office. "What is it?"

"Sit down!" It was a command, and she hurriedly complied, slipping into the chair that faced his desk as he stalked around behind it.

Edward stood poised for battle as he glared at his daughter seated there in front of him. CC looked so sweet and innocent that he wondered how she could have been so brazen. How could she have done it? Thomas Highland had just stopped by to inform him that he'd seen CC exiting the jail earlier that day. As it was highly irregular for a woman, especially a young, unmarried one, to visit such a place, he'd thought it important that Edward be informed. Edward agreed with his assessment. His daughter had had no business whatsoever going to the jail. He was outraged by her behavior, and he would punish her accordingly.

CC was growing more and more nervous as she watched the play of emotions on his face. He was angry with her, of that she had no doubt, but what she didn't understand was why. Unless . . .

"Father? Is something terribly wrong?"

"Why would you ask that?" Edward countered sharply.

"I don't know. It's just that you look very upset."

"Yes, you're right about that. I am upset."

"Is there something I can do to help you?"

"I doubt if you can help me with it, my dear. You see, you are the cause of my anger."

"Me?" CC was suddenly frightened.

"Yes. I had no idea that I had raised a liar for a daughter."

"A liar?" She swallowed nervously as she blanched.

"Yes. While you told me that you were going shopping earlier today, it appears that you had another goal in mind."

"Father, I—"

"Let me finish!" he ordered, barely suppressing the fury that was consuming him. "You told me you were shopping; however, Thomas Highland informs me that you were at the jail today, apparently visiting Lord Kincade. Is that true?" Edward demanded.

Cornered and seeing no way out, she answered truthfully. "Yes."

"For God's sake, CC!" he thundered. "No decent, self-respecting woman would go to a jail unescorted. It's unheard of! You've disgraced yourself and me!"

"I hardly think that I've disgraced you, Father," CC managed calmly, not bothering to deny any of his claims.

"My dear, you made a spectacle of yourself visiting that man in jail! He murdered Lord Radcliffe, and Lord knows what else he's done! I don't understand how you could do such a thing! I want you to go to your room and stay there."

447

"Father!" She came to her feet in protest. "You can't do this to me!"

"I most certainly can, and I just did. Go to your room and stay there until I've had time to calm down. If you don't, I swear, CC, I just might throttle you!"

CC's eyes widened at his threat. She had never provoked her father to such anger before, and she knew she'd better do as he said. "Yes, sir." Quickly and quietly, she left the study and hurried upstairs to seek refuge in her own chamber.

Edward watched her until she had disappeared up the stairs, and then he sat down heavily at his desk. Elbows resting on the desktop, Edward leaned forward to rest his head in his hands. He thought it extremely odd that CC had gone to the jail to visit Kincade. She had always claimed her dislike for him, and he wondered at her real reason for going. He was determined to find out, but first he knew he had to get his anger under control. Once he knew he could face her without losing his temper, he would try to get to the bottom of her scandalous behavior.

Things looked decidedly black, and Matthew was more worried than he'd ever been at any other time in his life. Noah was in dire trouble, and if he wanted to save him, there was only one course of action open to him. Since leaving the arraignment, he had combed the city trying to locate Ryan Graves. It wasn't until near sundown that he finally caught up with him in the taproom of the Green Dragon.

"Ryan! I need to speak with you right away . . . privately," Matt said as he approached the table where Ryan was sitting with two men Matt didn't recognize.

"Of course, Matthew," Ryan stood up and, after excusing himself from his other companions, directed Matt to a table in a deserted corner of the room. "What is it? Is there a problem?"

"You haven't heard?" Matt was stunned as he sat down opposite Ryan.

"Heard? Heard what? I traveled with our shipment today and only just returned," he explained quickly, wondering what he'd missed during his time away.

"Noah's been arrested and charged with murder!"

Ryan looked genuinely stunned by the news. "What?! When did this happen? And who is he supposed to have killed?"

"He was arrested last night," Matt stated. "He'd gone to face down Geoffrey Radcliffe over a personal grievance, and evidently things got out of hand. Radcliffe threatened him with a pistol, they fought over it, and it went off. The authorities found Noah standing over Geoffrey with the gun in his hand."

"Were there any witnesses?"

"Oh, yes, there were witnesses," he went on disgustedly. "Radcliffe's servant has given testimony that Noah forced his way into the house and threatened Radcliffe. He also stated that Radcliffe sent him for help because he was afraid of Noah."

"Has he been arraigned?"

"Yes, earlier today, but the magistrate refused to release him. It doesn't look good, Ryan. It doesn't look good at all. Not only do they have the servant's testimony, they also found out about the fight Noah had with Geoffrey at a party the other night. Because of that argument, in which Noah defended our cause, they've accused him of being involved with us."

Their gazes were solemn as they met across the table, and Ryan asked, "What do you want me to do?"

"Noah will get no justice in that court. I've already seen it in action. I've got to get him out of there!" Matt insisted. "You once said that if I ever needed your help . . ."

"And I meant it, Matthew. Let me see what I can arrange. I'll send you word at home as soon as I come up with something." His pledge was in earnest. "Stay there and wait until you hear from me."

"Thank you, Ryan."

Chapter Twenty-Eight

"Matthew, if you're going to accept my assistance, then things have to be done my way!" Ryan argued as he met with Matt several hours later at the Green Dragon.

Matt scowled blackly at the rebel leader. "But he's my brother! I want to help!"

"The best way you can help Noah is by staying completely out of it. Once he's been freed, just who do you think the authorities are going to question? You've already told me that they brought up the subject of your marriage to Faith during the arraignment. You have to be able to prove your innocence, so it's important that you know none of the arrangements."

Matt looked suitably chastened as he realized he would be the prime suspect.

"Now, do you want us to do it or not?" Ryan demanded curtly. Time was of the essence. If they were to get Noah Kincade out of jail tonight, he had to set his plan in motion soon.

Matt knew Ryan was right, but he found it irritating that he couldn't help Noah escape. He nodded his agreement. "Is there *anything* I can do?"

"Nothing; at least, nothing for right now. Once we've got him out of jail and safely in hiding, I'll arrange for a meeting between the two of you. Until then you know nothing, so act like it. Carry on with your usual activities."

"All right," he answered grimly as he thought of how long the next few hours were going to seem while he waited for word that Noah was free and safely away.

"Good." Ryan stood up, anxious to be about his mission. "If anything happens . . . you'll let me know?"

"Nothing's going to happen," he told Matt firmly.

"How can you be so sure?"

Ryan's smile was enigmatic. "Not all those working at the jail are the king's men."

With that he was gone, and Matthew was left alone to worry and wait.

"Kincade!"

The voice outside his window was little more than a hoarse whisper, and at first Noah thought he'd imagined it.

"Kincade!" It was slightly louder the second time. Realizing that it was real and not a figment of his imagination, he quickly got up from the cot and peered out into the darkness of the Boston night.

"Who is it?" he called back in hushed tones.

"Never mind who it is, just be ready!"

Noah was puzzled. "Ready for what?"

"We're getting you out of there!"

Stunned, his emotions in turmoil at the thought of being rescued from jail, he quickly lay back down on the cot and pretended nothing had happened. The thought of being broken out did not sit well with Noah, for he knew he was innocent of the charges against him. He felt that by fleeing, he would be admitting his guilt. Still, Noah realized that if he stayed and was convicted at his trial, he would be just as innocent, but he would also be dead. It didn't take Noah much time to decide to go along with his rescuers. Whoever they were, they were risking everything to help him, and he was going to do all he could to make sure they didn't fail.

Noah didn't know how his liberators managed it, but shortly after he'd been warned, a major ruckus broke out in the street in front of the jail. As the guard on duty went out to attempt to quell the violence, a man he'd never seen before rushed down the hall to his cell and unlocked the door.

"Who are you?" Noah asked as the man pushed the barred door wide and offered him his freedom.

"A friend," was his only reply.

Allowing his rescuer to take the lead, Noah followed him out the side door of the building to where two horses were tethered, awaiting them. Mounting up, they fled the scene without being noticed. Fearful of drawing unwanted attention to themselves, they passed through the streets of Boston at a measured pace. When his guide reined in behind a shabby two-story wooden building in a poor section of town near the docks, Noah followed suit.

"Come with me," the man directed.

Noah was quick to comply and within minutes found himself safely ensconced in a small, windowless room on the second floor. As his rescuer lit a candle, bathing their surroundings in a flickering yellow light, Noah eyed the room curiously, noting that the only furniture was a single bed and a small washstand. "What is this place?"

"It's one of our secure rendezvous points. You'll be staying here until we can arrange safe passage for you out of Boston."

Noah nodded in understanding and then asked, "Who are you?" His companion was tall and slim; his clothing, dark and nondescript as it was, revealed little about the man himself. Noah did not know him—in fact, he had never seen him before—and yet he had just risked his life to save him from almost certain death. Noah was humbled and grateful.

"A friend. My name doesn't matter," replied the man. "All that matters is that we get you out of here."

"Where will I be sent? Where will I be safe?"

"Either Philadelphia or New York; it just depends on how hard they look for you."

"Thank you," Noah told him solemnly. "I was beginning to think that I had very little hope of ever being free again."

"Well, it's not over yet by any means, but with any luck at all, you'll soon be free. For right now, you just stay in this room. We'll bring you everything you need."

"I will," he promised as the man started from the room.

"Graves will arrange for you to visit with your brother as soon as possible, but the authorities will no doubt suspect him first, so it may be a while."

The man's mention of Ryan Graves confirmed Noah's suspicion that Matthew and the rebels were the ones behind his rescue. "Will you tell Graves that I'm very grateful for his help?"

"You helped us. We're just returning the support." He put Noah more at ease. "You know, our country could use more men like you. . . ."

"Your country?"

The man smiled. "We'll be free of this British tyranny one day. The calls for revolution and independence are growing. In fact, if sanctions are brought to bear on Boston over the tea episode, I suspect the break may happen much sooner than we all think." He paused, studying Noah with fathomless dark eyes that seemed to be assessing his worth. "Give it some thought. You're young, and you've got a cool head on you. We Americans need all the help we can get. Think about it." He glanced about the room. "I've got to go now. Someone else will check back with you later tonight to make sure you're all right and to bring you a change of clothing. Just stay in here and be quiet, and everything will work out fine."

"Thanks."

They clasped hands, and then his rescuer departed, leaving Noah alone with his thoughts.

"Americans . . ." Noah frowned as he said the word softly

to himself, and he remembered the first time he'd heard the term used. It had been at Winthrop's ball. That night he had had a different opinion of the rebels, but now . . .

Shrugging out of his coat, Noah tossed it aside and moved to the bed. He stretched out upon it and was pleased to find that its comfort was a vast improvement over the hard cot he'd had in his cell. Folding his arms beneath his head, he stared up at the ceiling. His thoughts were confused as he realized that he was now a hunted man. Noah knew he would never be able to return to England and could no longer plan on restoring his wealth and position. A month ago that possibility would have devastated him, but now, to his surprise, the pain was less than he'd expected.

As Noah pondered the bleakness of his future, CC crept into his thoughts. His heart ached as he remembered her, warm and willing, in his arms. How perfect they had been together! He had hoped to win his freedom in court and then face her with the truth of his feelings, but now he knew any chance of ever being with her was lost. Despite CC's involvement with the rebels, she was still her father's daughter. Even if she had meant it when she'd told him she loved him, Noah knew it would be impossible to ask her to marry him now, for he had nothing to offer her—no home, no security, no future. From this point on, his life would be only danger and intrigue, and who knew how or when it would all end? His only hope was to trust in Graves to get him safely out of town. Beyond that . . . well, he decided wearily, he would deal with it later.

Closing his eyes, Noah sought sleep. Rest had been elusive in the miserable confines of the jail cell, and he knew he was going to have to be fresh and ready to move whenever they came for him. As he finally drifted off, his last waking thought was of CC and of how sorry he was that he had never had the chance to tell her that he loved her.

*　　　*　　　*

CC was wildly angry as she paced her room. It was dark, and still her father had not come to speak with her or allowed her to leave her room! She was growing distraught over the thought that Kincade might have already been released from jail, and she was desperate to let Ryan know about his possible treachery.

A sharp rap at her bedroom door broke through her thoughts, and she hurried to open it, hoping it was her father coming to tell her she could come out. To CC's dismay, she found only Anna standing in the hall with a dinner tray.

"Your father told me to bring this to you. He also said to tell you that he's not quite ready to speak with you yet, and he wants you to stay in your room until tomorrow." Anna explained her presence as she faced her mistress. Though she had seldom seen Miss CC in such a high temper, it was easy to tell that she was still angry, for her green eyes were sparkling with an inner fire, and her cheeks were flushed in agitation.

"What!?" CC couldn't believe it, and she planted her hands on her hips defiantly. "You can't be serious, Anna."

Anna gave her a sympathetic look as she moved past her into the room to place the tray on the bedside table. "I wish I was making it all up, Miss CC, but I'm not. Your father was still furious with you when he told me to bring your dinner up to you on this tray. What in the world did you do to make him so angry?"

"It's a long story, Anna . . ." she snapped in irritation, "and one I'd rather not discuss."

The maid nodded in deference to her wishes. "Can I get you anything else tonight? Would you like me to have a bath sent up?"

At the remembrance of Anna's first comment about CC's father, a plan had begun to form in CC's mind. She refused the offer of a bath. "No, not tonight. By the way . . . are you sure my father said that he didn't want to speak with me until tomorrow?"

"Yes, Miss CC."

"Well then, since I won't be interrupted tonight, I think I'll just eat and go on to bed."

"All right."

"Thanks for the dinner, Anna."

"Oh, you're welcome. I just hope everything calms down soon. I've never seen you and your father mad at each other before."

"It doesn't happen often," CC assured her, managing a cool smile, "and it will probably all be over by tomorrow."

"I hope so. Well, good night."

"Good night, Anna."

When the servant had gone from the room, CC locked the door behind her. Completely ignoring the meal, she rummaged through her armoire and pulled out her disguise. If her father was definitely not going to come up to see her tonight, there was no reason why she couldn't sneak out of the house to give Ryan the news and then make it back without being missed. She undressed quickly and pulled on her boy's clothes. After blowing out her lamp, CC opened the window and climbed out onto the welcoming branches of the tree. In short order, she was on the ground racing toward the Green Dragon in hopes of finding Ryan.

It was over an hour later that a totally frustrated CC stood in the stables of the inn. She had gone first to the inn, then to Ryan's house, and then back to the inn again, and all without success. No one had seen or heard from him since earlier in the afternoon. She tried desperately to figure out where else Graves might have gone. It occurred to her then that he might be meeting with some of the other rebel groups at the old house near the wharf. The ramshackle two-story was one of their most safe and secret meeting places. Realizing that it was her last hope, she started off as quickly as she could toward the waterfront.

* * *

The sound of violent pounding on the front door was not unexpected, but Faith, Matthew, and Ruth still exchanged nervous glances across the dinner table.

"Wait here, and don't say a word," Matt told them in quiet tones as he stood up and calmly went out into the hall to answer. "Who is it?" he asked through the closed, locked door.

"It's Constable Jeremy Roberts!" Came the reply. "Open up!"

"Of course." Matt gave every appearance of being completely at ease as he unlocked the portal and opened it. He was surprised to find that the law officer had several armed regulars with him. "It's good to see you again, Constable. Is there a problem?" Matt nodded toward the soldiers.

"I think you know what the problem is, Kincade," Roberts charged nervously.

"It's *Lord* Kincade, Constable Roberts," Matthew instructed haughtily, drawing himself up with dignity, "and I have no idea what it is you're talking about."

"I'm talking about your brother's escape."

"Noah? You say he's escaped?" He truly sounded shocked by the revelation.

"Indeed he has, Lord Kincade, and I think you just might know something about it," the constable declared, eyeing him suspiciously.

"Please, Constable Roberts . . . won't you come inside. I'm sure we can discuss this in a more civilized manner that way." Matt held the door wide to admit the officer.

"All right," Roberts grumbled. He was disappointed with Kincade's reaction and very distressed by the fact that he'd invited them inside. "My men will search the house and grounds while we talk."

"This is highly irregular," Matt protested indignantly.

"Your brother's an accused murderer, and his jailbreak was highly irregular, m'lord," he responded brusquely.

457

"I had nothing to do with it."

"We'll just see about that, now won't we?" he sneered at the English nobleman. "Men, check the house. Don't miss anything. I'll be with His Lordship in the parlor."

The soldiers quickly moved indoors and began to search the small home. They left no piece of furniture unturned and no item untouched in their zealousness to find the escaped prisoner.

Faith and Ruth grew nervous at the sight of the soldiers, and they hurried into the parlor to stay with Matthew.

"Faith and Ruth, this is Constable Roberts. Constable, this is my wife, Faith, and her mother, Ruth."

"Ladies," he greeted them shortly before turning his full attention to Matthew. "Now, Lord Kincade, I'd like the answers to some questions." He regarded Matt doubtfully.

"By all means, what can I do for you?"

"I want to know where your brother is."

"I wish I could help you, but I assure you I have no idea where Noah is. In fact, this is the first I'd heard that Noah had escaped. How did it happen?"

"Never mind." Roberts dismissed his question. "Tell me, when was the last time you saw your brother?"

"I went to his arraignment earlier today."

"Did you have the occasion to speak with him then?"

"No. It was not permitted," Matt informed him.

"And you haven't had any communication with him or from him since?"

"No, sir. I haven't heard a thing," he answered honestly.

"How about you ladies?"

Faith and Ruth both paled at his charge.

"Oh, no. We haven't spoken with or seen Noah since all of this happened," Faith replied quickly.

They were interrupted as the soldiers returned from their search.

"Did you find anything?" Roberts asked.

"No, sir. Not a thing."

"You checked everywhere? The attic . . . the cellar . . ."

"Yes, sir. There's nothing. There's no indication at all that anyone's been here."

"All right." Roberts turned back to Matthew. He had thought that the brother would be hiding out here, and it irritated him to find that he wasn't. "Don't think this is the end of it, Lord Kincade."

Matthew's expression was regal with disdain. "It most certainly is the end of it, sir. I know nothing of my brother's escape. I was not a party to it, and I do not know where he is. I believe your search has been completed, and I would appreciate it if you would leave my home now."

Roberts and his cohorts glared futilely at Matthew, but he ignored them as he moved into the hall and opened the door for them.

"Good night, gentlemen," he said curtly. He shut the door with firm finality behind them and then breathed a huge sigh of relief that they were gone.

As Edward Demorest sat in his study trying to enjoy his usual after-dinner liqueur, his mood was somber. He had dined alone this evening, and he hadn't enjoyed it. He admitted reluctantly to himself now that he had missed CC's company all evening—not that he wasn't still angry with her, for he was. Her behavior today had been totally outrageous and quite unbecoming of a woman of her position in society. But he wasn't used to being so completely alone, and he decided to make his peace with her tonight rather than wait until morning. Pleased that he'd convinced himself to make the move now, he set his snifter aside and strode from the room.

"CC." He knocked softly at her chamber door. "CC, I'd like to speak with you."

There was no answer to his knock, and he frowned slightly. He knew Anna had told him that she was planning on retiring early, but he'd never known her to be a very sound sleeper. Knocking a little louder, he called out to her again.

"CC. I'd like to speak with you. Please open the door."

He paused, awaiting her response, but silence was all that greeted him.

"CC?" Edward called her name. "CC, is something wrong?"

There was still no answer, and he began to grow worried. Anxiously, he tried the doorknob, and he was distressed to find the door locked.

"Mr. Demorest? Is there something the matter?" Anna stood at the bottom of the staircase as she called up to him.

"Yes. It's CC. She'd not answering. . . . Perhaps she's taken ill. Quick, bring me the extra set of keys."

"Yes, sir."

Within moments Anna was beside him with the set of master keys. Edward quickly sorted through them, located the one for CC's room, and hurriedly unlocked the door. Pushing it open, he strode forth into the darkened bedroom.

"CC? CC, my dear, if you're ill . . . Anna, quickly, light a lamp for me," he ordered.

Edward started in the direction of his daughter's bed, fully expecting to find CC there. As Anna lit the lamp, bathing the room in a golden glow, he was astounded to discover the bed empty and CC nowhere to be found.

"By God! She's not even here!" He wasn't sure if he was more astonished or furious. "Anna!" Edward rounded on the servant as he spied the untouched dinner tray on the table near the bed. "What do you know about this?!"

"Nothing, sir!" she answered quickly, defensively.

"The truth, Anna! I want the truth!" he bellowed as he realized how completely his daughter had defied him.

"That is the truth, sir!" she cried, fearful of losing her job. "I brought up the dinner tray as you told me to, and I offered to have a bath sent up. Miss CC said that she didn't want a bath, and that she was going to go on to bed early tonight since you weren't going to speak with her until tomorrow."

"I see." Edward's eyes narrowed as he looked about the room, noting her hastily discarded clothing and the open window. "You didn't see her or talk to her after that?"

"No, sir."

He knew then how she'd made her escape, and he became even more upset.

"Mr. Demorest, sir, do you suppose she's all right?"

"Don't worry about it, Anna. You go back downstairs and take care of your own duties. I'm going to wait here for my daughter's return." He stalked to the window and glanced out.

"Yes, sir." Anna scurried from the room, feeling sorry for CC when she got back.

Edward crossed the room to close and lock the door before blowing out the lamp. Settling down in the chair beside the bed, he folded his arms across his chest and sat back to wait. *If CC thought she'd witnessed the full potency of his anger over her visit to Kincade at the jail, she was wrong,* he vowed silently as he contemplated a suitable punishment for such an unruly, wayward young female.

Chapter Twenty-Nine

CC moved cautiously through the darkly shadowed rebel hideout. Though she could detect no sign of anyone's presence in the old two-story structure, she knew better than to assume that there was no one around. For years they'd been forced to meet in secret, and they were most adept at disguising their whereabouts. CC was aware that there were several windowless meeting rooms in the building, and it was in one of these that she hoped to finally locate Ryan.

CC ascended the staircase as quietly as possible, and when she reached the hall, she noted with relief that light was shining from beneath the door to one of the rooms. Quickly she rushed forth, anxious to impart her news about Noah's treachery so that precautions could be taken against any possible action by the Crown.

CC knew a momentary pang of sorrow over the fact that she had to tell Ryan of Noah's betrayal, but the memory of the scene at the jail between Noah and Eve assailed her then, erasing any kinder emotion she might have felt for him. She had always known that he was a double-dealer, and she felt foolish for having believed any of what Matthew had told her last night. She was glad now that she had not arrived at the jail before Eve. Who knows what kind of a fool she would have made of herself, professing her love to him? Her witnessing of his embrace with Eve had cured her of wanting him, and any love she had felt for him was buried beneath a hard shell of hate. It was in that frame of mind that CC knocked once on the door to announce her presence and then turned the knob to open it, calling out to Ryan as she did so.

Noah, try as he might, had only managed to get a few minutes sleep since being left there. Unable to rest, he had lain upon the bed trying to come to grips with what he really wanted from life. His entire plan for the future had been destroyed by the events of the past few days, and he had to admit to himself that he was not altogether sorry. Matthew's blunt assessment of his character had shocked him, and yet at the same time it had forced him to accept the ugly truth about himself. He had changed. He had become a different person, and Noah knew he didn't like the man he'd become.

Looking back objectively, Noah could see how the humiliation of his father's failure had rendered him a slave to his obsessive desire to "prove" his worth to those who'd shunned him. He understood his own motivation in striving to reestablish himself, but he knew now that the goal of returning to England possessing great wealth was a useless, fruitless achievement. The opinions of his so-called friends among the peerage were not important, for, had they been true friends, they would not have deserted him in the first place. Noah's thoughts drifted to remembrances of the life he'd led before his father's death. He realized now that his existence had been completely hedonistic, not unlike Geoffrey's here in the colonies, and he knew he could never go back to that. He had discovered that there was more to life. . . . There was justice and dedication and love. . . .

A sound in the hall interrupted Noah's thoughts, and thinking it to be one of Ryan's men returning to check on him, he quickly got up and started toward the door as it swung open.

CC stepped inside the room fully expecting to come face-to-face with Ryan and several other members of the group. Instead she found herself staring up at Noah. He looked so tall and so handsome that for a minute she froze, overwhelmed by his very nearness. Her hands went cold and clammy, and her heart began to pound in her breast. *What was he doing here?* Of all the people she'd expected to see when she came through the door, he had been the last. Her moment of disbelief was brief. He was a double-dealing traitor!

"You! What are you doing here!?" CC erupted in shocked fury.

"CC!" Noah was surprised, but thrilled, to see her. He had never suspected that she would be the one coming to check on him, and all he could think of was that he was finally going to have the chance to tell her everything. She looked beautiful to him even in her boyish garb, and he could hardly wait to take her in his arms and profess his love.

"I asked what you were doing here!" CC snapped, her emerald gaze a vicious glare as she stepped warily backward to maintain a definite distance between them. Trying to ignore the way her pulse was racing, she nervously glanced around the room, hoping someone else was there. To her dismay, they were alone. *Where was everyone?*

"You don't know?" Noah approached her slowly, a slight smile curving his handsome lips. "It's obvious, isn't it?"

"It's not obvious to me!" she retorted, feeling overwhelmed by his dominating presence in the small room.

Noah frowned as he considered her answer. Surely she knew about the jailbreak. . . . "CC, I'm here because this is where Ryan sent me," he explained simply.

"Surely you don't expect me to believe that. I know what a filthy, double-dealing liar you are!!" she declared, her green-eyed gaze scathing upon him as she remembered him heatedly embracing Eve several hours earlier. *How had he come to be here in the rebel hideout when he had been plotting with Eve?* CC was desperate to locate Ryan and find out the truth.

Noah knew CC had every right to be angry with him over the way he'd treated her when they were last together, but he had not expected this type of reaction from her. His only hope was to apologize for that night, but she gave him no opportunity.

"I'm going to find Ryan!" CC was seething as she started out the door, "And I'm going to tell him the truth about you!"

Surprised by her vehement accusations, Noah stood immobile for a moment. Only the thought that she was stalking out without an explanation goaded him to react. Grabbing her by the shoulders just as she would have left, Noah spun her around to face him.

"What the hell is the matter with you?" He gave CC a brief shake as he dragged her closer. Even as annoyed as he was with her, the feel of her slender shoulders beneath his hands sent shock waves of awareness through him.

"*You* are what's the matter with me! I know all about you and your deals and plans!! You're the lowest of the low, Kincade! You're nothing but a damned insidious traitor!" CC hissed, wishing she could break free and slap him.

"A traitor?!" Noah could only stare down at her in complete bafflement. CC thought him a traitor? The idea was as close to ridiculous as anything he'd ever heard.

"That's right!" she challenged, taking advantage of his momentary confusion to wrench herself free from his firm hold. "I'm going to find Ryan right now and let him know just how low-down and conniving you really are? Unless . . ." The thought suddenly struck her that Noah must have already set his betrayal into action and that her friends were probably even now being arrested by the authorities. She blanched as she stared up at him, her eyes dark and haunted in her pale face.

Noah read her distress and didn't understand it. "Unless what, CC? What the hell are you talking about?" Noah was

465

completely confused by her wild charges, and he raked a hand nervously through his hair as he stared down at her in consternation. Where in the world had she ever gotten the idea that he was a traitor?

"Unless Ryan and the others have already been arrested . . ." She backed toward the door, her very real fear reflected on her features. "No wonder I couldn't find anybody! You've already turned them in!"

"Turned who in, CC? I'm no traitor!" he protested, reaching out to snare her arm as she would have fled the room.

"You expect me to believe that after what I saw and heard this afternoon?!" CC struggled against his overwhelming strength as he drew her closer to him.

"Yes, I expect you to believe it, especially since it's the truth! And I'd also like to know just what it is you supposedly saw that convinced you I was so devious." Noah countered, trying to make sense out of her accusation. "Don't you know that I just sold the arms shipment to Ryan for half of what I'd originally asked?"

"Oh, I know all about that. You almost had me convinced that I'd been wrong about you." CC glared up at him mutinously. "Almost. I had forgotten for a moment what a despicable, amoral man you really are, but after seeing you with Eve today, you can be sure that won't ever happen again!"

"You saw me with Eve?"

"I went to the jail and accidentally walked in on the two of you. I saw you kissing her, and I heard you make a deal with her!"

Noah was stunned. CC had gone to the jail to see him? Why? He longed to know the answer, but first he had to find out what it was she thought he'd done.

"I made no deal with Eve. In fact, CC, when Eve left my cell, she was in quite a temper."

"If Eve was in a temper when she left you, it was probably

466

because she couldn't bed you right there! I saw you kissing her, Noah! I heard her say that she knew you were a man who liked to deal and that she could have you out of jail before the day was over!"

"Just what kind of deal do you think I made, CC?" Noah asked, his tone quieting as it became clear to him just what had happened. For some as yet unknown reason, CC had gone to the jail to see him and had evidently walked in just as Eve was trying to blackmail him into marrying her. He regretted that CC hadn't stayed past that one kiss, for, if she had, they wouldn't be having this confrontation right now.

"She was probably working for the authorities, trying to convince you to turn us in in exchange for your freedom! What else?" CC looked up at him, her gaze cold and accusing upon him.

"Ah, CC," he murmured in understanding as he lifted one hand to gently caress her cheek, "what else, indeed . . ."

CC slapped his hand away in irritation as she tried to deny the desire that was stirring within her. "Don't patronize me, Kincade!"

"I'm not patronizing you, CC. I'm trying to explain exactly what it was you thought you saw and heard this afternoon."

"I know what I saw and heard!"

"You're right about Eve kissing me, and you're right about her offering me a deal, too, but you're wrong about everything else."

CC looked at him skeptically as she began to doubt her long-held beliefs about him.

"Think about it," he urged as he sensed that she was calming. "If I had done what you accused me of, why in the world would I be here?"

His reasoning was maddeningly logical, but still CC didn't want to believe him.

Noah read her mistrust and went on. "I'm here, CC, because Matthew and Ryan arranged for my escape from

467

jail." As he revealed the truth of all that had happened, Noah studied her expression, hoping to see revealed there an acceptance on her part.

Despite her initial reluctance to accept his explanation, CC felt her fierce belief in his treachery begin to fade. However, the memory of the scene with Eve was still branded in her mind, and she knew that she could not completely accept what he was telling her. "But what about Eve? I heard—"

"I know exactly what you heard," he agreed steadily. "Eve offered me a deal of sorts that would have guaranteed my release from jail. I refused to take her up on her offer. Suffice it to say that when she left me, she was pleased at the thought that I was going to face the gallows for my crime."

"Why would you refuse her deal if it would have freed you?"

"There were too many strings attached."

"I don't understand."

"Eve witnessed the fight between Geoffrey and me."

"She did?! Why didn't she tell someone?" She looked up at him in surprise.

"She saw it all, all right, but she withheld her testimony in hopes of forcing me to marry her." There was a bitterness in his tone that betrayed his true feelings for the cunning, beauteous widow.

"What?" CC was truly shocked at his revelation.

Noah smiled thinly, but it was not an expression that mirrored happiness. It was a cynical sneer that reflected the contempt he had for the woman's sly maneuverings. "It seems Eve was at Geoffrey's the night I went there and quarreled with him. Geoffrey had just discovered that I had killed his brother in a duel in England. He was determined to seek revenge, and he drew a pistol. He planned to shoot me and then tell the authorities that I'd attacked him, but I wasn't about to let things end that easily. He didn't expect me to fight him for the gun, so at least I had that much on my side. The gun went off accidentally while we were struggling over it. The whole thing was entirely a matter of self-defense, but unfortunately, I was discovered in the very compromising position of having the murder weapon in my hand when the authorities arrived. Had Eve been a woman of honor, she would have come forth then to profess all she knew. Instead she maintained her silence, condemning me to arrest." He gazed down at CC standing so close to him, listening so intently. "I wasn't even aware she'd been there until she showed up at the jail this afternoon. Her deal was that she promised to tell all and see that the charges were dismissed if I would agree to marry her."

"And you turned her down?" CC knew Eve was capable of such treachery, but she thought Noah's refusal to save his own skin oddly out of character for him. He was a man who first and foremost took care of himself, with an eye always on profit. His decision was to remain in jail when he could have been freed. "I don't understand. You would have been free . . . safe. . . ."

"I would have been trading one prison for another, CC." Noah's voice was hoarse as he regarded her solemnly. "Death seemed far preferable to the prospect of a lifetime married to a woman I didn't love. I didn't want to spend the rest of my life knowing that I had sold myself to her for a price." His gray eyes were dark and filled with emotion as they met hers. "There is only one woman I've ever loved, CC, only one woman I've ever proposed to. . . ."

There in the smoky depths of his very serious regard she saw the truth of his feelings openly revealed for the first time. Her breath caught in her throat, and she found she could not answer.

"I love you, CC," Noah went on, finally professing the emotion that had tormented him for so long.

CC had dreamed of having his love for so long that she could only stand there and stare up at him. She wanted to ask him about the night at the inn when she had told him the truth of her love for him and yet he'd rejected her. She didn't understand why he hadn't told her of his love then.

When she didn't respond immediately to his declaration of love, Noah's heart sank. He was too late. He had feared as much but had held out a last shred of hope until now. Now he knew that there was no hope at all. She didn't love him, and he couldn't blame her. "I know I've treated you badly. I know I have no right to expect you to feel anything for me at all, but I had to tell you. I had to let you know before . . ." He looked away from her as he tried to bring his feelings under control.

CC heard the defeat in his tone and reached out to touch his arm. "Noah . . ."

He looked down at her hand on his arm before glancing up to her face, his expression wondering.

"Noah . . . I love you, too." She said it softly, yet with deep feeling as the hard protective shell that had encased her heart melted away.

It was his turn to be stunned, but only for an instant, before he swept her into his arms and crushed her to him. "I thought it was too late. . . . I thought I'd lost you," he told her huskily as he held her close.

"You haven't lost me, Noah. I'm yours forever." CC savored his embrace.

Her words sent a shaft of pain through him. *Forever*, she had said. It unnerved Noah to think that forever might only be right now. He bent to her and kissed her. It was a desperate kiss of desire and longing, and when it ended he still held her close, fearful of ever letting her go. Had he discovered the woman of his dreams, the love of his life, only to have to tear himself from her? How could he tell CC that now that they'd finally found each other, there could be no future for them? With an effort, he forced the possibility from his thoughts. They had now, and that was all that mattered.

"CC . . . love." He swung her up into his arms and carried

her to the bed. This would be their night—a night of loving and giving, a night with no misconceptions or lies. There were no more doubts or suspicions between them, no more half-truths. . . . They loved, and love conquered all.

Together they sank down upon the bed. All else faded into oblivion as they immersed themselves in each other. Each touch, each kiss took on special meaning as they whispered the long-denied endearments and pledges of devotion.

With the most exquisite of care, Noah stripped away the barrier of her clothing, revealing to his cherishing gaze the beauty of her womanly form. "You're lovely, CC. . . . You're the most beautiful woman I've ever seen. . . ." His voice was husky as he stared down at her, enthralled by the perfection of her breasts and the sweet invitation of her slightly parted thighs. "I love you."

"Oh, Noah, please . . . love me. . . . I need you so. . . ." She lifted her arms to encircle his neck and pull him down to her for a passionate kiss. Her lips parted under his, and her tongue met his in a sensual duel of desire.

As their mouths blended, he drew her against him. His caresses were almost worshipful as he stroked her with beloved reverence. Noah played upon her body as if he were the master, and she were a finely tuned instrument worthy of only the most delicate of touches. He held her enraptured, bringing her senses more and more alive with each delightfully arousing caress. His lips followed his hands, tasting and exploring every inch of her silken flesh as he sought to give her the ultimate in sensual pleasure.

CC began to move restlessly as the fire of need he was creating within her flamed uncontrollably to life. She wanted him. . . . She loved him. . . . She needed him. There was only Noah and the joy of their being together. Her hands moved over him hungrily, unbuttoning his shirt and slipping within to caress the hard, hair-roughened expanse of his chest. Suddenly she was impatient to have him undressed and naked beside her. She wanted to feel the hard, hot strength of him against her and know that he was hers, and hers alone. With eager hands, she pushed the shirt from his shoulders. Noah was momentarily distracted from his lovemaking by her actions, but he understood her need. He, too, wanted that ultimate closeness, and he stood to quickly finish stripping away the rest of his clothes.

CC's eyes were glowing as she watched Noah undress, and when at last he stood before her gloriously unclothed, she marveled at how perfectly he was made. There was no ounce of spare flesh on him. He was long and lean and firmly muscled. Her emerald gaze glowed with the fire of her inner need as it traced the width of his powerful shoulders and then followed the dark path of his chest hair down past his waist to the proof of his desire for her.

CC's heart quickened at the thought of being possessed by him, and she glanced up heatedly to find his gaze upon her. Their eyes met and held as Noah joined her on the bed once more. She knew a surge of wild passion as he moved above her and then settled his hot, hard weight against her welcoming softness. His mouth sought hers in a flaming, devouring exchange that told her of the power of his love.

Though his need was near to overwhelming, Noah held himself in check, going slowly so he could treasure every moment of their lovemaking. Easing a hand between them, he sought out the damp sweetness of her and he gloried in the knowledge that she was ready for him. With a slow, erotic rhythm, he caressed CC until she was moving hungrily beneath him. Knowing that she wanted him as badly as he wanted her drove him over the edge of self-restraint, and his need to bury himself within her could no longer be denied. Noah positioned himself before the portals of her love and thrust into the hot, velvet heart of her in one swift, sure movement. The moment was ecstasy. Enthralled, they blended and merged, taking and giving until the differences between them became nonexistent. They were one. When the excitement became too intense for them to bear any longer, they peaked, surrendering to the heated waves of rapturous splendor that pulsed through them. Wrapped in each other's arms, sated and secure, they drifted through the aftermath of love's splendor.

Reason returned slowly to Noah as he cradled CC against him. Though he wanted to stay there with her forever, loving her and holding her, he knew it was not to be. His situation was desperate. He was a hunted man . . . a man wanted for murder. He was going to be smuggled out of town like some illegal cargo, and his future was uncertain at best. He loved CC, yet he knew they could not hope to be together. What possible happiness could there be for her with him? He couldn't return to England or to Boston society. He had nothing he could give her . . . nothing . . . not even his name. The ecstasy of their moment of loving erased, he tried to ease himself slightly away from her, but CC stirred at his movements and gazed up at him.

"Noah . . . is something wrong?" she asked in a tender voice as she noticed a strange sadness in his eyes.

Noah grimaced inwardly at the question. Everything was wrong, but how could he tell her? How could he explain that at any moment Ryan or one of his men was going to show up, and he was going to be spirited away to God knows where?

"Noah . . . what is it?" CC could tell by his expression that he was tormented by something. She had no idea what the problem was, but she wanted to help him if she could.

"CC, I think we'd better get dressed." Noah climbed from the bed and, keeping his back to her, began to pull on his clothing. "Ryan may be sending someone over to check on me tonight, and I wouldn't want them to find us like this."

CC was completely confused and more than a little hurt by his behavior. She had thought they had worked through all the problems facing them. They had admitted their love! Didn't that count for something? Suddenly she was angry with him for shutting her out, and her temper flared.

"Is it something I did? Something I said?" Coming to her knees in the center of the bed, she faced him, her auburn hair streaming about her shoulders in tumbled disarray, her eyes flashing fire.

When Noah turned around to answer her, he was struck again by her loveliness, for she looked like an avenging angel. She was everything he'd ever wanted, and he wondered how he was going to tell her that he had to leave her and that it was over between them.

"CC, this has nothing to do with you. . . ." he hedged, his gaze fastened on the beauty of her.

"How can you say that?" she demanded. "You make wonderful love to me, then leave our bed without a word. You became cold and indifferent. . . ."

"CC, I am hardly indifferent to you, and if I seem cold, I'm sorry."

"Then tell me what's wrong. We love each other. If there's something troubling you, maybe I can help." Her plea was so heartfelt that Noah couldn't prevent himself from sitting down on the bed and drawing her back into his arms.

"Ah, love . . . everything is wrong." His voice was a hoarse whisper as he buried his face against the sweetness of her throat.

"What do you mean?"

"I love you, CC. There's nothing I want more than for us to spend the rest of our lives together, but that's not going to happen."

The certainty of his words was like a slap in the face to CC, and she stiffened in his embrace and drew back to look at him. "What do you mean?"

"I have nothing to offer you, darling." His words were despairing. Noah felt as if his heart were being torn from his chest. He wanted her, Gods knows he did, but his sense of honor would not allow him to make promises to her he would be unable to keep.

"I have your love. That's all I've ever wanted."

"What good is my love going to do you if I'm a wanted

man? Have you forgotten that I've just broken out of jail? I'm a criminal, wanted by the law. Ryan's going to get me out of Boston as soon as he can, but after that I'm going to be on the run. There can be no future for us."

Her eyes filled with tears. "But I love you! I want to be with you! It doesn't matter. . . ."

"It does matter!" Noah told her bitterly. "CC . . . I feel the same way you do. I love you. . . . I want to be with you, but I won't take you with me. It's too dangerous. If anything ever happened to you, I'd never forgive myself."

"Let me make that decision!" she demanded.

"No." He was curt. "I love you too much to put you at such risk."

"Then marry me now. I can stay here and wait for you. . . ." she pleaded, wanting more than anything to be his wife and to bear his name.

"No, love. It wouldn't be fair to you. I have no idea where I'll be going or what I'll be doing. The way things stand, I could be dead tomorrow."

"Oh, don't say that!" CC cried as she wrapped her arms about him in a fiercely protective embrace.

"I have to say it, CC. It's something you have to think about. You've got to understand. . . ." Noah pried her arms from about him and held her slightly away so he could meet her eyes. "I love you, darling. I'll never love anyone else. It's because of my love that I won't put you through all the torment."

"What's going to happen to you?" CC asked in a choked whisper as she struggled to fight back the tears burning in her eyes.

"I wish I knew," he told her, smoothing an errant lock of hair back from her face and then bending to brush his lips tenderly against hers.

"Noah, please, I'll go anywhere with you! I'll do anything. . . . Just don't say that we're going to be separated!" she agonized.

Before he could reply, the sound of someone entering the

house below tore them apart. "Get dressed," he ordered as he closed the door firmly and then quickly finished straightening his own clothing. "It's probably the messenger from Ryan."

CC was grateful she had been wearing the boy's garb, for it made it easier for her to dress, and she was completely clothed before the knock sounded at the door.

"Kincade?" Joshua Smith asked cautiously.

"Yes. Come in."

Noah greeted him with pleased surprise. "It's good to see you again, Smith."

"You, too," he returned, glancing questioningly from Noah to CC. "Did Ryan send you here, Miss CC?"

"No. As a matter of fact, I came here looking for Ryan and accidentally discovered Lord Kincade's presence."

Smith nodded. "Oh."

"What's the news?" Noah quickly asked, directing the conversation away from the subject of CC's presence.

"It looks like we may be able to get you out of town just before dawn."

"Is it definite?"

"We won't be sure until after midnight. Ryan will get back to us then with a definite answer, one way or the other."

"Us?"

"Yes. He gave me orders that I was to stay with you for now, just in case."

Noah fought to keep from scowling at the news. Smith was staying! Were he and CC never to have another moment alone together? Was it to end like this?

"I can stay with him if you've got something else you have to do, Joshua," CC offered, feeling the same terrible desperation that gripped Noah.

"No, I'm sorry, Miss CC. Ryan gave me explicit instructions that I was to stay here until we heard from him."

CC was crestfallen. The thought that she might never see Noah again left her dreams shattered, and she felt as if her life were ending.

"How's my brother?" Noah was asking. He was trying not to believe that CC would soon be forced to leave.

"They searched Matthew's house first, but of course they didn't find anything." Smith was smug, pleased that their plan had worked so well.

"Good." Noah was relieved that Matthew wasn't paying the price for his present predicament.

"I've brought us some food." He held up a saddlebag and then looked around the small room in annoyance. "Pity there's not a better place to sit than on the bed," he commented as he walked over and sat down. As he rummaged through the pouch for food, CC and Noah exchanged strained glances.

"Noah . . . I . . ."

"You'd better go now," he told her firmly, not wanting to put her reputation at any greater risk.

"All right." They were the most painful words she'd ever uttered. She wanted to throw herself into his arms and refuse to leave, but she knew it was impossible. Heartbroken, she picked up her tricorn and started from the room.

"I'll go down with you," Noah offered.

"Don't go downstairs, Kincade. Someone might catch sight of you through a window. Stay up here," Smith instructed, keeping his attention diverted to allow them a moment of privacy. Though he gave the impression of being a coldhearted man, Joshua knew love when he saw it. He knew that young Miss CC was carrying quite a flame for the Englishman, and he thought it quite a pity that things were turning out as they were.

Noah and CC moved in silence out into the darkened hallway, and they didn't speak until they were near the top of the staircase.

"Noah . . . please don't make me leave you!" Her tears were falling freely now as she gave up the fight to contain them. "Not now . . . not when we've just discovered how much we love each other! My life will be empty without you!"

"CC, it's the only way I can live with myself. If you're home with your father, I'll know you're safe and well."

"But Noah—"

"No more, CC!" he cut her off brusquely. "Do you think I want this any more than you do? Do you think I enjoy the thought that I may never hold you, or touch you, or kiss you again? It's tearing me apart to send you away, but it's the only solution!"

Without another word, he clasped her to him and covered her mouth with his in a potent kiss meant to brand her as his for all time.

"No matter what happens, CC, always remember that I love you. . . ." He said the words softly and then kissed her again, this time cherishingly. "Goodbye, my darling. . . ."

"Noah . . ."

"Go now before it becomes even more difficult!"

CC gave a choked sob and then touched his cheek one last time. Steeling herself against the emotions that were ravaging her very soul, she turned away to stuff her hair up under her hat.

"Goodbye, Noah . . . and please, please, be careful." Tears were coursing freely down her cheeks as she took one last look at him. Then she turned and raced away down the steps and out of the house, disappearing quickly into the night.

Miserable and dying inside, Noah watched her until she was out of sight. He felt as if someone had physically ripped his heart from his chest, and he drew a deep, shuddering breath as he started back to his room and Smith.

Unmindful of any attention she might attract, CC hurried away. She felt frozen and lifeless inside. Nothing seemed to matter without Noah . . . nothing. Eager to seek out what little comfort the familiar surroundings of her room could offer, she ran for home, unaware that her father was there in her chambers waiting for her.

Chapter Thirty

CC was exhausted as she finally climbed through her open window and then closed it behind her. As she moved about the dark, warm security of her own room, she realized vaguely that she'd been very lucky in not having been found out. As tired and filled with anguish as she was, CC wanted only to collapse upon the bed and cry out her misery, but she knew that it would not do to risk being discovered in her disguise. Moving wearily to her small bedside table, she lighted the lamp. The flickering flame wavered for a moment before shining full and bright, and it bathed the chamber in a soft golden glow. CC turned, ready to search through her armoire for a nightgown. She went completely still and stared in shock at the sight that greeted her. There, sitting in the chair near the bed, was her father.

"Father!" she gasped as she stood before him, her limbs suddenly quaking in fright. They had argued many times. They had even been very angry with each other on several occasions, like this afternoon, but never before had she seen such a look on his face. His expression was positively fiendish as he regarded her with eyes that seemed to glow red with fury.

"I see you've finally decided to return, my dear. That is you, isn't it?" Edward's tone was cutting as he regarded her in complete disgust. It was bad enough that she'd left the house in such an unorthodox manner without his permission, but to discover that she had been dressed like a man while doing it . . . well, it was more than he could countenance. How dare she?! And what was she up to?

Hastily, CC tugged the tricorn from her head, shaking her long hair free from its confines. "Yes, Father. It's me."

"I see," he stated rigidly. "I want to know where you've been, young lady. . . . And I use the term loosely at this point."

As distraught as she was over being parted from Noah, CC could think of no lies to cover for her outrageous behavior. Swallowing nervously, she didn't answer.

"I asked you where you've been!" he boomed as he came to his feet and stalked toward her.

"I'd prefer not to talk about it, if you don't mind, Father."

"You prefer not to talk about it. . . ." Edward was irate, and he repeated her statement in amazement. "*You* prefer not to talk about it! By God, daughter, were you the male you're pretending to be, I'd thrash you within an inch of your life right now!!"

CC cringed at the very real threat of physical violence in his voice. Edward came to stand before her, his hands clenched into fists at his sides as he fought for control.

"I want to know where you've been!" He loomed over her, barely containing his rage.

Drawing on her courage, she lifted her chin and looked up at him. "I can't tell you."

"Ah, but you will, little girl. I am going to know exactly what is going on here. It was bad enough that you shamed yourself earlier today by going to the jail, but this . . ." He gestured toward her mode of dress. "This is unforgivable!" Edward was bellowing now, and CC knew she had to do something to defuse the situation.

Finally gathering enough presence of mind to tell him a close rendition of the truth, CC hurried to offer, "I understand you're upset, Father, but the whole thing is really quite simple. There was a political meeting tonight, and I wanted to attend. I knew it wouldn't do if I went as CC Demorest, so I wore these clothes to keep my identity a secret. I'm sorry if I've upset you."

"Upset is not the word for what I'm feeling right now, dear girl! I have dedicated my life to raising you, and this is the thanks I get for it!" He gestured toward her clothing. "A political meeting, indeed!" Edward snorted his disbelief as he shook his head in sorrow, lamenting his erroneous judgment. "I've given you every educational opportunity. I've allowed you freedoms no other woman has ever enjoyed. Yet you respond this way. I was wrong in giving you the chance to voice your opinions. Instead of permitting you to express youself, I should have forced you into the traditional submissive role so well suited to your sex."

"Father . . . I . . ."

"Shut up!!" He silenced her viciously. "I don't want to hear another word from you. While I was sitting here alone in the dark waiting for you to return, I had quite some time to ponder your activities lately. Everything else aside, I find it most distressing that you are brazen enough to go out in public dressed as a man. I can only conclude that you are jeopardizing my good name, and that, Cecelia Marie, is something I will not tolerate." He glowered at her. "Since, despite all my efforts, you obviously have acquired no sense of decency, I'm afraid we're going to have to make some very drastic changes."

"What do you mean?" Her eyes rounded fearfully as she wondered what he was planning.

"First thing in the morning I'm going to book you passage to England. You will return to London and live with your Aunt Charlotte. She was always a stickler for decorum, and perhaps, just perhaps, she can correct all your faults. Under her strict tutelage you will learn to become a woman— someone your mother would have been proud of. . . ."

His last declaration hurt. "But Father . . ."

"Silence! I've made my decision. You will be leaving Boston at the earliest possible moment. Good night." He turned from her without another word and quit the room.

It was well past midnight, and Noah and Joshua shared the shuttered room in silence. After they had eaten earlier, Joshua had made several attempts to engage Noah in conversation, but Noah had been so filled with despair at the thought of being parted from CC that he had been unusually curt in his replies. Frustrated in his overtures, Joshua had lapsed back into his usual taciturn manner. They had remained silent from then on as they waited tensely for word from Ryan.

The hours since CC's departure had passed with maddening slowness for Noah, and his mood was black as he paced the small chamber. Never before had he known such an all-encompassing love for anyone. It was as if a vital part of him had been cut away, and he was at a loss to deal with it.

Though Noah had been honorable in his original intention of leaving CC behind, the more he thought about never seeing her again, the more impossible it became. How could he possibly exist without her now that he knew the true sweetness of her love? The answer came to him easily . . . he couldn't. No matter how noble he had tried to be in sending her away from him, Noah knew he couldn't live with that decision. Somehow, some way, he was going to see her one more time. When he did, if she still wanted to accompany him, he was going to take her with him. His thoughts were interrupted then by the sound of riders in the alley below.

"Joshua?" Ryan called out as he entered the house and started upstairs to find them.

"We're here, Ryan," Joshua answered, coming out into the hall to meet him, "and we've had no trouble."

"Good." The leader sounded slightly breathless.

"What's the word? Do we travel tonight?" Joshua asked, leading the way back into the room where Noah was waiting.

"As soon as we mount up," he told them as he handed Noah a bundle. "Here . . . I brought a dark cloak and hat for you. Hurry! We're to rendezvous near Long's Wharf as soon as possible."

"What about patrols? Aren't they still searching for him?" Joshua wondered how Noah was going to be able to get out of town undetected.

"Trust me." Ryan gave him a half smile. "All we have to do is get there. The rest should be simple. Let's go."

Noah was glad that things were going so smoothly, but he knew that he could not leave without seeing CC one last time. "There's just one problem, Ryan." He spoke up determinedly, causing the other men to pause and look back at him questioningly.

"Problem? What kind of problem?"

"I have something I have to do before I leave."

"What?" Ryan frowned at the interruption in his schedule.

"There's someone I have to see."

"I'm sorry, Kincade, but there's no time. We'll be lucky to get you out as it is without making a stop along the way."

"Either we stop at the Demorest house on our way to the rendezvous, or you can forget about me going along with your plan."

"The Demorests'?" Ryan looked at Noah as if he'd just lost his mind. "You're crazy! Edward Demorest is an ardent loyalist. We're not going anywhere near his house."

"Edward Demorest may be a loyalist, but CC isn't. I'm not leaving town until I've had the chance to speak with her again."

"Again?" He glanced at Joshua and then back at Noah.

"CC was here earlier. We're in love, and we're going to be married," Noah informed him. "I thought I would be able to leave her behind, but I find I can't. I want her to travel with me."

"CC go with you?" Ryan was surprised. "But it's impossible! I don't know if there will be room for another person."

"CC and I go together or I don't go at all."

"You're crazy!"

"I may well be." He shrugged off the comment. "Now, do we stop at the Demorests'?"

"All right, all right," Ryan told him in exasperation. "Let's just get out of here. Our connection will be waiting for us, and I don't know how long they can remain where they are without drawing attention to themselves."

Joshua listened to the exchange in silence and then smiled when Ryan finally gave in and agreed to Noah's plan. He had always liked CC. She was a spunky one and right smart, too. She would be getting herself a fine husband in this man.

Within minutes the three men were on their way. Traveling by the back streets, they finally neared their destination and reined in a short distance away from the Demorest house.

"Is CC going to meet you outside somewhere?" Ryan asked.

"No. She doesn't even know I'm coming for her," Noah answered, leaving him astonished.

"Then how the hell are you going to get her out of there? Go up and knock on the door and ask her to come out?" Ryan snapped as his gaze nervously combed the deserted streets and alleys for some sign that they were being followed. Luckily, he noted no one in the vicinity.

"Do you have any idea which room is hers?" Noah asked, ignoring Ryan's exasperation.

"I do." Joshua spoke up for the first time. "CC told me once that she had to sneak out to come to the meetings and that she had to climb down a tree outside her window to do it. There's a big tree on the far side. Why don't you see if it's the one?"

"Thanks, Joshua."

The older man nodded and gestured for him to hurry. "There's very little time. Go get your woman."

Noah cast him a grateful glance as he dismounted and then hurried toward the secluded grounds.

When her father had left her, CC had been too overwrought to sleep. Memories of Noah and the glory that could have been theirs had haunted her every thought, and once the shock of the confrontation with her father had faded, the tears had come. Heartbroken, she had sobbed out her torment until finally there had been no more tears to shed. Not only had she lost her love this night, she had also been stripped of the one other thing she cared about . . . her involvement with the rebels. She longed to flee but knew that there was nowhere to go. She was trapped, and unless some miracle happened, she would be shipped off to England, probably before the week was out.

Feeling miserable, CC got up from the bed and went to the armoire to select a nightgown. She had been so upset earlier that she had not bothered to change out of her trousers and shirt. Now, however, she felt wretchedly unkempt in the wrinkled, sorry outfit. She hoped that getting cleaned up and changing into a gown would help her feel a little better. Clutching a warm winter-weight nightgown, she moved to the washstand and poured herself a bowl of water. Her movements were lethargic as she unbuttoned the shirt and slipped it off.

It had been many a year since Noah had tried his hand at climbing trees. Gingerly testing each limb for strength as he went, he slowly made his way up through the maze of bare branches toward the lighted window on the second floor. He prayed silently that luck would be on his side and that the room with the light would be CC's. He breathed a deep sigh of relief when he finally maneuvered himself close enough to look in.

His view was unimpeded, and he stopped all motion at the

sight before him. There within the warmth of the room was the woman he loved. He watched as if mesmerized as she poured a bowl of water and then began to undress. When she slipped out of the shirt and let it fall, the lamplight bathed her pale flesh in a golden-honey glow. Desire flooded through him, and his grip on the tree limb tightened until his knuckles shown white. The beauty of her bared breasts enthralled him. Though he wanted nothing more than to spend the rest of his days admiring her loveliness, he knew regretfully that now was not the time. As quietly as possible, he reached out, pried the window open, and climbed inside.

CC went about her ablutions mechanically. She felt drained, emotionally and physically, and she hoped to get some rest when she'd completed her toilette. A good night's sleep always managed to make even the worst situations seem less dire.

The cold caress of a chilling draft swept down her spine, and CC shivered, wondering where the unexpected breeze had come from. Frowning slightly, she glanced up into the mirror. To her complete surprise, there was Noah standing behind her in the room just inside the window.

"Noah?" His name was a hushed whisper on her lips. She could not believe that he was actually there, and she stood immobile for a long moment just watching his reflection.

"CC, darling . . ." He went to her without further invitation, sweeping her into the warmth of his embrace. His mouth met hers in a frantic, passionate kiss that told her of his desperation and his devotion.

"Noah, what are you doing here?" she asked breathlessly when the kiss ended.

"I couldn't do it, CC."

"Couldn't do what?"

"Leave you."

"But you can't stay here in Boston, Noah! If the authorities catch you, you'll be hung."

"I know. Ryan's already made the arrangements to get me

out of town tonight, but I told him I wasn't going anywhere without you. I love you, darling, and whatever happens, I want us to be together."

"Oh, Noah." She kissed him again. The avidness of her excitement told him all he needed to know about her willingness to leave her home and loved ones behind to go with him.

"You'll come?"

"Oh, my darling, of course I'll come! I didn't know how I was going to live without you."

"What about leaving your father? Are you sure about that? I don't want there to be any regrets between us."

"I'm sure, Noah," CC told him solemnly.

"Then hurry. Joshua and Ryan are waiting for us below in the street. There isn't much time."

"Let me write Father a short note," she said as she pulled on her shirt and quickly buttoned it. She hurried to the desk to write a missive, apologizing to her father for having been such a disappointment to him and attempting to explain her reasons for her actions.

Noah had been tempted to help CC with the blouse, but he'd known better than to touch her. Just seeing her so unclothed had sent his passion for her soaring, and he knew he couldn't afford the distraction, at least not right now. Later would be soon enough . . . later, when they were man and wife.

"I think I'm ready." In a quiet gesture, she laid her quill pen aside and stood up.

"Is there anything you want to take with you?"

CC opened a jewelry box and took out several pieces of jewelry. "These were my mother's, and I want to keep them."

"Of course."

Grabbing up her tricorn, she hurriedly stuffed her hair up underneath it and then wrapped herself in the folds of a dark-colored cloak. "Let's go," she said, joining him at the window.

"You're positive?"

CC nodded in response. Noah climbed through the window and descended ahead of her. When he reached the ground he waited to help her, and then together they raced through the night to join Joshua and Ryan. Without a word, Noah mounted and then drew CC up to sit before him in the saddle. His arms tightly about her, he put his heels to his horse and followed Ryan's lead toward the wharf and freedom.

Though they were aware of the possibility of danger at every turn, the trip to the waterfront was made in safety. Parked in the dark shadows of an alley, a farm wagon laden with hay awaited them.

"This is it," Ryan told them as they all dismounted. "I know it won't be comfortable, but you should make it out alive, and that's all that really matters."

"Thank you, Ryan." Noah shook his hand. "Will you let Matthew know what happened and tell him I'll be in touch as soon as I can?"

"I will. You take care of CC." Ryan smiled at her.

"You have my word on that."

"I've arranged for your transportation as far as New York. Our contacts there are expecting you. They'll help you in any way they can. Now, you'd better be going. It will be dawn soon, and the farther you are out of town at sunup, the better."

Once more they shook hands. Goodbys said, CC and Noah climbed into the wagon. Lying close together, they remained perfectly still as the others covered them completely with hay. So camouflaged, they were spirited away from Boston undetected by the authorities, who were still searching the town for him.

Chapter Thirty-One
Epilogue

Caroline Chadwick set her teacup aside and gave Marianna Lord a shrewd look. "It occurs to me, Marianna, that you know much more about all this than you're letting on."

"Oh?" Marianna asked archly, her eyes twinkling merrily.

Margaret agreed with Caroline. "Marianna, if you know something about what's happened to CC, for heaven's sake, tell us! It's been almost six weeks since she disappeared. You know how worried we've been about her!"

Marianna faced her two friends, knowing that she could delay no longer in relaying what she'd just heard. "I've been sworn to secrecy. . . ."

"Yes, yes," they goaded her excitedly, hoping for some news of their friend. "You know you can trust us completely."

"Well, I wasn't supposed to tell anyone, but I got a letter. . . ."

"A letter? From CC?"

At Marianna's positive nod, they were beside themselves with curiosity.

"Well, tell all, Marianna! For heaven's sake, you know

how worried we've been about her ever since she disappeared that night!" Caroline snapped in irritation.

"It was positively horrible. Why, I've imagined all kinds of terrible things!" Margaret shuddered.

"Well, darlings, what happened to CC is far from terrible!" Marianna smiled knowingly.

"What happened?" Caroline and Margaret were both on the edge of their seats waiting to hear.

"Did you happen to notice that CC disappeared the day after Lord Kincade broke out of jail?" Marianna asked enticingly, allowing them to draw their own conclusions.

"You don't suppose . . . ?"

"Lord Kincade and CC?"

Margaret and Caroline exchanged amazed looks as Marianna nodded in confirmation. "Thank goodness she wrote me this short note. I just got it yesterday; that's why I sent for you both. I know how desperate we've all been for some word about her. Her father's been horrendously closemouthed about the whole situation. He's become a regular recluse these past weeks."

"I know. I stopped by for a visit, but he wouldn't see me," Caroline offered, miffed at having been slighted. "Did she really run off with Lord Kincade? How exciting! The man is so devilishly good-looking! Why, if he'd asked me, I would have gone, too!"

"I know," Margaret sighed. "Noah Kincade is so wonderful. I couldn't believe it when they told me he'd been arrested for Geoffrey's murder. It just didn't seem possible."

"I don't believe for one moment that he shot Geoffrey down in cold blood. Whatever happened between them that night, it wasn't murder," Marianna declared supportively.

"I don't suppose we'll ever learn all that happened. Frankly, I'm just glad the man got away. I wouldn't have been able to bear it had he been convicted and sentenced to hang. Why, I might have been tempted to break him out of jail myself!" Caroline chuckled.

"You would have had help, darling," Margaret laughed. "But tell us, Marianna, what's happened with CC?"

"She couldn't go into detail, for obvious reasons. All I know is that they left Boston together and were married. . . ."

"An elopement . . . how exciting! CC and Lord Kincade!" Margaret sighed. "How romantic."

"I know. They'll make a handsome couple, all right."

"Did CC say where they were going or what they were going to do?"

"No. She just wanted to let me know that she was safe and ecstatically happy."

"I'll bet she is," Caroline agreed. "Perhaps one day the charges against him will be dropped, and they'll be able to return."

"I hope so. There's a new investigation going on now regarding that night. It seems that two men were arrested shortly before Geoffrey was shot. Apparently they were hired indirectly by a servant of Geoffrey's named Bartley to kill Kincade. They attacked him and his brother, Matthew, but luckily, didn't succeed. Matthew Kincade turned them over to the authorities."

"Geoffrey wanted Noah Kincade dead?"

"Evidently. Now, the most startling revelation of the whole thing is that this Bartley, who hired the killers, is the same one who swears Lord Kincade killed Geoffrey in cold blood. I don't know what's behind all this intrigue, but I feel sure that when they get to the bottom of the whole thing, Noah Kincade will be vindicated."

"It would be wonderful. I'd love for CC to come back as Lady Kincade," Marianna said dreamily. "Wouldn't Eve Woodham just see green?"

"She certainly would," Caroline remarked. "Have you noticed her lately? She's gotten so outlandish! She's chasing any and every man with well-lined pockets."

"I don't doubt it. With Geoffrey dead and Lord Kincade gone . . . why, the poor woman must be just inconsolable!"

"I'll bet there are a lot of men willing to try to console her."

"I wonder how much consolation she'll need?"

"Plenty!"

The three friends laughed together.

"Someday soon that woman is going to get what's coming to her, and when she does . . ."

"We're all going to enjoy it," Caroline concluded.

"Indeed we will."

CC raised up on one elbow to gaze down at her beloved husband, studying his handsome features with sensual appreciation. "You know, we've been married for almost six weeks now. Does that make us 'old married folks'?"

"Hardly," Noah drawled as he drew her down for a soft kiss.

"Then you aren't tired of me yet?" CC's emerald eyes were glowing with love for this man who was now her husband.

"No, not yet," he teased, bringing her down full upon him and relishing the feel of her soft, naked breasts crushed against his bare chest.

"Good," CC murmured as her lips explored his in a slow, sensual caress.

"CC . . ." Noah's tone had gone from lighthearted to serious as he considered the decision he'd made about their future. CC had seemed happy just being with him during the long weeks of flight from Boston and subsequent secret rendezvous with the *Lorelei* in New York, but he knew these last few idyllic days of living safely aboard the ship could not last forever. The news he'd received from Lyle about the state of affairs in Boston had not been good. War was imminent. Noah knew they could never remain casual bystanders when their help would be so desperately needed by their friends.

CC gazed down at him, noting the slight frown marring

his handsome features, and a moment of worry sliced through the warmth of their loving embrace. "What is it, darling?"

"I spoke at length with Lyle today, and he told me that things are not looking good in Boston. Sanctions are a foregone conclusion, and the port is going to be completely closed down."

"They're going to close the port?" She was aghast. How would anyone survive? Boston, her home, was a shipping town. . . . The port was its life's blood. "My God, if they do that, war will be inevitable!"

Noah nodded and then spoke solemnly. "I know what this means to you, CC, and I'm sorry that we can't go back to help. . . ."

"Oh, Noah, please—" she interrupted, but he cut her off.

"Let me finish, love," he insisted. "I've instructed Lyle to send word to Graves that we're willing to transport whatever he needs."

CC stared at him in amazement and for the first time understood the true depth of his love for her and the completeness of his transformation. "You have?"

"Yes. Our friends will be needing all the help we can give them."

"Oh, Noah! I love you so much!"

"You don't have any regrets about coming away with me?"

"Never." She kissed him softly.

"You don't miss your father or your life there?"

"I'd be lying if I told you that I didn't. I do miss my father. I didn't like leaving him that way, but, Noah, nothing is more important to me than being with you. You are the only person who matters in my life."

"I love you, CC."

"And I love you, my very dearest husband."

The warmth of the moment surrounding them, they were lost in a haze of blissful ecstasy as they joined and mated in a joyous celebration of their devotion. Together they rode their desire to the heights, seeking, and ultimately finding, the rapturous enchantment of love's greatest delight. When the thrill of passion's promise had passed, they rested in peace-filled contentment, knowing that no matter what the future held, they would be happy as long as they had each other.

MORE TANTALIZING ROMANCES
From Zebra Books

SATIN SURRENDER (1861, $3.95)
by Carol Finch

Dante Fowler found innocent Erica Bennett in his bed in the most fashionable whorehouse in New Orleans. Expecting a woman of experience, Dante instead stole the innocence of the most magnificent creature he'd ever seen. He would forever make her succumb to . . . *Satin Surrender*.

CAPTIVE BRIDE (1984, $3.95)
by Carol Finch

Feisty Rozalyn DuBois had to pretend affection for roguish Dominic Baudelair; her only wish was to trick him into falling in love and then drop him cold. But Dominic had his own plans: To become the richest trapper in the territory by making Rozalyn his *Captive Bride*.

MOONLIT SPLENDOR (2008, $3.95)
by Wanda Owen

When the handsome stranger emerged from the shadows and pulled Charmaine Lamoureux into his strong embrace, she knew she should scream, but instead she sighed with pleasure at his seductive caresses. She would be wed against her will on the morrow — but tonight she would succumb to this passionate MOONLIT SPLENDOR.

UNTAMED CAPTIVE (2159, $3.95)
by Elaine Barbieri

Cheyenne warrior Black Wolf fully intended to make Faith Durham, the lily-skinned white woman he'd captured, pay for her people's crimes against the Indians. Then he looked into her sky-blue eyes and it was impossible to stem his desire . . . he was compelled to make her surrender as his UNTAMED CAPTIVE.

WILD FOR LOVE (2161, $3.95)
by Linda Benjamin

All Callandra wanted was to go to Yellowstone and hunt for buried treasure. Then her wagon broke down and she had no choice but to get mixed up with that arrogant golden-haired cowboy, Trace McCord. But before she knew it, the only treasure she wanted was to make him hers forever.

Available wherever paperbacks are sold, or order direct from the Publisher. Send cover price plus 50¢ per copy for mailing and handling to Zebra Books, Dept. 2160, 475 Park Avenue South, New York, N.Y. 10016. Residents of New York, New Jersey and Pennsylvania must include sales tax. DO NOT SEND CASH.

SWEET MEDICINE'S PROPHECY
by Karen A. Bale

#1: SUNDANCER'S PASSION (1778, $3.95)

Stalking Horse was the strongest and most desirable of the tribe, and Sun Dancer surrounded him with her spell-binding radiance. But the innocence of their love gave way to passion—and passion, to betrayal. Would their relationship ever survive the ultimate sin?

#2: LITTLE FLOWER'S DESIRE (1779, $3.95)

Taken captive by savage Crows, Little Flower fell in love with the enemy, handsome brave Young Eagle. Though their hearts spoke what they could not say, they could only dream of what could never be. . . .

#4: SAVAGE FURY (1768, $3.95)

Aeneva's rage knew no bounds when her handsome mate Trent commanded her to tend their tepee as he rode into danger. But under cover of night, she stole away to be with Trent and share whatever perils fate dealt them.

#5: SUN DANCER'S LEGACY (1878, $3.95)

Aeneva's and Trenton's adopted daughter Anna becomes the light of their lives. As she grows into womanhood, she falls in love with blond Steven Randall. Together they discover the secrets of their passion, the bitterness of betrayal—and fight to fulfill the prophecy that is Anna's birthright.